D1394973

A
SONG
FROM
DEAD
LIPS

A SONG FROM DEAD LIPS

WILLIAM SHAW

Quercus

First published in Great Britain in 2013 by

Quercus
55 Baker Street
7th Floor, South Block
London
W1U 8EW

A CIP catalogue record for this book is available
from the British Library

HB ISBN 978 1 78206 416 9
TPB ISBN 978 1 78206 417 6
EBOOK ISBN 978 1 78206 418 3

10 9 8 7 6 5 4 3 2 1

Printed and bound in Great Britain by Clays Ltd, St Ives plc

Typeset by Ellipsis Books Limited, Glasgow

For the late, great Tom Hibbert

1968

ONE

'Why didn't you go when I told you, before we left the house?'
The question is aimed at a small, short-trousered boy, moving angrily down the pavement. Nanny, hair wild in the October wind, drives the huge Silver Cross pram with her right hand and drags the little boy along the pavement with the left. Baby has abandoned Nee-Noo, his felt elephant, and is grizzling under the yellow blanket. They had gone to the park. None of the other nannies had been there. It was too cold, but the children's mother insisted they go for a walk every morning before their elevenses. Mother believed in fresh air and exercise, though she herself preferred to stay home, sucking Park Drives and talking for hours and hours on the phone like it doesn't cost anything and playing patience.

'I told you to go, didn't I?' Nanny struggles onward, crab-fashion, each arm extended, one pushing, the other pulling. 'Didn't I?'

'I didn't want to go when you said.'

Nanny is dressed in the ugly navy cape she hates. Her shoes are black tasselled loafers that should only be worn by grannies. Make-up is not permitted. Skirts below the knee. And as for the daddy. Wandering hands.

The boy already has the assurance of one who appears to know that Nanny is just a paid employee. Three pounds ten a week plus board and can be treated as such.

'I need to go now.' The boy's consonants are clear and clipped. He comes from stock that believes that giving orders requires plainness of speech.

I

'Can't you just hold it?' demands Nanny. The first leaves of autumn blow past the three of them. 'Just for five little minutes?'

The boy considers for a second, then answers simply, 'No.'

'Show me what a strong boy you are.'

'I am a strong boy but I need to wee-wee,' he says in a voice too deep for one his age.

Nanny wishes she was better at this. She is young and inexperienced. She took the job to escape life in the English provinces. Imagining Carnaby Street, she got St John's Wood and a small, spoilt boy who wears a blazer, woollen shorts and garters on his socks, and a father who wants to grasp her bum when the boy's mother is not looking. Homesick and lonely, the seventeen-year-old's only pleasure is her nights listening to Radio Luxembourg. The radio tells her there are more people like her somewhere in England and that stops her from going mad. Last night the disc jockey played 'Fire' by The Crazy World of Arthur Brown and she wished her world was crazy like that, that the whole world would burst into flames.

They give her Sundays off, and what's the point of that? Nothing happens on Sundays. She went down Kensington on her last day off just to look at all the clothes in the dark windows of the shops. She couldn't have afforded any of what they sold anyway. She daydreams that David Bailey is going to spot her, dress her up in beautiful clothes to take her photograph and make her famous, but no one's going to notice her looking like a middle-aged witch.

London just means she's more aware of everything that's happening out of her reach.

'What are you singing? It sounds horrid. Stop singing.'

Had she been singing? It was probably that Arthur Brown song going round in her head. She decides to try to ignore the boy, pushing onward up the pavement. She notices, under her yellow cotton blanket, Baby beginning to cry. It is almost feeding time.

'You were singing your pop music. Pop music is a horrid noise.' He parrots his mother.

2

In the Soviet Union, they say, pop music is banned. Brezhnev will send you to Siberia for listening to it. The same in Spain and Greece. Only they just lock you up there. And pull your fingernails out. And you're not allowed to wear miniskirts either. Mother just bangs on the door when she plays hers and tells her to stop that degenerate swill. If all the teenagers in England got together they could kill everyone over thirty. Everyone old should die. Even her dad. She wouldn't care. Were those blackberries on the hedge she was dragging the boy past poisonous?

'I need to go.' The boy pipes up again. It is so inconvenient of him. In this part of London you can't just wee anywhere. The young nanny looks around, wondering if she could knock on one of the doors of the white-painted houses with the posh cars parked outside and ask to use their WC. But she is shy and unsure of herself.

'I'm going to wet my shorts,' the boy announces. 'I really am.'

Mummy, Baby and Alasdair have elevenses together before Mummy's mah-jong and sherry session with her friends. It would not do to arrive back home with him wet. She grabs the boy's hand tighter. 'This way,' she says, yanking little Alasdair determinedly halfway across Hall Road.

'Ow. You're hurting me.'

'No I'm not. Hurry.'

She is tired and angry. The place she has chosen to cross is a poor one. It is on a slight curve of the main road. She cannot see the traffic coming towards them from the north.

'Quick,' says Nanny, now halfway across and beginning to realise the danger. But the little boy in grey shorts and jacket is fiercely strong, pulling against her as she tries to manoeuvre her two charges across the remaining tarmac.

In this absurd tug of war she is winning, but as she approaches the kerb on the other side, the momentary concentration it takes to tip up the wheels of the enormous pram gives Alasdair the chance to slip her hand.

3

'Alasdair. Come here now!' she screams.

Alasdair ignores her and stands, arms folded, in the middle of the road.

'You stupid boy.' Nanny pushes the pram onto the safety of the pavement before lunging to grab Alasdair. The child leaps back further, grinning. Nyah-nyah.

Around the corner spins the inevitable black cab, doing at least forty, orange light on 'For Hire'. Even at that speed, Nanny can see the horror on the cabbie's face as he swerves, eyes wide.

On the tarmac, Alasdair is too shocked to move. He stands alone, face suddenly white, eyes wide.

The taxi skids to a halt thirty yards down the road near a red phone box. Luckily, he had been a good driver. He had kept control of the vehicle even when its wheels hit the kerb and bounced back into the road. There is a second of absolute, total, world-stopped stillness before the driver's window slides down, and the tweed-capped head emerges, craning backwards towards the teenage nanny who has now captured the wayward heir in her arms.

'You stupid fucking bint.' And then for emphasis, in a voice still tremulous with shock, the taxi driver shouts again: 'You stupid stupid stupid fucking bint.'

'See what you did?' shouts Nanny. 'See what you did?'

The boy's lip is trembling. She turns left down a side street looking for privacy. He does not resist her now.

'Stupid boy.' If he were her younger brother she would have whacked him a good one by now.

A little way down the side street she has ducked down, she notices a smaller driveway to some flats behind. They are modern, built on a bombsite, and newer than the big Victorian houses on the main road, but their proportions are mean and ugly in comparison and already they have a neglected air. A piece of cardboard taped to the front door says *Concierge bell not working*. Even here it's hoity-toity. Not caretaker, mind you. This is N.W.8. A row of small padlocked sheds stands on the left-hand side of the small entrance. Beyond that, down the short muddy pathway to where a few clothes lines criss-cross an area of tarmac, there is a pile of rubbish. A rusting bicycle, sodden cardboard, an old stained mattress, springs emerging from the cotton.

She pulls the boy down the alley and looks to left and right and up at the net-curtained windows of the yellow-bricked flats. No one seems to be watching them.

'There,' she shoves the boy by the shoulder. 'Do it there.'

'Here?' says the boy, looking at the pile of rubbish.

'Yes. There. Hurry up.'

She is still shaking. She imagines the boy's body flying upwards, struck by the cab. A limp shape on the black roadway. There would have been such a fuss. And of course she would have got all the blame. She pulls a hanky from her pocket and wipes the wet from her eyes. There is a pause.

'I can't if you're watching.'

'I'm not watching,' she protests. She turns her back and waits for the boy to pee.

She knows what will happen, of course. The boy will tell on her for calling him stupid, for letting go of his hand in the middle of the road. 'Listen. I promise I won't tell your mummy that you were a naughty boy in the road. That can be our secret, can't it?'

The boy doesn't answer.

'I don't need to tell her. So let's keep it between ourselves.'

The boy is still silent.

'I've got a packet of Spangles in my room. I'll give you some.'

'I don't want to wee here,' says the boy solemnly.

'Oh for goodness' sake.' She turns angrily. He is standing there, hands at his undone flies, looking straight at the pile of debris. He looks pale. It must be the shock from the near miss with the taxi, she assumes. 'What's wrong with here? I thought you wanted to go?' She assumes this is part of some upper-class tic he has learned. We only urinate in the proper place. 'Get on with it. Baby needs to have her feed.'

'I don't want to wee-wee on the lady,' he says.

For a second, Nanny does not understand what he is saying. What lady?

The boy starts to cry. It's a whining noise that lacks his usual volume and indignation. Something is wrong. Then, as she bends down to the height of the small child, she catches sight of a dark glimmer, from under the bottom of the dirty orange mattress. In the darkness she makes out a nose, a lip, curled up, frozen in Elvis-like half-sneer. A woman's face, eyes open and glistening unblinkingly in the squalor of the pile of rubbish.

Amazingly, Baby has drifted back to sleep through the shouting and the squealing of brakes of the near miss on Hall Road, but Nanny's brief staccato scream is enough to wake him now. She begins to howl up a storm. Curtains twitch. Faces appear at the windows of the flats above.

TWO

It had been a mistake to go to work yesterday.

Breen had not been himself. He had not been ready. He had been tired. He had stayed on too long after his shift because he had not wanted to go back home to be alone.

The details of what had happened last night were not clear to him. There had been a knife. There had been blood. There had been fear. Afterwards, he had scribbled notes in the hospital corridor but when he had tried to read them later at home they made little sense. He could not understand why he had behaved the way he did.

The nurse had said Sergeant Prosser would be OK. They were only flesh wounds though he had bled a lot. Breen had hung around the hospital to see him for himself but it was 1.30 in the morning and the nurse in her starched white hat had hissed, 'He's asleep, poor man. Go home to bed, get some sleep yourself and let the bugger be.'

He had not slept.

Now, stepping off the Number 30, he walked slowly into the wind. A route he'd taken a thousand times before. Each street corner was familiar, yet vivid. Things he had never noticed before included a paving stone cracked in three by two parallel lines, a front door with a postcard of the Virgin Mary on it, held with rusty drawing pins. The quality of greyness in the morning light seemed more menacing.

A few yards ahead, a GPO van pulled up. By the time Breen was level with it, the driver was already pulling thick wads of letters from the belly of the postbox, stuffing them into a hessian sack. As he passed, one single white letter slipped from his hand and fell on the pavement. Immediately, a gust of wind caught it and flipped it over, sent it skeetering back from where Breen had just come.

'You dropped one,' called Breen, pointing at the letter that was tumbling away down the street.

The postman didn't even look up, just gave the tiniest shrug, then clipped up the top of the postbag. Breen set off running after the letter. The first time he was close to it another blast lifted it tumbling down the street again. The second time he caught up with it, stamping his shoe down on the envelope. 'Got it,' he shouted, but when he looked round the postman and his van were already gone. He posted the letter back into the box and walked on.

Turning off into Wigmore Street, his skin began to feel clammy and his scalp had started to prickle. His pace slowed. He tried to suck in air more evenly, exhale more slowly. He paused and took out a packet of No. 6. Cigarette number one. A scabby-footed pigeon pecking at a crust of sandwich fluttered away, wing beats startlingly loud. He looked around for a bench or something to sit on to catch his breath, but there wasn't one. And he was already late.

The familiar music of one-finger typing and unanswered telephones. The smell of smoke and floor polish.

The desk sergeant didn't even look up from his paper as Breen walked past. He almost managed to make it to his desk before anyone said anything. It was big John Carmichael who spotted him first, new leather jacket, white shirt pinching slightly at his fleshy neck, fag stuck to his lower lip.

'What happened, Paddy?' he asked quietly.

'Anyone know how Prosser is?' Breen asked.

Jones, the youngest one in the office, looked up and said, 'Look what the cat sicked up.'

He thought he heard someone mutter the word 'cunt'.

Jones, red-faced with anger at him, said, 'He says you ran and left him on his own to face the Chink with the blade.'

8

All eyes on him, Breen moved past them and sat at his desk. The morning light filtered through the canvas blinds. Olivetti typewriters filled with triplicate forms, white on top, yellow in the middle and pink underneath. The picture of the Queen. Blackstone's Police Manual and Butterworth's Police Procedure. Green enamel lampshades hanging from the ceiling, comfortably coated in dust.

'You just bottled it and ran out on a fellow copper.'

'Shut up, Jones. More to it than that, isn't there, Paddy?'

Jones said, 'I'm just saying what happened, that's all.'

A black-and-white photograph of a charred arm sat at the top of Breen's in-tray. His stomach lurched. He turned it upside down.

'Prosser should get a medal. As for you . . .'

'Now, now,' said Carmichael. 'Come on. How are you then, Paddy?'

'I'm OK.'

'Why you even sticking up for him, Carmichael?'

'We were worried about you, mate.'

'Reckon not.'

'Stop it, Jones.'

'Prosser said you ran so fast he thought you were training for the Mexico Olympics.'

'Have you seen him?'

'Went to the hospital this morning. He's OK. No thanks to you. What in hell were you thinking?'

'Come on, lads. Give the man a break. We all have our bad days.'

Jones snorted. 'Be fucked.'

'Language!' shouted Marilyn from the other side of the room. 'That's enough.'

'Oooooh,' hooted Jones. 'I'll give you some language, love.'

The door to Bailey's office opened. All heads looked down. The one-fingered typing restarted.

'Ah,' said Bailey. 'I was wondering what the noise was. Breen. Inside, please.' He nodded towards his office.

★

9

He closed the door behind Breen, then sat slowly in a chair behind his desk. He was a thin man with a lined face and deep-set eyes. A white speck of toothpaste stuck in the corner of his mouth. Stubble left in the cracks of skin by his safety razor.

'Have you written your report into what happened last night?'

'Not yet, sir.'

Bailey chewed his bottom lip, then said, 'Make sure you write it all down while it's fresh in your mind.'

In Breen's two years in D Division, he had seen younger men leapfrog Bailey, becoming Superintendents, joining C1 or one of the other close-knit units like the Flying Squad. Men promoted over his head, men going places, who walked with the swing of people who know they are on the rise. Bailey played by the rules. He was from the army generation. Honest, stiff-backed, hard-working. If he smoked, it was Senior Service, never an American brand.

'I visited Prosser this morning in hospital.' Bailey rolled a yellow pencil back and forth on the table. 'He's not so badly hurt. He'll be up on his feet in no time. Naturally, he wouldn't tell me precisely what happened.'

'No, sir.'

Bailey looked Breen in the eye. 'So I'm asking you.'

A pause. Breen looked at Bailey's desk and saw there was a dark blue folder with his name written on the front. His records. 'It was dark,' Breen said. 'There were two men in the shop. One of them pulled a knife.'

Bailey took off his black-rimmed spectacles and polished them with a cotton handkerchief, lifting them occasionally to breathe moisture onto the glass.

'I'm quite aware of what the men are saying. They think it's your fault Prosser was injured. They think you were windy and left him to face the assailant alone.'

'Yes, sir.'

'Well?'

'What, sir?'

'Please don't be obtuse, Sergeant. I expect that from a man like Prosser, but not you. Start at the beginning. You presumably heard there was a robbery in progress?'

Breen couldn't help looking at that speck of toothpaste. 'Yes, sir. On the radio.'

'What were you doing in a car? Your shift was long over.'

What had he been doing? He was not sure. Above all, he hadn't wanted to go home to an empty flat to start to clear out his father's belongings. 'I was driving around looking for vagrants, sir.'

'Oh, for pity's sake.'

'We think that the body in the fire last week was probably a tramp. I thought if I could find one . . .'

Bailey shook his head. 'That's not proper CID work,' he said. 'Uniform can do that.'

'Yes, sir.'

'So you drove to the shop in response to a call from Control. Did you and Prosser enter the shop together?'

Breen hesitated again. 'No, sir.'

'Why not?'

'Prosser got there first, sir.'

'He's an idiot,' said Bailey. 'He should have waited for another officer.'

'He must have known I was just behind.'

'How could he have known that? He's a liability. But you went in after him? What, two, three minutes?'

'I suppose it must have been . . .'

'And?'

'And there was this man holding a knife. He had his arm round Prosser's neck and was holding the knife out at me.' Breen realised he was holding out his right hand in front of him over the desk, prodding it towards Bailey. He laid his hand back on his lap.

'And?'

And? How could he explain what happened next? He had no idea why he panicked. He ran. Back out of the shop towards his car, crouching down behind it, heart thumping, hands shaking. How was he supposed to put that into words?

'I made an exit, sir.'

Bailey gave a small grunt. 'So I suppose it's true what they're saying. You left Prosser on his own?'

'Yes, sir.'

'That's when Prosser was wounded, fighting off the assailant?'

'Yes.'

Bailey replaced his spectacles and looked at Breen. 'This was what time?'

'Just gone nine.'

'You left another officer alone with an armed and dangerous man? The men will not like that one bit.'

'Yes, sir.'

Bailey looked at him but said nothing.

'Is that all, sir?'

'You've been on the force, what, twelve years?' Tugging at his ear.

'Thirteen.' Enough to be due a small pension to supplement his income as a factory nightwatchman, or a PE teacher in a comprehensive. What other jobs did ex-policemen do?

'This kind of incident can wreck a career for ever.'

'Maybe I should take a couple of days off,' said Breen. 'Get back on top of things. I've had a lot going on.'

Bailey's face twitched. 'You were perfectly entitled to take time off when your father died,' he said quietly. 'If you'd have taken a couple of days off then maybe this would never have happened . . . but I'm not giving you time off now. That would be a mistake.' Bailey went back to rolling the pencil back and forth over the blotting paper on his desk. 'These things are no good,' he said. 'If you turn your back on them, they fester. People talk. Tell me, why doesn't Prosser like you?'

'I wasn't aware he didn't, sir.'

'Don't play simple, Breen. You know he doesn't like you.'

'I'm not one of the lads, I suppose.'

Bailey opened the folder and picked through sheets of paper. 'You don't live on our turf, do you?'

'Stoke Newington, sir. I was stationed there before I moved to Marylebone.'

Bailey stood and walked slowly to his windowsill. He grew African violets there. They were lined up in a small row of terracotta pots sitting on jam-jar lids. The east-facing light was ideal for them. He kept a small bucket outside the door to the yard that collected rainwater for the plants. Tap water was too strong for them, he said.

'Prosser is not a good policeman. He's uncouth and does what he pleases,' said Bailey, his back still to Breen. 'Nor am I convinced of his integrity. I barely recognise the force I joined these days.'

A familiar speech. They'd all heard it a hundred times.

'You, on the other hand . . . until now you've been a diligent old-fashioned copper. Steady. One stupid incident and Prosser's a hero. And as for you. Talk starts. It doesn't go away unless you make it. Better to face it down.'

'Yes, sir.'

He turned to face Breen again. 'How's the investigation into the body in the fire going?'

'Nothing yet, sir.'

Bailey grunted again, overfilling one of the plant pots so water spilled over its saucer onto the carpet. 'Bugger,' he said. 'Pass me a tissue, will you?' He pointed to a box of tissues on his desk. Breen pulled one out and handed it to him.

'We are a small team here at Marylebone. There is not room for enmity and division. Whatever his merits, Sergeant Prosser is popular. He has influence. An incident like this only boosts his reputation at the expense of yours. We don't want that, do we?'

On his desk, positioned so Breen could see it too, Bailey kept a silver-framed photograph of his wife, round-faced, soft-skinned, smiling.

'Report. On my desk this afternoon.'

★

13

'You resigned yet, then?' said Jones. People looked up, curious.

'Shut up, Jones, or I'll clock you one,' said Carmichael.

Breen said nothing. Marilyn brought a beige folder over to his desk. Pink Marks and Spencer's pullover. Bullet bra. Bleached hair with occasional roots.

'What's this?'

'Missing Persons file you asked for. You OK?' she added quietly.

'I'm OK,' answered Breen. 'Your boyfriend got a job yet?'

She scowled. 'I've warned him unless he does he'll be out.'

'Good for you, Marilyn.'

'Hasta la bloody vista, know what I mean?'

She leaned in, straightening the folder she had just left on his desk. 'What Jones and the rest is saying, I don't believe it. Not for a minute. Don't you worry.'

'But it's true,' said Breen.

'It can't be.'

'Can I ask you something? Do you think I'm old-fashioned?'

She laughed. 'Sort of. I don't mind though.'

'What, like, stuck in the mud?'

Not answering, she turned her back on him and returned to her desk. The tidiest in the whole room.

He looked at the Missing Persons folder, not opening it yet. The same night Breen's father had gone into hospital there had been a fire in one of the bombed-out houses in Carlton Vale. Locals had been complaining that truanting kids from Kynaston Tech had been setting light to the derelict houses all summer, but when the firemen had dampened the flames they found human remains on what was left of the first floor. The can of lighter fuel next to the body suggested it had been a dosser attempting to light a fire to keep himself warm. The burned body remained unidentified. No time for that now. He put the folder aside. He had Bailey's report to write.

Breen placed a sheet of carbon paper between two sheets and wound them into his typewriter. He typed 'Detective Sergeant C. Breen 14/10/68', then stared at the blank page for a minute. He had read the shaky writing that filled six pages of his notebook several times and still failed to make sense of it.

Marilyn's phone rang. Distracted, Breen watched her answer it, saw the softness of her face disappear as she listened. 'Right,' she said. She picked up a notebook and started writing out details in shorthand. 'OK,' she said, pencil still in hand, 'got it,' and put the phone down. It rattled on the cradle. She looked up at Breen.

'One just come in,' she said. She stood and walked straight to Bailey's office.

'Sir?' She knocked on the glass of his door.

Bailey stood, square-shouldered, in the middle of the office. He was cleaning his glasses with his handkerchief again, listening with the rest of them as Marilyn read from her notes.

'A young naked woman,' Marilyn said. 'Found under debris. St John's Wood. Discovered by a woman. Approximately eleven a.m. Local resident called it in. Body appears recent.'

It was 11.20 now, according to the bakelite clock that hung above the door.

'Aye, aye,' said Carmichael. 'Young naked woman. Best not send Jones. He's never seen one of them.'

''K off.'

'Some things we don't joke about in this office, Carmichael.'

'No, sir.' Carmichael smirked, looking downwards. Tobacco suede Chelsea boots, finger loop at the ankles.

'May we continue?'

'Go ahead,' said Carmichael.

No one liked Bailey, but people hadn't used to be so obvious about their feelings.

Bailey cleared his throat and turned to Marilyn again. 'Any sign of a weapon?'

'Didn't say, sir.'

Bailey gazed around the room, looking from face to face. Then he made up his mind. 'Breen, by rights I think this one's yours.'

'Me, sir? You already put me on the arson one, sir.'

Bailey sniffed. 'I'm aware of that. However, as you might have noticed we're a little short-staffed today. Nothing wrong with you taking on another case, is there, Sergeant?'

'No, sir.'

'Specially as you're the reason we're short,' muttered Jones.

'I'm sure you're keen to show you're up to it, aren't you, Paddy?' said the inspector.

'Yes, sir,' he said.

Bailey pursed his lips for a second as if deep in thought. Eventually he said, 'Jones? You'll assist on the murder squad.'

'Assist Breen, sir?'

'Yes. Assist.'

Jones glowered at Bailey. 'Yes, sir. If you say so.'

'Good.' And turned back to his office and his African violets and closed the door behind him.

They stood there for a second, saying nothing, until Marilyn said to Jones, 'You know what he's trying to do, don't you? Stop you acting like a total spacker about what happened to Prosser.'

'Thanks for making that perfectly clear, Marilyn,' said Jones. 'Only it ain't going to work.'

'I know,' said Marilyn. 'You're still going to be a spacker either way.'

Breen began looking through the drawers of his desk for a fresh notebook. There was a prescription for some painkillers for his father and a pile of raffle tickets from the D Division Christmas Ball 1967, but no notebook.

Jones, nylon blazer and brown slacks, dark hair Brylcreemed down below his collar, came up and stood close to him and said quietly, 'I said I'd go and do an errand for Prosser. On account of him being in hospital. 'Cause he got stabbed. I'll be along this afternoon, if you can handle it until then, that is.'

'Fine by me,' said Breen. 'Anyone got a spare notebook?'

THREE

Two local constables from the St John's Wood station stood at the entrance to the alleyway into the back of the flats. They were still waiting for the tarp to cover the victim with.

'A kid found her,' volunteered one of the constables. 'The body was covered up by a mattress. All sorts of people must have walked past her from the back of Cora Mansions this morning, but he spotted her on account of his height. Being short, you see?'

At the beginning of an investigation, local constables were especially keen.

'So she could have been there a while, I reckon.'

'Thanks.'

The body was out of sight beyond the line of sheds. Breen noticed a man setting up a camera on a tripod.

'Anybody know who she is?'

'No, sir. Unidentified so far.'

'Anybody gone round the houses yet?'

The policeman, a pale-looking youngster, raised an eyebrow. 'We was waiting for you, sir.'

Breen stepped back. On the fire escape at the back of Cora Mansions, a woman in a pale housecoat stood leaning over the metal banister looking down at the group of men working around the body. 'You going to take a look, sir?'

A ginger cat sat on the roof of one of the sheds, glaring at the activity. The police camera's flash went off.

The cameraman was lowering his tripod to alter the angle of his shot. The police doctor looked up from his kitbag. 'Bugger me,' he said. 'Paddy Breen. Heard you were last seen running away from the scene of the crime. What are you doing here?'

'Good to see you too, Dr Wellington,' said Breen.

'If I die,' said Wellington, 'please don't let me be found with my naked behind sticking up to the sky. What a way to go.' Early forties. Balding. Hair swept over the top. Rakish sideburns and a cravat.

They had moved the mattress off the body and stood it against the brick wall next to her. The woman – not much more than a girl really – lay awkwardly, head jammed down on the earth, legs above her, tangled in a rusted bicycle frame. Absurd in her nakedness. Drizzle trickled unevenly from her upturned bottom down her pale, dead back. A small drip of blood had dried at the upturned corner of her mouth. Her pale blue eyes were wide and glassy.

Breen looked away. 'Excuse me,' he said.

He managed to walk four paces before he was sick into a patch of straggly nettles a little further down the alleyway. There had not been much in his stomach besides coffee. When he pulled a handkerchief from his pocket to wipe his mouth, he felt his hand shaking.

'You all right, sir?' said a constable.

Breen looked away. His nostrils, throat and mouth stung. His stomach churned. 'Yes, I'm fine.'

'Christ,' said Wellington.

'I think it's just a bug . . .'

He bent over and vomited again. He spat a long dribble of saliva onto the grass next to his small, pink pile of sick.

'I think that's what the college boys call contaminating the site, Breen,' called Wellington, rummaging in his equipment bag and eventually pulling out first a thermometer and then a small jar of Vaseline.

'Do you want a cough drop, sir?' said the local copper.

Still leaning over the patch of weeds he answered, 'No, I'll be fine,' spitting onto the grass again to try to clear the stinging taste from his mouth.

He straightened himself up, stomach aching from the convulsions.

'Was she killed here, or dumped?' he asked Wellington. His voice was quiet, not much more than a whisper.

'Dumped,' said the doctor.

'Yes?'

'Well, I don't think she bloody walked here looking like that. Looks like she was lying on her side for an hour or so after she was killed. Come here. Only don't go chucking up on the evidence, Breen.'

Breen took a deep breath, stood up straight and approached the corpse again. 'Look here,' said Wellington, leaning over the woman. 'Blood pooling in the tissue of her left-hand side.' He pointed to a blueness in the skin on her pale thigh. 'A prettier corpse than the last pile of bones you brought me,' he said.

Still leaning, he reached out and, holding it between finger and thumb, inserted the thermometer into the dead girl's anus. 'Convenient, at least,' said Wellington, twisting the glass rod a few times to push it in further. 'This won't hurt a bit,' he muttered.

Breen quelled the spasm in his throat.

'Charming,' muttered one of the coppers.

Satisfied that it was in far enough, Wellington stood and looked at his watch. 'You don't look well, Breen,' he said. 'You want me to take your temperature too? When she's finished with it?'

'I'm fine, thank you, Dr Wellington. Thank you for asking.'

'How was she killed?'

'I'll go a tenner on asphyxiation. No other signs of injury so far.'

'Strangled, like?' said a constable.

Wellington glanced at the young man, irritated. He was not an investigating officer and had no right butting in. 'Possibly,' he said. 'Faint petechiae on the face. Blood spots. Her head appears to be congested with blood.'

The rain was starting to come down harder now, forming puddles in the dirty earth. Water dripped off the dead girl's white fingers. Wellington carried on counting the seconds on his watch.

★

For constables who spent most of their time on the beat, a murder was a treat. They crowded round, eager, notebooks at the ready. Breen started by dividing them into two groups. The first were to start with a fingertip search of the whole back alley, working out onto the road and then spreading out from there.

'What are we looking for?' said one.

Breen paused. He felt another lurch in his stomach.

'Anything,' he said.

The policemen looked at each other, puzzled. Breen pulled out his handkerchief again and held it to his mouth. He turned his back to them and stared hard at the ground as the world around seemed to dip and weave.

A voice behind him. 'Sir?'

'Give me a minute,' he muttered.

He could hear the buzz of conversation growing behind him. Someone laughed.

'Clothes,' he said. The murmuring stopped. He took another breath of air. 'Clothes. Dress. Blouse. Bra. Knickers.' He paused, rubbed his eyes with the back of his hand, then continued. 'She's naked, isn't she? Where are her clothes? Handbag. Coat. Purse. Think of anything a girl carries around. Lipstick. Powder. Women's things. You –' he pointed to a ruddy-faced copper who looked a little older than the rest. 'You're in charge of checking out these flats' bins, OK?'

A groan.

'Shrubbery. Front gardens. Knock on doors and ask to look in back gardens. Any railways or canals round here?'

'There's the underground up there.'

'Good. How far?'

''Bout a quarter-mile.'

'You. Call up the Transport Police. Give them my name. Say we want to search the banks, especially around road bridges. You two do the canal.'

'Yes, sir.'

'You . . .' Breen pointed to one of the constables.

'Me, sir?' He'd picked the tallest, a lanky lad with thick eyebrows.

'You take a note of the locations where they have searched and write down exactly where anything is found.'

'Right, sir,' the lad said, pleased to have been picked.

'Can't I do that?' said the one who'd been given the bins. 'Only I got a bad back.'

'You stick to the bins. You'll be fine. Anybody finds anything, report it back to . . . What's your name?' The copper mumbled his name. 'Towels. Sacks. Blankets. Sheets. Anything she might have been wrapped in before she was dumped. Or just anything that you think shouldn't be there . . .' he tailed off.

Still they stood there, waiting for more instructions.

'Right then. Start by that wall,' he said. 'In a line. Move towards the street. And then . . . spread out.'

Finally they shuffled off, happier now he'd told them what to do. He turned to the second group. 'Door-to-door,' he said.

This time they huffed like kids who had been picked for the fat boy's team. Like all beat policemen, they abhorred knocking on doors, talking politely to members of the public. He gave them four questions. Did anybody have any idea who the dead girl might be? How long had that rubbish been piled by the sheds? Had anyone heard anything suspicious last night? Had anybody seen or noticed anyone different around the flats in the last few weeks? There were almost certainly better questions, but he couldn't think of any, right now. He told the constables to start with the ground floor flats and work up. After that they could begin to move on up the road.

When they had set off to do what he had asked, he went to sit in the police car and lit a cigarette. Breen smoked five cigarettes a day. No more. He liked using them to divide up the day, plus it made a packet of No. 6's last four days. Today he was already on his second. He sat behind the driving wheel, leaning forward to lay his head on the cool plastic. The sight of a dead body had never affected him like this before. He was not well.

After a minute he sat back and pulled out the clean notebook and the pencil. He sat for a while, holding the pencil in one hand and the cigarette in the other.

A few minutes after Wellington had left, an ambulance arrived, bell ringing, to take the body away. It parked in the middle of the street. The flash of its blue lights shone off the last damp leaves on the lime trees. As always, a small crowd had gathered to watch the goings-on. A young man dressed in football kit, and a woman with a headscarf and shopping trolley. A pair of young girls joined them to watch the gurney pass, rattling on the uneven ground. Dressed in big woollen coats and loud scarves the girls clutched each other by the arms as the dead girl passed them, covered by a black sheet. Craning her neck to see past them, a nanny dressed in a dark uniform stood smoking a cigarette just a few yards back from the rest of them. They seemed to be there just to feast on the sadness of the scene. Jones had arrived. He was picking through the debris, where the body had lain.

After a while, Breen started to feel cold, so he switched on the Cortina's engine. The hum of the engine was reassuring.

A knocking on the driver-side window. It was one of the constables. 'Are you all right, sir?'

He wound it down.

'I said are you OK?'

'I'm fine,' said Breen. He wiped his eyes with the cuff of his jacket. 'I just needed a couple of minutes to think.'

'Yes, sir. Only, there's a woman on the second floor. I think you should speak to her.'

He squinted up at her, leaning down towards the car's open window. 'Did she hear something?'

'She was the woman who called it in, sir. And she says new people moved in round here.'

'And?'

'And I think you should speak to her, sir.'

He turned off the car's motor. 'Do you have a mint or something?'

'No, sir. Sorry.'

Breen shook himself, then adjusted the rear-view mirror to look at himself. He got out of the car to follow the copper.

The second-floor flats had their own walkway that ran along the front of the building. Faces peered out from behind doors as they passed. Breen had never minded it before. To be a policeman is to be watched. You were like a car crash. People stopped to gape.

The constable stopped in front of a green-painted door with a knocker in the shape of a pixie and a doorbell to one side. He rang the bell. A woman opened the door a crack. 'This is Detective Sergeant Breen,' said the copper.

Breen stepped forward. 'Good afternoon, Mrs . . . Miss . . . ?'

'Shankley,' said the policeman reading from his notebook.

'Miss,' said Miss Shankley, unchaining the door and standing back to let them in. Breen recognised her now. She was the woman in the housecoat who had watched them from the fire escape. She led them down a short corridor into a living room cluttered with china ornaments. Cheap plaster heads of leering Moors, one-eyed pirates, swarthy fishermen and swashbuckling highwaymen stared down from the walls. Shiny porcelain animals stood on every available surface.

Breen walked over to the window. The net curtains were drawn back. A family of white china cats sat on the sill.

'We've never had anything like this happen round here. Would you like a cigarette?' Breen shook his head and the constable did the same. 'I have filter tips if you'd prefer? No?' Picking up a packet of Woodbines from the mantelpiece above the gas fire, the woman sat herself in an armchair opposite the television. On top, a pair of toby jugs stared at each other.

'Any idea who she is?' asked Breen. He looked back out of the window. The small crowd was still there, peering round the sheds at the policemen as they picked through the rubbish on which the girl's body had lain.

'I heard,' the woman leaned forward, flicking a lighter, 'that she was a prostitute.' She wore thick foundation that ended abruptly at the side of her face and at the line of her chin.

'You heard?'

'It's talk. In the building.' She smoothed down her housecoat over her knees.

'Who was doing the talking, Miss Shankley?' Breen looked down at her.

The woman pouted. 'I just heard it on the stairs. It's amazing what you pick up.'

Breen looked down at his shoes. He wished she would ask them both to sit down, but she just sat there puffing on her cigarette. He had barely slept last night. He said, 'Anything we know that could identify her is extremely important. Who did you hear it from?'

She sniffed, then said, 'If you must know, it was Mr Rider.'

The constable looked at his notebook. 'Flat number 31,' he said. 'Floor above.'

'That's right. Are you going to mention that to him? Only, I'd appreciate if you didn't tell him it was me as said so, you understand. I don't want to cast any aspersions. This is a nice block.' Miss Shankley tipped the ash of her cigarette into a large ashtray. 'How was she killed?'

'We can't say yet.'

'Was she interfered with?'

'I'm not sure.'

'There was a woman abducted in a van on Abbey Road a few years ago. It turned out to be a young man who was a bit soft in the head who worked in the bakery. I don't think he lives around here now, though.'

The woman sighed. The sound of a telephone ringing in the flat next door travelled through the walls.

'This has been a terrible experience. It's really shocking for everybody who lives here, you know.'

'What were you doing when you found the body?'

'Not me, no. I didn't find the body. It was the girl.'

Breen frowned. He looked over at the constable. 'The body was first spotted by a young woman who was walking with a child,' he said.

'She was screaming her head off. I came out to see what all the fuss was about,' said Miss Shankley. 'She was standing down there bawling her eyes out with these two poor little children.'

'Who is this girl?'

The constable shrugged. 'Miss Shankley said she was wearing a dark uniform. Possibly a nurse or a nanny.'

'She ran off,' said Miss Shankley.

Breen remembered the girl he had seen before, watching the body being removed. He went to the window and looked down but the girl was nowhere to be seen. 'Have you passed her description to the other constables?'

'Not yet, no, sir.'

'The constable here said you had something to tell me.'

'Well, yes, but I'm not sure it's important,' said Miss Shankley with a prim smile.

'It might be,' said the copper.

'Yes, of course. It might be. Who am I to say? You are the professionals, after all.'

Breen rubbed his head. 'Do you mind if I sit down?' he asked.

'I'm sorry. Rude of me,' she said. The sofa had plastic covers that squeaked as he lowered himself onto them.

'I feel so dreadful for the girl,' Miss Shankley said. 'Even if she was, you know . . . I mean, being found naked too. So degrading. It was never like this when I moved in. It was lovely, this block. We used to have street parties down there.'

'My colleague said you . . .'

'You told me you had noticed some new people move into the building.'

'Not this building, thank heavens,' she said. 'No, no. The house behind.' She stood and pointed out of the window.

Breen stood again, slowly, took a couple of paces to the window and looked out to where she was pointing. Behind the lock-ups, behind where the dead girl had been found and the wall against which the rubbish was stacked, was a white Victorian house, half hidden by a large lime tree that stood between the new flats and the older building. Paint was peeling from the wall closest to them and a leaky overflow pipe had left a green stain down the white wall.

Miss Shankley stubbed out her cigarette, smoothed her housecoat, then stood up. She picked up the ashtray and disappeared to the kitchen to empty it.

'When did they move in?' called Breen.

'Two weeks ago. Two and a half now. On the Wednesday.'

'You're very precise about that.'

'You notice things,' she said, re-entering the living room with the ashtray wiped clean.

'Like what?'

'Well, you notice things that are unusual, don't you?'

'Not everyone does,' said the copper.

'I suppose not,' said Miss Shankley, smiling as she smoothed down her housecoat.

'Unusual?' asked Breen.

She lowered her voice. 'They're dark,' she said, as if they might hear if she spoke too loud.

'Dark?'

'Black. You know. Africans,' she said, as if he hadn't understood.

'I see,' said Breen. He sat back down on the sofa. 'Africans?'

'Well, they told me they were from Africa,' said Miss Shankley.

'Oh.' He sat back on the sofa. On the walls were three mallards, all different sizes, flying up in a diagonal line. He closed his eyes and rubbed each side of his nose with the finger and thumb of his left hand, then looked at his watch. It was past one o'clock. Lunchtimes in the pub were routine. He would not mind missing that today.

'Is that all you want to know?' asked the woman, disappointed at his silence.

'I'm just wondering why they told you they were African,' he said.

'Well, you see, at first I thought they were Jamaican. We had a Jamaican family move in last year. There was a lot of fuss about that. They didn't stay. Perhaps they didn't like it here. Well, it's not their sort of place, is it? We were very relieved when they moved. I'm sure they were too.'

Breen put his hands in his mac pockets. 'So . . . you told your new neighbours to go back to Jamaica and they told you they were Africans?'

'I beg your pardon?' said Miss Shankley, lifting her chin a little higher.

'Nothing. I think that's all for now,' he said, standing.

'It was just a neighbourly conversation, that's all,' said Miss Shankley.

'But they're new in the area and you think that they've got something to do with the dead girl?'

'I didn't say anything of the kind, officer,' she said, mouth hard and small. 'I just thought you should know that there were people who were not from round here who had recently moved in.'

'And we're grateful for you being so observant,' the constable butted in.

The woman sat on her plastic-covered armchair, pouting.

'Did the constable here ask if you heard anything out of the ordinary last night?' said Breen, pausing in the hallway.

'I asked her all your questions, sir. She says the rubbish has been like that for weeks. And she sleeps with earplugs in.'

'I have nothing against Africans,' said Miss Shankley. 'But they have the whole of Africa to live in.'

'Just one more question. What time do you get up in the morning?'

'Around six. I listen to the radio.'

'Do you remember if you looked out of the window?'

'Probably.'

'There's a mattress down there. It's orange.'

Breen pointed out of the window. Miss Shankley got up and stood beside him. The mattress was still leaning against the wall where the police had propped it when they uncovered the woman's body. 'Do you remember seeing where that was when you got up this morning?'

'Why would I notice a thing like that? You know,' said Miss Shankley, 'I saw you being sick in the bushes down there, Sergeant. I noticed that, clearly enough. I'd have thought you'd have got used to it by now.' Then to the copper, 'Is he all right? He's still looking a bit peaky if you ask me.'

'I think we're done, Constable,' said Breen.

'I'm a woman on my own. I find all this very disturbing.' She led them to the front door and as she held it open for them she said to the other policeman, 'Rivers of blood, you know.'

'What?' said the copper.

'Immigrants,' said the woman. 'What Mr Powell said. They don't have any place here. You wait. What if there were as many niggers in the country as bloody Irish? They let a thousand Pakis in the other day. Think about it. It's going to be trouble. You'll see.'

On the walkway outside, the copper said, 'Mind you, I think she's got a point. We all do.'

'What?' said Breen.

'You know. All the coons coming over. People don't like it. Not just Enoch Powell. They're taking our jobs. And they're bringing crime with them. They're taking over all the knocking shops too. And selling drugs.'

He strode on ahead down the walkway, then stopped and turned, waiting for Breen to catch up.

'My father was an immigrant,' said Breen.

'Yeah, but he definitely wasn't a coon, sir.'

Breen started up the stairs to speak to Mr Rider at number 31, the man who had told Miss Shankley that the dead girl was a prostitute, but there was no answer. The neighbour's front door opened and an old woman peered out and said, 'He's not in.'

'We going to knock on the darkie's door now?' said the constable.

★

When they went to try the door of the white house behind the sheds, no one was in there either.

'We could break in?' suggested the copper.

'We could,' said Breen. 'If this was *Z-Cars.*'

'Just an idea.'

Breen squatted down and pushed back the black painted letter flap to peer into the house but there was a letter box on the other side, blocking the view.

Back inside the police car, Breen wound down the passenger window and watched the policemen, standing awkwardly in doorways as they talked to the residents, slowly working their way down the street.

FOUR

West London was full of colour. Each year the colours got louder. Girls in green leather miniskirts, boys in paisley shirts and white loafers. New boutiques selling orange plastic chairs from Denmark. Brash billboards with sexy girls in blue bikinis fighting the inch war. A glimpse of a front room in a Georgian house where patterned wallpaper had been overpainted in yellow and a huge red paper lampshade hung from the ceiling. Pale blue Triumphs and bright red Minis parked in the streets.

Around Clerkenwell the colour faded. The old monochromes of post-war London returned. Still flat-capped and grey, East London continued about its business.

The bus back to Stoke Newington was crowded and fractious. He stood downstairs, hanging onto the strap until the bus emptied out at Angel. For the rest of the journey he sat next to a young woman who was crammed into a seat surrounded by shopping bags full of new clothes. She was pretty in a Bardot-ish way. He found himself looking at her reflection in the glass of the bus window. On the other side of the glass, the orange street lights were bleary in the wetness.

He lived in a cul-de-sac behind the police station where he had worked before he took the job with D Division. Basement flat.

There had been no chance yet to put away his father's things. A carton of bandages still sat on the dresser and his walking frame was still by the door. On the telephone table a pile of the notes he had left for the women he had paid to look after his father while he was at work. The nurse's folded zed bed, tucked into the corner of the room. A tangle of wires from a single socket powered the radio-gram, two standard lamps, the electric clock and the television.

His father had stayed here for the last six years of his life but had never liked it. He had lived on his own in Fulham until the day he had forgotten about a pan of sausages and set fire to the kitchen of his flat. Breen had had to move out of the police section house on Mare Street to rent this place. It had a spare bedroom that his father could use until he was well enough to move back on his own. That had never happened.

It seemed too early to start moving his father's belongings. They still cluttered the flat: his photographs and books, his records by Italian tenors, his poetry and his novels and his collection of walking sticks, even the leather armchair Breen was sitting in now.

Normally Breen enjoyed cooking for himself. From the age of ten or eleven he had taken over cooking the meals for himself and his father. Tonight, though, he just heated a can of beans. He went to cut a slice of bread to go with it, but the loaf in the bread bin was sprouting grey mould.

He ate the beans on their own in front of *Olympic Grandstand*. He was watching a girl from the USSR who was doing floor exercises to some thumping piano music – she was beautiful in a scary, Soviet kind of way – when the electricity clicked off. The light on the television shrank to a small line, then a single dot, then disappeared into blackness.

Breen sat there a minute, eyes adjusted to the darkness. The sounds of the street seemed louder now. When his eyes began to make out dull shapes, he stood and felt around for the electric meter by the front door. He usually left a pile of half crowns on top but they were all gone. He dug one out of his pocket, fed it into the slot and turned the handle. The television came back to life, blaring a national anthem he didn't recognise.

After he'd washed the plate and put it on the rack he smoked his fifth and last cigarette, then dressed in his pyjamas and went to bed, worn thin by the day.

He sat in bed looking through his police notebooks, one for the dead man, the other for the dead girl. He hadn't even begun to write his report about what had happened to Prosser last night. He fell asleep trying to remember what he had meant when he had written 'Ask about the doors'.

Four hours later he woke, unable to return to sleep. He switched on the light by the table, and lay awake for a few minutes, then he got up and shaved.

Outside it was dark. He walked down Kingsland High Street, deserted at two in the morning but for the occasional car, pavements silver with rain. The late summer was slipping into winter with little in the way of autumn in between.

He passed shops with their wooden shutters down, barrows chained to trees, piles of rubbish and dogs that growled from behind locked gates. Below the pavement, water trickled noisily through drains.

At Dalston Junction he arrived at Joe's All Night Bagel Shop. It never closed, serving tea and coffee to lorry drivers delivering at Ridley Road market and to the taxi drivers waiting for the early shift to begin. The front of the cafe was painted bright red. In the window was a handwritten sign that read 7 *days without a bagel makes one weak.*

Joe, leaning on the counter reading a novel, looked up as he came in. 'Hello, my friend,' he said, and spooned coffee into a mug without asking. Joe only served instant. When Breen had told him he should buy one of the machines like the coffee shops in the West End and start serving real coffee, he had said, 'And maybe get a skiffle band to play for my customers too.'

'Teacakes are half price,' said Joe as he filled the mug with hot water from an urn. Breen never ate here, but Joe always offered something.

'What's the news?' asked Breen.

'My daughter is about to make me a grandfather,' said Joe. 'What's happening with you?'

'I'm in the shit.'

Joe said, 'Don't tell me your problems. I have enough of my own,' and went back to reading his novel. Breen added a spoonful of sugar to his coffee, stirred, then stood at the counter slowly sipping it. The bell went and a young greaser couple in black leathers came in, ordered egg and chips and sat down on opposite sides of a small table, staring at each other while they waited for Joe to cook their food. The guy had long hair and huge sideburns, like some reincarnated Viking warrior. He stubbed out a cigarette and leaned over and started to kiss the young woman on the mouth. Older men gaped enviously over cooling tea. In all their lives they had never had the chance to be as young as this, to wear leather and to fondle beautiful women so brazenly in public. As if to tease them further, under the table, the man forced his right hand between the black leather of the young woman's thighs. She slapped it away and broke the kiss, laughing loudly.

The doorbell rang again. This time it was a young man in a tweed cap that looked too small for him, brim pointing upwards. He approached the counter and asked for a cup of tea.

'Cor, look at them two.' He nodded at the pair of greasers who were kissing again. 'I bet she fucks him,' he said quietly. 'What you think? I bet she likes it too. I bet she fucks anyone. I'd fuck her.'

Joe said nothing. While he served the tea, the young man said in a quiet voice. 'Hey, I got something good for you. Do you want to buy any watches? Gold watches going cheap.'

Joe replaced the large teapot on the table and said, 'What do I need to tell the time for? This bloody place never bloody closes.' He turned back to the chip basket, lifting it from the hot fat.

The young man blinked a couple of times. It could have been a nervous tic. 'I thought you Yids liked a bit of tom.'

'A bit of tom? God save us. Talk English, schmuck. You watch too much television.'

'Tom. Tomfoolery,' the guy whispered. 'You know, jewellery.'

'Oh, for goodness' sake go home,' said Joe quietly. The chips were still too pale. He dropped them back into the bubbling oil.

Next the young man turned to Breen. When he'd come in, Breen had thought he was only about twenty. Now he looked closer he could see fine lines around his eyes, and veins breaking in the skin. 'What about you, mate? Nice stuff.'

Joe said, over his shoulder, 'You're barking up the wrong tree there, my friend. I told you, if you know what's best for yourself, get lost.'

The young man was offended. 'I'm just trying to earn a living like the rest of you,' he said.

Joe snorted. He cracked first one egg, then a second, onto the hotplate and wiped his brow with his forearm.

'Shockproof,' said the man to Breen, picking up his mug of tea. 'Gold straps. Roman numerals. Guaranteed to five yards underwater.'

Breen put down his coffee and reached inside his jacket pocket. For a second the man's face lit up, thinking he was about to make a sale, until Breen pulled out his wallet and opened it. 'Do as he says. Get lost.'

The man slapped his cup back down, spilling brown tea over Joe's Formica counter, and was gone into the night in half a second.

'You could have waited till he paid,' muttered Joe.

'Keep your hair on,' said Breen, putting his warrant card back into his jacket pocket. 'I'll get it.'

Joe wiped down the surface with a grey dishcloth. 'Flash that flipping thing around in here any more and I won't have any customers at all.' He put two plates onto the counter and tipped the chips onto them, then slid two eggs from the hotplate. 'Egg and chips twice,' he called.

The greaser couple broke from their kiss and the man stood to fetch the plates. Breen pulled out his notebook and flicked through the pages he had written. His notes were densely scribbled and unmethodical. It was as if he had forgotten how he used to arrive at a scene and patiently record first the time of day, then the position of the corpse, and so on. Across the bottom of a page he had written 'River Tiber'. He borrowed a pencil from Joe and turned to a clean page and started sketching what he remembered of the scene behind the flats. He had added diagrams to police notebooks before, but never drawings, even though he had a talent for it. Art had been one of the few subjects he had done well in at school. His father had never been able to hide his disappointment at the mediocrity of his son's academic results, but the day before the funeral, Breen had discovered a small roll of the drawings he had done at school carefully tied in red ribbon, tucked in a box his father had brought with him to the flat.

He drew the downward curve of her back and the pure roundness of her behind, her arms folded awkwardly. 'What you drawing?' said Joe.

Breen closed the notebook rapidly and put it back into his pocket.

It was quiet now. In an hour or so the morning shift would start arriving on their way to work. Joe went to his LP collection and spent a while looking through it, pulling out a record, replacing it, eventually picking out another. There was a record player just to the right of the counter. Joe took the black disc out of its sleeve and laid it on the turntable, then lifted the needle and dropped it carefully.

There was a moment of crackle, then a piano began to play slow descending notes. A cello joined in for a short phrase, then the rest of the string quartet, until they all gave way to the cello exchanging conversational phrases with the piano.

The woman looked up, 'What in hell's that?'

'Leave it,' said her boyfriend, pausing from his chips.

Joe came out front and sat down on a plastic chair and took out a cigarette and tapped it quietly on the table in front of him, then lit it and smoked as the music played. No one spoke. The only other noise was the clatter of cutlery on plate and the sigh of one of the old insomniacs who gathered at Joe's in the smaller hours. It was one of those times when the unsatisfactory complexity of the world fades far enough into the distance for the moment to become a thing in itself. Making a shape out of such sadness seemed to offer a safety from it. Breen sat and listened as his coffee cooled. The moment lasted for two or three whole minutes before the bell rang and a bobby on his beat came in, the door's bell ringing dissonantly against the music.

'Aye, aye, Joe,' said the copper. 'Cup of tea. Two sugars. An' turn down that old racket, why don't you?'

On Wednesday morning the first post brought a letter from his father's solicitor. There were no surprises. He knew the contents of his father's will already. A few shares that were not worth much and around two thousand pounds that had been left over after paying for the nurses to look after him. Enough to give up the police, if he wanted, and live off what was left over for a year or maybe more. Maybe go to Ireland. He had never been. Or maybe buy a car. He had never owned one of those either. He put the letter in a drawer and walked up to Church Street to catch the bus to St John's Wood.

Mr Rider was in this time.

He was a small, round, middle-aged man who lived alone. He wore a Marylebone Cricket Club tie with a brown cardigan and opened the door with a smoking briar pipe in his hand.

'And?' he said.

'May I ask a couple of questions, sir?'

He eyed Breen up and down and pulled on his pipe. Breen took out his warrant card and showed it to him. The man peered at it. 'What about?'

'The murder of a young woman.'

'Ah. Yes. Of course.' He opened the door and beckoned Breen in.

Rider's apartment was spartan: no television in the living room, no pictures on the walls. A complete set of *Encyclopaedia Britannica* and six volumes of *The Second World War* by Winston Churchill filled the bookshelf above a desk on which sat a solitary black and white photograph, framed in silver, of a young woman in army uniform.

'You said the murdered woman was a prostitute. I wonder how you knew.'

'I beg your pardon?' Mr Rider stood still, blinking at Breen.

Breen repeated what he had said.

Mr Rider opened and shut his mouth, then fiddled in his trouser pocket for a box of matches, before saying, 'I didn't.'

'You didn't what, Mr Rider?'

The room was thick with the reek of pipe smoke. There were no flowers or ornaments; a man's room. The kind of absence of a woman's touch that he recognised from his own childhood. 'I didn't know she was a . . . ah . . . prostitute.'

'But apparently you told people that you thought she was.'

'No I didn't.' Pause. 'I suppose I may have. I was just guessing. Rather silly of me, really, I see now. It sort of shakes you up, when something like this happens.'

'What made you think she was a prostitute?'

Mr Rider struck a match to relight his briar pipe, sucking on it furiously. 'I mean, there are prostitutes not far from here. After all, you do notice them.'

'You notice them?'

'What do you mean?'

'Do you use their services, Mr Rider?'

The small man blushed and shook his head. 'No. Certainly not.'

'I wouldn't necessarily think the worse of you if you did. I just want to know.'

The man shook his head again. 'No. No. I don't.'

'So you have no particular reason for thinking the dead woman was a prostitute?'

The man said nothing.

'People like to assume the worst of the dead; that it's their fault for getting killed,' said Breen. A strangled girl. A burned-alive man.

'I beg your pardon?'

'Can I ask where you were on Sunday night?'

'Sunday night?'

38

'Yes.'

'The night the girl was killed?'

'That's right.'

'I'd have to think.' The man reached into his trouser pocket and pulled out a small knife and started excavating the bowl of his pipe.

'Take your time,' said Breen.

'I don't know. Probably went for a walk. Came back here. Had supper. Listened to the wireless. The Light Programme. Same as always.'

'Nothing more definite than that?'

'I don't have particularly definite days,' said the man with a small, high giggle. 'I'm retired. A widower. I live alone. I suppose it's rather odd to a young man like you, but the days just pass.'

'Try and think.'

'I'm trying,' said the man abruptly and with that the knife slipped. The man gave a small squeak and put his left thumb into his mouth. A dribble of blood trickled down his chin.

'You've hurt yourself, Mr Rider.'

'It's nothing,' he said quietly, but to do so meant taking his thumb out of his mouth. Blood spilled down his old skin onto a thin Persian rug.

'Hold your hand up. It'll slow the blood,' said Breen.

Breen went to the bathroom. He found Elastoplast where he would have expected it, in a small cabinet in which Mr Rider also kept his toothbrush, his razor, a tin of Eno Fruit Salts and an old empty bottle of Yardley English Lavender. A women's perfume.

He returned with the plasters. 'I can manage perfectly well myself,' snapped the man as blood splodged onto the white cuff of his shirt.

Outside again, Breen made it to the end of the walkway, then stopped. For a few minutes he sat on the cold stairs writing his notes. When he looked back he found that he had written a list. 'Pipe. Blood rug. Woman in photo. People think worst of dead. Lonely.'

Two pages that would sound ridiculous if he was ever required to read it out in court.

Breen looked up at the sound of footsteps. A man he recognised as one of the residents, clutching a stiff broom. 'You going to be there all day?' he said.

Breen closed his notebook, put it back into his pocket and stood, then watched the man patiently sweeping the stairs, one at a time.

The debris had all been cleared away. A search of the ground had turned up nothing. Now there was just a patch of bare earth next to the sheds.

The local constables were gathering again in the yard. Jones was there too, hands in his suit pockets, chatting to a couple of the uniformed men. Breen arrived at the bottom of the stairs just as a dustbin lorry was reversing slowly down the small opening between the sheds and the building. Somebody had scrawled on the back of the lorry's dark green paint, *Thunderbird 3*.

'What's going on?'

'Three guesses,' called one of the binmen jumping off the back of the lorry. Wearing a large canvas apron and a big pair of leather gloves, he waddled to a pair of steel doors and banged back the bolt. There was a huge iron bin that collected the refuse from half of the flats inside.

'Leave it,' Breen said. 'I don't want it taking away.' He called to a nearby constable, 'What happened to that copper I told to go through the rubbish?'

'Off sick I heard. Bad back, so he said.'

'Off sick?'

'Yep.'

'Why didn't anybody tell me?'

'Dunno.'

The binman stood with a chain, ready to latch it onto the big bin. Breen ran over. 'Leave it alone. Come back another time.'

'No skin off mine.'

'What's going on?' Miss Shankley was leaning over the railings above.

'Sergeant Breen is arresting your dustbins,' said Jones.

The binman banged on the side of the lorry. 'Ride 'em out, cowboy,' he shouted. 'Police orders.'

'We need to examine the contents,' Breen said.

'Now the buggers won't be back for another week. It'll stink the place up,' Miss Shankley called down.

Breen walked across the yard and pulled off the ladder that hung on hooks against the wall.

'Careful with that,' Miss Shankley shouted.

Leaning the ladder against the side of the bin, he said to the young freckle-faced constable who was still standing nearby, 'In you go.'

'Me, sir?'

'Yes.'

'Inside that?'

'See what you can find.'

Jones said, ''K that for a lark. She was dumped, Wellington said. Chances are, you get your uniform all mucky for squat, mate. We're not going to find anything round here anyway.'

'We need to check the bins,' said Breen, ignoring him. 'Up,' he ordered.

'It reeks, sir.'

The other coppers jeered. 'Go on, Pigpen.'

'So. What are we going to do then, sir?' one of the local constables asked Breen.

'Keep on with the door-to-door.'

A half-dozen local officers were milling around, fecklessly waiting. Breen had asked for more but this was all he had been sent today. The assumption that the girl was going to turn out to be a dead prostitute was already having its effect. The force would not waste resources.

'Move, then,' ordered Breen.

A couple of them groaned. The novelty of an escape from the

drudgery of the beat had already worn off. The officers were a mixture of the young and inexperienced and older coppers who didn't like any officer telling them the way to do things.

Breen asked them to gather round. A circle of men surrounded him. 'We'll do this street, then move on to Abbey Road. OK? Take a house each and work your way down. Be imaginative. Try and find out if anyone—'

'Sir?' interrupted one.

'Yes?'

'We already done this street yesterday.'

'Yes, I know,' answered Breen. 'And?'

'And like I said, we already done that.'

'We questioned the occupants in daylight, just after the murder,' he said. 'Half the people would have been at work. They'll have been home now and had a chance to talk about it some more. Now we need to do it all over again to find out what they're saying today. We haven't even found the nanny who first found the body yet. Ask around. See if anyone knows where she lives. Keep going over and over until we find something.'

'Two to one she's not even from round here,' muttered Jones.

There was grumbling from the younger ones at the back. Breen ignored it. 'Find out what they're saying. Find out . . . what they think about it all.'

'What they think about it?' said one of the older coppers incredulously.

There were a couple of sniggers. They preferred it when they had a list of questions they could go through one by one.

'Yes. What they think about it all. About the murder. About who she might have been.'

'You're the boss.'

The policemen drifted off back down the street away from them.

'Short odds she's a judy like that guy upstairs says,' Jones said

42

to Breen. 'If this was Prosser's case he'd have already checked the streetwalkers.'

'Then why don't you ask Carmichael who the prostitutes are round here? He's on Vice. He might have heard something.'

'You're the one who's all matey with Carmichael,' Jones said. 'Why don't you?'

Breen only half heard him. He was standing by the line of lockups, close to where the body was found and looking around him. He pulled an *A–Z* from the pocket of his coat and flicked through the pages until he found the one Cora Mansions was on. He looked from the page up at the streets around him. The alleyway at the back of the flats was narrow, too narrow for a car. If somebody had brought the victim in off the street they must have carried her. Strange place to choose to hide a body.

'I do hope you're not feeling poorly again, Sergeant.' He looked up. Miss Shankley, housecoat flapping in the gentle breeze, was on the rear fire escape again.

'Fine, thank you, Miss Shankley.'

'Glad to hear it. No collywobbles today, then?'

'Miss Shankley,' he called up to her. 'Is one of these sheds yours?'

'Third from the left.'

He went to the door and examined it. 'It has a new padlock.'

'Should bloody hope so.'

'Why's that?'

'Wait a mo.' She turned, then disappeared inside her flat. Two minutes later she had descended the front stairs and was standing next to him, tiptoeing around the muddy puddles in her fur-lined house slippers.

'They've all got new locks,' said Breen. All had been fitted with new brass hasps too. *Ask about the doors.*

'They were all broken into, weren't they?' said Miss Shankley as she arrived at his side.

'Were they?'

'Three, four weeks ago. We had your lot round about it. Surprised

43

you didn't know that. It was a bloody nuisance. Took the caretaker that long to get round to fixing it. I'm really not sure why we pay a service charge at all. He drinks, you know. Thinks we don't notice.'

Looking closer, under a new coat of paint, Breen could see the marks in the wood where each door had been prised open. He ran his fingers over splintered wood that had been covered with filler and sanded down. 'So somebody came along and busted all these doors?'

'You can see why we don't like strangers round here,' said Miss Shankley, nodding her head in the direction of the white house behind. 'Things go missing.'

'Oh yes. Your new neighbours. The ones that arrived, I think you said, two and a half weeks ago. That's a week after your doors were busted in.'

'I never actually said it was them, did I? You're deliberately misconstruing me.'

The sheds were small. The doors all opened outwards.

'I mean, it's not people like us who go around entering and breaking,' said Miss Shankley.

'Did you lose much stuff in the break-in?'

'No. Don't keep nothing valuable in there. Paint pots. Household items that needed mending. That sort of thing.' Breen remembered all the fearsome china ornaments in her flat and imagined a space crowded with limbless tigers and headless pirates.

'Is that all?' said Miss Shankley.

He held up the *A–Z* and pointed at the space to the north of the flats.

'What's this building here?' he asked, pointing to the map. Taking his eyes off it, he looked down past the lock-ups to the wall that separated the flats. You could see a roofline of what looked like a workshop of some kind rising above the brick wall.

'That's that recording studio.'

Breen looked blank.

'EMI. The Beatles. You know.'

Breen frowned.

'Bloody nuisance,' said Miss Shankley, turning away.

'Tell me one thing,' Breen asked her. 'What day were the locks fixed?'

'Last Friday, would you believe.' Breen did the calculation. The killing would have taken place two days later.

'How did you keep the shed safe before the caretaker fixed the locks?'

'Weren't any point really, was there? Nothing left in there worth having.'

'So your door was easy to open – until three or four days ago?'

'Wide to the world. Some people complained about them banging in the wind. Can't say I heard them, but it weren't my fault, was it?' She turned and waddled away back into the courtyard.

'Which people?' called Breen.

'Them people.' She thumbed her nose at the white Georgian building behind the sheds.

He walked up Garden Road and turned left onto Abbey Road. Twenty yards from the junction, a young girl of eight or nine in khaki shorts stood crying under an elm tree.

Other trees had lost their leaves in the rain of the last few days, but this one stood greenly straight, alone on the pavement. Breen walked past, then stopped and turned. The girl was still snivelling, eyes red.

'What's the matter?' Breen called back at her.

'My cat's stuck up the tree,' said the girl.

Breen looked up. 'I can't see it.'

'She's right at the top. Been there for hours.'

'She's just enjoying the view.'

'No she ain't.'

'She'll come down in a bit,' said Breen.

'No she won't.' The girl wiped her nose on the sleeve of her jumper.

'She will. You'll see.'

'No she won't.'

Breen walked on. By the next corner he stopped and looked back. She was still there, looking up at the tree, wetness shining on her face.

There was a low white wall behind which cars were parked. From a distance, it looked as if the paint was old and peeling. When he walked closer he saw that in fact the paint was relatively new, but hundreds of words were scratched into the surface. He peered to make them out. 'Mo'. 'Susan 4 George'. 'I luv you John Mary B'.

He squatted down to read more. 'Nina 4 Beatles'. 'John xxx Lisa'. 'Mary and Beth woz here 10/9/68'. 'USA loves you'. 'Wenna+Izzie always All we need is ❤'. 'Pippi and Carolyn 1968'. 'I shagged a Beatle' – 'LIAR' – 'NOT TRUE'. Painstakingly carved: 'Those who make revolutions halfway dig their own graves'. 'Hands off!!! I sor them 1st'. 'Paul call me! V. important!! Greenwich 4328'. 'Bob Dylan' – 'cant sing'. 'Kirby Hill girls love u'. 'I was alone I took a ride'. 'Kiwis are No 1 Beatles Fans'. 'YOU SAVED MY LIFE'. 'Jill = Scruffs'. 'Apple rules'. 'Leprosy I'm not half the man I used to be Since I became an amputee' – 'THAT IS SICK' – 'How DARE you?'. 'I am the walrus' – 'no i am'. 'WE LOVE CYNTHIA' . . . About thirty-five feet of wall, covered in these messages.

He walked round into the small car park. There were more words on the other side too.

'We paint over it every few months,' said a voice. Breen looked up.

The front of the recording studio was a large Georgian house, set back from the road. Standing on the steps leading up to the front door was a man in a brown caretaker's coat, holding a clipboard. There was a pile of musical instruments at the bottom of the stairs: cellos and double basses.

'Don't know why we bother. It's like that again in a few weeks.' He leaned forward and checked the labels on the instrument cases, then made some marks on his clipboard.

'Mostly girls?' said Breen.

'Ninety-five per cent.'

'How do they know when the Beatles are here?'

The man shrugged. 'Sometimes they're how we know when the Beatles are due. When they start arriving we know that means the Beatles will be in today.'

Breen wandered up to him and showed his warrant card.

'Oh yeah?'

'If I showed you a photo, would you be able to tell me if it was one of the girls?' he said.

'Don't bother. Another copper showed us it already. The dead girl.'

'You didn't recognise it?'

'No. There's so many of them. We don't pay them any mind, really. They're OK. Don't do any harm.'

The man picked up a pair of cello cases and walked them up the stairs.

'Is there anyone else I should ask?'

'Almost certainly,' he said, returning to pick up a double bass. 'But I don't know who that would be. Best thing you could do is come back when the Beatles are here. Then you'll see them all, all the girls.'

'When's that going to be?'

'No idea. Sorry.'

'What is it they all want?' asked Breen.

'Who? The girls?'

'Yes.'

'They just want to be close to them.' He walked the instrument up the stairs through the front door and returned again.

'Do you want a hand?'

'You're not allowed to touch the instruments. Union regulations.'

The man paused and took a tobacco tin out of his pocket. 'It's like they think if they can only get to them, everything will make sense. People think they must have the answer to everything. It would drive me mad. Wouldn't it you?'

'Yes, it would.'

'They try and break in sometimes. We've had one or two who made it past the doors.'

'What happens then?'

'Nothing really. They just stand there. They don't know what to do when they're actually in front of them.' He licked his cigarette paper and spun the cigarette between his fingers, then went inside the building.

Breen left him and walked further up Abbey Road. It was a genteel street of mansion houses and dull apartment blocks with few people on the pavements outside them. A butcher, blood on his apron, came out of a corner shop and started yanking down the shutters of his shop. Breen checked his watch. It was Wednesday, half-day closing. The place would be dead soon. He lit today's second cigarette as he passed Hall Road and carried on until he reached Langford Place, then stopped for a minute, finishing the smoke before turning back.

The girl was still there, weeping beneath the elm tree. Breen walked past her a second time, then stopped. He turned round yet again and walked back.

'Does your mother know you're here?' said Breen.

The girl shook her head.

'Wouldn't she be worried?'

The girl shook her head again.

'It must be a very special cat.'

This time the girl nodded.

Breen returned to the alley behind the flats where the dead girl had been found. The ladder was still leaning against the large bin. 'You in there?' he called, but the policeman who was supposed to be going through the contents inside the bin had vanished. The wooden extension ladder was heavier than he expected it to be, but he found a way to balance it on his shoulder.

'You. Where you taking that now?'

Miss Shankley was leaning over her rear balcony.

'I'm just borrowing it for a few minutes, that's all,' he called back.

'Mind you do. That's private property.'

By the time he reached the tree, the weight of the ladder was digging hard into the top of his shoulder. He dropped the ladder down onto the pavement and looked up at the elm. The lower branches started at around ten feet up; they were dense. It was hard to see a place on which he could balance the top.

'What are you doing?' asked the girl.

'What does it look like I'm doing?'

'Keep your hair on. Just asking.'

Breen jammed the ladder up into the branches. Halfway up, one side of the ladder slipped off the small branch that had been holding it. Breen gripped tight as the ladder twisted. 'Hold the ladder steady,' he ordered the girl.

She didn't move.

'If you don't hold the bottom of the ladder, I can't go up it to try to find your cat.'

The girl put one hand on the ladder.

'Both hands. Don't let it move. OK?'

The girl looked up at Breen and nodded.

A couple more rungs and Breen was in among the thick branches. They looked impossibly dense. He took a few seconds to choose a limb that seemed to offer a little more space than its neighbours, then cautiously wrapped his hand around it. The wood felt hard and cold next to his skin. Pulling himself up on it, he found a foothold for his right foot on the crook of a branch.

'Are you sure this cat of yours is up here?'

'Yes. He is.'

He looked up again. Leaving the safety of the ladder, he squeezed his left foot next to his right. Now he was in the tree, past the limbless trunk.

He paused again, considering his next step. He found himself smiling. He hadn't smiled in weeks, it felt like.

The bark of the tree was creviced but his fingers were too big to fit between the cracks. He would have to rely on branches. He chose one above his head. Feeling bolder now, he looked for another to take the weight of his left foot. Raising his body upwards, his right shoe slipped suddenly from the branch, sending the weight of his body sideways, cracking into the trunk.

'Ow,' he said quietly to himself.

He had been careless. He would have to keep his feet directly on top of each branch. Leather soles had no grip.

He waited until he had caught his breath, then looked up again. 'I can't see him.'

'He's right at the top.'

Again, he placed his left foot back on the same branch, more firmly this time. Hauling himself up with his arms, he was able to raise his body higher now into the leafless branches at the centre of the tree. His body was twisted now, top half facing one way, legs the other, but there was something satisfying about having reached this place, above the traffic, away from the street. He must have climbed trees when he was a child. But when? He couldn't remember.

'What's he doing up there?' A voice from below.

'Rescuing my cat.'

He was only perhaps fifteen feet above the ground but it felt more. Beyond the street, he could see the traffic clearly, the elderly man tugging a dog away from a bus-stop sign, the veteran with one leg swinging down the pavement on his crutches. If it hadn't been for the ladder and the girl holding it, no one would know he was there. Through the leaves he could see Grove End Road. A mansion house on the corner. In a first-floor flat, a woman in a blue dress was standing at a cooker stirring something. The kitchen looked warm and cosy. A rich chicken soup, perhaps, or stew and dumplings. He could almost smell it. Was she cooking for a lover or for herself?

He tore his eyes away and looked up again. The sky behind them made the branches look even blacker.

'What's his name?' he called down.

'Whose name?'

'The cat, of course.'

'Loopy.'

'Loopy?'

'That's right.'

So here he was, halfway up a tree, calling out to a cat called Loopy. He peered into the dark branches and thought he saw, clutching the main trunk like a sailor in a storm, a small black shape. Hard to make it out through the leaves, but as his eyes adjusted to the darkness it gradually came into focus. Claws dug into the bark, a small black cat looking down at Breen over its shoulder.

To be honest, Breen decided, the cat looked perfectly fine there. If anything, there was something scornful in its expression. He looked down again at the girl. Scruffy, thin-cheeked, hopeful.

'Loopy. Loopy. Come here, Loopy.'

The cat didn't move. It continued to stare at Breen, unimpressed. He would have to climb higher, he decided.

SIX

It occurred to him, as he waited to be X-rayed, that he was in the same hospital where the dead girl still lay. She was somewhere below the floorboards beneath him. She would be still, naked, blue and cold, lips dark, breasts flat, lying on her back in darkness. There would be rough, bloodless stitches where Wellington had opened her up, perhaps, like snips of barbed wire. She was waiting in a drawer for Breen to find something.

He closed his eyes.

'You all right?' said the nurse cheerily. He was in a side room on the ground floor; he sat on the bed, arm lying in his lap. 'You look a bit done in.'

'Collarbone. This chap here. Hurts like bugger, I expect.' A doctor, a young man with a pipe tucked into the top pocket of his white coat, sent pain tearing up his arm as he prodded and poked. 'What in heaven's name were you doing?'

Sitting on the day bed, he told them about the girl and the cat and the tree.

'Sleeve,' said the nurse.

Automatically Breen moved his bad arm and flinched. 'Ow,' he said.

'Other one,' she giggled.

'And you're a police detective?' said the doctor.

'Yes.'

'And you were up a tree trying to rescue a girl's cat?'

'That's so sweet,' said the nurse, wielding the syringe. 'Just a little prick.'

'Is this one the last? I really should be going,' said the doctor.

'Two more. One abscess, one chest pain. I think that's it for tonight.'

'I lost my balance trying to grab him,' said Breen.

'At least you tried,' said the nurse. 'That's the main thing.'

'Is it?'

'Of course it is.'

The doctor left, clacking his heels down the corridor.

'Do you think I could have a coffee?'

'Sorry.' The nurse smiled. 'No coffee. No, no, no. Not for you.' She put the syringe down on the trolley and picked up a clipboard.

'Can I have some water then?'

Again she shook her head. 'Nil by mouth. You'll probably need anaesthetics, poor old you. We'll know if we have to just as soon as they've taken your X-ray.'

'And how long will that be?'

'I really can't say. There's quite a queue. I think it's great that you were helping rescue a cat.'

'You mean other people don't?'

'Of course they do,' she said. 'Anyone we should contact?'

She tutted in a sympathetic manner at his reply as she left the room and he was relieved she was gone. The hubbub of the hospital, the complaining doctor, the chattering patients, the rattling of trolleys, even the careless platitudes of the nurse, were oddly lulling.

He stood up and walked out of the side room, holding his arm to his chest. It was evening. A food trolley was doing the rounds; they were placing trays of lukewarm cottage pie and boiled vegetables on the beds of patients who were not going home for a while. Jelly and condensed milk for afters. He walked to the nurses' station. 'Is there a phone I can use?'

The nurse pointed him down a corridor, past the double doors towards a visitors' room, where a grey-skinned man sat in his pyjamas smoking a pipe and holding the hands of a bored-looking young girl.

It was not easy using a telephone with one hand. With the receiver wedged under his chin, he placed sixpence in the slot and dialled. When Marilyn answered he pressed Button A and heard the coin drop.

'I heard the news,' she said. 'Oh, Paddy? What are we going to do with you?'

'The car's in Garden Road. They brought me here in an ambulance. Can someone pick up the keys from me?'

'Do you want me to come and drive you home?'

'It's all right. I might be here ages, for all I know. I have to have an X-ray but they won't find anything. I'll be fine.'

'It'd be no trouble. I'd like to.'

'I'll be fine.'

'Bailey wants to know what you were doing up a tree.'

'He's heard, then?'

'Everyone heard, Paddy.'

'And everyone's having a good laugh, I suppose?'

'Bailey isn't laughing exactly.'

'No, I don't suppose he is.'

He finally left the hospital at a quarter to eleven at night. A taxi dropped him off at his flat, where he struggled for a bit with the key, and when he went to bed it was too painful trying to take his shirt off, so he slept in it, fitfully, unable to turn over without it hurting.

At two he woke and thought he heard the sound of his father, struggling to make it to the toilet. He had found him once or twice on the floor, shivering with cold. Then, as he was about to get out of bed, he remembered it couldn't have been his father and lay back to fall in and out of dreams full of monsters and men with knives.

'Here, kitty, kitty, kitty.'

'Get lost.'

'Ooh. Can you find my pussy, you big strong policeman?'

'I hear you've had a break in the case with your dead bird,' said Jones.

'You heard what?'

'A break. Get it?'

'Opportunity Knocks for Constable Jones,' said Carmichael. 'What's new, pussycat, whoa-uh-oh-uh-oh-oh!'

Marilyn said, 'There's a woman from Garden Road called up says you stole her ladder.' She came and stood by his desk. 'You shouldn't be at work. You hurt yourself.'

'Just bruises,' he said. 'Doctor says I'm fine.' The doctor had given him a sling and told him to take a week off, but he could not bear the idea of a week in the flat on his own. His father's stuff all around. Besides, if he was off sick the dead woman would be passed on to another officer. Probably Prosser. So he had not put the sling back on this morning. Instead he'd folded it and placed it in the drawer among his vests.

Prosser emerged from Bailey's room. 'Snap,' he said quietly. There would be bandages under his shirt sleeve.

Breen's shoulder ached dully and he had to be careful not to move too quickly. The two men stood facing each other. The walking wounded.

'How are you doing?' he said to Prosser.

The office was suddenly quiet. Prosser was the longest serving of the CID Sergeants at Marylebone. Early forties. Tweed jacket with leather elbow patches. Just split up from his wife. Unlike Breen or Carmichael, he still lived in one of the police flats off Pembridge Square and spent his evenings playing declaration whist or pool at the table with the younger officers at the section house across the road. They all loved him. One of the lads.

'Me?' said Prosser, walking over to drop a folder on Jones's desk. 'I'm fine. It's you we've got to worry about, is what I'm hearing.'

Marilyn looked up from her desk and broke the silence. 'Meeting at nine sharp on the St John's Wood murder. Papers got wind of it last night,' she said.

Jones whispered something to Prosser, and Prosser looked at Breen and laughed.

'Carmichael,' Bailey said, emerging from his office. 'I need a word.'

'Right away, sir.'

Breen crossed the room to his desk; there was a metal fire bucket standing on it. Inside was a note that read *In case you feel a bit queasy*. The note had been written on a sheet of Izal toilet paper, scrawled in pencil above where it read *Now Wash Your Hands Please*. Next to the bucket lay Dr Wellington's report.

Breen looked up at Prosser and Jones. Jones was trying not to laugh; Prosser just smiled. Turning to the report, Breen pulled out two black-and-white ten-by-eights of the dead woman's face. Frizzy-haired, eyes closed, about sixteen or seventeen years old, maybe older, with square cheekbones that cut across her otherwise round, soft face. She had the flaccid look the dead have.

He was reading Wellington's one-page report when Carmichael came back and sat at his desk.

'What did Bailey want?' asked Prosser.

'He wanted to know how I was so successful with the women.'

Marilyn snorted.

'Your wife especially, Jones.'

'Really funny.'

'He wanted to know why I drive a brand-new Lotus Cortina and you only have a clapped-out Morris.'

'You haven't got a Lotus Cortina,' said Jones.

'No, but I'm going to, one of these days.'

'Seriously.'

'He's getting his knickers in a twist about me doing stuff with the Drug Squad.'

Breen looked up. 'When did you start working with the Drug Squad?'

'It's not official, like. I just been giving them a bit of help. You know. And Bailey don't like it unless he's had the forms in triplicate.'

Bailey appeared at the door of his office. He glared at Breen, then said, 'Right, Breen, Jones. What have we got?' The team crowded into Bailey's office.

★

What have we got? Facts that were too sparse to suggest any sense of direction. The policemen had returned from their search yesterday with a pair of knickers; they were large, white and matronly, and from the state of them had obviously been lying on the ground for far longer than the dead woman. Nothing else had been found.

The victim remained unidentified. The door-to-door enquiries had come up with two individuals – in addition to Mr Rider – who suggested that the dead body was a prostitute. This, Breen considered, was a possibility. Streetwalkers used Hall Road, only five minutes' walk away, but Carmichael said that nobody had reported any prostitutes missing.

What the body was doing out there in the open was a mystery. It was a half-hearted place to leave a corpse, barely concealed in such a public place. It suggested a lack of planning by the person, or people, who'd murdered her. The murder had been badly thought through. Or at least, the disposal of the body had been.

'No decent leads, really. It's enough to make you sick,' said Jones. People snickered.

'Enough of that,' said Bailey.

'Ha-very-ha,' said Carmichael.

'I said. Enough.'

A woman police officer entered the room. Everyone stopped for a second and looked at her. Though there was a women's unit at Marylebone, they were only on admin tasks and social work. If a crime involved a kid you'd ask one of them in. Apart from that, they never came into the CID office.

The woman blushed. She was gawky-looking; a thin, angular face, and dark hair cut into a lank bob.

Bailey scowled and said, 'You're early. I'll be with you in a minute, Miss . . . ?'

'Tozer, sir.'

'We're wasting our time there,' said Jones. 'Going over the same ground. She was dumped, Wellington said.'

'Breen?' said Bailey.

'I don't agree. Until we know where else to look, it's our best bet.'

'Waste of time, I say.'

'What about the woman who discovered the body?' asked Bailey.

'It wasn't a woman. It was a girl. A nanny. No name yet. We're looking.'

The one thing the door-to-door enquiries had established beyond doubt was that the orange mattress that had lain over her had been there before she had been dumped. Several people had noticed it, lying against the wall on top of the pile of rubbish.

Breen picked up the forensics report and started to summarise it for everyone in the room. In it, Wellington said pretty much what he'd said the day before yesterday to Breen. She had been strangled. He estimated that she had died between 6 p.m. and 10 p.m. on the previous day – around fifteen hours before she was discovered. The fact that blood had settled on one side suggested she was not dumped until at least two hours after she was killed, which meant that she had not been dumped until 8 p.m. at the earliest on the previous day, by which time the alley would have been dark.

'Nobody's going to dump a naked bird in broad daylight,' said Carmichael.

'She's not just a naked bird,' blurted the woman constable. A broad West Country accent made her voice sound doubly out of place.

Everyone stared.

'No, you're right. She's a naked dead bird,' said Carmichael. People laughed. Tozer coloured but didn't lift her glare from Carmichael's face.

'That's sufficient, thank you,' said Bailey. 'Wait outside please, Constable, until we're ready.'

The woman left. Breen picked up from where he'd left off. There were no obvious signs of penetration, though Wellington hadn't ruled out a sexual assault. He looked at the woman constable through the glass. She was standing outside, looking at her feet, embarrassed.

'Missing persons?' asked Bailey.

Jones answered. 'No one there matching the victim's description in the last two weeks.'

'A pretty, young, naked woman stirs the prurient instinct. With that kind of attention it is useful to make progress fast. OK, everyone. Back to work,' said Bailey with a sigh. 'And Breen?'

'Yes, sir?'

'That woman constable outside has applied to join CID.'

There was an immediate hush in the room.

'Like it or not, she's been made a TDC,' said Bailey. Temporary Detective Constable. She was a probationer.

'You're joking?' said Carmichael.

'It is not my doing, you can be quite sure of that.'

'Hell's teeth.'

'She will be on the murder squad with you and Jones, Breen.'

'Oooh,' came the catcalls. 'Breen has got a girlfriend.'

'What?' said Carmichael. 'We've got to work with a bloody plonk?'

'I should imagine Breen needs all the help he can get.'

'But she's a woman, sir,' continued Carmichael.

'Well spotted, Carmichael.'

'So's Breen,' said Jones.

'That will be all, thank you,' said Bailey, closing the door behind him.

SEVEN

It was a new Cortina, F reg, pale blue with a white door, the letters 'POLICE' picked out in black on the side.

The Temporary Detective Constable got in and tossed her hat into the back of the car, not saying anything.

'Right.' This was a new one on him.

He opened the door, sat down and turned the engine on, then went to put the car into reverse and almost passed out from the pain of the motion. 'God,' he said.

'You all right, sir?'

The nerves in his shoulder were screaming. His skin prickled with a sudden sweat.

'Sir?'

He breathed deeply and reached his good arm up to adjust the rear-view mirror so he could reverse without turning his head.

Gingerly putting the car into first, he made it out onto the street and up to the traffic lights without having to change gear again.

'Sure you're OK?' she said.

'Fine.'

'Your arm. I heard you fell out of a tree,' she said in her rural accent.

'Yes.'

'Bet it hurts.'

'Yes,' he said. 'A bit.'

They didn't talk again until they were halfway up Lisson Grove.

'She wasn't raped, then? The dead girl?'

He looked at her. She was young, probably only in her early twenties. 'We're not sure yet.'

'Got any leads?'

'Not so far,' he said.

She nodded, then said, 'You're still in second. You should change up.'

He dropped his arm down to the stick and the left side of his body flooded with pain again. He wasn't sure he could do this.

There was a traffic jam ahead. He tried to see what was causing it, but a large bread van blocked the view.

'They said she was naked. Did you see her?'

'Yes,' he said.

'Was she pretty?'

He looked at her. 'Not particularly, I don't think. People look different when they're dead.'

Now the car was going slowly he needed to change down again. Cautiously he moved his hand down to the gears. Another sudden stab of pain. He braked to avoid hitting the car in front, stalling the engine.

'What's wrong?'

He laid his head on the steering wheel of the stationary car. 'I'm not sure I can drive. I can't seem to change gear. My arm's too sore.'

'From when you fell . . . ?'

'Does everyone know about it?'

She nodded. Somewhere behind a car horn sounded. Breen switched the hazard lights on and cars slowly started moving around them. After a while she dug in her bag. 'Got an aspirin if you want,' she said.

They had given him painkillers at the hospital, but he wasn't due another one until lunch. 'We're going to have to go back to the station.'

'You going to call in sick?'

'I can't drive.'

Looking at him, she said. 'Who'll take over this case?'

'Sergeant Prosser, I suppose.'

She scowled and pulled out a packet of cigarettes from her bag, offering him one. Usually he didn't smoke so early in the morning. He took one, though. First of the day. It would help with the pain.

'What if I did it?' she said.

'What?'

'Drive the car.'

'But you can't.'

'Been driving tractors since I was eight, sir. Otherwise you'll have to go back to the station, won't you?'

He nodded. If he went back now he would be sent home sick. 'Women officers aren't authorised to drive cars.'

'Just for today. You'll probably be all right tomorrow, won't you?' She lit the cigarette for him, throwing the match out of the sidelight. 'No one has to know.'

Cars coming the other way stared, wondering why a police car was stopped in the middle of the road, lights flashing.

'Tell you what,' she said. 'I'll change over just before we get there if you like.'

The car inched forward until they reached the cause of the jam. Big new Greater London Council blocks were starting to spring up all over London; they were building new flats here too. These were small fry compared to some of them, just four storeys high, and already half built. A lorry unloading bricks blocked half the road and a workman was directing cars around it, but he was doing so in a half-hearted, haphazard way, one or two vehicles at a time.

Tozer honked the horn, but the sudden burst of noise didn't help. The workman trying to direct the traffic panicked. He tried to make a Commer van that was coming towards them back up to let the four or five cars in front of the police car come through, but there was a big red Number 2 bus right behind the van. There was no space for it to move backwards.

'For pity's sake.' The policewoman wound down her window and shouted, 'Oi! Get a bloody move on! Want some chewing gum, sir?'

'No thanks.'

A gust of wind blew a pale white curtain of concrete dust across the road into the constable's open window. She wound it up, swearing, brushing the pale flecks from her woollen suit.

Now a foreman had come out and was adding to the confusion by shouting at the workman directing traffic and pointing to the police car.

'Cathal Breen,' the constable said, pronouncing the 'th' in the name. 'When they said your name first, I thought it sounded like you were a woman,' she said. 'Kathleen. No offence meant.'

He looked over at her. 'It's pronounced *Cah-hal*,' he said.

'Cathal. What kind of a name is that?' she asked.

'Irish,' he said. 'My parents came over before the war. What about you?'

'My parents?' asked the woman, turning towards him, a puzzled look on her face.

'No, your name.'

'Tozer,' she said, looking ahead again. 'Helen Tozer. Pleased to meet you.'

The traffic started to move again. He hoped she wasn't going to talk this much all the time.

'The girls say you went mental a couple of days back, is that true?'

He looked at her. 'Mental?'

'Sorry, sir. I mean . . . You did something, and Prosser ended up getting stabbed.'

'You know Prosser?'

'God, yeah. We all know Prossie. He lives in police flats near the women's section house. Since his wife walked out on him he's always hanging round.'

'Do you like him?'

'Not much.'

'I went mental? Is that what they say?'

'Yep.'

He watched a crocodile of schoolchildren in blazers and caps walking up the pavement.

'I'm just saying, you know,' said Tozer. The traffic cleared. She accelerated past a man on a motorbike.

'Do you have to drive so fast?' said Breen.

'They said Prossie went into a shop on his own where there was a robbery taking place.'

He still had to write the report for Bailey. Martin & Dawes. The modern men's outfitters. By the time he arrived, Prosser's car was already there and the back door to the shop was wide open; Prosser was inside. The thieves had been calmly loading rails of clothes into the back of a parked van.

'Chinks with knives, they said. Bloody hell. I hate knives,' said Tozer.

Two Chinese men; one kitchen knife, eight-inch blade. He was on the car radio outside calling for back-up when Prosser had emerged a minute later, covered in his own blood. The thieves had made it out of the front of the shop, abandoning the van. Pure fury in Prosser's eyes as he looked at Breen.

'Personally, I wouldn't say it was your fault, exactly,' she said. 'If he'd done it according to the book, he shouldn't have gone in there until you got there.'

'Bully for you. Slow down.'

'Like I said, just saying.' She swung a quick right and pulled up by the murder scene. 'This where she was found, then?'

He sat in the car, looking ahead.

'Sir?'

'Near the end of the sheds over there.'

She was silent for a while. 'You would have thought somebody would have noticed their daughter had gone missing,' she said eventually. 'I mean.'

'You'd be surprised,' said Breen, looking out of the car window. Rain had started to spatter against it.

'Be honest, sir, I think we're wasting our time around here. Like Jones said this morning. Body was just dumped, wasn't it? Whoever put it here could have come from miles off.'

64

'You think that?'

'I mean, I know it's not my place, sir. Only I can't help—'

'If the body was dumped, why here?'

Tozer frowned. 'Just chance, I reckon. Someone was looking for a badly lit spot. That's my point. There's no reason to restrict our search to this area.'

'Tozer, isn't it?'

'Yes, sir.'

'You've been in CID half an hour . . .'

'Sorry, sir.' She stared at the steering wheel.

'Look. See these shed doors?'

'Yes, sir.'

'Until last Friday, all the locks were broken. The doors were all open. They'd been that way for a month or more. Anyone walking past would have been able to see that. But they were fixed two days before the murder. I'm guessing whoever dumped her was expecting to be able to leave her in one of these sheds for a few hours, maybe a day, until they could take her somewhere else. It would have to be someone local to have noticed that the doors were all open. And then they got here and found they'd all been locked . . .'

'. . . And panicked and dumped the body under a mattress?'

'Yes. Which means the murderer could be someone who walks down this road a lot. Probably every day. OK?'

'Right.' She nodded, and looked up and down the street with renewed interest. 'Wow. So it could be someone living in any of these houses?'

'Possibly.'

At that moment the door of the shabby Victorian house next to the lock-ups opened, and a large black man emerged, pausing on the doorstep to look up and down the street. You couldn't fail to notice him. Blacks were not common around this neighbourhood; besides, he was dressed conspicuously, in a beige linen Nehru jacket, whose thin vicar-ish collar circled his large neck. It was the sort of suit that you saw African leaders wearing in the newspapers; businesslike,

65

but deliberately un-British. The man, carrying a fat brown leather briefcase, checked his watch and then surveyed the street again.

Breen opened the car door and called after him, 'Sir?' The black man appeared not to hear at first, or maybe pretended not to. Breen shouted louder. 'Hey! Sir!'

The man turned, slowly, with great deliberateness towards Breen. He was a large man; his chest strained at the linen of his suit. 'Yes?'

'Detective Sergeant Breen,' he called. 'I'm investigating the death of a young woman whose body was found close to your front door.'

The man stood at the top of his front steps and looked back down at Breen. He smiled. 'You need to speak to me now?'

'It is a murder we're talking about,' said Breen.

A taxi was driving slowly towards them, 'For Hire' lit in orange on its roof, checking house numbers.

'Of course, of course,' said the man, nodding. 'But I am late for an appointment now. Would it be possible to arrange a time?' He spoke in the kind of accent that one only acquires in an English public school. 'Shall we say, eleven a.m. tomorrow?'

'First things first. What's your name?' said Tozer, pulling her pencil out from the elastic around her notebook. Breen looked at her, eyebrows raised.

'Samuel Ezeoke,' said the man. 'And yours is?'

'How do you spell that?'

The man said slowly, 'E-Z-E-O-K-E. Pronounced *Ez-ay-oak-ay*. My first name is Samuel. S-A-M-U-E-L,' spelling it out as if to a child.

'Can I have your employer's address?' asked Constable Tozer.

'My employer's address?' said Ezeoke, eyes wide.

'So he can vouch for you.'

'Because I'm an African?' Ezeoke reached into his jacket pocket and removed a small silver case from which he pulled a single business card.

As she read the card, Tozer coloured.

Back in the car, thin-lipped, Tozer muttered, 'How was I to know he was a bloody surgeon?'

Breen sat in the passenger seat, flicking through the pages of an *A–Z*. 'What were you doing back there? You're not supposed to be doing the questioning.'

'Thought I was helping,' she muttered.

'Well, you weren't.' He looked at her.

She was chewing her lip, looking miserable. He sighed. He did not know how to handle women.

The rest of the morning they spent driving around the local streets, peering into backyards and alleyways. She was talking again.

'My old boss says they're going to start a big investigation of CID for being bent,' said Tozer.

'They've been saying that for years,' said Breen, looking out of the passenger window.

'Are they bent?'

'Some.'

'That's terrible,' she said. He turned away from the window and looked at her. She was so fresh-faced and eager it hurt.

'Is that the tree you fell out of, sir?'

'Yes.'

'Doesn't look that big,' she said.

He reached in his pocket and took out the orange bottle of painkillers the hospital had given him.

'Don't you want some water with them?'

'I'm OK,' he said, though bitterness lingered in his mouth after he'd swallowed.

'The police doctor said you were sick when you saw the body. Is that right?'

'Have you ever seen a dead body?'

She shook her head. 'Not really. Seen loads of dead animals in my time on the farm. Millions of them.'

'It's not the same.'

'I think I'd be all right if I saw one,' the woman said. 'Not that I think it's wrong for you to throw up. Everybody should be upset, the way I see it. Sir?' She interrupted her own flow. 'That's EMI Studios, isn't it?'

'Do you ever stop talking?'

'Sorry. If other people don't talk much I end up just filling the space. Loads of girls hang out there, though, don't they? Hoping to see the stars. Do you think she could have been one of them?'

'You don't think we might have considered that?' he said.

'Right. Sorry.'

Why did her eagerness irritate him so much? There was nothing wrong with being enthusiastic.

She said, 'Mind you, that don't mean she wasn't one of them.'

'No. You're right,' he said. 'I've been thinking that.'

'You hungry?' she said, changing the subject again before he could begin to explain why. 'I could murder a lardy cake.' She gazed at the window of a bakery window they were driving past.

He wondered how much more of this he could stand. Maybe he could persuade Jones to drive him. Jones wouldn't like it, but Bailey might be pleased if he tried to make an effort with Jones. And at least they understood each other.

A little after midday they walked over to the canteen at St John's Wood Police Station, where the officers who were still going door to door were taking a break. Breen lit cigarette number two.

'It's yummy, sir. Sure you don't want a bite?' She held out her cake. It was thick and rich, dripping with grease.

'No, thank you.'

As they sat on metal chairs drinking tea from enamel mugs, a young red-faced copper approached them. 'Sir?'

Breen recognised him as one of the men he'd spoken to yesterday. He was clutching a mug in one hand and a dirty, crumpled brown-paper bag in the other.

'I was looking for you yesterday, only I heard you fell out of a tree, sir,' he said with a smirk.

'Well?'

''Cause I found this, sir. In one of the bins you asked me to look through.'

Breen unwrapped the top of the bag and pulled out a black cotton evening dress.

Breen and Tozer looked at the dress, then at each other.

'Which bin?' asked Breen.

The flat had two refuse chutes that dropped rubbish down into bins below.

'The far one, sir. Not the one by where the girl was found, know what I mean?'

Breen handed the dress to Tozer and struggled to pull out a notebook from his jacket pocket. Holding it with his sore arm, he flicked through until he found a drawing he'd made of the flats with all the occupants marked on it.

'Why would anybody throw this away?' said Tozer. 'I mean, it's in good nick.'

'Why is it so clean?' said Breen. 'If it was in the bins?'

'It was in that bag I just give you, sir.'

Breen put down the bag. 'Why didn't you tell me that before I stuck my own prints all over it?'

'I do something wrong, sir?'

'Never mind.'

'Bourne and Hollingsworth. Oxford Street.' Tozer was reading the dress's label. 'Size fourteen.'

'What?'

'Wellington's report said she was seven stone ten, didn't it? Might be a bit big for her.'

'When did you read Wellington's report?'

'This morning, before you got in.'

'Why?'

'Why shouldn't I?' She fingered the hem. 'I had always imagined the girl as a Carnaby Street type. But then she was naked, wasn't she? So how would I know? Still. This dress doesn't even look like it's been worn, hardly. Why would anybody just chuck it away?'

She laid the rumpled dress out on the worn top of one the tables and then stood back suddenly. 'Oh,' she said.

In the middle of the dress, just below the seam that joined the top to the skirt, was a stain; a small pale blot.

She leaned forward and peered.

'What?' Breen asked.

She picked up the dress and examined it closely. Then put it back down and leaned over towards him, whispering, 'Do you think it's . . . you know?'

He picked up the dress and looked at the stain.

'You know.' Then even quieter: 'Spunk, sir.'

He blinked at her. He must have been looking shocked that a girl would have used the word, because she said, 'No need to be like that, sir. We have that stuff in Devon too.'

EIGHT

In his small office in the hospital basement, Wellington was delighted by the find. 'A-ha,' he said.

'"A-ha" what?'

'Another Onan shall new crimes invent, and noble seed in selfish joys be spent.' He sat behind the desk and pulled the dress towards him, holding a small magnifier to his eye.

'I was wondering if it was sperm.'

'Yes, yes. Women present, Paddy. But yes. Sperm.'

'You think it may be?'

'I'll be sure whether in two hours. I'll do an acid phosphatase test. You realise that if this is the victim's dress, this may be an indication of some particular deviance? An inability to penetrate?'

Wellington raised the dress to his nose and sniffed it.

In the car, hands on the wheel, Tozer said, 'He seemed happy.'

'Yes. You did well, Constable.'

'Thank you, sir. Where next?'

'Soho,' said Breen, settling back into his seat.

Without looking, she reached her left hand behind her and felt for her handbag, 'There's a packet of Juicy Fruit in there,' she said, dumping it on his lap. 'Could you pass me some? Have some yourself, if you like.'

He looked at her like she was mad. 'I'm not going rooting in your handbag.'

'Right. Sorry.'

He pushed the bag over to her. She dug around with one hand

while driving with the other. He was thinking, why shouldn't a woman her age know what sperm looked like? It was 1968, after all. If she had been coy about it, like women were supposed to be, it might have gone unnoticed. He wasn't sure if he was disturbed by this, or fascinated.

'You're quiet, aren't you?'

'Yes,' he said.

She parked the car in Soho Square. 'Wait here. I'll be back in an hour,' he said.

'What am I supposed to do for an hour?'

'I don't know. Do some shopping?'

'You're joking, aren't you?' she said.

In the square a group of people in their twenties and thirties were giving away pale blue bits of paper. A young man with a beard and a duffel coat stood with a sign that read *Free your mind*. A girl in a headscarf and a badge with a red clenched fist handed one of the leaflets to Breen. 'You should come,' she said, and smiled.

He read it: 'ANTIUNIVERSITY of London. Courses: Future of Capitalism. Black Power. Counterculture. Revolution. Imperialism. Faculty includes Allen Ginsberg, Stokely Carmichael, C. L. R. James, R. D. Laing, Jeff Nuttall. No formal requirements. £8 10/- for each course.' He handed it back. 'Not me. I'm too stuck in the mud for a revolution,' he said.

She shrugged and took it back from him, holding it out for the next passer-by.

Detective Sergeant Carmichael was waiting for him in Pollo's, sitting on the red-and-black-striped vinyl banquette seats. Pollo's had always been one of Breen's favourites. An Italian. *Italiano*. Gaggia coffee machine, the works. Proof, against all the evidence of his Irish ancestry, that Catholics could have class.

'You're late,' said Carmichael. 'He's only gone and left now.'

'Who?'

'The man I invited you to meet.'

72

'Sorry. Had to drop by to see Wellington. Who were you fixing me up with, anyway?'

'Pilch.'

'Pilch? Drug Squad Pilch?'

'I was putting in a word for you, believe it or not,' said Carmichael.

'A word for me? Why?'

'Because D Division is a mess. Everybody knows it. Especially CID. It's going to blow up, sooner or later. Bailey doesn't run it, Prosser does. He has all the ranks running around after him. And call a spade a spade, he really don't like you much. You'd be better off out.'

'Drug Squad? Not my thing.'

'He's a coming man, mark my words. On the up-and-up. And let's face it, you need some help right now. You should get off murder anyway.'

'I don't think so,' said Breen.

'Murder is murder. But drugs is going to be big, I tell you.'

'So you say.'

'Stands to reason. We're on the tip of the iceberg. Come aboard, Paddy. Ship's about to sail. Murder is just the same old same old. And I'm on vice. That's even worse. Vice is done for. This is the permissive society. When there's people starkers on stage up the Shaftesbury Theatre singing about the age of the Hairy-Arse, who needs to pay for it any more? Did you go? No? I did. God, there's some ugly bloody women in that. I felt like shouting, "For God's sake put your clothes back on." In a couple of years we'll be like Sweden, I tell you. The point is, nobody even has to pay for it these days. These young girls, nowadays they'll fuck anybody. Drugs though. Nobby Pilcher's got it right. Growth industry. I'm serious, Paddy. You need to get out of D Div.'

The restaurant had filled. All the tables were taken. A queue formed outside on Old Compton Street.

Soho was changing; it was full of advertising men and film makers who didn't wear jackets and drank wine with their meals.

Grown men wore flared trousers and scent. They carried notebooks and diaries with them wherever they went. They slouched. They smoked cigars.

'And I'll stick up for you, you know that. But . . .'

'I know.'

'We all fuck up sometimes. But you need a fresh start.' Carmichael cracked a breadstick, sending crumbs flying. 'I'm sorry 'bout your dad an' everything.'

'Thanks.'

'I know he never liked me much. But all the same.'

Breen didn't contradict him. His father had never liked Carmichael and had thought even less of him after Breen followed him into the police.

The waitress appeared. Carmichael ordered lasagne with chips and a pint of Harp.

'Nothing,' said Breen. 'I'm OK.'

'Not eating?'

'No. I'm not hungry.'

'You got to eat, Paddy. You're bloody skin and bones.'

Breen ordered a spaghetti al burro and a glass of Chianti.

'Give him a bolognese. He needs a bit of *carne*.' She disappeared with the order. 'I just want to help,' said Carmichael. 'That's all.'

'I know,' said Breen. They had trained at Hendon together in the fifties. Looking at the advertising men and go-getters around him, he realised that Carmichael was one of them. He fitted in here. He was a professional. A go-getter.

'Seriously. You used to be one of us.'

'My dad was sick.'

'We all know that. But we're a tight bunch, coppers. And you're either one of us or you're not.'

'And I'm not.'

'Not what I'm saying. But all of us at the nick, we're all tight. Used to be, anyway. These days the lads all think you're Lord Snooty and all of his pals.'

'There was nobody else to look after him.'

'And all I'm saying is if you were still one of us, they'd be, "Oh, Paddy had a wobble but it could have happened to any of us." People would be giving you a second chance.' The drinks came and Carmichael sucked three inches off his pint, then wiped his mouth with the back of his hand. 'Your dad's dead now. It's time to clean the slate. Don't forget, I can put in a word with Pilch for you.' Carmichael took out a packet of Pall Malls and removed a cigarette, tapping it on the table a few times before he put it in his mouth to light it. 'So. Arm OK?'

Breen nodded.

'What's that girl like?'

'She hasn't stopped talking once.'

'I mean. A plonk on CID. How can you be expected to work like that?'

'She's not that bad.'

Carmichael raised his eyebrows.

'No, seriously. She's OK. She's keen.' To his surprise, Breen realised he was sticking up for Constable Tozer. He was on the verge of explaining to Carmichael about what she'd spotted on the black dress but Carmichael butted in.

'You can't have women on CID. It's not going to work. What would happen if you ran into some serious trouble?'

'She might run away, you mean?'

It took a second, then Carmichael said, 'Ha, very funny. Why are you always trying to be so bloody obtuse? I'm offering you a chance here and you're throwing it back in my face.'

They looked at each other. He had deliberately irritated Carmichael. 'Sorry, John,' he said. 'I'm a bit tired.'

'World's changing, Paddy. Just say you'll think about it, OK? About Drug Squad.'

Sitting at the next table was a slender young man with shoulder-length hair, a flowered shirt and a gaudy women's scarf wrapped around his neck. He was talking to a large middle-aged man in a pale suit. The waitress simpered round the hippie-looking one, so Breen reckoned he was probably an actor or a musician. He didn't look like he was even twenty years old.

Carmichael caught him looking at them. 'Swinging bloody London,' he said.

It was as if some kind of coup had taken place. The young and the beautiful had seized power. They had their own TV programmes, their own radio stations, their own shops, their own language. In his early thirties, Breen felt cheated. Jealous even.

Nodding vigorously, the large man in the suit laughed loudly at something the young man said.

The food arrived. Breen looked at his plate, a pile of pasta slathered in meat sauce, and regretted ordering it. He picked up the fork and tried to lift the spaghetti. The pasta slid straight off his fork.

'Eat up,' said Carmichael. 'You need feeding.'

Afterwards, Breen walked north towards Tottenham Court Road. The sun came out as he reached Soho Square and the small square park was filled with the unexpectedly vivid browns and greens of all the fallen leaves. The suddenness of colour left him feeling exhausted. He reached a damp park bench on the path that ran through the middle of the square and sat down.

He put his head between his knees and closed his eyes. He felt bloated after the meal with Carmichael. After a few breaths he sat back and opened his eyes again. A pigeon fluttered down in front of him, cocking its head expectantly, flashing the wild iridescent pinkness of its neck feathers. The world seemed to contain a new level of indiscriminate significance he had never noticed before.

When you were a policeman you were trained to spot things that were out of the ordinary: a man waiting outside a bank, a broken window, a car with an unusual registration number. Right now, everything seemed to be out of the ordinary.

The small crowd of students was still giving away leaflets. One of them was strumming a guitar hung on string around his neck.

He waited another minute, and the sudden brightness passed. Clouds obscured the sun again, though the unfathomable sense of unease stayed with him, filling his chest again.

'You OK?'

He looked up. Constable Tozer stood by the bench. 'I had a cheese sandwich. It was horrible. What did you have?'

He stood.

'So anyway. I went to Bourne and Hollingsworth.'

'Buy anything?'

'No.' She grinned. 'I asked about the dress.'

'What? On your own?'

'It's only just over the road. I couldn't face finishing my cheese sandwich so I thought I'd drop in.'

'You're supposed to have a CID officer with you. You know that. You're just probationary. You're not supposed to do anything without my say-so.'

Tozer's smile vanished. Now she looked hurt. 'I just thought it would be good, that's all. What's the point of me just hanging around doing nothing?'

'It's procedure, that's all,' he said, realising as he said it that it was the sort of thing that Bailey would say. 'Well? What did you find out?'

'No luck. I found a floor manager in women's wear. She said they hadn't sold anything like that in a couple of years.'

'OK. Next time, you should ask.'

'Yes, sir. Only . . .'

'Only what?'

'You're not going to like this either, then.'

'What?'

She drew a circle on the tarmac path with her right toe. 'I've got somewhere else we could go, if you like.'

'What do you mean?'

'Beatles Fan Club. It's a ten-minute walk from here. I called them

77

up.' She nodded towards the police box just at the north side of Soho Square.

'You did?'

'Only took a minute.'

'You shouldn't . . .' He swallowed his words, remembering how he'd defended her to Carmichael in the restaurant a few minutes earlier.

'You were having lunch. I was just wasting my time otherwise.'

'OK, OK.'

In the car as she hurtled down Tottenham Court Road, he thought: men like Carmichael had grown up in houses full of women. They understood the company of sisters and their friends. At the age when Breen had been puzzling over the underwear section of the Littlewoods catalogue in the privacy of his bedroom, Carmichael had already heard what girls talked about amongst themselves. He knew how to charm them, to cajole them. To Breen, women could be a different species.

He looked at his watch. 'I suppose we've got the time.' He peered at her in the autumn sunlight and said, 'Is that make-up you have on?'

She smiled. 'Maybe.'

'Did you have that on earlier?'

'No.' A small smile.

'Is it in case the Beatles are there?'

'Don't be daft.' She laughed.

The address turned out to be a nondescript new block in Covent Garden, a narrow street that had recently started to fill with shops selling flowery shirts and flared trousers. The office was on the first floor.

'Welcome,' said the woman at the desk, in a voice that had little in the way of welcome in it. 'I've been expecting you.' She was young and plump in a motherly way, soft-skinned and pink, with dark hair and two yellow plastic hoop earrings. Her name was Miss Judith Pattison and she sat behind a typewriter in a room that smelt of copying ink and Miss Dior. On the wall there was a framed photograph of the Beatles as they used to be three or four years ago, clean-shaven and smiling; they were on a beach somewhere, blue sky above them, blue water behind them. John Lennon was wearing a straw hat turned up at the front. Each had signed their name in black felt tip pen. One of them had written: 'To Rudith Miss Pattison. Wish you were here!' They were looking right at the camera. Did he resent it, that four young men could look so aggressively at ease?

The room was crammed with filing cabinets and heaps of paper. A huge tower of brown envelopes sat on the floor; next to it were piles of photographs and a newsletter titled *Official Beatles Fan Club*. The filing cabinets had more mounds teetering on top of them. From the room next door came the clattering of keys and the blaring of a transistor radio.

'You'll have to excuse the mess,' said Miss Pattison, peering out from behind more papers. 'We're extremely busy. Can I get you a cup of tea?' She spoke with a hint of a Liverpudlian accent.

'. . . *To Daphne who works in a well-known carpet manufacturer's in Manchester who says, "Dear Mister Skewball, can you play anything by the Hollies . . ."*'

'Turn it down,' bellowed Miss Pattison over the noise of a roaring electric kettle.

'We were wondering if you could take a look at the photograph,' said Constable Tozer.

Miss Pattison placed a tea bag in each cup. 'You said on the phone you think she's one of ours?'

'We're not sure. It's possible,' said Breen, explaining where the body was found. 'And she was around sixteen or seventeen years old.'

The electric kettle roared. 'I do hope she isn't one of ours. It would feel personal.'

A sparrow landed on the windowsill outside; someone must have left crumbs out for the birds, because when it flew off again, its beak was full.

'That sounds such a terrible thing to say, though, doesn't it? Of course she must be somebody's, if she's not one of ours.'

'Can I ask you something?' Tozer interrupted. 'Do you actually know the Beatles, then?'

Miss Pattison returned Constable Tozer's smile and nodded. 'They're not round so much these days, of course. They have their own lives.'

'Do they come here?' Tozer asked looking around, awed.

'Goodness, no,' said Miss Pattison. 'We tend to go to them.'

'To their homes?' Breen glared at her, but she wasn't paying attention.

'If necessary, yes.'

'That must be so fab. I would love—'

Breen coughed.

'Sorry.'

'OK then.' He pulled out the photograph. It seemed a small, mean thing compared to the shiny black-and-whites of these four handsome men, who grinned, hands in pockets, for the camera. She was lifeless, in every way opposite.

Miss Pattison sighed. 'It's such a terrible, terrible thing,' she said. She picked up the photo and looked at it, then stood up with it in her hand and walked to the window so she could see it better.

Tozer spotted a signed photo of George Harrison on Miss Pattison's desk. She picked it up and looked at the sunken-cheeked, moustached young man, and the rounded squiggle of a biro mark across the bottom of it. 'George is my favourite,' she said, then looked up, caught Breen's eye and hastily put the photo back. 'Sorry.'

Miss Pattison was still, brow furrowed, looking at the other photograph; the dead one. The unglamorous one. 'Do you recognise her?' asked Breen.

'No. But we have tens of thousands of girls. I can't know every one.'

Breen tried a different approach. 'Have you ever come across any men who try and take advantage of the fans, perhaps?'

'Take advantage?' said Miss Pattison. 'What? Rapists?'

'Possibly.'

'Was she raped?'

'She may have been.'

'How awful.'

'There might be someone out there who the fans know . . . somebody who they were already suspicious of.'

'We have fifty thousand members. Do you expect us to call them up? Or write to their parents?'

'Fifty thousand? You have a newsletter. Couldn't you put a notice in that?'

'Oh no. That would not be at all suitable. Not at all.'

'Suitable? A girl is dead.'

'And I am sorry. But our newsletter is not the place to discuss it.'

'There must be other people we could show this photograph to?'

'You can leave the photo with us if you like. Perhaps someone will recognise it.' Miss Pattison folded her arms. This was her world. She was not going to be helpful.

'Are they doing a Christmas record for the fans again this year?' asked Tozer.

Miss Pattison broke into a sudden smile. 'Of course.'

'I have all of them. I think they're super.'

'You're a fan?' Miss Pattison's eyebrows danced.

'Of course,' said Tozer.

'A member?'

'Yes.'

Miss Pattison paused. 'What did you say your name was again?'

'Tozer. Helen Tozer.'

Miss Pattison stood and walked through the door into the next room. 'Wait there,' she called, leaving them alone in her office.

Breen blinked. The smell of the woman's scent was eye-watering.

'Do you like The Beatles, sir?' asked Tozer. 'Or are you more of a Rolling Stones man?'

'Neither.'

'Bob Dylan?'

Breen paused a second. 'Are you really a member of this fan club?'

Tozer looked at him like he was impossibly old.

Miss Pattison returned beaming with two brown folders in her hands. She read from the top one. 'Helen Tozer. Coombe Barton Farm, Kingsteignton, Devon.'

'That's me!' said Tozer in a high squeak. 'Farm girl.'

'You're one of the older fans, then?' Miss Pattison said approvingly. 'The newer ones don't get envelopes. They just get index cards.'

Tozer smiled back at her.

'And up to date with your subs as well,' said Miss Pattison. 'Good girl.' Breen looked at the policewoman, surprised. Returning to her desk, Miss Pattison read. 'Join date: September 1963.' A broad smile filled her face. 'My, my.' Then she looked at the second folder. 'Now look at this. I have an Alexandra Tozer. Same address.'

'That's my little sister,' said Tozer. 'She was the reason I joined. She was a much bigger fan than I am.'

'She sent in a photograph of herself. A lot of you do that.' She pulled out a photograph of a girl, around fifteen or sixteen years old, standing in a snowy field. She was wearing a short tartan miniskirt and woollen tights, a blue denim hat with a little peak on it, and smiling at the camera. Her features had none of the solidity of her older sister; she was willowy and pale-skinned. 'I see she's stopped sending her subscriptions,' Miss Pattison said disapprovingly. 'That is a shame. We lose a few more every year.'

'Yes,' said Tozer.

'You should persuade her to join again, you know.'

There was a pause. 'Don't think so,' said Tozer.

Miss Pattison did not notice the way Tozer avoided her gaze as she answered. Breen recognised a familiar rawness in Tozer's voice, something which had always been there but which he had never noticed before. He stood and said, 'We'll be in touch, Miss Pattison.'

Tozer remained seated. She reached her hand across the table and took one of Miss Pattison's. Miss Pattison looked slightly startled by the physical contact, but Tozer smiled at her confidently and said, 'I know it's hard and that you're busy, but you will ask around, won't you?'

Miss Pattison hesitated. 'Well . . .'

'For a fan? Please?' Tozer took the girl's photo, wrote her own name and a phone number underneath and passed it to the woman.

'For a fan?' Miss Pattison was murmuring. 'Yes, of course I will.' She smiled back at Tozer. 'For a fan.'

Breen clattered down the concrete stairs, glad to be out of that stuffy room.

'You all right, sir?'

'You keep asking me that.' It was late in the afternoon now. A man was wheeling a barrow with a single half-empty crate of apples on it north from Covent Garden.

'Well, frankly, sir, you look done in.'

'I'm fine.'

They wandered down towards the market where the last of the costermongers were packing up. The day was ending. Soon the next batch of lorries would be arriving from somewhere in Kent, stacked with onions and potatoes. Tozer took out the signed photo of George Harrison that Miss Pattison had given her as they left and looked at it. 'I think he's gorgeous, even with the beard. I bet you don't even have a favourite Beatle, do you, sir?'

Breen shook his head. 'I missed all that,' he said. 'Too old.'

'I never met anyone who didn't have a favourite Beatle. Even my gran has her favourite.'

'Who's that?'

'Paul McCartney, course,' she said. 'Go on. You have to have one.'

The rain shone on the cobblestones outside. 'I'm not really much of a pop music fan,' he said apologetically.

'Go on, you have to pick one.'

He laughed. 'Um . . . I don't know. Ringo Starr?'

She stuck her tongue out. 'No, no. You're not taking this seriously. You'd never be a Ringo. You're more of a John Lennon man.'

'Am I?' He paused.

'Clearly. You're the troubled one.'

She didn't seem to mind his awkwardness. He asked, 'Who is your sister Alexandra's favourite Beatle?'

She went quiet.

'Your sister, Alexandra?'

Tozer looked away and said, 'Oh God. She was Lennon all the way. Even had the hat, didn't you notice?'

'No,' said Breen. For the second time he noted the tense: 'was'.

The smell of old cabbages hung in the air in the old market. They walked around for a while in silence. Eventually Breen said, 'When we saw the dead girl, you told me you'd never seen a dead body before.'

'I hadn't,' Tozer said. She looked at him curiously, then walked on.

They drifted slowly back towards the car. On King Street two men stood in the side doorway of a shop that had been converted into a hippie nightclub. It announced itself in painted letters on the door: *Middle Earth*. The men were clutching electric guitars; one had long shoulder-length hair and an Afghan, the other big corkscrews of hair, pale blue circular glasses and a gold-braided military jacket a horseman in the Light Brigade might have worn.

One of the guitar cases was painted as a Union Jack. If it was supposed to be ironic, the irony was lost on Breen. To be English and young is to be superior. Britannia waives the rules. At the best of times, Breen had felt alien in this country. Faced by this, doubly so. These people were only a few years younger than Breen, but they lived in a different world. Men of Breen's generation had grown up wanting to wear better suits than their fathers. This lot didn't want suits. They weren't looking for careers, weren't waiting to enter the world of middle age. Gazing at Breen they seemed to say, 'Everything you stand for is ridiculous.' Even though Breen wasn't sure he had ever stood for very much at all. Maybe that was what fired their contempt.

The shop's glass was covered in gaudy posters for groups with names like The Pink Floyd, The Nice and The Pretty Things, hiding whatever lay behind. The two hippies didn't take their eyes off Breen and Tozer as they walked past. Peace and love be fucked.

England dividing itself on new lines.

Later, they stopped at the station to check in to see if Wellington had been in touch.

Marilyn was turning the handle of the Roneo machine with a bored look on her face.

She looked from Tozer to Breen and back again. 'You two a team now?' she said to Breen.

'She's just a probationer.'

'Put the kettle on then, love,' said Marilyn to Tozer. 'I'm parched.'

'I'm fine, thanks,' said Tozer. 'Put it on yourself.'

'That's nice, isn't it?' she said, still cranking the Roneo. 'I heard you had her going round asking questions with you.'

'Her is standing right here,' said Tozer.

Breen looked from Tozer and back to Marilyn again, aware that he was being drawn into something that could only end badly.

'I always end up making the tea for you lot,' Marilyn said. 'Why shouldn't she?'

'Because I don't even want tea.'

Marilyn paused her cranking and glared at Tozer.

'So, I'll make it, then?' said Breen eventually. Both the women stared at him.

In the kitchen down the corridor, he rummaged through the cupboards looking for the tea bags. 'Has Wellington been in touch?' he called to Marilyn.

Marilyn left the Roneo and came and leaned against the doorway, watching him. 'He called an hour ago. He said it was what you thought it was. He wouldn't tell me what, though. Said it wasn't my business.'

Breen opened a tin but it was full of Nescafé.

'In the box on the left,' she said. Breen found the wooden box and pulled open the top, then looked for cups to put the tea bags in. Marilyn let him rummage a little while longer, then said, 'Top cupboard,' over her shoulder, returning to the office.

Breen brought two cups back into the office, spilling tea on his trousers as he walked. He placed them on Marilyn's desk, wiping the liquid off the material.

'Where's mine then?' said Tozer.

'The plonk has Breen making her tea now,' Jones jeered.

'You said you didn't want one,' protested Breen.

'That was when she wanted me to make them.'

'Oh for God's sake,' Marilyn said.

'It was a joke. Just a joke.'

'Don't be so pathetic.' She turned her back on Tozer. 'So what was Wellington on about then?'

Breen had never known Marilyn be so rude. He couldn't understand it. 'Constable Tozer here, who you think so little of, discovered a stain on the dress,' he said, finding himself sticking up for her a second time in one day.

Tozer stopped smiling and shook her head. 'Don't, sir.'

'And correctly identified it as sperm.'

'Sir,' hissed Tozer, tugging at his sleeve.

'It was in those dustbins, the ones you suggested we shouldn't bother going through, Jones.'

'But, sir . . .'

'What's that?' said Jones. 'What did she find on the dress?'

'I suppose the question you'd have to ask is how come she knew what it was,' said Marilyn, picking up her cup of tea. 'I mean . . .'

'Ooooh,' said Jones, standing and rubbing his hands together. All eyes were now on Tozer.

'See?' Tozer reddened.

'A man's you-know-what?'

'You'd probably need to see a lot of that stuff to know what it looked like.'

'You dirty bitch.'

The woman constable glared at Breen. 'Thanks very much, sir.'

'Where did you see that, Tozer?' Whistles and catcalls. Tozer ran from the room, slamming the door behind her.

'Tou-chy,' said Jones.

'I'd heard she was a bit of a slag.'

Breen stood there looking around the room, at all the grinning faces. 'Give the girl a bloody chance,' he said.

'I don't think Constable Tozer is going to make it in CID, somehow,' said Marilyn, smiling, back on the Roneo machine. Click-whirr. Click-whirr.

'She was trying to help solve a murder.'

Jones lit a cigarette and said, 'So it looks like someone in the blocks then? In Cora Mansions?'

Breen walked to the door, opening it and holding it open, waiting to see if Tozer was coming back. 'You'd ruled that out, if you remember,' he said. 'You changed your mind, then?'

'Maybe I was wrong. We're all wrong sometimes.'

Breen turned and nodded. 'What beats me is why someone who lives in the block would dump a body there,' he said. 'I mean, everybody who lives there would have known that the locks on the shed doors were fixed, surely?'

He looked back down the corridor. No sign of Tozer. She had disappeared.

'Maybe they were just trying to put the body in one of the sheds and were disturbed?' said Jones.

'Maybe.'

'Oh. Forgot to say. I found the girl who discovered the body.' Jones stood up and walked over to where Breen was standing and handed him a piece of paper with an address on it and a phone number.

'I'll do it.' Breen read the address: a house on Abbey Road.

'Look out for the woman of the house; she's a posh gob. She said I'd called at an inconvenient time and should have made an appointment.'

'Got any Sellotape, Marilyn?' called Breen. He let the door swing shut.

Without pausing from turning the handle of the copying machine, she said, 'Bottom drawer, left-hand side.' Blue-printed sheets fell out of the Roneo into a growing pile.

Marilyn stopped for breath. The noise stopped. She reached out for a packet of No. 6's on the top of the cabinet and lit one. 'My boyfriend came by and bought me this'. Holding out her right hand, cigarette between the fingers, she showed off a small diamond ring.

Breen said, 'That's nice.'

'I think it's hideous,' said Marilyn, frowning, holding the ring up to her face. 'I'm never sure what to think when he buys me jewellery. He's up to no good. You think I should chuck him, Paddy?'

'Don't ask me.'

Marilyn wrinkled her nose and turned away. Breen began sticking pieces of paper to the wall to form a large rectangle. Fetching a pencil from his desk, he started drawing a rough picture of Cora Mansions on the paper.

'Look at the famous Irish artist,' said Jones. 'Leonard O'Davinci. Get it? Leonard O'Davinci?'

When he'd finished, Breen got out his notebook and started flicking through it. 'Who have we got alibis for?' he said.

Jones was interested now. He pulled out his own notebook and started reeling off names. There were thirty-eight flats in the block, seven of which were unoccupied. Breen found a green biro and used it to cross out all of the names they could eliminate.

'I mean, firstly, are we sure it's the dead girl's dress?' said Breen.

'It's a dress. And she was starkers,' said Jones.

By the end of it there were eight names on the list. Five of them were on the side of the flats which would have been closest to the rubbish chute under which the dress had been found. Three had not been in when police called. Two were men who lived alone and who had not been able to provide alibis. Mr Rider was one of them. Breen circled his name.

'What about the bag?' said Jones. 'You said the dress was in a bag.'

Breen opened his briefcase and pulled out the bag. It was an ordinary brown paper bag with pale blue stripes printed on it; there was no name anywhere.

'What if I was to go round the shops with it and check which ones use bags like that? I mean, they're all paper bags, but they're all a bit different. You never know.'

'Nice idea,' said Breen.

Jones nodded.

Prosser was sitting opposite Jones, eyeing them. 'Nice idea,' he said, imitating Breen's voice.

Jones blushed like a schoolboy caught out talking to a girl by his mates. 'Just a thought, that's all.'

Bailey had heard the sound of voices and went to the open door of his office. 'Have you seen Carmichael anywhere?'

'No, sir.'

'And you? Everything OK?' He stood in his doorway holding a small metal watering can.

'Yes, sir.'

'Good,' said Bailey, looking at them all, frowning, then turning his back on them.

Marilyn came up and said to Breen, 'Your girlfriend is crying in the ladies' toilets.'

'She's not my girlfriend.'

On the ground floor, where the women's toilets were, Breen stood outside the door. 'Tozer?' he called. 'I'm sorry. I didn't think. I shouldn't have told them.'

A sergeant in uniform came out of the gents next door to it, wiping his hands on his blue serge trousers.

'Helen?'

The sergeant looked at Breen with a knowing smile and winked at him. 'Girl trouble.'

'Mind your own bloody business,' Breen snapped.

'Pardon me for speaking.'

Breen waited until he'd disappeared down the corridor, laughing, then said, 'You in there?'

No answer. He sighed.

'I'm sorry. I was only trying to stick up for you.'

A voice from inside the toilets. 'Mr Popularity Contest sticking up for me is all I fucking need.'

NINE

Door-to-doors eliminated two more of the flats early the next morning; one was a single woman who had been out playing cards at a friend's house. The other was a young girl who had been visiting in-laws while her husband worked shifts.

Miss Shankley was there at her front door, arms folded, as Breen walked past. 'You stole my ladder.'

'I'm sorry. I had meant to bring it back. Only.' He raised his sore arm.

'I heard,' she said. 'Well, it's gone now. Someone filched it, didn't they?'

He took out his wallet and counted out three pound notes. 'Will that cover a new one?'

'But then I've got all the bother of getting it. What are you lot doing back here? I thought you'd finished.'

'Just routine,' said Breen.

Miss Shankley looked at him. 'You think it's one of us, don't you? You think it's one of the people here.'

Breen didn't answer.

'I'm a woman living here on my own. If there's some murderer living in our block you should tell us. I heard you're looking for a sex pervert.'

'Who told you that?'

'I heard, that's all.' You could never trust other coppers to keep their mouths shut.

★

At eleven, he and Tozer stood outside Mr Ezeoke's house, Breen with a raincoat held up over his head. He felt weary.

'I mean, why couldn't you pretend that it was you that knew what it was? Nobody would have blinked if it was a feller said it.'

'I was just trying to give credit where it's due.'

'Well. Thanks a bunch. Sir.'

It was one of the things that had buzzed around his mind: how exactly she had known. Distracting thoughts. They were not the only ones though. Several times he had switched on the light, picked up the notebook he had left by the side of the bed and stared at the pages he had written after visiting the Fan Club.

Samuel Ezeoke opened the front door and beckoned them into a large hallway. Cardboard boxes were stacked against one wall. 'Ezinwa?' he called out up the dark wood stairs. 'We have guests. Let me take your coats. Please excuse the mess. We have only been in this house a short time and we are still unpacking.' His accent seemed more English than Breen's or Tozer's.

Breen stamped to get the drips off him.

'So tell me why you need to speak to me,' said the man.

'We still haven't identified the victim, so we're talking to people again to try and see if there's some detail that they may have overlooked.'

A stern-looking woman emerged down the stairs, dressed in a long skirt and white blouse with her hair tucked under a brightly coloured headscarf. She was tall and slender.

'Ezi, they want to ask again about the killing of that poor girl.' He turned to the two policemen. 'This is my wife, Ezinwa.'

His wife's face softened. 'Such a terrible thing to happen. I talked to a policeman the day before yesterday but I am afraid I was not able to be very useful. We have only lived in this neighbourhood a short time.' Unlike her husband, who spoke perfect English, hers was strongly accented.

Breen had grown up in an England of cautious floral prints. The Ezeokes' living room was a long way from that: loud and unfamiliar.

It housed the biggest Pye TV Breen had ever seen and a walnut veneer music centre with a stack of LPs leaning up against it. The one at the front had a bright yellow cover: *Dancing Time No. 5 Commander in Chief Stephen Osita Osadebe and his Nigerian Sound Makers*. Large, dark wood sculptures sat on the mantelpiece. On the wall, a huge mask, wood stained white, eyes dark holes, raffia hanging from the bottom of it. Vibrant modern paintings hung unevenly on the wall. One, on the wall opposite the front window, showed a row of exaggeratedly curvaceous woman dancers, lines flying away from them in all directions. Two or three paintings were still leaning against the walls, ready to be hung; Breen remembered the Ezeokes had only moved into the house two or three weeks earlier. A gold-framed black-and-white photograph of a round-faced, bearded man in a pressed suit, sitting in front of a flag, hung slightly crookedly in an alcove. Above hung a huge ceremonial horsehair fly whisk. The place was crammed. It was like they owned more things than could possibly fit into a room this size.

'Please. Would you like a refreshment? Tea, coffee, Coca-Cola?' asked Mrs Ezeoke. She towered over Constable Tozer. Despite the African-ness of her looks, her hair tied up in a headscarf that knotted at the back above the neck, her long-limbed grace, she seemed determined to sound as English as any of them.

'Now,' said Mr Ezeoke. 'You are having some difficulties uncovering the identity of the dead girl?'

Tozer bristled. 'I wouldn't describe them as difficulties.'

Ezeoke smiled. 'I apologise. My wife tells me I often speak out of turn.'

'These are extraordinary paintings, Mr Ezeoke,' said Breen, gazing around him.

'You like them?' beamed the man.

They were thick with colour; strong black lines formed shapes that suggested large-bottomed women, pounding food in pots, or dancing. 'They are by great Biafran artists. This one is by Uche

Okeke and this,' he pointed to a smaller white canvas, 'is by Chike Aniakor. Have you heard of them perhaps?'

Breen shook his head. 'I'm sorry . . .'

'You will.' Ezeoke laughed loudly.' 'One day these canvases will be worth many thousands of pounds.'

Breen stared at the paintings' clashing colours.

'You are from Biafra?' He tried to picture the country on a map of Africa but he had no idea where it was; he knew he had heard the name a lot in the news over the last year.

'Yes,' he answered.'I am proud to say I am.' His wife came in with a tray of drinks and a plate of biscuits, laid out on a paper doily.

'Eat, please.' She smiled. 'My husband grew up here in England. But he is becoming more African than I am.'

'My wife, on the other hand, has gone native here. Please take one,' he said.'I cannot have one until you do.' Ezeoke laughed again.

Breen took a Chocolate Bourbon, Tozer a Chocolate Finger; Ezeoke leaned forward and took three pink wafer biscuits in his large hands.

'Biafra. It's at war, I think?' said Breen.

'Of course,' said the surgeon. 'My country is fighting a war of independence. Right now I can't even travel home to see my relations. It's a tragedy.'

'It must be hard for you.'

Their host could not answer immediately; he had put one of the pink wafers in his mouth and was chewing it. Crumbs fell from his lips. He picked up a glass of lemonade that his wife had poured for him and swilled down the biscuit. When he had managed to swallow it down, he said, 'The British made lines on a map that have no relevance to a modern Africa, and for that we are paying with our lives. I am too old to fight, myself, but yes, many of my relatives are engaged in the struggle back home.'

'Old man, you are too old to fight but not too old to be polite. Don't make a pig of yourself eating all the biscuits,' said Mrs Ezeoke.

Breen tried to remember anything he had read about the war. It was confused, in his mind, with Vietnam. Facts came only in fragments. Hostilities had started last year. Part of Nigeria had seceded but he could not remember why, or which side had the upper hand.

'It would have been better if your government had recognised our country, of course,' said Mr Ezeoke. 'It would have been over in a few weeks if you had, and fewer people would have had to die. But you chose not to and supported the genocide instead. Because you're still imperialists who want our oil. You'll regret that. When we win, the countries who supported us will be the ones we let buy our oil.'

His wife clucked her tongue. '*Mechie onu*. These police officers have not come here to hear your political opinions. They are looking for a murderer.'

'I am sorry.' He smiled at Breen. 'My wife is right. I wish I could help you more.'

Breen showed them the photo of the dead girl. Mrs Ezeoke sat on the arm of her husband's chair and looked at it with him. He furrowed his brow, then shook his head. 'I'm sorry,' said Sam Ezeoke. 'I wish I could say I recognised her.'

His wife tutted. 'She is young. How terrible.'

They were sitting around a small, ornately carved African table, geometric patterns carved into the dark wood. An immense glass ashtray sat in the middle of it.

'I've got a question,' Breen said. 'Had you noticed that the doors of the sheds next to where the body was found were open?'

'My God yes,' said Mrs Ezeoke, leaning forward on the sofa. 'The doors were banging all night. Every night. My husband almost got into a fight with one of the residents there when he complained because we could not sleep.'

The surgeon chuckled. 'It was not that vulgar, Ezi. I was most polite.'

Breen pulled out his notebook and flicked through the pages. 'Would that have been with a Mrs . . .' He found the name. 'Miss Shankley?'

'I didn't ask her name,' said Ezeoke. 'I don't think she was interested in mine either. Though of course I could have spelled it out for her if she asked.' He giggled. 'She told me to go home.' The giggles turned to laughter.

His wife scowled and muttered, 'This is not a joke, *nna*.'

'Of course it is a joke. You cannot expect me to take people like her seriously.'

The doorbell rang. Mr Ezeoke excused himself and went to answer it. Breen and Tozer could hear him speaking loudly to someone in the hallway.

'I am sorry about my husband,' said the woman. 'He is all talk. He would not admit it but he was very offended by the woman he spoke to in those flats. Very upset. She was very rude to him.' She smoothed down her skirt and said more quietly, 'I think she would not be rude to him if she was in hospital and her life depended on his work.'

Breen stood to go, and as he did so Ezeoke entered the room with another older grey-haired man.

'Are you going?'

'We'll leave you. You have guests.'

'This is my good friend Eddie Okonkwo. A staunch supporter of the Biafran cause. Eddie, this policeman is a fan of the Uli school of art.'

'Are you? I have more in my shop,' said the wiry man, holding out his hand to shake. 'You must come and visit me.'

'Well . . .'

'If you like African art, I sell it.' He pulled out a business card and handed it to Breen. *Afro Art Boutique. Fine African Antiques and Art. E. Okonkwo. Notting Hill 4732.* An address on Portobello Road. 'I am very fashionable,' said Okonkwo with a smile. 'All the in people come to my shop. Brian Jones. Terence Donovan. Susannah York. You know Susannah York? She is very, very beautiful.'

'Brian Jones?' said Tozer.

96

'Of course,' said Okonkwo. 'My Ashanti stools are very popular. You should come before I have to put the prices up.' He laughed.

'Eddie. Must you turn everything into commerce?' said Ezeoke.

'Just one question. Where you were on Sunday evening?' Breen asked Ezeoke.

'I had dinner in town with a colleague and came back here around eleven.'

'And your wife can confirm that?'

'Naturally.'

'You were here alone until midnight, *nna*. I was with my uncle.'

'Of course. I forgot,' said Ezeoke.

'My uncle gets homesick. I have to go and cook Biafran chop for him.'

'It's true. She does. She is the best cook in London,' said Okonkwo. 'You're . . . ?'

'Yes. I am her uncle,' beamed Okonkwo.

'And your colleague will be happy to confirm you were having dinner with him? Can you give me his name?'

'*Her* name. Mrs Frances Briggs. Her husband is Senior Registrar at my hospital.'

Breen noticed Mrs Ezeoke run her tongue around the inside of her upper lip.

They shook hands on the doorstep. The rain had eased off.

'That was strange,' said Tozer.

'Was it?' said Breen.

'Didn't you think? All that African stuff.'

Breen shrugged.

'Don't you think they must feel so out of place in England?'

'If they do, I sympathise.'

'And him going on about how rubbish the British are for supporting the other side, but he's happy enough to come here and live off us.'

'He's a surgeon. He probably pays more tax in a year than a copper would in a lifetime. He's not exactly living off us.'

'You know what I mean,' Tozer said.

They walked down Garden Road to where their car was parked.

Straight away, Jones appeared out of the alleyway from Cora Mansions. He was out of breath. 'Paddy,' he said. 'Been looking for you everywhere. I think we've got him.'

'What?' Breen and Tozer followed him past the sheds into the courtyard.

'The murderer.'

'Bloody hell,' said Tozer.

Miss Shankley was there at the bottom of the stairs, dressed in her housecoat as always, arms crossed, cigarette in her fist.

'Carters,' said Jones. He was excited, unable to stand still, shifting his weight from foot to foot.

'What d'you mean?' said Tozer.

'Come out of the way.' Breen took his arm to pull him out of earshot of Miss Shankley. She craned her neck towards them, still trying to hear.

'You know I said I'd go and ask about the bag?' said Jones. 'Struck lucky. Fifth shop I went into, the guy said it wasn't his, but he knew where it was from. Carters hardware in St John's Wood High Street. I talked to the bloke who owns it. He says he buys them special thickness for tools, on account of them being so heavy.'

'Good work,' said Breen.

'Thanks.' A smile. 'I got him to check his books, and you'll never guess who's got an account with him.'

'Go on.'

'Your Mr Rider.'

'God,' said Tozer.

'Plus – and you'll like this – plus, I asked Miss Shankley there, Rider doesn't have one of the sheds.' Miss Shankley caught the sound of her name and smiled. 'So he probably wouldn't have known the doors had even been fixed. So maybe he was trying to stuff her into one of the sheds after all. Shall we bring him in?'

'This is it, then,' said Tozer.

'We arrest him, right?' said Jones.

Breen turned to Tozer. 'Tell Marilyn we need a search warrant for his flat. Give her the address. Is he in?'

Breen could see Miss Shankley following his gaze upwards to the top floor.

'No. He goes out for a walk every morning, apparently.'

'Who said that?'

'His neighbour. He goes out every morning, regular. Back at one for lunch.'

Breen looked at his watch.

'Get one on the front and one on the back, just in case he's back early. Keep it discreet.'

'Why? Where are you going?'

'To talk to the nanny.'

'Haven't we got enough?'

'Maybe,' said Breen.

Tozer nodded. 'Cautious, isn't he?' she said to Jones.

Jones snorted. 'I'll say he bloody is.'

'If he comes back,' said Breen, 'ask him to come to the station to answer some questions. If he refuses, pull him in.'

'It was my idea,' said Jones to Tozer. 'You know, to go and check on the bags.'

'Super,' said Tozer.

They were both excited; Breen should have been too. Heading the squad that caught the murderer would do something to clear his slate. And even though he'd initially neglected to search the bins, Jones could now claim his part in the result. But Breen still felt the same pressing anxiety he felt from yesterday, the same leadenness.

'Maybe we'll go to the pub after, yeah?' Jones said to Tozer. 'Celebrate. Us CID boys will show you how it's done.'

'What's going on?' called Miss Shankley from the bottom of the stairs. 'You should be telling us.'

'Oh God,' said Tozer when they had walked round the corner.

'See the way Jones was looking at me? Now they all think they can buy me a drink and then you know what. And he's married, isn't he?'

'And that's my fault?'

'Yes. It is, matter of fact.'

TEN

Mrs Broughton wore a collared blue dress with buttons at the front and a mid-length pleated skirt. Her black hair was held firmly in place by a layer of spray.

'She is a very silly girl indeed,' she said.

A Wedgwood teapot sat on the coffee table in front of her. There was a scent of geraniums in the air from a row of plants on the windowsill. She, Breen and Tozer all had cups full of tea in front of them. The silly girl, whose name turned out to be Joan, sat uncomfortably on the piano stool, fidgeting. She was dressed in her nanny's uniform: a black woollen jacket and a grey skirt. Her cheeks were flushed.

'Why she didn't think it important to tell me that my children had seen a dead woman I can't think.'

The girl sat silently. Outside in the hallway a grandfather clock that had probably been in the family for generations ticked through each heavy second.

'I am sending her home to her parents. I have told the agency that I shall not be using them again. She is not suitable.'

'Have you been here long?' Breen asked the girl.

'She has been here almost two months,' answered Mrs Broughton. She sat on the floral print couch, one arm lying across its back. 'I suppose I'll have to pay her till the end of the week. It's very inconvenient.'

Breen observed the girl chewing slowly on the inside of her lip. He looked at her hands. Her nails were short and bitten. Unhappiness in the young is never well concealed.

'My husband has a senior position in the Foreign Office,' Mrs Broughton said. 'He would loathe it if there were a whiff of scandal about this. There is no reason for this to be in the newspapers, is there, officer?'

'I doubt they'd be particularly interested.'

'One small mercy, I suppose.'

'May we speak to Joan alone?' asked Breen.

'Alone? We are *in loco parentis*, for now at least. I think we should be there.'

'I'd prefer to talk to her on her own. There will be a woman constable present.'

A pause. A small smile. 'Well, I suppose so.' But she showed no sign of finishing her tea and leaving the room.

'Perhaps we might talk to you in your room,' Breen said to the nanny.

The girl nodded silently, looking at her feet, then stood.

'She'll show you the way,' said Mrs Broughton, leaning forward to open a silver cigarette box that lay next to the teapot. 'Please don't leave without seeing me first, officer.'

Up the stairs in gilded frames hung dark portraits and joyless, damp-looking landscapes. The opposite of Ezeoke's paintings.

The girl lived at the top of the house in a room whose ceiling was so low Breen could not stand up straight. Around the walls were Sellotaped pictures of pop stars and models cut from magazines. Breen recognised only Twiggy and Jean Shrimpton. There was a red Dansette on the shelves and an untidy pile of singles on the floor. A crochet hook and some wool sat on a chair. A spider plant that was badly in need of water. A small chest of drawers with clothes half pulled out. A small brown leather suitcase, half packed.

'Going home then?' said Breen.

'So I hear,' said the girl. She walked to the wall and started carefully peeling off the photos.

'Mind if I sit down?'

The girl nodded slightly. There was only one chair, so Breen sat on it.

'I'll take the bed then, shall I?' said Tozer. The metal bed squeaked as she sat down.

The girl's eyes were red; she rubbed the sleeve of her woollen jacket across them to dry them. Tozer pulled a hanky out of her sleeve and offered it to her.

'I'm sorry. I meant to call the police. Only I was worried what she'd say.'

'Why?'

She said nothing, lips scrunched up, and reached for another photo. A pop group clustered round a drum kit that had *The Small Faces* painted on it.

'It's OK. We won't tell her,' said Tozer.

The girl paused in her packing. ''Cause Alasdair had to have a wee-wee in an alleyway, 'cause I was talking to some boys in the playground and didn't take them to the toilet when we were still in the park,' she blurted. 'And we were almost home but he was desperate.'

'Alasdair?'

'Their son. I look after him.'

'And Mrs Broughton wouldn't have liked the idea of her son ...?'

The girl shook her head. 'And now she's calling me deceitful 'cause I didn't tell her. And a liar. And she's the one who said she was going to pay me four pounds a week and she only pays me three pounds ten.'

Tozer stood and put her arm around the girl. 'If I were you, I'd be glad to be out of here.'

The girl shucked the constable's arm off her shoulders, continued in her work. 'They'll tell the agency, and all. And I won't get another job now.'

'There are other jobs,' said Tozer.

The girl nodded. 'I hate this place anyway. London's a dump.

Everbody says it's cool but it isn't. This room smells and Mr Broughton is a letch. He tries to see me when I'm in the shower.'

'Never,' said Tozer.

'He does. I've seen him. You can see out of the kids' bedroom right into the bathroom if you leave the window open. And you have to if you're having a shower because it gets all steamy. I've seen him in there, peeking through the curtains.'

'What? Peeping Tom?'

She nodded and giggled. 'And he has wandering hands, know what I mean? When she isn't looking.'

'That's disgusting,' said Tozer.

The girl grinned, half embarrassed.

'What does he do?'

'Puts his hand on my bum.'

'What a perver.'

'I know.'

'A groper.'

The girl laughed out loud this time.

'You're best off out of it.'

'Yeah.'

'Tell me,' said Breen, interrupting. 'What do you remember of when you first saw the body?'

'I didn't see much. Just her face. She had creepy eyes.'

'Did you recognise her?'

She shook her head.

'The rest of her was covered by the mattress?'

'Yes. You could have only noticed her if you were crouching down. Or if you were a little boy.'

'Did you see anyone there?'

'No. No one.'

'So. Why did you run away?'

'I don't know. I was scared. And I didn't want to get caught up. I was late. Mrs Broughton would have killed me if I was late. She doesn't like me very much.'

'Unlike Mr Broughton,' said Tozer.

The girl laughed again, losing a little shyness each time.

'Do you ever talk to the girls who wait over the road?' Breen said.

'Sometimes. They don't like me much, though.'

'Why not?'

'They're real cliquey. I'm not one of them, am I?'

'What do you mean?'

She bit the inside of her lip. 'They're a bunch of loonies, if you ask me. Some of them sleep outside at night. And the clothes. They look awful, if you ask me. They're all super-rich but they wear these dirty clothes. They give me the creeps.'

'You ever seen the Beatles there yourself?' asked Tozer.

The girl shook her head. 'Mrs Broughton don't like me going over there. She saw me there once and gave me a real talking-to. She complains to the council about them. Says they're spoiling it all round here.'

Breen pulled out the photograph of the dead girl. 'Could you look at it for me?'

She looked and shrugged. 'No. Not seen her before. Not until Monday, anyway. Is she dead in the photo?' She stared at it, fascinated. Then she handed it back and continued putting away her belongings.

She now had a pile of all the photographs she had put on the walls. She laid them carefully inside the lid of her suitcase. Then she unplugged her Dansette and fastened the lid with a click. 'How old was she?' she asked.

'Around sixteen, seventeen, we think.'

'You haven't found out who she is, then?'

'No. Not yet. But we're close.'

'Same age as me,' said the girl. 'Scary, isn't it?'

'Yes,' said Tozer. 'It is.'

'Was she hurt bad? You know. Before she died.'

'I don't think so,' said Tozer.

'I dreamed about her,' said the girl. 'Couple of times.'

'Oh yes?' said Tozer.

'Yeah. Both times I'm looking at her and she wakes up. Only she's still dead, like. In one she started singing.'

'Singing?' said Tozer.

'Sorry. Didn't mean to say about that.'

'It's OK. It must have been a nasty shock.'

'It was a weird song. In a language I didn't understand. And I think if only I can understand the words she's singing I'll be able to help her. But they're all gobbledygook.'

'And what happened then?'

'I don't know. I think I woke up.'

She turned and sat on her suitcase, trying to close it.

'Are you going to catch him? The one who did it to her?'

'You know what?' said Tozer. 'I think we've got him already.'

'Wow. Who is it?'

'Tomorrow's papers. Keep them peeled. I think we've got the bugger.'

'Cor,' said the girl.

'Enough,' said Breen.

They left her alone in her room, sitting on her bed.

'We have, though, haven't we? Got him?'

On the way out they paused to say goodbye to Mrs Broughton. She was still on the sofa, a pack of patience cards dealt out in front of her now on the coffee table. A novel by Alistair MacLean, spine cracked, beside the ashtray.

'What did she have to say for herself?'

'Not a lot,' said Breen.

'She never does,' said Mrs Broughton.

'Right.'

'She's a waste of time, that girl. Girls today are lazy. They just want to be models or film stars. They don't understand the meaning of service. Will that be all?' She moved a card from one pile to the next. Breen turned to go.

'She did mention that your husband is a Peeping Tom, though,' announced Tozer.

'I beg your pardon?' The woman sat there on the sofa, her mouth an O of red lipstick.

'It's not legal to spy on teenage girls when they're in the shower, you know. You might want to tell him that. I wouldn't say anything to the agency about the girl if I were you. She could make a complaint against you. That's the kind of thing the papers would be much more interested in.'

Mrs Broughton found her voice. 'How dare you!'

Breen took Tozer's arm and pulled her towards the door. 'We'll see ourselves out, Mrs Broughton.'

Mrs Broughton was standing now, patience cards knocked onto the floor, mouth opening and closing in fury.

'I mean. I mean, for God's sake.'

'Well, it's true, isn't it?'

'You can't do that.'

'Why not?'

Breen fumbled with the handset in the car. 'Can you check with Marilyn to see if a search warrant has been issued yet?' he asked the controller.

'I mean,' Tozer said. 'Why bloody not? Sometimes I think all of you must be perverts.'

He remembered last night, lying in bed, thinking about her.

'Scratch the surface and it's bloody everywhere,' she said.

'There's a difference between a harmless fumble and actually killing someone.'

'Says who?' said Tozer.

Breen opened his mouth to answer, but decided against it. His shoulder ached. He looked in the glove compartment for an aspirin.

'Still, I mean, we got Rider for it.'

'If the link to the dress is right, then yes,' said Breen.

She picked a piece of gum from a packet and started to roll it between finger and thumb. 'What's he like?'

'Shy. Buttoned-up. One of the old guard.'

'See? It's them. The ones who never learned to let their hair down.' When the chewing gum was rolled tight she popped it into her mouth.

'There's nothing wrong with not letting your hair down,' he said.

She chewed for a little bit, then said, 'God. Do you believe that? I think if you don't let yourself go once in a while, all that rage and fury just builds up inside you until you go off. Like an H-bomb.' She looked at her watch. It was only a quarter past twelve. 'Can we head back there now?' she said.

Just then their call sign came on the radio. Delta One Five. Breen picked up the handset. 'That you, Paddy Breen?' said the voice. 'Better get down to the nick. Jones has just pulled in your suspect.'

'Damn.'

As always, the traffic was thick.

If he did it by the book, Jones would wait for them to start the questioning, but he didn't trust Jones to do it by the book. 'Stick the siren on,' he said.

'Yippie-ay-yay,' she said.

She drove south, diving between traffic. He banged sideways against the door as she looped round a roundabout. When he tried to reach out to steady himself with his bad arm, pain flooded through it. 'Slow down.'

'Always wanted to do the siren,' she shouted back.

ELEVEN

The room was too small. The one they normally used for questioning was being decorated so they were using a storeroom on the second floor instead. Each time anyone came in, Breen had to shuffle his chair out of the way. With filing cabinets lined up along the far wall, there was little standing room.

'You said to nab him if he made a move,' said Jones.

The room was bright. One of the two neon strips above their heads buzzed. It had a dark blueish patch near one end of the tube and would occasionally flicker off and on.

When Breen had interviewed Rider in his flat he had been full of the quiet confidence of his years. Early sixties, roughly. Retired on sick pay. Now he looked smaller, jacketless, dressed in shirtsleeves and tie. He was bleeding from a cut on his upper lip.

'He was rude,' said Mr Rider. He looked confused and frightened. 'I was just walking on Primrose Hill. I've not done anything wrong.'

'Has he said anything yet?'

'Only that he shouldn't be here,' said Jones.

'It's a mistake,' said Mr Rider. 'You've made a very serious mistake.'

'Why is he bleeding?'

'Nobody is telling me why I am here. You've no right to bring me here without asking me.' Mr Rider's voice had a reedy, wheedling tone. There was a patch of sweat under his right armpit.

'Did Constable Jones explain that we were asking you to come to the police station for questioning?'

'He just grabbed me and marched me to the police car. In front of the whole world.'

'Why is he bleeding? Tozer? Can you get some cotton wool from First Aid?'

'He didn't give any reason at all.'

'He banged his head getting into the car, Paddy. That's all. Just a bump.'

'He shoved me. He deliberately pushed me.' Rider's voice sounded curiously childlike. Breen looked at the man's hands. They were trembling.

Breen looked away at Jones; Jones shrugged as if to say, 'So what?'

'We have a warrant to search your flat,' said Breen.

'Search it for what?'

'Would you mind giving Constable Jones the keys?'

'I'm not giving that thug anything. He hurt me.'

'If you don't give the keys to us, I'm afraid he'll have to break the door down. As I said, we have a warrant, so he is allowed to do that. You don't want that to happen, do you?'

'I've done nothing wrong!' the man screamed, his voice suddenly loud. 'This is all a mistake.'

Jones held out his hand. 'Just give me the keys, if you don't mind.'

From the corridor outside came the sound of laughter. 'I should let you know, I'm in the Conservative Club and I happen to be very good friends with my MP.'

'If we're making a mistake,' said Breen, 'you've got nothing at all to worry about.'

'Why would I trust you with my keys? You're a thug.'

'Go, then,' said Breen to Jones.

'No!' screeched Rider. 'Wait.'

'Keep your ruddy hair on,' said Jones.

Rider seemed to be thinking, weighing up the situation. Eventually he dug in his pockets and handed the keys over; just two keys on a single ring. 'Top one's a bit sticky,' he said. 'You have to pull the door towards you. I expect the place to be tidy when you've finished.'

Rider seemed to relax a little when Jones had left the room. He was replaced by Tozer who arrived with a wad of cotton wool and a small bowl of water. She dunked the wool into the water, but Rider snapped, 'I'll do it myself, thank you very much.'

'Suit yourself,' she said.

'Do I really have to be here?'

'It would be useful if you could answer a few questions,' said Breen. 'If, for any reason, this results in a trial, it's always to your advantage to have cooperated with the police.'

'Trial?' said Mr Rider. 'But I've done nothing wrong.'

'Then you won't mind answering a few questions.' The ache had not gone down in his shoulder. If anything, it was worse.

'I suppose I can spare a few minutes,' Mr Rider said. He padded the cut on his lip, then dropped the cotton wool. It fell into the bowl of water, turning it a thin pink.

'We found a dress,' said Breen. 'A black dress. It was discarded in one of the bins at Cora Mansions.'

The statement had an immediate effect on the man. His eyes widened and the florid colour seemed to vanish from his face. 'I beg your pardon?'

'You put it there.'

'No I didn't,' he said.

Breen felt his skin prickle. The man was lying. The sudden change in his demeanour at the mention of the dress. The flat denial. The heaviness that had been building all day vanished. The old excitement he used to feel broke surface.

'Why did you throw it away?'

'I didn't,' he insisted. 'This is absurd.' His voice was trembling.

Breen leaned forward, interested. He had found it hard to imagine Rider as a killer, but they were on to something now.

'Take your time. Tell us about it when you're ready.'

Tozer seemed to have picked up something too. Standing behind Rider, she focused entirely on the man, eyes on the back of his head.

'I haven't got anything to tell.'

Breen looked at his watch and made a note of the time on the pad in front of him.

III

'What is going on?' said Rider. 'Please.'

'A girl's dress,' Breen said.

'A girl?' said Rider.

'That's right.'

'A girl?'

'A girl who you assaulted.'

'Assaulted?'

'Possibly raped.'

A second's stillness in the room. Everything stopped while the man seemed to be trying to understand what Breen was saying. 'No,' he said, frowning, examining Breen's face. 'No. My God. No.'

The man had looked frightened before; now he looked doubly so. 'You think it was the dead girl's? Oh my Lord.'

'We found sperm on the dress.'

For a second the man looked like he was about to choke; where before his skin had been almost white, now it flushed red.

'Tell us about what happened. Did you mean to kill her, or was it an accident?'

For a long time Rider looked straight down at the table, shaking. Then he leaned forward across to Breen and whispered something in his ear. He said it so quietly Breen couldn't make it out.

'Sorry?'

Rider leaned forward again. It took a while for Breen to understand what he'd said: 'It was not the girl's dress.'

And as he sat back, big tears began to drip down Mr Rider's cheeks.

Breen's brief moment of confidence that he might have understood what had happened to the dead girl vanished.

He said to Tozer, 'Go and get a glass of water for Mr Rider.'

'But—'

'Now,' said Breen quietly. 'Please.'

To his relief, she did what she was told without any more objections. With Tozer gone, the sound of Rider's embarrassed sobs seemed to fill the room. Sucking in air, blowing it out again.

'Tell me about the dress,' said Breen.

The man shook his head rapidly from side to side.

'We can clear this all up if you just tell me.'

'No,' he said. 'I. Can't.'

'Try.'

'I can't.'

'You have to.'

'I have not done anything wrong.' He was trying to get control of himself but the sobs kept rising. 'It was my wife's dress,' he said suddenly between gulps of air.

'But she's dead, your wife?'

Rider nodded. 'Tumour. Two years ago. I moved to Cora Mansions to try and start again, but somehow I can't.'

Now Breen remembered the black-and-white photo of the woman in the living room. It had been set between two candles. A shrine of sorts.

'Sometimes I pretend . . .'

'I'm sorry,' said Breen.

'It's funny. We used to row all the time when she was alive. Now she's gone I can't cope without her. I miss her so much.'

Breen found his handkerchief and handed it across the small table.

Still staring at the table, he whispered, 'Sometimes I imagine. And then I'm awfully ashamed of myself.'

'That's why you threw the dress away?'

Instead of answering, the man began to cry again. Breen stood and watched his shoulders rising and falling. All his fault. Just because everything appeared to fit together didn't mean it did.

When Tozer came back into the room, banging the door into Breen's chair, Rider was wiping his face with Breen's handkerchief.

'Constable Tozer can arrange a ride home for you, if you like,' said Breen.

'What?' said Tozer.

The man stood, wiped his eyes one last time with Breen's handkerchief, then shook his head. 'I'd rather not arrive back in

113

a police car, if you don't mind. It was bad enough going in one coming here. They were all watching me. I won't be able to look people in the eye.'

'We could drop you somewhere?'

Rider shook his head. Breen led him down the stairs and out of the police station. From the steps he watched him walking fast, taking small steps, eager to get as far away as he could. He turned right at the end of the building and disappeared from sight.

'What happened in there?' said Tozer. 'Why's he going home?'

'I'm a bloody fool,' said Breen.

On Friday morning he woke absurdly early again.

It was dark. He made himself a coffee and took it into his father's room, sitting on his father's empty bed. He thought of Rider, alone, with his wife's dress. A life skewed by absence.

There was a tiny photograph of his mother on the bedside table, not much bigger than a postage stamp in a small silver frame. A smiling, wild-haired woman sitting on a stone wall somewhere, presumably in Ireland. This was the only likeness of her he had; because she had died when he was so young, he had no memories of her.

His father, as his mind unravelled, had gradually lost her too. She had been unremembered by him, bit by bit, until there was nothing of her left. In his last days, Breen had seen his father lift the photograph up and examine it, close to his eyes, as if trying to peer inside it to recover what had gone. Mr Rider, on the other hand, could not forget his wife.

Policemen usually married young; that way you could apply for a police flat. Like Prosser and Jones. Breen had only had girlfriends before his father had moved in. After he lived with his dad, it was harder to find the opportunity to date. But there had never been anyone whom he could imagine missing as much as Rider missed his wife, or his father had missed his mother.

At the police station, as he walked in, the desk sergeant looked at his watch and said, 'Blimey, Paddy, you're up with the birdies again.'

He switched on the light in the CID room and took four sheets of paper from Marilyn's desk and Sellotaped them together. Propping up an *A–Z* against his in-tray, he drew a map of the streets around Garden Road. He made steady strokes with the pencil, pausing occasionally to check his work across the map. When he'd finished, he went back to Marilyn's desk and picked up four more sheets and drew a second map of the streets around Carlton Vale where the man had been found burned to death.

Marilyn came in at a little after 8.30. 'Do you sleep here now? Cup of tea?'

Breen shook his head without looking up. Writing on bits of paper and arranging them on his desk, looking for obscure signs, for overlooked facts. With Rider he had been too eager to believe in the easy connection between a dress and the murder.

She brought him a cup anyway. 'What's with all these drawings and diagrams? I'm going to have to order more paper if you carry on like this. You OK, Paddy? You look done in.'

Breen didn't answer. He picked out his first cigarette of the day. It was early, for him, but he felt the need. As he pulled it out, he noticed there were only four cigarettes in the pack of ten. That was odd. He had only bought the packet yesterday morning. He thought back and tried to remember if he had offered anyone else a cigarette during the day.

'Houston calling Apollo?'

'Sorry. Can you call the social services, Marilyn? Check we've got a list of all the hostels here?' He passed her the second map he'd drawn.

'Is this for the dosser? The burned guy?'

'Yes.'

She took the map off him. 'You probably won't find out who he was, you know,' she said.

'Maybe,' he said.

'Why him?'

'It's our job, isn't it?' he said, but when he glanced up at her she was looking at him with a disbelieving air.

At nine he lit the cigarette he'd taken out of the packet and took a long pull, feeling the nicotine calm him. Then he called Devon and Cornwall Constabulary. 'Do you have any record of an incident involving a girl called Alexandra Tozer?' he asked a woman down a line so poor and crackly that he had to spell out the name twice. They promised they would call back.

Jones came in late with a hangover. 'Started the weekend early, Jonesy?' said Marilyn.

'Lightweight,' said Prosser.

'I don't know how you do it.' Jones grinned. 'And you were on brandy too.'

'Like I said, lightweight.'

Bailey emerged from his office. 'Constable Jones. What time do you call this?'

'Sorry, sir. Won't happen again.'

'Bad news about Sergeant Breen's case, eh, sir?' said Prosser. 'Turns out he was chasing the wrong suspect.'

'So it seems. Will there be any fall-out?' asked Bailey.

Breen shook his head. 'No, sir.'

'Sure?'

'Quite sure.' The man would be too embarrassed by what he'd done to make a complaint.

'That's something.' Bailey nodded and returned to his room.

'Imagine tickling the pickle like that, on your dead wife's dress,' said Jones. 'That's sick.'

'Feel big, do you, beating up old men?'

'He fell.' Jones smiled. 'Not my fault.'

'You shouldn't have treated him like that,' said Breen. 'It was cruel. If I catch you doing something like that I'll report you.'

'He's an old wanker.'

116

'Language,' said Marilyn. Prosser looked straight at Breen and slowly shook his head.

Breen's phone rang.

'Actually, I think what that old man did is quite romantic, in a way,' Marilyn said as she picked up the handset.

At ten he found Tozer in the canteen talking to two policewomen from A4, the women's branch.

She smiled at him. 'Where are we going?'

'I need to talk to you,' he said.

'Oooh,' said one of the girls.

'Who's the lucky one?' said the other.

'Is it about my driving?' Tozer said.

'No. Nothing like that.'

'What she mean, driving?' said one of the girls.

'About what I said to Mrs Broughton? No? What, then?'

'Not here,' he said.

'Oooh,' said the girls again.

'Shut up,' Tozer told them.

'Let's go for a coffee somewhere else.'

On the way out of the back of the building, Breen heard someone shouting his name. Prosser pushed open the swing door and was coming after them.

'Go on,' he said to Tozer. 'Get in the car.'

'What?' he said to Prosser.

Prosser grabbed him by his bad arm and said, quietly, 'Lay off Jones. Nobody who bad-mouths their fellow officers in front of everybody like that belongs in the force.'

'Let go of my arm,' said Breen.

'Let go of my arm? You're a bloody joke, Paddy Breen.'

Breen looked Prosser in the eye and said, 'Jones beat up an old man. He didn't fall. You know that.'

'This isn't primary school, Paddy. Jones was doing his job. Which makes him twice the policeman you'll ever be.' Prosser released his grip on Breen's arm. 'About time you started sticking up for coppers ...'

Breen turned his back and started walking across the tarmac.

'Instead of just running away,' Prosser called.

'What did Prosser want?' said Tozer, when they were changing seats a hundred yards up Gloucester Road.

'I've been meaning to ask. Have you been taking my cigarettes?' Breen demanded.

'What?' she said, looking at him.

'Have you?'

'Bloody hell. Is that what you wanted to talk to me about?'

'No. But, have you?' he asked again.

'No.' Then: 'Well, maybe a couple. I ran out. Sorry. I didn't think you'd mind.'

'It's OK. Just ask.'

She started the engine. 'You mean you actually count the number of cigarettes you have left?' she said.

They went to the cafe in Paddington Rec and ordered a tea and a coffee.

'Anything else?' said the woman behind the counter.

'What's that?' said Tozer, pointing at the counter. *Cake 4d.*

'Lemon drizzle.'

'Ooh,' said Tozer. 'I'll have one of them.' The woman picked it up with her fingers and put it on a white plate. The radio finished playing a song by Matt Monro.

'Let's go somewhere quieter,' said Breen.

'What's this about?'

They took their drinks to the bandstand, an old, rickety wooden hexagon whose roof kept off the rain. Breen sat down on the bare boards and crossed his legs. Tozer sat down a couple of feet away. 'This is very mysterious,' she said. She pulled a chunk off the cake. 'Want some?' she said, tucking her legs under her.

Breen shook his head. He hadn't noticed her legs before. They were long and thin, but not in a bony way. He pulled his eyes away from them. 'Why did you apply to CID?' he asked.

'It's interesting work. It's why I joined in the first place. Are you disappointed it wasn't Rider?' she asked.

'More disappointed in myself. Just because things fit together doesn't mean they're right.'

'I was gutted,' she said. 'I thought it was him.'

He looked at the thin rain falling down, making rings in the dark puddles around them. 'Tell me about your sister,' he said.

She pursed her lips and looked away. After a minute she said, 'Why should I?'

'Because if we're working together on the death of a young girl, I'd like to know about her.'

'How did you know?'

'You change when you talk about her. Plus you talk about her in the past.'

'So?' she reached out for her tea, fumbled it and knocked the mug over. The brown pool dripped away quickly through the gaps in the worn boards.

'Alexandra Tozer. She was murdered in 1964.'

Quietly she said, 'You got no business—'

'Yes I have.'

Tozer turned away. When she wasn't looking, he found himself glancing back down at her legs again. 'It has nothing to do with the job,' she said.

'Yes it does.' A wet pigeon landed on the bandstand handrail and cocked its head, eyeing Tozer's cake. 'She had been raped. She was found naked like our girl.'

Tozer chewed her lip. 'Yes. And?'

'Is it why you have a go at senior officers like Carmichael, even though you're only two years out of Hendon?'

'He called the victim "a naked bird".' She took a make-up compact out of her bag; he watched her checking her eyes, one by one.

'I'm sorry for what happened to you,' he said.

'Yeah, yeah,' she answered.

'No. Really. It's just . . .'

'Just what? Is it I'm just probationary again?'

'No. But it could complicate things.'

'My sister is a complication?'

'That's not what I'm saying.'

'You had no right,' she said quietly.

'Yes, I did.'

'You went poking into my life.'

'I had to. You weren't telling me about it. If it's going to affect your ability to take a rational view of this case, I need to know.'

'Are you saying I'm irrational?'

'Maybe.'

'And you're the really rational one?'

'That's not the point.'

She stood up suddenly, snapping the compact shut. The pigeon, startled, flew off. 'So what *is* the fucking point?'

He sat, shocked, as she turned away from him. 'Where are you going?'

She didn't answer, just walked down the wooden stairs onto the grass of the park and away through the drizzle.

'Tozer,' shouted Breen after her, standing, but she had disappeared down a curve in the path. 'Constable Tozer,' he shouted again.

He picked up the two empty mugs and took them back to the cafe, then walked back to where Tozer had parked the car. The police car had gone.

He stood there, in the drizzle, waiting for her to return. He moved to the shelter of the porch of a nearby house, but the wind still blew the water into his clothes. After five minutes, with the rain starting to soak through his mac, it was clear she wasn't going to come back.

The road was quiet. By the time he'd trudged to Maida Vale, water trickling into his shoes and he was soaked through. His brogues

continued to fill with water as he walked. To try to hail a taxi he had
to stand on the edge of the pavement in the downpour, holding his
hand out as the cars splashed past.

TWELVE

'Been swimming?' said Marilyn.

'Give over.' He undid his shoelaces, peeled off his socks and draped them over the radiator.

'Protocol is protocol. I should have been told.' He could hear Bailey talking on the phone from his room.

'Have you seen Tozer?'

'This is not the first time this has happened,' Bailey was saying.

'No. Why? Have you lost her?'

'There is a right way to do that and a wrong way.' When Bailey lost his temper he spoke in clipped phrases. 'That's not an excuse. If I started ordering your officers around there would be anarchy. We have procedures. We have ways of doing things.'

'Good riddance to bad rubbish,' said Marilyn.

The office was still, people listening. Jones sat in front of a typewriter, forefingers poised over the untouched keys. Marilyn stood in the middle of the room, a mug of tea in one hand and a cigarette in the other.

'What's going on?' asked Breen.

'This is chaos. This kind of thing will make us a laughing stock.'

Marilyn made a face. 'Some raid going on in Montagu Square' she said. 'I just put the call in to him now from New Scotland Yard. By the sound of it, the boss hadn't had a whiff of it.'

'He'd only do his nut about it because they weren't doing the paperwork proper,' said Prosser.

Jones's phone rang; he picked it up.

'Did you know anything about this?' Breen asked Marilyn.

'Not a peep,' Marilyn said. 'Did you?'

'No.'

'Are you trying to suggest that there would have been a security risk if you'd told me about it? Are you?'

'You're not serious? You're having me on?' said Jones down the phone.

'What's going on?'

Jones put the receiver down with a whoop. 'Fuck-ing hell,' he said. 'You'll never guess.'

'What?'

'You'll never guess who Pilcher's mob are just pulling into Paddington Green.'

'Who?'

'Only John Lennon and his Nip bird.'

'Pilch? John Lennon?'

'What for?'

'Drugs. They just raided John Lennon for drugs. They're on the way there now. That's why the boss has his knickers twisted.'

'Drugs?'

'John fucking Lennon and that Yoko Boko bird.'

'Yoko Boko? What the fuck's that?'

'Pilch has only gone and done it now. Like to hear him singing now.'

'Help! I need somebody. Help,' sang Prosser.

Big laugh.

'I'm down. I'm really down. I'm going down . . .'

More hilarity. Some of the younger officers were practically crying now.

Jones banged his desk and joined in, singing, 'All you need is love.'

'What the hell's that, Jones?' said Prosser.

'It's a Beatles song, isn't it?'

'Yeah but it ain't funny, you moron.'

Jones looked stung.

Marilyn handed Breen a large brown envelope. 'It's the artist's drawing of the girl,' she said. More quietly, she added, 'If you want, we could go for a drink later. Some of the boys are going out.'

'I don't think they want to go out for a drink with me that much.'

'We could go somewhere else then.'

'Oi, oi,' said Jones. 'I thought you had a boyfriend, Marilyn.'

'I was just trying to cheer him up.'

'I know how you could put a smile on my face, Marilyn,' said one of the other men.

'You lot disgust me.'

The *Evening News* and the *Evening Standard* wouldn't print a photograph of a dead body, but they would print a likeness. His best bet now to identify the girl was to ask the public. He had booked a police artist to create an image of the victim, but when he took the pastel drawing out of the envelope he stopped for a second and frowned.

He didn't recognise the woman in the drawing at all. She was pale, bony, thin-faced, and seemed much older than the dead woman he'd seen at the scene of the crime. For a minute he stared at it, not sure if his brain was playing tricks on him.

'This isn't her,' he said eventually.

'Let's see,' said Marilyn. She held the drawing in one hand and Breen's photo of the dead girl, the one he'd been using to show members of the public, in the other. 'Not really. Is it?'

'Not in a million miles.'

'Has she, you know, changed? It's been a couple of days now.'

'She's in the fridge. Bodies don't change. Not for a while at least.'

'I see what you mean.' She looked from one picture to the next.

'It's like he's drawn someone completely different.' The woman had a thin, aquiline nose.

Marilyn went back to her desk, picked up the phone and started making calls.

Breen went back to his desk and sat down. It was getting dark already. The days were getting shorter. He opened his drawer and picked out his pencils, then the pencil sharpener which he had inherited with the desk. It had been at the bottom of his filing cabinet, one of those large ones with a handle. Now he clamped it to the edge of the surface and started sharpening his pencils, one by one. It was satisfying, leaving each with a shining point. On an impulse he leaned forward and smelt the pencil sharpener. A sudden rich aroma of dry cedarwood.

'What are you doing?' said Jones.

Breen looked up sheepisly. 'I was smelling the shavings.'

Jones looked at him. 'Bloody hell.' He went back to his work. 'Smelling the bloody shavings.'

'You'll never believe it,' Marilyn called across the room. 'He's only gone and drawn the wrong body.' Heads looked up from their desks. 'Two unidentifieds down at the university morgue. One numbered 97617, the other numbered 97611. Only, the last number looks just like a seven so they pulled out the wrong one for him. Weren't his fault.'

'Pity's sake.'

'They say they're sorry.'

'Bet they do.' He looked at the drawing again. The fluid strokes, the oddly inappropriate flourish of an eyelash, the pale glisten on the dead lips. The care of the artist's hand.

'And how soon can he do another one?'

She got back on the phone to him. 'I'm trying to book him in now, but he won't be able to do it until Monday.'

Breen groaned. 'Can't he do it Saturday?'

'He don't work weekends,' she said.

That meant next Tuesday's papers at the earliest, so the newspaper with her picture on it would not be on sale until over a week after the murder. Already opportunities were fading. The longer it took, the less chance there was of a result.

'How you doing with that women's libber of yours, Paddy?' asked Jones. 'Wouldn't mind seeing her burning her bra.'

'You're pathetic,' said Carmichael.

'Only joking,' said Jones.

'Nothing to see there. She's flatter than a bloody snooker table,' said Carmichael.

'You should know,' said Jones.

'She's nothing but trouble.'

'Didn't she let you poke her, then?'

Marilyn cupped her hand over the handset and said, 'Do you mind, boys? I'm trying to make a phone call.'

'Unlike Marilyn. Now I'd like to see her burning her bra. She's got something you could get a hold of,' said Prosser, ignoring her. 'She's got nipples like a Lockheed Starfighter.'

'Go on, Marilyn,' said Jones. 'They're wasted on your boyfriend.'

'They'd be wasted on you, mate.' Marilyn flicked a V-sign and carried on with the call.

'I heard Pilch didn't find nothing,' said Jones. 'That he had to take his own gear along, just so he could find something, know what I mean?'

Carmichael glared at him. 'Who the hell told you that?'

Breen looked at Carmichael. 'That true, John?'

Carmichael said, 'Course it bloody isn't. What are you saying, Paddy?'

Breen didn't answer.

'Spit it out, Paddy. You'll turn into Bailey if you don't watch it.'

Bailey emerged from his office looking pale. 'What's that?'

'Nothing, sir.'

'Why have you got no shoes on, Sergeant Breen?' he asked. Breen looked down at his bare feet.

Prosser interrupted. 'Sir. I got a question.'

Bailey sighed. 'Yes?'

'Is it true we're all getting women drivers now, Inspector?'

'What on earth are you talking about, Sergeant?' Bailey blinked.

Breen knew what Prosser was doing. 'This is called sticking up for your fellow officers, is it?' he said quietly.

Prosser just winked back and smiled. 'I must have got the wrong end of the stick,' said Prosser to Bailey. 'Only I just heard that you were letting us have women drivers.'

'Don't be ridiculous, Sergeant Prosser. That would be against regulations.'

'My mistake, Inspector.'

After Bailey had gone back in his office, Prosser walked over to Breen's desk and said, 'Just kidding, Paddy. Keep your hair on. Though just think how angry he'd be if he found out.'

'What's all that about women drivers, Prossy?' said Jones.

'Never you mind,' said Prosser.

Breen picked up the artist's drawing again and looked at it. From the photograph, he started drawing the dead girl's face with his sharp pencil, first the roundness of her face, then shading the curves of her skin. There was an ill-tempered silence in the CID room.

Somewhere out on the stairway, one of the old guys from the force was whistling some old music-hall song in one of those high, quavery tones, all vibrato and swoop. The voice broke into song: 'You are my lily and my rose . . .'

Later, Breen was drinking instant coffee in the canteen and smoking cigarette number three when Marilyn came up and sat down next to him with a cup of tea and a piece of shortcake. 'I'm sorry about that mix-up with the drawing, Paddy.'

'It's not your fault.' She was wearing a tartan polyester dress with a bow at the neckline. Breen noticed she wasn't wearing the ring her boyfriend had given her.

'So what happened? You just tried to have a word with her and she buggered off?'

'Yes.'

'She's a mad cow. Bailey will sack her. You should tell him. What were you having a word with her about anyway?'

'It was personal.'

'Personal? What? Bloody hell. You and her?'

'No. Nothing like that.'

'Thank God. I thought for a minute . . .'

'No.'

Marilyn dunked her shortbread into her tea and then sucked at it for a little while. 'You and her. I think you fancy her.'

'No I don't,' he said.

'You got to watch things, Paddy. Your dad just died. It's a classic. You're vulnerable.'

'Give over, Marilyn. I don't fancy her.'

'I'd keep well away, Paddy. She's a weirdo. You can see it a mile off.'

It was late afternoon now. Some people seemed to live in the canteen. There was an elderly officer who always seemed to be sitting by one of the windows doing *The Times* crossword, sucking on a Bic. Breen had no idea what he did. Some of the cleaning staff had arrived and were having a tea before their shift started.

She unwrapped another biscuit and dunked it in her tea. 'You ever want a change, Paddy?'

'Change?'

'I was thinking of jacking it in and going to college.'

'Really?'

'I've had enough of it, you know?'

'They're only playing, you know. They're not serious. It's just banter.'

She took a sugar cube, held it in her tea until it had turned brown and then popped it into her mouth. 'I'm bored, too, be honest.'

'Bored? What are you going to do?'

She smiled. 'You'll laugh.'

'No I won't.'

She fiddled with the sleeve of her dress. 'I was thinking of studying sociology.'

Breen was surprised. 'Sociology? Where did that come from?'

'I've always been interested in that stuff. Émile Durkheim. Karl Marx.' She licked her finger and dipped it in the biscuit crumbs on the wrapper, then sucked the end of her finger. In his mind, he had not left space in Marilyn's life for anything beyond her feckless boyfriend and her police work. 'Everything can't just go on the way it is. Don't you want things to change?'

'Change?'

'Yes. You know.'

'Of course I do,' he said. 'Why wouldn't I?'

'Me too. I don't just want to be a typist all my life.'

Breen nodded.

She smiled at him. 'Sure you don't want to go out for a drink, Paddy? Nothing else. Just a drink? Big John and some of the boys are going out tonight. They're all excited about having nicked a pop star.'

It was almost clocking-off time. He didn't want to, but perhaps he should. Maybe Carmichael was right. He should get out among the men more.

He was about to say yes and go for a quick half with them and Marilyn when Tozer walked into the canteen.

She came straight up to Breen as if nothing at all had happened and said, 'Do you want anything from the counter?'

'We're fine, thank you very much,' said Marilyn. 'And where have you bloody been?'

Tozer ignored her, came back a minute later with a cheese sandwich and a mug of tea, and sat down in a chair next to Marilyn.

'How's it going?'

Marilyn said, 'Fine till a minute ago. You can't just bugger off and leave a senior officer behind when you're supposed to be accompanying him, you know.'

Tozer shrugged. Breen looked at Tozer's sandwich. It had been on the counter too long and its white crust corners, cut on the diagonal, were beginning to curl at the edges. Tozer picked up the stale sandwich all the same and took a large bite out of it.

'So,' Breen said. 'Where have you been all day?'

Tozer looked him in the eye. 'Oh, here and there,' she said through a mouthful of crumbs.

'For God's sake,' said Marilyn.

'Oh,' Tozer said, after she'd swallowed her first bite. 'You might want this.' She opened up her handbag and pulled out an open notebook, handing it to Breen. On the page was written in red biro, in her curling, girlish hand: *Morwenna Jane Sullivan. Address, Verden an der Aller, Germany, 13 June 1951.*

Miss Pattison had called.

She had shown the photo of the dead girl to a few select fans. Within a day a girl coming to pick up a competition prize had said she recognised her. She hadn't known her well; she had only met her twice outside EMI. According to Miss Pattison, all she told her was that she thought her name was Morwenna but she was definitely a Gemini, which she remembered because she was a Gemini too.

'Miss Pattison said the police would want to talk to her but the girl said she wasn't interested in that and disappeared.'

'What was the fan's name?'

'You see, she put her name down in the competition entry as Miss P. Lane. Only there's no P. Lanes in the fan club. And then I figured it out. Penny Lane. Get it?'

'Get what?'

'Oh for God's sake, sir, haven't you even heard of "Penny Lane"?'

'Course I have. Just pulling your leg.'

'Very amusing.'

'What about that drink then, Paddy?' said Marilyn. 'Later?'

'Another time maybe. What about Morwenna?'

'I was just going to say. No Penny Lanes, but I searched through every single file and I found eighteen bloody Morwennas. Who'd have thought? I'd never even heard that name. I mean, who calls a girl Morwenna? But only one Gemini. Bingo. Verden an der Aller. You think her family's in Germany?'

Marilyn stood, took her mug back to the counter and left the canteen without saying another word.

'Military, more likely,' said Breen. 'Stationed out there when she was born. What about the girl who recognised her? Do you have an address for her?'

'Went there. Turned out the address was that squat in Hamilton Terrace, you know?' A group of students had taken over a huge empty Regency house in one of the posher roads in St John's Wood a few months earlier; there had been a flurry of complaints at the time but they had died down. Breen was surprised to learn that the students were still there. 'I did knock but I spoke to this guy who said she didn't live there any more. He would, though, wouldn't he?'

Breen nodded.

'I got a photograph of her, mind.' She reached into her handbag and pulled out a small black-and-white photograph. Three girls standing in line, each holding a copy of a single in front of them, smiling shyly into the camera. 'Miss Pattison took it. For the newsletter she sends out. Our Penny Lane's the one on the left.' A girl with long mousy hair, standing in a sheepskin coat, holding the record to her bosom.

'She's OK once you get to know her, Miss Pattison.'

'Right.' Breen looked at the photograph.

'See?'

'See what?'

She frowned. 'You thought I was just a nutter, didn't you?'

'I never said that,' said Breen. 'That wasn't what I was trying to say at all.'

She looked away. 'I'm still bloody starving. Haven't eaten since that bit of cake and I never finished that. Are there any more sandwiches left?'

'You just had one.'

'So?'

'Let me get you one,' said Breen, standing. And then said, 'Tozer?'

'What?'

'That was good, what you did.'

'I know.' She grinned. Then: 'Ask if they've got any pickle, can you?'

The woman at the serving counter glared at him when he made it to the front of the queue with his tray. 'Don't know what you're looking so flipping happy about,' she said to Breen, wiping greasy hands on her nylon apron.

Back at his desk he called the Ministry of Defence; the woman in the records office said she'd do her best. He was making a note of the conversation in his notebook when Marilyn passed close to his desk and whispered, 'Only saying. She's on the pill. It's common knowledge. You know what that means.'

'What?'

'Helen Tozer. She's an S-L-A-G.'

Marilyn raised her eyebrows meaningfully and then turned her back.

THIRTEEN

Breen opened the front door. 'Sorry,' he said. 'The place is a bit of a mess. I've been meaning to give it a clean.'

'You live here on your own?' Tozer had offered to give him a ride home. When she had pulled up outside, he had invited her in for a coffee.

'I moved out when my dad got ill. He needed looking after.'

She nodded. 'Carmichael thinks that's what sent you doolally, your dad dying.' He noticed she was wearing mascara. When had she put that on? When she was in the car, waiting for him to bring his briefcase downstairs from the office? If so, what did it mean when a girl got made-up? Did it mean she was interested in you?

'Doolally, he said?'

'Sort of.'

'I didn't know you knew Carmichael?'

'We go out for a drink with the lads sometimes. How come you never go?'

He picked up a pile of newspapers from the armchair and stuffed them into a bin. 'I haven't had much time. I was looking after my dad.'

He stood there pursing his lips for a second before he said, 'So. Do you want a cup of coffee? It's real.' He bought his coffee beans from a Turkish shop at Dalston Junction and ground them himself.

'Friday night. I was hoping for something stronger. Got anything?'

'Stronger? Sorry, no.'

Standing in the middle of the carpet was a dining chair. Surrounding it were circles of paper, with big words picked out in coloured biro, or pencil drawings. There were dozens of them. Some were names of people: Miss Shankley. Samuel Ezeoke. Some were words: 'Locks'. 'Lighter Fuel'. 'Kynaston Tech'. He'd done another drawing of the dead girl's body from memory in blue biro.

She picked up one of the pieces of paper. It was a map he'd been drawing of Cora Mansions. 'What's all this?'

'Don't move it,' he said, too loudly. 'I'm still working on it.' He yanked it away from her and replaced it on the carpet.

'Sorry,' she said. 'I was curious, that's all.'

She found the biro drawing of the naked girl. Her behind pointing upwards. The plump curves looked suddenly prurient.

'I am just trying to think things through.'

'With all this?'

'It's about trying to see the connections.'

'It's very good,' she said. 'I didn't know you were an artist.'

'I was going to go to art school, only my dad didn't think much of that. So I joined the police instead, only he didn't think much of that either.'

'So.' She pointed to the map. 'You still think whoever did it is from round there? Even after Mr Rider?'

'Yes,' he said, placing his foot over the writing on one of the sheets of paper and hoping she hadn't spotted it.

Without asking, she sat in the chair and gazed around her. There must have been a hundred different pieces of paper around the room, some in pencil, some in blue biro, others in green or red. He realised how mad it must look. What had he been thinking, inviting her in?

'Why don't we go out for a drink instead?' he said. 'Just leave that stuff and we could go out?'

'Super idea. I could do with a drink after today.'

'Pubs round here are pretty rough.'

'I'll feel right at home then,' she said, standing up.

When her back was to him, he reached down and picked up the sheet of paper on which he'd written her sister's name, crunching it up into a ball and slipping it into his pocket.

★

Walking down Stoke Newington High Street, she said, 'You asked me if I'd ever seen a dead body.'

'Yes.'

'You think I lied to you about that?'

'Did you?'

'I never lied. They never let me see my sister, after they found her. They said it would upset me.'

'I'm sorry,' said Breen.

''S OK. I don't mind.'

A car drove past at speed. There was a puddle by the gutter; Breen grabbed Tozer's arm and pulled her back from the edge of the pavement just before the wheel hit the water, splashing it in an arc onto the slabs where she would have been walking.

'Thank you,' she said. 'You can let go now.'

He released her arm.

They had stopped outside a small shop selling doll parts. A hundred different eyes peered out from a green baize board, some large, some small, some blue, some grey. There were plump porcelain arms and odd, pot-bellied body shapes to attach them to. A row of pouting, empty-eyed heads sat along the top of a small shelf. 'She just didn't come home from school one day and that was that.'

Breen nodded. They opened the door into the lounge bar of the Red Lion, on the bend of the street. A few codgers stared at Tozer and shifted on their bar stools. Conversation faltered. Women rarely came in this pub, even in the lounge bar. The room was dark, a fug of smoke drifting at eye level. The sound of the click of snooker balls came from the public bar behind the frosted glass.

He returned with a double rum and black for her and a pint for himself. Though the other customers had started talking again, they still craned their necks to peer at them.

'Do you like London, sir?' she asked, head cocked on one side.

'Don't call me sir,' he said. 'I mean,' he added. 'We're not at the station now.'

'OK. Do you like London . . .' She smiled and paused. 'I don't like "Cathal". Mind if I call you Paddy?'

135

'You wouldn't be the first. Nobody ever called me Cathal except my dad.' His mother had given him the name, his father said; his father had worried that it would make him stand out.

'It's a funny name.'

'My father didn't think so.'

'Sorry. I didn't mean to offend you.'

He took out a cigarette and offered her one. 'Doesn't matter.' He felt foolish now, bristling over a name he'd hated all through growing up. She took one of his cigarettes and he lit them both.

'Well, Cathal?' she asked. 'Do you like London?'

'I've never lived anywhere else. What about you? Do you miss the countryside?'

She smiled. 'You should try it.'

He shook his head. 'Wouldn't know what to do there,' he said.

'No. I don't think you would.' She picked up her rum and black and the beer mat was stuck to the bottom of it: *A Double Diamond Works Wonders*. She peeled it off, put it back onto the table and took a large gulp from her glass. 'Cheers,' she said.

'Cheers.'

She took another sip from hers, then said, 'Right then. I'll tell you all about it all. But I don't want you telling anyone else, OK? You tell Bailey and he'll take me right off, and you know it. Only thing his lot think us women police are good for is putting parking tickets on cars.'

Breen looked at her. She looked good with a bit of make-up on. 'If I think anyone has a problem that might affect the investigation, I'm supposed to let him know.'

She looked down at her drink and said quietly, 'You're the one who went doolally, not me.'

Breen smiled. 'Bailey knows about that.'

She looked up at him. 'Does he know about you chucking up when you saw the body?'

He took a sip of his beer. 'OK.'

'Promise you won't say?'

'Promise.' He wondered if he was making a mistake.

She paused, took a third gulp. 'Where should I start?'

'Anywhere.'

She fiddled with the winder of her watch for a couple of seconds then spoke again. 'It was the same as how it always starts. Alex didn't come home one night.' She paused and twisted the winder some more. 'Dad was furious the first night. He was convinced she had run off with one of the boys from the Tech.'

'How old was she?'

'Sixteen. The boys were always sniffing around her. She was gorgeous, Alexandra was, in an aloof kind of way. Always boys around her. Had Mum's looks. I take after Dad.' She smiled. 'And she loved it all, of course, all the attention, though she never showed it. I was older, and I would have jumped for any of them, but she was always offhand. Which they all loved, of course. I could never be that casual around boys. One time two boys asked her out, to go to the local barn dance. She said yes to them both. She didn't care that they were furious with her. And fair play, she danced with them both. And told both of them to buy me drinks and all. Just to show she had the power and I had not. Sorry. I'm going off, aren't I?'

'It doesn't matter. It's all part of it.'

'I like to talk about her. I never can when I'm at home. Nobody mentions her no more.'

'You really have barn dances?'

'God, yes. All the time. Accordion players and set dances and the lot. Do you dance?'

'Not really.'

'What about Irish dancing?'

'Not on your life. How old were you when this happened?'

'Eighteen years and six days when she disappeared. I was studying agriculture at the local tech. It was just after my birthday. I was going to be a farm girl. Can you imagine that?'

He shook his head.

'Poor Dad had wanted a son to take over the place. He ended up with me and Alex. After that Mum couldn't have any more. I was the elder so I was going to do what he wanted. She was the beautiful one who always had it easy. It's like that with the second child, isn't it? The first one has to figure everything out for themselves. The second one dances along afterwards. Not that I minded, really. Not much, anyway. She was the beautiful one.'

She pulled out a cigarette from her handbag and offered one to Breen. Breen shook his head.

'It was a Tuesday. Dad drove round Newton Abbot going into all the scrumpy bars, of which there are a few, let me tell you, pulling out the boys and accusing them of running off with his daughter. You should meet my dad. He's sort of big. Ever drunk scrumpy?'

Breen shook his head again.

'I wouldn't. It's piss.' She finished the glass. 'Mind if I give you the money to get another?' she said.

He shook his head. 'I'll get it.'

'Can you see if they got any crisps?' she called.

The middle-aged, bleach-haired barmaid was at the off-sales counter, handing over lemonade and a packet of cigarettes to a scabby-headed boy. 'They for your dad?' she said, handing him the cigarettes.

'Who do you think they're for?'

'They better chuffing be,' said the barmaid. 'I'll give you a slap if I see you smoking them.'

She returned to the main bar and served Breen. 'Three and six. You're from round here, in't you?'

'Yes.'

'Copper, in't you?'

'Yes.'

'Thought so. I know all the coppers round here.'

'What? All of them?' Tozer called out. 'You must be a bit of a live wire then.'

A few of the customers laughed. 'She bloody is, an' all.'

'Oi, shut up or you're banned, the lot of you,' said the barmaid with a grin. 'You live by the station, don't you?'

'That's right.'

'Thought so. My sister used to look after your dad.'

He tried to remember the name of the pale girl who used to clean for him back when he worked at the local station, but he couldn't. 'How is she?'

'She's marrying an accountant.'

'I'm sorry to hear that,' he said.

'Sorry to hear about your dad too. My sister liked him. She said your dad used to recite poetry to her.'

Where other memories had vanished, his father had been left with odd chunks of the poems he must have learned as a child. Unexpected, haunting lines that occasionally fell from his mouth like reproaches: 'The Light of Lights looks always on the motive, not the deed, the Shadow of Shadows on the deed alone.'

'He's in a better place now,' said the barmaid, and turned to pull another pint with arms that looked used to heavy work.

When Breen came back with the drink and the crisps, Tozer opened the packet, dug around for the blue twist of salt and poured it over them. She munched a few in silence.

'Your father sounds like he could be a scary fellow, then,' said Breen.

'Oh, my dad ain't really scary. He's a lamb. It's just he is tall and he does carry a shotgun round with him, but that's only to knock the crows off the hurdles.' She closed her eyes as if seeing something more clearly in her mind. 'He used to be a very careful man. We had the best-kept cows in South Devon. He was always winning prizes at the County Show. We got a whole wall full of rosettes. Best Guernsey Cow in Milk. Best Guernsey Group of Three. You know? Champion Local Dairy Animal. Now he just goes through the motions. It's not the same.'

She fell silent. The smoke fug thickened around them. The hubbub of the pub had reasserted itself now. Tozer's joke about the barmaid had broken the ice. Breen's beer had left a ring of wetness on the dark wood table. He put his finger in the spilt liquid and drew lines out from the circle so that it looked like an infant's drawing of the sun, rays spreading outwards.

'They found her on the second day, in the woods just a couple of hundred yards from our house.'

He thought of the girl under the mattress. The drizzle trickling down her cold body.

'I was at school when they found her. I remember Mrs Wilton, our headmistress, coming to get me out of maths class. Her face was as pale as a nun's arse and I remember she had a biro mark right next to her mouth from chewing a pen or something, and I couldn't stop staring at it all the time she talked. I knew even before she opened her mouth, though, that they must have found her, just by looking at her. Alex had been raped and knifed. There were bruises all over her. That's why they didn't want me to see her. He had piled sticks and leaves on top of her and just left her. They say the foxes had been at her.'

She said all this in a matter-of-fact voice, but took another large gulp from her rum and black at the end of it. Breen thought: her sister must have struggled a long time with injuries like that.

They sat in silence together for a while.

'Was that why you joined the police, then?'

'What? To find who killed my sister? Not at the beginning.'

A bearded tramp stuck his head round the door. The barmaid shouted a single word: 'Out.' The head disappeared again.

'I fell in love.'

Breen watched her twisting a stud round in her earlobe. A small gold dot on pink skin.

'Not really love at all, actually. Stupid. This copper fancied me. He was a detective sergeant, as it happens. He was on the case.'

'Oh.'

'That summer, the house was full of policemen. They were always round the place. We thought they were going to find Alex's killer.

140

We loved them, me and Mum and Dad. We couldn't do enough for them. Our house was like their bloody country club. We were the best bloody thing that happened to them.'

The pub was quiet. People talked in low voices to each other. There was only the noise of traffic passing in the High Street, and the occasional click of balls from the table next door.

'We used to serve them tea and toast with cream on it. I could swear they were all a stone heavier by the end of the winter. I loved it. All the talk of evidence and stuff. My dad says I've always been a bit of a tomboy. I liked the company.'

In the public bar, someone broke a glass. The sound of ironic cheering followed.

'I wouldn't say he was good looking, even, but he was important. And he fancied me. And I'm eighteen. And if a man like that says he loves you, you're supposed to like them back. Do you want more crisps?'

When Breen returned from the bar with two more packets, she said, 'I found I liked the police, though. Being around with them. Everything that had happened to my family was wrong and they were there to put it right. So I started saying I wanted to join too.'

'What did your father say?'

'He was OK about it. He's pretty much given up on the farm these days, since Alex was killed. She was found on our land, see? In the spinney down by the railway track. She'd been there those two days. I think that's what spoiled it for him.' She looked down.

'And the boyfriend? Was he keen on you joining the police?'

'I thought he was, at the beginning. Then, first time I came back from training in Bristol with my uniform and all, he met me at the station and asked me to marry him. He expected me to chuck it all in and go to live with him in a police house in Torquay. And have lots of little police babies. I think he thought it was just a phase.'

'And?'

'And I was only, what, nineteen? Me and all the police wives waiting for the boys to come home drunk on a Friday night? He never took it seriously, me wanting to join the police. So I chucked him.'

'How did he take it?'

She put a handful of crisps in her mouth and chewed on them thoughtfully. 'Not great. He'd bought a ring and everything.'

'What about the investigation?'

She pursed her lips. 'One time they thought they'd found the boy who did it. It's strange. You can focus all your hatred on someone real. You think that makes it easier, but actually it just makes things even more complicated. Turned out to be soft in the head. If you'd asked him if he'd killed John F. Kennedy he'd have said yes. They let him go after a week. After that, nothing.'

'Oi, copper,' said a voice. A middle-aged man with a mournful face was looking over at them from the bar. 'You going to be in here long? Only, Val here –' he nodded at the barmaid – 'says we got to be on our best behaviour till you're gone.'

There was a laugh. 'Take as long as you like,' said the barmaid. 'It makes a change.'

'Charming.'

Tozer fished out her purse for the money to buy another drink. Breen shook his head and took a ten-shilling note from his pocket. He returned with the third round and asked, 'Did you have any thoughts about who killed your sister?'

'You deal with people like me all the time. You must know what goes through our heads.'

'Yes. I do.'

'Never being sure why someone was killed. It's nothing that ever adds up. We start to look at everyone we see. Everyone we know. You look at the guy who drives the milk tanker up to the farm. The boys who ride motorbikes up on the farm tracks. The old guys with the fishing rods who go down to the estuary.'

The bell rang for last orders. 'We should head back,' Breen said quietly.

'Even my dad, you know? That thought enters your head, eventually. You start to doubt everything.'

The old guys shuffled to the bar for their last pint.

'You got any food in your place?' said Tozer. 'I'm starving.'

Breen thought: a can of tinned tomatoes, a loaf that was probably stale, a tin of herrings, a piece of elderly cheese and a couple of onions.

Joe's All Night Bagel Shop was busy, full of people who'd dropped in after work, but Tozer was the only woman in the place. A couple of Chinese men sat at one table playing cards. A gaggle of Pakistanis were bickering loudly as they drank tea in the corner together.

'Oi, keep it down,' shouted Joe as he brought Tozer's fry-up.

'It's like the bloody United Nations in here,' said Tozer, looking around her wonderingly.

'Isn't it?' said Joe. 'Nobody agrees with anyone else here.' He turned and shouted again at the Pakistanis, then asked Breen, 'What's wrong with your arm? Someone have a go at you?'

Tozer tucked into her food. Sausages, beans, double egg, fried onions, mashed potatoes. Breen watched her eat, amazed.

'What if the person who did it was a lover?' asked Tozer, wiping her mouth with the back of her hand. Breen wondered for a second whether she was talking about their case or that of her murdered sister, until she added, 'That's why no one came forward to say she's gone. Because he's not reporting it.'

He nodded. 'That's what gets me too. And why the parents didn't come forward.'

'How long is it going to take to track them down?'

'Not long. We should know something on Monday.'

They sat in silence a while. He watched her work her way through the plate, and as she did so, the cafe quietened, other customers leaving for their homes or for their night shifts. When the last of the baked beans was hoovered away, she sat back in her chair.

'You've got to be patient,' he said. 'Something will crack.'

'Will it?' she said, looking at him darkly. 'It hasn't for four years with my sister. I don't think it ever will.'

'Sorry. I meant in our case.'

'I know,' she said.

Joe's daughter was working tonight. She was standing behind the counter doing dishes with her growing belly pushed against the sink; it looked like the baby would be due very soon. Joe left her to it, lifting the counter with a broom in his hand and walking into the restaurant area. He swept the floor carefully with long strokes, avoiding Breen and Tozer's table, pausing occasionally to lift chairs out of the way.

In the kitchen, Joe's daughter had the radio on. After the weather forecast that said it would rain, the news was all about the Mexico Olympics, where two black American athletes had raised their fists in Black Power salutes at the medal ceremony. *It's a vulgar political display. Of course they should be suspended immediately and sent home,'* a commentator was complaining.

'Oh, shut your idiotic hole,' said Joe angrily, switching off the radio.

'I really thought it was him, you know,' said Tozer. 'Rider. Even though I half knew the dress wasn't hers. I just wanted to think it was him. Poor old git. Do you think he's OK?'

Breen said, 'You have to get used to it. You never see the whole picture. Just parts of it. You have to make up the rest. You have to make assumptions. And mostly you're wrong. But if you don't start filling in the parts that aren't there, you'll never get it right. You have no choice.'

'That's what all the bits of paper are, aren't they?'

'In a way. I sit there sometimes and I'm trying to figure out which order they should be in. Whether they're connected. That's all. They help me think.'

'You do that for every case, then?'

'No,' he said. 'I just started doing it. I never really had the space before, I suppose, when my dad was alive.'

144

The cafe was quiet now, except for the sound of Joe's daughter stacking dishes in the kitchen. Joe came back into the restaurant, pulled up a chair next to Breen and started to roll a cigarette.

'You look tired, Joe,' said Breen.

'Hope I don't look as bad as you,' said Joe, licking the cigarette paper. He nodded at Tozer. 'Who is your friend?'

'This is Constable Tozer,' said Breen. 'We're working on a case together.'

'Oh yeah?' said Joe, pulling a packet of Swan Vestas from his jacket pocket.

'We're just working together, like he said.'

'That's good.' He put the roll-up, so thin there could barely have been a strand of tobacco running through it, into his mouth and struck a match and sucked. He exhaled smoke through his nose, then said to Tozer, 'And all this time I just thought Mr Breen here was kidding when he said he worked for the police.'

'Well,' said Tozer, 'there are some I've met who aren't that sure of whether he works for them or against them.'

Joe smiled at her. 'I can understand that.'

'Got another coffee, Joe?'

'In a minute,' he said, giving his cigarette another tug.

They walked back to the car together.

'So you've given up on detective constables then?'

'Mostly,' she said.

A milk float whined along the road, bottles chinking in their crates as it ran over cobbles. They walked back up towards Breen's flat, not saying much.

'You can stay at mine,' said Breen.

She stiffened. 'I'm not like that. Whatever they're saying.'

'No. I didn't mean that. If you don't think you're OK to drive.'

'I'm fine.'

'I've got a spare room, that's all,' he said. 'If you want.' Though that was not what he had meant at all and he was sure she knew it. Whether it had been the beer or not, several times that evening he had imagined her naked, her scrawny arms around him. It would feel good to wake up with a woman. It felt like it had been a long time.

'I'll see you Monday, sir.'

'Right.' He paused. 'Goodnight then.'

'Night.'

She turned to go.

'Tozer?'

She stopped. 'I'm going home, sir.'

'No. I wasn't . . . I just wanted to say again. Good work.'

She looked at him and smiled. 'Yep,' she said, and carried on walking.'

That night, as he lay in bed, Breen was conscious that life since his father had died seemed to have become a series of unconnected episodes. It shook his sense of the simple causality that his job rested on: that every crime required a criminal. Tozer's sister had been killed. No one had been found. What if dead bodies just appeared on heaps of rubbish down side streets, without cause?

He wished he had not tried it on with Tozer. She had rejected him. He was looking for patterns, covering walls and floors with pieces of paper, but if he could not understand how to make the most basic human connection of all, how could he be expected to make sense of other people's lives?

Saturday morning was always hectic. Laundry and groceries.

The only men who went to launderettes were single, bachelors and widowers. They ignored each other and got on with the job, left as soon as they could. Every Saturday Breen took his bag of washing into the launderette next to Fine Fare. This morning he had to wait for over an hour for a machine to come free. Joe's daughter waddled in with a plastic basket full of sheets. She fussed about him, helping him load the washing into the machine even though she looked huge with the baby.

'When's it due?'

'Two weeks.'

'Joe must be excited,' Breen said. 'He'll be a grandfather.'

'You know my dad. He'd die before he let anyone know he was happy.'

'But he is, though, I know.'

She smiled at him. Joe's family had disappeared in the concentration camps. He didn't feel he had the right to be happy, she had once told Breen.

'He'll miss you when you have the baby.'

'I won't miss it. I'm sick of the place,' she said. 'I wish he'd give it up.'

When his machine was finally turning, she sat down heavily on the wooden bench next to him and took out a paper bag of liquorice allsorts, offering him one.

'That woman you came in with last night,' she said.

'Yes?'

'It was good to see you with a girl.'

'She's just a colleague,' said Breen.

She smiled and picked through the bag to choose a pink one.

'I've never seen you with a girl before, Paddy,' she said, chewing her sweet. 'That's all I'm saying.'

'I've had girlfriends,' he said. 'Plenty. There was this girl worked in Hammersmith Library. But she wanted to go out all the time and I couldn't after my dad moved in.'

He offered her a cigarette. She took one and put it behind her ear. 'I'll have it when I finish my sweet,' she said. He lit his and kept the matches out to light hers with when she was ready.

'What about all those girls who used to come in and look after your dad for you?'

'You can't exactly ask a girl who you pay to wipe your dad's arse out for a date, can you?'

'I bet you'd like a girlfriend though.'

'I thought you were spoken for,' said Breen.

She laughed. 'I'm serious.' When she finished her sweet, she took the cigarette from behind her ear and he struck a match for her.

'I like it on my own,' said Breen. 'I'm used to it.'

She inhaled and held the smoke in for a second, one hand on her large belly. After she blew it back out, she said, 'That's what my dad says. He's rubbish at lying too.'

A red light on her machine came on, and she stood up to add more powder from the cup.

'Let me have your shirts to iron,' she said. 'You'll never manage that on your own with your bad arm.'

'I'll be fine,' he said. 'You've got enough to be doing.'

'Suit yourself.'

That afternoon he played some of his father's 78s on the radiogram. When his clothes were safely in the dryer he had gone to the school shop up the road and bought a new pack of pencils and a sketch pad. He opened it now, put the small photograph of his mother in front of him and started trying to sketch her. As the pencil moved over the paper, he sat in his father's old chair listening to John McCormack sing 'Kathleen Mavourneen', his rich, vibrant, ridiculous tenor singing, 'Then why art thou silent, thou voice of my heart?' He knew every absurd phrase and swoop. His father had played them occasionally. It was the closest he'd ever got to indulging himself in emotion.

And the long hiss afterwards as the needle spun around in the groove.

He was out of cigarettes.

FOURTEEN

Monday morning, Jones came in a little after a quarter to nine with a black eye, skin around it yellow and purple. 'Bloody hell,' said Prosser.

He smiled sheepishly. 'I walked into a door.'

'That's a terrible thing to call your missus,' said Carmichael, looking back down at his paper.

Breen's phone rang.

'I walked into a door.'

'Whatever you say.'

'Hello?'

'I walked into an effing door, right?' Jones carefully hung his jacket on a wire coat hanger, then put the hanger on the hatstand.

Breen tried to hear the voice on the other end of the line. It was the woman from the Ministry of Defence.

'Keep your ginger hair on. You walked into a door.'

'Thank you.'

Breen cupped his hand over the receiver. 'Quiet,' he shouted.

The voices stopped for a few seconds at least. Breen picked up a pencil and said, 'Fire away.'

Jones sat down at his desk and carefully placed a sheet of carbon paper between two forms.

'A door with a skirt on.'

'Will you just shut up!' Jones shouted, red-faced.

Breen wrote down: 'Major Sullivan. Seventh Armoured Signal Regiment.'

'Where's he stationed?'

'He's retired,' said the woman on the other end of the line. 'He retired right after that posting in Germany, as a matter of fact. I've got an address, though, if you want it.'

Bailey stuck his head round the door. 'What are you lot all doing sat on your behinds?' he said.

When he'd gone, Carmichael pulled a face and repeated Bailey's words in his Kenneth Williams voice. Nobody laughed. It was one of those mornings.

Breen looked at the address he'd written down.

'Cornwall?' said Jones. 'Can't you just phone them?'

'It's been a week. I want to know why they haven't reported their daughter missing. I think we should talk to them, face-to-face.'

'Can't you let the wurzels in Devon and Cornwall do it for you?'

'I think we should go,' he said.

Jones scratched the side of his face thoughtfully. 'It wouldn't take two of us, though, would it?'

Breen was relieved. 'It's OK.'

'Cornwall?' said Tozer. 'That's where she came from?'

There was no mention of their brittle parting on Friday night. It was as if it had not happened. 'Liskeard. Is that far from where you live?' he asked.

'Not that near. 'Bout an hour and a half away.'

'If I can clear it with Bailey for you to come, will you drive me there?'

'You serious?' she said.

The next morning she examined a Ford Zephyr that he had booked out for the journey. It had seen better days. 'I've driven combines that go faster,' she said.

It was early but they wanted to get out of London before the morning traffic was too bad. Tozer swore constantly as she crunched through the gears as they drove out along to the Great West Road.

New cars parked outside new factories and offices. Union Jacks flip-flapping lazily. Neat lawns in front of the offices. They hit traffic at Gillette Corner and crawled for almost an hour towards the new section of the M4. Near London Airport they were stationary again as the planes flew overhead.

'What's that one?'

'It's a Britannia,' said Breen.

'And that one?'

'It's a Comet.'

'What about that?'

'It's a Britannia too. No, sorry, a Constellation.'

'I never met a man who didn't know the names of planes. You been in a plane?' asked Tozer.

'No.'

'But you know what their names are.'

'Not all of them.'

'I think that's fab.'

'That's a Comet. BOAC.'

'We went on holiday to Sardinia. The Pineta Beach Hotel. I don't know what plane it was, though. It was the summer after Alex was killed. Mum wanted to do something to cheer us all up so we went on a package. Dead modern. Dad got food poisoning and Mum got heatstroke on the miniature golf course. Don't laugh. It's true. I swear it. I spent my time on my own by the pool being chatted up by Eyeties.'

A gang of seven or eight greasers roared past the stationary traffic, weaving between cars, hair sweeping backward in the wind.

'I didn't mind, actually. One of them was all right. He was very strong and brown. He got me drunk one night on the beach and tried to feel my bosoms. And worse. I may have been drunk but I gave him such a slap . . .'

The traffic was moving again. 'Was this before or after you started going out with the detective sergeant?'

'During. I wrote postcards home to my policeman every day. I think I used up every card they had in the hotel.'

Slowly at first, but gradually speeding up, the cars and lorries around them began to hurtle westwards.

'I got drunk a lot that holiday. All three of us did. That's all we did, really. Dad almost drowned in the pool one day he was so drunk. He's not used to it. Doesn't drink much normally. A bottle of Bass with Sunday dinner.'

Tozer weaved from the left lane to the right again, working her way through the speeding traffic. The motorway verge blurred. As she indicated to pull out to overtake a gravel lorry in front, Breen said, 'Do you always drive like this?'

'I'm only going sixty.' She moved lanes again, accelerating past the lorry and moving back into the left lane ahead of it. Breen's good hand dug into the leather of the seat. He tried to look at the speedometer but her hands were in the way.

'When the holiday ended we were relieved, I think. We all felt uncomfortable pretending that everything was OK. Back to mud and cowpats, getting up at five in the morning for the milking. We felt guilty for trying to have fun. My mum said, "I don't think we'll be going again."' She laughed. 'That's the Tozer family motto. "I don't think we'll be doing that again." Is there anything wrong with my driving?'

'Nothing.'

'You seem to be really tense.'

He looked at her. 'I'm fine.' The motorway ended at Maidenhead and they carried on along the A4. On the slower roads, he relaxed a little.

While she was filling up the car at a service station in Reading, Breen went to the gents to splash water on his face. There was no towel to dry himself on, so he pressed his skin against the sleeve of his grey jacket.

'Were you close to your dad?' she asked, when they were driving again.

He peered at a map. 'I think it should be signposted for the A33 at the next roundabout.'

'And?'

'And what?'

'Your dad? Were you close?'

'He was not an easy man to be close with. But I was, yes.' If she'd asked that when he was alive he would have answered differently. Now he was gone he realised how close he had been.

In Dorset, they stopped at a village shop and bought fresh rolls and a quarter-pound of cheddar which they shared sitting in a car park, washing it down with swigs of lemonade.

'The boys at the station say you've changed.'

'Do they?'

'Jones says you and Carmichael used to be best mates.'

'We are best mates. Still.'

'He said you and Carmichael once got mad with Bailey and put a bit of bicycle inner tube over the exhaust pipe of his car.'

'That was Carmichael, mostly.'

She laughed. 'Why?'

'You know, police practical jokes.'

'Did it work?'

'It was like his car farted all down the street.'

'Fab!' She laughed.

She lifted the bottle of lemonade and took a swig from it, then held it out to him. He looked at her backwash of breadcrumbs floating in the clear liquid and said, 'You finish it.'

'You sure?' she said. 'Thanks.'

By two in the afternoon they were at Honiton, where an overturned horsebox had blocked the road, and they sat in traffic for twenty minutes before turning off down a small lane. Breen tried to follow the small yellow lines on the map but he was soon lost.

'This road isn't even on the map,' he said. The lanes were deep and dark, cut into the hilly landscape, huge hedges rising on either side so he couldn't see the lie of the land. They became like tunnels, burrowing underground, roofed by branches of oak and hawthorn. After what seemed like hours of driving around they found a signpost to Exeter and followed it back to the main road.

It was past four by the time they reached Exeter. 'What shall we do? It'll be another hour at least before we get to Liskeard,' said Tozer.

Breen felt exhausted from the long journey and his stomach rumbled with hunger, but he said, 'Let's go on. We'll find a motel somewhere afterwards.'

'I told you already, I'm not that kind of girl, sir.'

'What?'

'You said let's go and find a room and I said I'm not that kind of girl.'

'No. I didn't mean that.'

'I know. That was a joke. Sir.'

'Right.' He nodded. She was teasing him, at least.

The countryside turned wilder after Exeter. They crawled up onto the moor in the grey evening light. Tozer drove determinedly, peering over the steering wheel into the darkening landscape. She seemed to know her way around these roads, navigating confidently over the narrow bridges and ever-curving bends, slowing to avoid the occasional sheep. Now the hills were covered in dark brown bracken, turning black in the evening light, and stunted trees, silhouettes, bent into the shape of the wind. Grey stone walls climbed high up steep slopes around them.

It had been dark for over an hour by the time they reached Liskeard. It was a market town, the buildings low and small. There was a hard, worn look about the place. Tozer stopped by a large corner pub, where two old boys in threadbare tweed jackets and woollen caps stood by an alleyway.

Tozer got out. 'Can you tell me where Fonthill House is?'

'Fonthill House?'

One took off his cap and scratched at his scalp. 'That up Shute Hill?'

'Mebbe,' said the other.

'It's a Major and Mrs Sullivan,' said Breen from the open car window.

Another man emerged from the gloom. 'Here, these two want to find a place called Fonthill House. A Major and Mrs . . .'

'Sullivan,' said Breen.

'Aye, I know them,' said the third man. 'He's that one on the Bodmin Road. Blow-ins. I did some grass mowing for him Michaelmas gone. Wouldn't make that mistake again.'

'Why not?'

'Skinflint said I'd not done it proper.'

'Never.'

'Cheeky bugger.'

'Where's that?' said Tozer. For the first time Tozer's accent sounded almost cosmopolitan.

The gents all offered various directions up the lanes, pointing out of town.

FIFTEEN

It was a huge grey-rendered Victorian house, a squat toad of a building that lurked behind a high granite wall. They drove in through the rusted gate down a narrow driveway choked with leggy rhododendron and laurels.

In the headlights, the garden wore a tired look. Leaves piled where the breeze had taken them. Grand cedars and Corsican pines had struggled against the wind for a century. In front of the house, in the centre of a circular driveway, stood a large iron fountain. The pond around it was thick with overgrowth.

Gabled windows looked out from a slated roof. Attached to one chimney, a long scaffolding pole, on which a television aerial waved gently in the wind. On the ground floor, huge sash windows looked out over lawns that dipped away from the house. A soaked wicker chair sat alone, facing away from the house, looking out across the valley behind.

They pulled up alongside a brand-new maroon Jaguar, tyres crunching on gravel. Next to the new car, the house looked ramshackle and unkempt. It felt absurd to be here, to be a detective announcing a death at a country house. It was something out of a slim paperback. There was a single light on the ground floor. Breen thought he saw a shape peering out at them as they parked. Almost as soon as he tugged on the wire pull of the bell at the wooden porch, another light came on in the hallway and the large front door opened.

The woman was in her early forties, fair-haired, slim and beautiful. She was dressed in slacks, a black polo neck and a wide-lapelled flowery jacket that looked like it must have been bought at Biba or some other trendy London boutique. There was a large bronze bangle on her left wrist. 'Yes?' she said, frowning.

'My name is Detective Sergeant Breen. This is Constable Tozer.'

'And?'

'Are you Mrs Julia Sullivan? Married to Major Mallory Sullivan?'

'Why?'

An elderly golden retriever limped to the door, barked once hoarsely, then seemed to lose interest, wandering away.

'Could we come in? We have something important we wish to discuss.' He knew how pompous he must be sounding. But it was easier to begin that way.

'Mal?' she called. 'We have visitors.' There was wine on her breath.

A man appeared in a doorway, frowning. 'What kind of time is this?'

Breen saw the likeness immediately. The dead girl's round face, her thick eyebrows, her solidity. She had none of her mother's lean beauty.

'Behave, Mal,' she said, quietly.

'Well?'

'It's about your daughter.'

'Yes? What's she done now?' said the major. Breen could now imagine the girl's dead face as something not dead. Her face was his face. His angry scowl could have been hers.

'Mal, for God's sake,' said Mrs Sullivan, still quietly.

'Shoplifting or —'

'I'm afraid we think she's dead,' interrupted Breen.

Gravity seemed to swell. The woman said, 'God,' but so quietly Breen could barely hear her.

By her side, the major stood stiffly, a puzzled look on his face.

'I'm afraid she was murdered.'

Major Sullivan reached for his wife's hand but she slapped it away, wrapping her arms around herself. 'Come in,' she said.

They walked into the living room. A room with a fire dying in

157

the grate. She walked straight to the sideboard, took a glass and poured herself a large whisky.

Breen assumed she was going to gulp it down to steady her nerves. Instead she turned and jerked the whole glass into her husband's face. 'Idiot,' she said.

He stood there, stunned, blinking against the pain in his eyes.

'This is all your fault.'

Whisky dripped from his face onto his shirt.

'That's hardly fair,' he said, like a schoolboy complaining about a detention.

'None of it's bloody fair,' she said, and she went to the sideboard and poured herself another glass without asking if anyone else wanted one.

'Tea would be an idea, perhaps,' Tozer said. 'Where is the kitchen? Come and sit down, Mrs Sullivan.'

'Tea?' said the major, still blinking. 'Yes.' And Breen followed him across the hallway, through the dining room and into a kitchen at the back of the house where the washing-up was still stacked in a wooden drainer and where four empty beer bottles stood on the pine table.

He watched the major fill the kettle from a tap with a bit of pink rubber fastened to it to stop it splashing, and place it on the range. 'It's an awful shock, you know,' he said.

'Of course.'

'What did she mean, it's all your fault?'

'I don't really know. She's like this when she's upset, you see.'

The major opened a series of terracotta pots, searching for tea. He was apparently not familiar with the kitchen.

'When did you last hear from your daughter?'

'Months, really, I suppose.'

He had found the one with the tea. Breen watched his hands shaking as he spooned it into a large white teapot.

'Can I ask why you were not in touch with her?'

'Wenna is difficult. We don't see eye to eye on everything. Didn't. God. What happened?' he asked for the first time.

'She was strangled. We don't know who by.'

'Christ.'

'Her body was found a week ago. I'm afraid it's taken us this long to discover her identity.'

'Oh Lord. Julia will be destroyed by this.'

He sloshed milk into four mugs, spilling it on the tray, then poured the tea too early, hands trembling.

'Why were you not in touch?'

'We argued, you see? From the start, she was wild. She didn't like rules much. Didn't like me. No good at school. Played pop music all hours. From when she was a teenager, we'd have a row, then she'd run off. For a couple of days or so at first. First time we found her living in the tree house I'd built for her in the woods. Proper girl scout. Then for longer. You know. Oh, where's the blasted sugar?' Opening doors, a packet of Rich Tea fell out onto the floor. He placed it back into a cupboard that must have had at least ten more packet of biscuits in it.

The major picked up the tray, cups rattling as he walked with it. 'You mind opening the door?' he said. In control, but barely.

The television was showing *Softly, Softly*. Breen stared. Police officer rings doorbell. Fact and fiction merging, overconnecting, in his state of tiredness. Every few seconds the wind rattled the window-panes, and as it did so, the TV picture faded to a fuzz briefly as the aerial swung on its pole, high above them.

The room smelt of old dog, cigarettes and spilt alcohol. A log fire was barely alight in the large fireplace. There was an empty red wine bottle on a Pembrokeshire table. A full ashtray was balanced on the side of the sofa. Empty glasses here and there. An evening of watching television and getting drunk enough to face their bed. Or beds.

'I'm afraid the tea's a bit weak, dear,' said the major. 'Not much good in the kitchen.' His eyes were red from the whisky, and there were still blotches of it on his clothes, but it was as if he was pretending it hadn't happened.

'I don't want bloody tea,' she said miserably.

'Right you are.'

Above the fireplace there was a portrait of Julia Sullivan. In it she was wrapped in a blanket, presumably naked underneath, painted in the lush style of Singer Sargent, making her look saucy and aristocratic. There were shelves of modern novels and poetry. On the other hand, there was a cabinet with three twelve-bore guns and a .303 rifle, and next to that, more orderly, a shelf full of military histories, another about fly fishing. A school photograph; a long line of boys in front of some gabled building. A regimental crest, mounted on wood.

'I am sorry it was so hard to track us down,' said Mrs Sullivan, attempting to light a cigarette. Her shaking hands extinguished the flame each time. Tozer pulled her lighter out of her bag and held it.

'What did you mean just now when you said it was all Major Sullivan's fault?' said Breen.

'Well, I obviously didn't mean literally,' she said. 'That would be ridiculous.'

'What did you mean, then?'

'She couldn't stand him,' she said. 'That's why she always ran away.'

The major sighed heavily and sat down in an armchair next to the retriever, leaning down to rub the dog's belly. The dog growled softly.

'We do have questions, I'm afraid,' said Breen.

'Perhaps you could leave them for tomorrow. It's late,' said the major. 'It has been a shock.'

'May we sit down? Just for a minute.'

Gruffly: 'Yes.'

Breen moved a copy of a society magazine so he could sit in a large armchair and told them the few details he had. A date, a means of death, a murderer who wished to conceal the identity of his victim by leaving her naked, a lack of other clues. A single tear made a track down Mrs Sullivan's cheek. The major sat stolidly, back straight, embarrassed by everything.

'We will need to build up a picture of what she was like. What friends she had as a child.'

'Yes.'

'One main question for now. Do you remember when you last spoke to your daughter?'

'I'd have to check my diary,' said the major.

'July the fourth. American Independence Day,' said Mrs Sullivan. 'The day you drove her back to London.'

'I suppose you're right.'

'She had come from London on a visit. I'd hoped she would stay.' She blew smoke out of her nose, looking at her husband with unconcealed bitterness.

'That'll be it,' said the major. He wrinkled his nose.

'A broken heart. Tears and tantrums,' said her mother. 'You know how it is. Your world is ending.'

'She'd split up with a boyfriend?'

There was a pause. Major Sullivan and his wife exchanged a glance. 'She never told us anything about her love life, of course. She was off her food.'

The major grimaced. 'Love life,' he said.

'She stayed two nights and then twisted Mal's arm to drive her back up to London. I don't enjoy driving.'

'Last time I saw her,' said the major.

'Where did she want to be taken?'

'She wanted Mal to help move her belongings from the room she'd been staying in with her lover.'

'Hovel, more like,' said the major. 'A house full of long hairs and draft dodgers.'

'Mal. Behave.'

'Where did you take her to?'

'Similar kind of spot. Edgware Road. Basement that reeked of mould. She moved out a couple of weeks later. Never told us where.'

'And this boyfriend?'

The two looked at each other again.

'Not really a boyfriend,' said Mrs Sullivan.

'How do you mean?'

'She was determined to be everything I didn't want her to be,' said Major Sullivan.

His wife said quietly, 'Morwenna believed she was a Sapphist. I don't know. I think it may have been a phase . . .'

'She was in love with . . . another girl?'

Mrs Sullivan nodded. 'Not that I cared. Unlike Mal.'

'Do you have any idea who her friend was?'

'She didn't talk to us about it.'

'No idea,' said the major.

'And you haven't spoken since?'

The woman shook her head.

'Any letters?'

Again, she shook her head.

'And you, sir?'

He looked at the floor. 'Not a dickie bird.'

The woman rolled her eyes at her husband's turn of phrase.

'So you had no idea where she was staying in the days before she died?'

'Isn't that what I just said?'

'Mal, for goodness' sake.'

'She was difficult.'

'Mal. She's dead.'

He looked down at the floor.

'Where is she now?'

'Her body is at University College Hospital. We would like you to identify her as soon as you feel up to it.'

Asleep in front of the fire, the old golden retriever twitched his paws, chasing squirrels in a dog dream.

'She had fallen in with a bad lot,' said the major.

'You don't know that,' said Mrs Sullivan. 'You just make that up.'

'Squatters and ne'er-do-wells, I used to say. Thrill seekers.'

'Please, Mal. For pity's sake.'

'She did ring a couple of times after we saw her, to say hello. But she hadn't done that for a long time.'

Breen said, 'She was a fan of The Beatles. We believe she may have spent some time with other fans.'

The major snorted. 'The bloody Beatles.'

'Yes, she was a fan. She loved all sorts of music.'

'If you can call it that.'

'Mal!' she shouted. 'Stop it, stop it, stop it. She's bloody dead, you idiot.'

There was a long silence before he said, 'Sorry. Yes.'

'You are such a bloody fool.'

The major sat, wounded and inept.

'And we did try to find her, didn't we, Mal?'

'Yes. We did.'

'Mal had some business in London. I suggested he look for her.'

'When was this?'

'Three weeks ago, maybe.'

'Why didn't you go?'

'Mal didn't want me to.'

'It was work. I had an important meeting. She would have been deathly bored.'

Breen said, 'Can I ask where were you on October the thirteenth?'

'Me?'

'Yes, sir.'

'Was that the day she . . . ?'

'Yes.'

'Sunday the thirteenth of October,' said Breen again.

'For God's sake. I was here. Wasn't I? I'm hopeless on days of the week.'

'He was here,' said his wife. 'It was the bloody parish council meeting, remember?'

163

'That's right. Parish council meeting. State of the village-hall roof. Vandalism of the bus stop. That kind of thing.'

'Mallory has been playing the country squire since we moved into this ridiculous pile.'

'And, Major Sullivan, you went to London . . . ?'

'That would have been the week before.'

'You went up Thursday and came back Friday.'

'When you went to London, where did you look?'

'I went back to that place on Westbourne Grove. And then the place on the Edgware Road.'

'Did you talk to people there?'

'Of course. But no one knew where she was. At least, they wouldn't tell someone like me. I'm the establishment. They were all on pot or something awful.'

'Can we have that address?'

'Can we do this in the morning? It's late. We've had a terrible shock.'

'She was an idealist,' said her mother, rubbing her mouth. 'Concerned about Vietnam and all sorts of things like that.'

'All that left-wing mush.'

'You see, I was wondering whether she might have been arrested on a demonstration or something. I thought it might be a way of finding her. So Mal went to the police, too, while he was up there and reported her as a missing person.'

'Really?' Tozer looked at Breen.

'That's right.'

A motorbike roared up the lane outside the house. Breen noticed that the gaps in the old sash windows had been stuffed with newspaper to keep them from rattling in the wind.

'You see,' said Breen, 'we had no record of her as a missing person.'

'You didn't?'

There was a pause. 'I don't suppose police records are always up to date,' said the major.

'If you'd reported her in early October . . . You definitely reported her missing?'

'Well, not exactly,' said the major.

They all looked at the major. 'Mal?'

'You see, I was going to go and report her missing, but then it seemed a bit silly. Because she'd been out of touch before.'

'Oh, Mal.'

'And she always did get back in touch. Eventually. I didn't want to bother the police. I thought she was bound to turn up, sooner or later.'

'You lied to me. You said you'd gone.'

'I didn't want you to worry. I thought I'd be able to find her myself. Or she'd just turn up out of the blue.'

'You're sodding unbelievable.'

'She was always running off, wasn't she, Julia?'

'I hate you. You bloody liar.'

He looked at Breen sorrowfully, giving a small shrug as if to say, 'See what I have to put up with?'

'And you had no other leads to go on,' said Breen, 'apart from this address you dropped her off at?'

Julia, still glaring at her husband, shook her head.

'No names of her girlfriends?'

'Please,' said the major, 'we're exhausted.' He stood and poured himself a whisky.

'Don't get sloshed, Mal.'

'The pot is calling the kettle black, dear.'

Julia Sullivan snorted. 'I knew I shouldn't have let you go alone.'

'It wouldn't have made any bloody difference anyway, would it?'

Tozer said, 'May I use your telephone, Major?'

'It's in the hallway.'

'Any brothers or sisters?'

Julia Sullivan gulped air.

'That's enough. I'm going to have to ask you to leave now,' said the major.

165

Julia Sullivan stood, followed her husband to the whisky bottle and poured herself another two fingers.

Breen stood. 'We'll need to make arrangements for you to identify her.'

'Oh God.'

'Out. Now.'

She dropped back down onto the sofa and sat, legs tucked under her, glass in her lap, staring down at it, saying nothing. A half-completed crossword on the table. A copy of the *Radio Times*. A big damp house with a couple and their dog.

The major strode to the living-room door and opened it. 'Please. Just go away. Leave us alone.'

'If there are any diaries, letters, anything you have that would help us understand who she was. We will return them to you.'

They left Julia slumped on the sofa in the living room and joined Tozer, who was standing in the hallway. The major closed the door carefully behind him and said quietly, 'Morwenna had one brother, you see. He died in a motorcycle accident this May.'

'I am very sorry. This must be very hard for you both,' said Tozer.

'Yes.'

'Shall we say eleven o'clock?'

The major stood in the porch, backlit from the hallway, and shook hands awkwardly.

'We need to find a bed and breakfast.'

'We're going to the farm. I just spoke to my mother on the phone.'

'I could still find a hotel.'

'It'll be fine. Much nicer than a B and B.'

Breen would have preferred the anonymity of a motel room, but he was too exhausted to argue. They drove down the dark lanes, lights on full beam. There were no other cars on the road. Looking out of the side window, Breen could see nothing, only a heavy blackness. At the brow of a hill Tozer braked sharply as a big pale bird almost flew into the windscreen, blinded by the light.

'Barn owl,' she said, and picked up speed again only to brake once more. A sheep stood in the middle of the road, eyes glowing like moonstones in the headlights.

Eventually they joined a bigger road, with the occasional car coming the other way, full beam lights dimming as they rounded corners before the starless dark returned.

'She was drunk.'

'Yes.'

'Just saying.'

'Why did he lie? About going to the police about her?' he asked.

'Families are complicated. Fathers and daughters.'

'I wouldn't know.'

'Take it from me.'

'He was hiding something.'

'Maybe.'

'And they didn't ask why,' said Breen.

'What do you mean?'

'Wouldn't you expect a man to ask the why questions? Why do you think they killed her? Why?'

'To be told a member of your family is dead is a terrible thing,' she said. 'He was in a diz.'

'A lesbian daughter, at that.'

'Tomorrow.'

'Yes.' He was too tired to think any further. 'Tomorrow.'

The darkness around them was total. He had never seen such a blackness. He lay his head against the side of the car and closed his eyes as Tozer drove down winding roads.

He was woken by her, gently knocking his shoulder. They were at a farmhouse where a woman stood in the light of a low door.

Tozer's voice, fuzzing into his head: 'Don't tell her about our case. It'll only upset her. I'll invent something.'

It seemed to take an age for Breen to remember where he was. He stared blearily at Tozer. She was outside now, throwing her arms

167

round the woman at the door, kissing her on the neck. By the time he had made it out of the door, Tozer was already pulling their two suitcases from the boot.

It was a cottage with small windows, roughly rendered. 'Don't stand in the cold. Come on in,' said the woman, a rounder, shorter, older version of her daughter, with a thicker Devon accent.

Breen tried to take a case off Tozer; it seemed unmanly to let a woman carry his suitcase in front of her mother, but she ignored his outstretched left hand. 'He in Alex's room, Ma?'

'That's right.'

She disappeared into a door to the side of the wainscoted hallway that ran like a passageway through the middle of the house. Breen stood inside the front door, blinking in the light.

'You'll be hungry, then?' said Mrs Tozer. 'Edward?' she called, come out here.

Helen Tozer's skinniness came from her father. He emerged from the living room which was on the opposite side to the door into which Helen had disappeared. Old corduroy trousers and a woollen shirt. Inside, an old television chattered in semi-darkness; the only other light was the pink glow of a two-bar electric fire. 'Pleased to meet you,' said the man, holding out a hand.

Breen placed his palm into the leathery skin of the older man's hand and allowed it to be shaken slowly. He smelt of tobacco and livestock.

'It's very kind of you to put me up,' said Breen.

The man nodded silently and then went back to his television.

Mrs Tozer led Breen back into the kitchen, a low-beamed room with a range at one end. 'What's for supper, Ma?' said Tozer, emerging down the narrowest staircase Breen had ever seen.

'Beef stew and dumplings.'

'Home,' said Tozer.

'You should try it more often,' her mother said, wiping her hands on a tea towel.

'I'm busy,' said her daughter, leaning over and dipping a finger into a pot on the range. She pulled out her finger and licked it. 'I'm starved,' she said.

Breen lay that night in a narrow bed, under low eaves. A small, uneven room with a latch on the door. A Persian rug, worn but clean. His bed was warm already from the hot-water bottle Tozer's mother had put in it, wrapped in a knitted cover, though the room was far from cold, warmed from the kitchen range below. The scent of soap and fresh bread. Cotton sheets that had been waving in clean air as they dried. A sprig of dried lavender hanging from the wall close to the head of the bed, its scent deliciously thick. A full belly and a soft pillow.

This was a house of women. He savoured the unfamiliar feeling for a few seconds before he fell into a rich, enveloping void.

SIXTEEN

A long time later there was music. It had been in his head for some time. Plush and colourful, strange and new, it took on unexpected shapes and shades, twisting into new moods, and he rose through it slowly to consciousness.

There were words too, that made sense at first only in a dreamlike way. He lay not so much listening as absorbing, soaking in the curiosity of it, until finally he rose to a delicious lucidity in which the notes and the songs became clearer. It was about days being few and filled with tears but sung in a strangely upbeat kind of way.

A girl's voice sang along to the music, something about it being so long since a girl had been gone.

The sun was shining through thin curtains. Helen Tozer was singing along to records in the room next door; her bedroom must have been the other side of the wooden partition.

He rose, still in his pyjamas, looking for the bathroom. She was sitting cross-legged on her bedroom floor, LP and single covers scattered around her. In front of her was a small pink plastic record player.

'Sleepyhead,' she said.

'What time is it?'

'Gone eight.'

She was already dressed in a pair of jeans and a cotton blouse. The song ended. She carefully lifted the needle off the LP before the next track started, took the record off the player and replaced it in its sleeve, then picked up another, reading down the names of the tracks.

'I don't remember. Do you like the Stones?' she asked, not looking up.

Breen shrugged. He yawned. Sleep was hard to shake.

She lowered the needle onto the start of another song, ignoring him, listening intently to the music, nodding her head gently in rhythm. He watched her with distant fascination, as a child might watch a bird digging for worms, then returned to his room, took his washbag and walked to the bathroom down the hallway.

Mrs Tozer was below in the kitchen, doing something with empty jam jars. She greeted him with a beaming face, like he was a prodigal returning. 'It's the Devon air, I expect.'

'What?'

'You sleeping so long. The air's thicker here. It tires you out if you ain't used to it.'

'Does it?'

'Definitely. And makes you hungry too, I expect. You eat bacon and eggs?'

'Definitely.'

She smiled at him and rubbed her hands on a towel, then pulled open the fridge door and lifted out a plate piled with bacon and set to work.

'Thank you for putting me up at such short notice.'

'It's a pleasure. You bring our Helen back to us. She's been away so long.'

'She brought me, really. I can't drive at the moment.'

'Yes. I see. I heard you been in the wars.'

'Sort of.'

'Helen says your father died recently.'

'Did she?'

'Maybe she shouldn't have said.'

'It's OK.'

'I'm sorry. It's terrible losing someone close.' A sheepdog poked its head into the open back door. She shooed it away. 'She's a chatterbox. She can't help it. Always has been.'

'I know.'

She laughed. 'Course you do. When she was a child she kept the milk-tanker driver waiting twenty minutes while she told him the story of Dracula and the Three Bears.'

The pan started to sizzle on the range. She laid three slices of bacon in it, one after the other. The kitchen was plain but Breen had the sense that behind the built-in cupboards, doors covered in layers of glossy cream paint, lurked provisions that could see an army through a long winter.

'Would you like two eggs, dearie?'

'One is plenty.'

'Mushrooms? Picked them this morning.'

'Lovely.'

'Was he old?'

'What?'

'Your father?'

'Sixty-seven.'

'And were you close?'

'He brought me up.'

'Was there no one to help?'

He was startled by a large shape moving past the small back window of the kitchen until he realised it was just a cow.

'No. No family here. He was a loner.'

'He must have been a great man, then, raising a fine man like you on his own.'

He nodded. 'I suppose he was.'

'Would you like beans?'

'No thanks.'

'You must miss him.'

'I do. Very much.'

'The space left by the ones we love is bigger than we ever think it will be.' Her face was unsmiling.

Tozer came downstairs when Breen was finishing the plate. She took it and washed it up, and dried it. He sat watching her bending over the sink, rinsing crockery under the taps. 'What are you talking about?'

'This and that,' said her mother.

'What size are your feet?' she turned and asked Breen, as she picked up a tea towel.

'Eight, why?'

'Do you want to go for a walk round the farm? We've got a while before we have to go.'

'That would be nice.'

There was a pile of wellingtons in a shed at the back of the farmhouse, some single, some in pairs, some so ancient the rubber barely held together. She managed to find a pair that were only one size bigger than Breen's feet; he sat on a bench in the backyard of the farm, watched by a beady-eyed cockerel, and put them on.

Arriving at night, he had had no idea where they were. Now he could see the land around them. The Tozers' farm filled a small valley that ran down towards a muddy estuary below the house.

The roundness of the hills made them look like they'd been drawn by a child. Fringing the far side of the water, a long forbidding wood, leaves turning yellow and red.

'This was my kingdom,' said Tozer. She had donned an old duffel coat and wore a red scarf around her neck. 'I know every inch.'

The cows had been through the yard a few hours earlier; the ground under their feet had become a thin colloidal ooze, sucking their boots until they reached untrampled grass. There stood a field full of black-and-white cows that gazed at them dumbly. Breen's London had never touched the senses in such a way as this place did; a thick, autumnal smell of decay filled the air.

'How's your arm?'

'Not too bad.'

One of the cows started ambling towards them with a slow step that looked menacing to Breen. Another joined in. Tozer seemed not to notice.

'My father, he's like a sore tooth. Even more than last time I was here. He doesn't say a word. He said anything to you?'

'No. Just a hello last night. I haven't seen him this morning.'

The cows came nearer. They seemed much bigger close to, thick with meat and muscle, nostrils emitting drool and steam.

'He's getting worse, I reckon. He used to laugh all the time. One time I was in this nativity play at school and I had the part of one of the three shepherds. I was so proud because I was playing the part of a farmer. Follow the star, you know? Only with my big police girl's feet, I tripped up on one of the cows that were lowing and fell right on top of Mary. I knocked Jesus's head right off. It was this doll, see? And the head rolled right across the stage and ended up under the piano. One of the shepherds had to fish it out with his crook. And you could have heard a pin drop.'

The cows were too close for Breen now. He had fallen back, walking slower, letting Tozer go on ahead alone.

'And then my dad started laughing. Not just tittering. Real loud laughing. Everybody shushing him, and he just couldn't stop. Half of me was dead embarrassed. Half of me was pleased I'd made him laugh so much.'

She turned and looked at Breen, standing there hesitant, and then back at the two cows that now blocked their way forward.

'Are those animals OK?'

'You'm a bit scared, in't you?' Extra Devon accent for comic effect.

'Yes.'

She laughed. 'They're only heifers.' She turned back to the cows. 'Ga'an,' she shouted, waving her arms. 'Get gone.' Instantly, the cows bowed their heads, jerked around and skedaddled back over the field. Breen followed her, avoiding the cowpats.

Halfway across the field she paused and stared at a distant clump of trees tucked in the fold of a hill, where three fields came together.

'Is that it?' he asked her. 'The place where they found your sister?'

She nodded, turning away from him so he could only see her back. A large wide-winged bird circled over the clump of trees.

'How did they reckon he took her there? Or was she there already?'

She felt in her coat pocket for her packet of cigarettes, pulled one out. 'I don't know. I really don't. I've tried thinking it through a million times and I don't know.'

The field dipped down towards the estuary. The tide was out and flocks of birds were picking at the dark brown mud that stretched out far into the distance. Thousands of them, small clumps of grey and brown against the dark mud.

Tozer began making her way along the edge, keeping away from the mud by ducking under the scrawny oak limbs.

'Me and Alex used to swim there. We taught ourselves. Neither of our parents could swim. Each summer it was like a competition. First one in.'

'Isn't it muddy?'

'Bit.'

'Didn't you mind?'

'No. She went in one hot day in May when the water was still freezing. I beat her next year by going in in April. God it was cold, though. Made your bones hurt.'

'So you won?'

'No. She beat me in the end.'

He stopped. There was a piece of china under his foot. Picking it up he examined it; a cracked triangle of blue willow pattern, fringed by a little weed on each edge. A piece of a small angular bridge. He looked around him. There were dozens of small worn pieces of pottery among the stones, and frosty bits of glass too, green and brown and blue.

'The New Year before she was killed, Mum and Dad were out at a party, so we had a party of our own. Just me and her. Fireworks and everything. Well, some sparklers,' she said. 'We'd sneaked a couple of bottles of Bulmers into the barn and built a fire out back. Happy New Year. I drank too much and fell asleep by the fire and missed it all. She woke me up some time after midnight, stark naked in the moonlight, teeth chattering. She said, "Pinch, punch, first of the month . . . and oh, by the way, I beat you." She had gone in at five minutes past. She was soaking. Her skin was blue. I remember her, standing there, skinny as a ghost, goose bumps, shaking with the cold. But she'd beat me.'

'That could have been dangerous.'

'Says the man who is scared of cows . . .'

'I wasn't scared.'

'You mean she could have killed herself or something?' she said.

'No.'

'She could have saved someone else the bother?'

She walked on ahead, down the narrow causeway of rocks and shells. Breen tottered along behind her, trying to avoid falling. His socks had fallen down into his wellingtons and his feet were cold.

'I thought if I got in at the stroke of midnight next year I'd beat her and she'd never be able to beat me again. Never got the chance. She caught bronchitis, though. Served her bloody right.'

Birds hung in the air above the farm, like the one he'd seen over the spinney where they'd found her sister's body. She saw him looking at them and said, 'Butcher birds.'

They rounded a corner, startling a group of ducks who took off, squawking angrily. They flew off across the mudflats, out towards the sea.

'It's beautiful here,' he said, because it was true and because he thought she'd like to hear him say it.

'Isn't it?' she said. She picked up a stick and beat a path through brambles, back into a field. 'I can't stay here any more, though. It's all ruined for me.'

The car splashed through mud on the way out of the Tozers' farm, engine roaring up the steep road out of the valley up towards Dartmoor and then west towards Cornwall.

In daylight, the countryside looked no less wild. Dead bracken and granite rocks. Stunted trees bent in the wind. Ground that looked thick with water. Sheep huddled against stone walls. It made Breen feel cold just looking at it. The sun disappeared into cloud. They had left the warmth of the lower valleys behind. As they approached Liskeard, a low mist closed in.

In the daylight, Tozer took the lanes fast, braking for bends at the last minute which did nothing for Breen's nerves.

Driving up the lane out of the town towards the Sullivans' house, they came to another bend. Suddenly, round the hedge-blind corner, a car came roaring out of the mist.

Breen tried to shout 'Brake!' but nothing came out. There was not enough time anyway because the other car was coming so fast. Hemmed by high banks on either side, the lane left little room for escape.

Tozer yanked the steering wheel to the left. Branches cracked across the windscreen. A dazzle of glass exploded all around. In that millisecond Breen wondered if he had put his seat belt on. Or if the car was even fitted with them.

Again, at what seemed the same moment, his body was thrown forward towards the glove compartment. Then sideways. He was conscious of a loud bang, and the world distorting as the other vehicle smashed into them. The smell of brake asbestos and rubber.

And then suddenly it was still. No birdsong, just the sound of another car engine roaring down the hill, away, noise gradually receding. And pain in his arm.

Someone began swearing quietly. 'Oh, fuck.'

Must be Tozer. He was relieved to hear her voice.

'Fuck, fuck, fuck.' Almost like a song sung to soothe a child. 'We were lucky, hey?'

Cautiously he opened his eyes.

SEVENTEEN

'You OK?' Tozer was looking at him. She was shiny, light glinting off her skin.

Breen lifted his good hand to his face. It was peppered with splinters of glass. She too was covered with glittering shards.

Breen was trembling like a kitten.

'You OK?' she said again. She had managed to steer the front of the car out of the path of the oncoming vehicle, leaving the rear of the Zephyr still in the middle of the road. The speeding car had smashed into their tail panel, jerking the car's chassis back round so that it stopped halfway across the lane.

'I think so,' he said. As he shook, small pieces of glass clattered off his clothes into the footwell of the car.

'Stay still,' she said. 'Don't move a muscle.' She reached round to the back of the car and picked her handbag off the back seat. Rummaging through it, she pulled out a pair of tweezers and a pack of tissues. Leaning forward, she placed one hand on his shoulder and carefully picked a lump of glass out of his cheek. He felt the blood start to trickle down his face from where she'd pulled it out.

She dabbed her face with the tissue, then gave it to him.

He asked, 'Did you see the car?'

'Only just. I mean. Christ.'

'Was that a Jaguar?'

'They almost buggering killed us, Paddy.'

'Yes.'

'Do you think he meant to?'

Glass was everywhere. Carefully he picked it out from his sling

178

with his good hand and threw the fragments onto the bonnet in front of them.

'This thing still drive?'

She put it into reverse and manoeuvred the car back around. 'Should I follow them?'

'Drive to their house. That's the nearest phone,' he said.

'Your voice is sort of shaky.'

She crunched the car into first and drove, one hand on the wheel, the other pushing out pieces of the broken windscreen so she could see better. The rear wheel arch, crushed against the tyre, made a grinding noise as they drove. Fortunately they were only a few hundred yards away from the house. As they pulled into the gravel driveway Breen noted that the Sullivans' car was not there.

'It was them, wasn't it?' said Tozer.

Unable to open his stoved-in door, he clambered out awkwardly over the driver's seat. Looking back at the car he saw that one headlight had gone completely, the windscreen was shattered and the rear panel fin on the driver's side had been torn off.

He went to the front door and twisted the handle. It was locked. 'Hello?' he called, thumping on the door.

No answer.

'Hello? Anyone there?'

He left the door and walked around the house. The back door into the kitchen was locked too.

'Here,' said Tozer. One of the sash windows in the living room was loose. She pulled a penknife out of her handbag and ran it between the frames, dislodging the newspaper that had been stuffed there to stop it rattling. Freed, the latch moved aside easily. Together they heaved the lower frame up.

In the hallway, he picked up the Sullivans' telephone, an old, heavy Bakelite job, dialled 999 and gave his warrant number and a description of the major's Jaguar. Afterwards, he lowered himself into the chair by the grandfather clock, where Mrs Sullivan had sat sobbing last night.

'We should find some sticking plasters. Your face is still bleeding.'

'I'm fine,' he said.

'He almost killed us. We were almost dead there. I mean . . . God. He was going bloody fast, wasn't he?'

'Did you see him?'

'No,' she said. 'Not really.'

'How many were in the car?'

'I didn't have time to count, precisely. Do you think he did it, then?'

'If he's run, it doesn't look good.'

'My God. Think of that. A father killing his own daughter. That's something dark.'

Breen looked down at his hands. They were still trembling. The grandfather clock seemed to tick absurdly loudly.

'Six inches to the right and they'd have smashed straight into us.' She looked up. 'What was that?'

He touched his face with his hand. 'Has it stopped bleeding yet?'

'That. What was it?'

'What do you mean?'

'That.'

'I didn't hear anything.'

'A kind of noise.'

Breen listened. Nothing.

'Can't you hear it?'

'No.'

'Hello?' called Tozer.

This time it was there, above their heads. A slight creaking of wood.

'And again – listen.'

Unmistakably, a slight banging sound.

Breen set off up the stairs, taking them two at a time, Tozer close behind. There was a landing with carpet, a corridor with doors off it. The main bedroom was at the top of the stairs, facing the front of the house.

Through the open door, Breen saw bedsheets pulled off the mattress onto the floor. The next thing he noticed, from where he stood at the top of the stairs, were two pallid, naked legs lying on the floor; the rest of whoever it was lay behind the bed.

'Hello?'

The legs were not moving. He walked slowly through the doorway and into the bedroom, more slowly still towards the furthest of the room's twin beds, until he could peer over and see who lay there.

It was not the major driving the car, that was certain. He lay on his front. His face, surrounded by an oval of blood, seemed to have melted into the floorboards, his head like half an orange on a plate. The shotgun must have been fired at close range. It had simply disintegrated the front of the major's head. All that was left was the back of his skull, which had hit the ground as he fell forwards.

'Oh,' said Tozer, hand in front of her mouth.

He had a pyjama shirt on but, for some reason, no trousers. The shirt had soaked up some of the blood from the floor, turning almost black. For a few seconds, Breen was able to remain separate from what he was seeing. The physics of the major's position, for instance, made no sense to him; the gun had been fired at him at close range, and yet he had fallen forwards. A blast that severe would knock a man back right off his feet. But then he turned to the wallpapered wall and there was a perfect silhouette of the Major's head picked out in shot. He had been executed close to the wall, his body slamming against it so hard that he had rebounded forwards to where he now lay. Still oddly calm and no longer shaking, Breen knelt down and felt the man's wrist. It was warm but, unsurprisingly, there was not the faintest quiver of a pulse.

At the touch of dead flesh though, the calm deserted him. He dropped the arm back down into the congealing blood, left the room quickly and was sick in a flowerpot on the landing. Mrs Tozer's bacon and eggs.

'Oh, Christ,' said Tozer, right behind him.

When he'd finished, he sat down on the stairs. Tozer took the stair above his and put her hand on his shoulder. He could feel her shaking with shock almost as badly as he was.

'Fine pair we make.'

'Poor man.' He retched again.

'It's amazing you keep any food down at all.'

There were small framed woodcuts on the stairs. A tree, climbing boys stealing eggs from a nest. A fish on a plate. 'Shall we call . . .' He stopped.

'What?'

'That noise again,' he whispered.

'I'm not sure.'

He put his hand to his lips. They listened.

'Oh my God. Do you think it's her?'

Another louder noise.

A whisper: 'If that was her, who was in the car?'

He stood, took a deep breath and felt his stomach churn again. He turned to go back into the bedroom.

There were two beds, side by side, his and hers. Hers had been slept in. By it were two black-and-white photos in frames: one of the dead girl, Morwenna, serious-faced in school uniform, the other of a boy, presumably her dead brother.

He stopped his tiptoeing and looked around. There was a huge black-and-white photograph of Julia Sullivan on the wall opposite the bed; in it she was dressed in a large white floppy hat and a white lace dress. The lace dress was open, showing a single breast. Her dressing table was set between the beds; a large mirror with two silver candlesticks on either side. More framed photographs: a boy, beaming, clutching the tiller of a sailing dinghy; a small girl looking down from a slide. She had a Jane Austen and a copy of *Wide Sargasso Sea* on her bedside table; he had an Agatha Christie and an Ian Fleming.

Again, this time unmistakably, a soft sound.

Breen jumped. Tozer whispered, 'Oh, Jesus.'

The noise came from behind a door. You could see daylight under the bottom of it, a thin line above the bare floorboards. But halfway along, the line of light was interrupted; a dark shape on the other side.

'Go call this in,' whispered Breen.

'What?'

'Please. Go. Give them the address and tell them to come quick.'

She hesitated still.

'Now.'

She left. He stood looking at the door and listening to Tozer clatter down the stairs. He waited until she was safely out of the way, until he heard her speaking into the telephone, before he spoke.

'Who's there?'

No answer.

'Open the door and come out.'

Still no answer. But again the noise, louder this time.

'I'm a police officer and there are more police on the way.'

He tried to sound in control.

'I'm coming in.'

The handle turned easily but when he tried to push open the door it would not give. Someone was blocking it on the other side.

Saying, 'I'm not going to hurt you,' he tiptoed back to the dressing table and returned with one of the silver candlesticks.

At the door he pushed again, hard this time. Whoever it was on the other side of the door seemed to be pushing their full weight against it.

'Stand back,' he said, stepped back himself, then heaved his good shoulder against the door with all his strength, candlestick raised in his left hand. With all his weight behind it, the door slid open.

There wasn't a person in the room. It was the golden retriever. It had been shot in the side of the head, flesh and bone exposed, but was still half alive. The dog had been trying to open the door, scratching against the woodwork with a bloody paw. Pushing it back, Breen had crushed the dying dog against the side of the bath.

Now it panted slowly and gently. He squatted down and stroked its matted fur.

It took an age for more police to arrive. By the time they did, in car after car, the dog was dead.

EIGHTEEN

The local CID man, Block, was showy. He had a handlebar moustache, a tweed jacket with leather elbow patches, a flamboyant
green cravat and he chewed gum, which he removed carefully and
wrapped in a piece of silver paper.

'We haven't had anything this good in a long time,' he said.

Tozer had found plasters in the bathroom cabinet and put one on
Breen's face, just by his left eye.

'I imagined it was like this round here all the time,' said Breen.

'Charmed, I'm sure. I mean, what are we looking at? Burglary?
Doubtful. Crime of passion? Much more like it, wouldn't you say?'

'I came to tell them their daughter was dead. Last night.'

'Right. Right. So you said. And how did they react? Was there
animosity? Anger? Remorse? What?'

Tozer said, 'If she did this half an hour ago, no, three-quarters of
an hour now, she could be miles away in that Jag. You lot wouldn't
want to let a murderer get away because you were wasting time,
would you?'

'Who's she?'

'TDC Tozer. She's with me. She hasn't learned to keep her own
opinions to herself.'

Tozer glared at him.

'You local?' Block asked her.

'No,' said Tozer.

'It's like he's got no ruddy face left at all, Sarge.'

Sergeant Block turned his back on Breen and Tozer and faced
his men. 'Well, it's not a shaving accident, is it? Twelve-bore at close

range. Very nasty. Very messy. OK. Think, boys. Was there another man, do you think? Any sign of a mystery lover? You say the Jaguar is missing? Find the car registration. First priority. Chop-chop.'

'It's not just missing. It almost killed us.'

'It was G-reg,' said Breen.

'Nice. Brand new?'

'Yes. And there were two twelve-bores and a 303 in the gun cabinet in the living room last night. There's only one gun there now,' Breen added.

'Sarge. Don't know if it's important but someone's been sick in this geranium on the landing.'

'Make a note of it.'

'That was me,' said Breen.

'Dearie me. I thought you Londoners were made of sterner stuff. Has the snapper arrived yet?'

'Look at this picture of her.' A local copper was standing in front of the big photo of Mrs Sullivan. 'Can we take it to the station for reference?'

'She's a bit of a looker, ain't she, Sarge? Nice personality.'

'Sarge? Photographer will be here direc'ly. He got held up in Exeter.'

'Pair of nice personalities, more like.'

'Bit on the small side for my taste, Constable. What sort of woman has a picture of herself with her mammaries sticking out in her own bedroom?'

'The wife of a lucky man.'

'I wouldn't say lucky from the state of him.'

With difficulty, Breen took out his notebook and began scribbling.

'She used to be a model, sir, according to people in the town.'

Block looked straight at Breen and said, 'This is a Devon and Cornwall job now, Sergeant.'

'We have an outstanding inquiry about the murder of a girl. The victim's daughter.'

'That's as may be, and of course we're always happy to help our friends in the Metropolitan Police, but the murder of Major Sullivan is our business, you understand.'

The local constables paused, waiting for Breen's reply.

'Naturally,' said Breen.

'Good. Right, boys. What have we learned? She's a slut, gentlemen. An exhibitionist. Cherchay le homme. I'll give you two guineas to one there's another man involved. Can someone get that bloody dog out of here? It stinks. The dog that Sergeant Breen and his glamorous assistant here thought was the killer. "Help!"' squealed Block, '"Come quick. There's someone else in the house."'

'I'll be downstairs,' said Breen.

The house was full now, policemen crashing through every room, all keen to be in on the investigation, yanking out drawers or spilling stuff out of cupboards, then trampling through the debris.

In the hallway, a policeman was talking on the Sullivans' phone. 'Yeah, boy. That's right. Half his bloody head has gone. You should see it. Bloody blood everywhere. It's like it's been sawn right in half. Gun must have been right by his head.'

They walked outside. Half a dozen cars were parked at all angles around the fountain now.

'Bunch of bloody bumpkins,' said Tozer.

The mist had closed even tighter around the house. The garden seemed to float in its own cloud.

'What are you doing?' asked Tozer.

'Writing everything down.' He was making notes in his book.

'Everything?'

'You never know what's going to be important.'

'Is that a drawing?' He had sketched the dead major, faceless, head down. 'That's brilliant, that is.'

Holding the notebook away from him, he squinted at it. There was something about the randomness of the shaky, half-controlled pencil strokes that made it feel like it had been drawn by a different person.

'Poor bugger. You don't look brilliant either.'

'I didn't use to be sick when I saw dead people.'

The warmth of the morning had been chilled by the encroaching mist.

'Before, I could shut things out and just get on with the job. It's like I've lost a skin.'

She put her handbag down on a cast-iron table that sat next to the deck chair on the lawn. 'It's like what happened to me when Alex died,' she said, lighting a cigarette. 'Only in reverse. I grew another skin.'

'I could never live in a place like this,' he said. 'I need to have people around me.'

'I wouldn't mind,' she said. 'It's a beautiful house.'

A pair of jays chuckled in a bare ash tree.

'What about neighbours? If there are any. They'd have noticed two gunshots.'

'Probably not,' she said. 'Specially now it's shooting season. Everyone round these parts has a shotgun. Popping off all the time at vermin this time of year.'

The lawn was sodden. A pile of leaves had gathered on one side, blown there by the wind. 'Where do you reckon she's gone then?'

'She could be going to London to see her girl. I'd told her the body was at University College.'

'You sure it's her that killed him?'

'We don't know anything for sure.'

Breen looked in his notebook and read back what he'd written: *Curtains drawn. Cup of tea. Gin bottle in bin. Gordons. 2 bttls empty wine. Beaujolais. M. shot by 12-bore from less than two feet away. Dog second barrel? New car. Job? Money?*

'Maybe I should just take you home?' said Tozer.

They walked once around the house before returning to the front door. In the hallway, another copper was on the phone. 'One cheese and onion, one ham, two ham and cheese, one bacon. The one with bacon has tomato ketchup. Got any pasties? Never mind. Crisps?

How much is that? You're jokin'. I thought you had a special rate for us coppers . . . Yeah, that's a bit more like it.'

Breen peered into the living room. The place was still being unmethodically turned upside down. The drawers from the desk were wide open and there were papers all over the floor. He guessed they were trying to find some document that had the full car registration number on it. If she was still in the car, they would need to pass a description out to other forces.

When the constable had finished ordering food, Breen finally got on the phone to Marilyn. 'Tell Jones to put someone down at the morgue at University College. She may be headed there.'

There was the sound of a siren from outside. The constable who'd been ordering the sandwiches was driving away to collect them.

'Yee-haw,' said a lanky copper, smoking a cigarette in the living room. 'Did you give him an order, lover?' he asked Tozer.

She shook her head. 'Nobody asked me.'

'You can have a nibble of mine then.'

'I'd rather starve.'

Breen squatted down and started looking through the papers they had discarded on the floor.

'Charmer. What are you doing later?'

'Nothing that involves you.'

'Leave her be. She's a cow,' said an older copper.

'I never forget a face, but I'll make an exception for you.'

Tozer snorted.

Breen knelt, going through a pile of bills splayed on the floor. A local grocer had written: *No credit until this bill is paid!!!!* Another note from a garage said: *Final demand.* There was a Coutts bank statement mixed in with the pile; on 16 August the Sullivans had been overdrawn by £662 14s. 6d.

Breen moved towards the bookshelves. More Austen. An old thumbed copy of *Kennedy's Latin Primer*. *The Strange Death of Liberal England*. He noted a couple of titles, then spotted a leather-bound photo album, tucked beside *Brewer's Phrase & Fable*.

He sat on the sofa with the album on his knees and started turning the pages. In the first pages there were many photos of Julia. These weren't snaps. They were taken in studios with expensive cameras, presumably when she was modelling, out-takes of her laughing, or having a cigarette while someone adjusted her hair. As a young woman she had been beautiful.

These gave way to more amateurish photographs. They were of a gang of friends, raucous and daring, who enjoyed striking poses for photos on picnics and at parties. Breen recognised the types. The men from the war who had never settled back into ordinary lives. Men who drank and rode on motorbikes. Women who were attracted to their rawness. One showed Julia at a fancy dress party in a daringly brief bikini, with a papier mâché head on a plate and a knife in the other hand. Salome? In one, a woman stood at an easel, painting a portrait of Julia outside a house. In another, a man sat on a porch strumming a guitar. Another, possibly the same man, sat at a typewriter dressed only in underpants.

Breen realised that many of the photographs appeared to have been taken at the same building, a pretty wooden Swiss-style chalet with an old-fashioned wood stove and window boxes. It was surrounded by woods. At first Breen thought the house must be somewhere abroad, but the more he looked, the more he saw the little details: a pint of milk, a copy of *The Times* on a dining table.

Then Mallory began appearing as part of the gang. The first photo of him was of a younger Mallory in an old open-top MG, grinning at the camera. Another of him on a yacht, knife between his teeth. One at the chalet, dressed as a tribesman in a grass skirt, holding a spear. It was taken before his chest had turned to flab.

A couple of pages later there was a photograph of a wedding, Julia Sullivan, unashamedly pregnant, cradling her bump with one hand and holding a posy in the other. It was a military chapel. There followed snapshots of babies: Morwenna and her brother Nicholas, dates of birth written below in a feminine hand. Then of the children growing up. A birthday party, with hats and bunting, obviously taken at the wooden chalet. Nicholas in a tin pedal car. Morwenna on a pony. By now the gang of friends had disappeared. The photographs were all of Mallory, Julia and the children.

The photos of Morwenna showed her becoming more tomboyish as the years went past. Her hair grew shorter; she was rarely pictured in dresses or skirts. In one she solemnly held a large, dead fish by the tail.

In one of the more recent ones she stood in the doorway of a tree house, arms on hips like Peter Pan, far above the ground. It was taken from below, her looking down triumphantly at the photographer. She was wearing a woollen check shirt and work boots. Near the back he found a recent one: a portrait of her gazing sullenly at the camera, clearly taken in the house they lived in now. He teased those last two out from their corners and put them in his pocket.

'What's that you've got?' said Block. 'This is our crime scene, remember, not yours.'

'I need a photo of the dead girl. I'll send it back to you when I've had a copy made.'

The sergeant grunted.

Breen picked up some of the paperwork that had been scattered over the floor by the policemen. It was letters, mostly. He returned to the couch and began to leaf through them. One was from an insurance agent informing them that the contents of Fonthill House were now valued at £2,000 and saying that the premium was overdue. Several others were about Fonthill and came from a solicitor in Exeter and were addressed to Mrs Sullivan. Flicking through them, he learned that they had bought the house just two years earlier for £11,000. There were no details of the mortgage; it appeared they had bought the property outright. He noted down the solicitor's address.

After another ten minutes looking through the jumbled correspondence, he said to Tozer, 'I'm done here. Let's take a look at the girl's bedroom before they turn that upside down too.'

They found it easily enough. So far the children's bedrooms had remained unscathed. They were both at the back of the house. One was clearly the boy's. It had photographs of Lamborghinis and Lotuses on the walls. An Exeter City Football Club calendar. A microscope. A dartboard. A crane made of Meccano. A half-built radio-control plane. A picture of Sitting Bull.

Morwenna's was next to it. There was a wardrobe full of children's clothes, and a shelf full of books like *The Little House on the Prairie* and *Black Beauty*, but little else in the room that suggested a life lived into double figures. A purple gonk lay on the bed.

He opened the chest of drawers. The top drawers were completely empty. Old clothes filled the lower ones, but there was nothing that interested Breen. Her bedside table had a drawer, but that too was empty. There had once been pictures on the walls torn out from teenage magazines, of the Beatles no doubt, and photographs pinned above her bed. All that remained were small marks in the paint where the Sellotape had been removed and the pins pulled out.

'It's like she'd already been erased,' Breen said.

A little while later, they were in the kitchen, looking through the dresser drawers, when a shout came from the master bedroom: 'Tell that girl to put the kettle on.'

Breen opened a cupboard. Yesterday it had been full of packets of Rich Tea biscuits. Now it was empty.

'She's taken biscuits,' he said.

'What?'

'She's taken packets of biscuits with her. Rich Tea. About a dozen.'

'So? Maybe she likes Rich Tea biscuits.'

'She could have left us some,' complained a copper.

An officer came in and looked around. 'Didn't you hear? Put the tea on. He'll be back with the sarnies any mo, speed he was driving.'

Nobody moved. Eyes turned towards Tozer.

'Fuck's sake,' she muttered.

★

'Got it,' shouted a copper, sticking his head around the hallway door. He was holding a piece of paper. 'I got the registration number. Sir?'

Block bowled downstairs and snatched the piece of paper from him.

'Well, well. It looks like the Metropolitan Police aren't useless at everything,' he said.

'What do you mean?'

'One of your lot did Major Sullivan for going through a red light. Maroon Jaguar. Registration ALP 367G. Good work. Phone that in, Constable.' And he handed the piece of paper back to the constable. 'Get it out on the phone, now.'

'Can I see that?' said Breen.

The constable looked at Block; the sergeant nodded. 'Make sure we get it back, though.'

The Jaguar had been pulled over after passing through a red light on Edgware Road. Breen noted the name of the officer who had issued the ticket.

When Tozer emerged from the kitchen, a scowl on her face and a tray filled with cups of tea in her hands, Breen held the document up for her.

'What is it?'

'Look at the date.'

She read it. 12 October 1968. It took a little while longer before the penny dropped.

'Hell,' she said. 'He was in London the day before his daughter was murdered.'

Breen nodded.

'That was a Saturday. He told us he went to London the week before, but didn't say anything about being there on the twelfth,' said Tozer.

'No. We only asked him where he was on the Sunday.'

'She said he was back here.'

'Maybe he was. Maybe he came back. It's a fast car. He could have driven up there and back in a day.'

'Was it him, then?' she asked.

Across the room, a voice called, 'Get a move on. That tea will be cold by the time it gets to us.'

NINETEEN

That evening Tozer suggested they eat out at a carvery in Newton Abbot. 'Can't stand being around my dad too long. I don't know how my mum does it. He's like a ghost. Mum thinks his hearing's going, but I just think he can't be bothered to listen any more.'

The restaurant was mock half-timbered, with loudspeakers that wired Mantovani to every corner. The walls were covered with antique copper bed pans and horse brasses. Red-fringed lamps sat on each table. Theirs was table 11, according to the triangular plastic sign next to their cruet set.

'Mum wants me to move back. I'm not sure I could take it. I do like it here, don't get me wrong, but I think I'd go nuts.'

The side of Breen's head where the glass had cut him was throbbing.

'You're quiet.'

He nodded. 'I just feel tired.'

'You should see a doctor.'

'I did. He told me to rest.'

Tozer lit a cigarette, looked around for a waiter and said, 'I could kill a drink.' Breen pulled the two photographs he had of Morwenna out of his wallet and looked at them.

'So,' said Tozer. 'Why do you think she killed him?'

'What if it wasn't her?'

She shrugged her shoulders. 'Yes, but it were, weren't it?'

An elderly pair of women sat silently spooning soup, one plump and the other thin, tipping their bowls away from themselves as they scooped up the last drops.

'I mean, how can you kill a man you've lived with all those years? Like that too. From right close to him. I've never seen anything so disgusting in my life. Do you want to eat à la carte, or shall we go for the buffet?'

Bored, she took the lid off the mustard pot and peered inside.

'She must have really hated him,' she said.

'If it was her . . .'

'Helen bloody Tozer!' Their waitress finally appeared, dressed in a black shirt with a white pinny tied round her waist. Big pink plastic earrings dangled from her ears. 'Look at you.'

'Val? You work here?'

'Almost two years. Silver service and everything. Oh, God. You look fab. You're so bloody thin. You living in London now, your mum said. What's that like? I heard it's full of wogs . . . You having starters?'

They ordered a carafe of red wine. 'School friend,' Tozer said, when she'd disappeared to fetch it. 'Well, not friend really. We were on the same hockey team.'

'I could tell you some stories about Helen,' the waitress said to Breen, bringing the wine back to the table. 'We were mad girls, weren't we?'

'Speak for yourself, Val.'

She poured a drop for Breen to taste, then held out her left hand. 'Look at this, Hel.'

'You married? Who to?'

'Guess!'

'I don't know. Honestly, I don't.'

'Course you do. Go on, guess.'

'Kevvo?'

'God, no. Not in a million years. He lives in a caravan now up Bovey Tracey after his mother kicked him out for stealing out of her purse. Honest.'

'Dennis?'

'Helen! Act serious.'

'Who was that boy you were caught with by your dad? Rich?'

Shaking head. 'No way. Come on, Hel. It's obvious.'

Breen noticed a large man in a dinner suit trying to get the waitress's attention.

'Sorry. Um. I give up.'

'Graham.'

'Graham with the three fingers on one hand?'

'Yeah.'

'Wasn't he the one who used to peek over the shower stalls when we were changing for sports?'

Val laughed. 'Yeah.'

'I never knew you were interested in him.'

The fat man took a knife and hit a wine glass with it three times, *ping ping ping*.

'I was too. Don't you remember? I always thought he was nice.'

'I remember you saying he gave you the creeps.'

'Hel. I never did. I must have been joking. I was always nuts about him.'

'Were you?'

She pulled a purse out from her apron and opened it. 'Here. That's my little boy. Graham Junior.'

'Excuse me, miss!'

'Sorry, Hel. I'll be right back.'

The moment she was gone Tozer rolled her eyes. 'We should have gone to Torquay. Less chance of bumping into anyone I know.'

The two ladies who were eating together passed their table, returning from the carvery, one behind the other, with plates piled perilously high. Breen read the short typewritten menu the waitress had left on their table, trying to decide what to have.

She returned with a notebook and pencil and stood there, scratching her head with the blunt end. 'And what about you, Hel? Any romance in the air?' she asked, looking meaningfully from Breen to Tozer and back again.

'We're just down here on work.'

'Oh. Right.'

'Who are those photos of?'

'Just somebody,' said Breen.

'Made up your mind yet?'

When she returned with two hot plates so they could take them to the carvery, she said, 'So, Hel. There's no special man in your life, then?'

'No.'

The waitress pulled a sad face. 'Don't worry. It'll happen. And who knows, you might strike it lucky like I did.'

'Super,' said Tozer. She stuck out her tongue when the waitress turned her back.

Breen was still there looking at the photographs when Tozer returned, plate piled with beef, Yorkshire pudding, roast potatoes, mashed potatoes, cabbage, parsnips, turnips, coleslaw and fried onions.

'You should eat something, sir. Keep your strength up.'

'Where's this taken?' He was looking at the photo of Morwenna standing at the doorway to her tree house.

'You think it's important?'

'I don't know what's important right now. I can't get anything into focus.'

Tozer started eating, sawing through a thick lump of beef.

'Actually it's more like it's all in focus, and I can't sort out what's important or not.'

'Sounds like a trip.'

'What?'

'LSD. What the hippies take. We had a lecture about it the other day. You take a pill, you can't tell what's real and what's not.'

'Sounds terrifying.'

'Some people like it, though. Mind-expanding.'

Breen lifted up his bare plate. 'If we'd not gone to tell them about their daughter, that man would still be alive.'

Tozer slurped in a big chunk of beef and a bit of gravy trickled down her chin. 'Oop,' she laughed, picking up her napkin and wiping her face. 'Yes, but that doesn't make it our fault.'

Breen stood up with his plate.

The man at the carvery wore a big white chef's hat and held a newly lit cigarette. He put it in an ashtray on the next table while he drew off a thick slice of beef. The fat on it looked pale and waxy. Breen watched the knife carving slowly through the flesh.

'I don't really want meat.'

'Sorry?'

'No meat.'

'No meat?'

'That's right. I'll have vegetables.'

'This is a carvery, sir.' There was a long pause. The man glared, put down the carving knife and fork and lifted up a spoon instead. 'Potatoes, sir?'

'Thanks.'

'Carrots?'

'OK.'

'Cabbage?'

'I'm fine, thank you.'

'Nothing else? Nice bit of gravy?'

'No thanks.'

He sat down to find that their waitress had pulled up a chair and joined them at the table. 'Ciggy break,' she said. 'What's London like?'

They walked back to the farm in the dark. Tozer knew a way that cut across the back of the town, across small wooden footbridges, through damp marsh land and along the side of the river.

Breen jumped as a startled bird clattered out of the reeds close to their feet, sending him into a puddle; the water went in over the top of his brogues. 'Damn,' he said.

Tozer laughed.

He joined in. He was a little drunk. After the carafe of wine they had had brandies. The air was still and warm. The day had been a tough one, but he was oddly happy. It was funny, because when he first met Tozer, he had disliked her. She was too opinionated for a woman. Too awkward. These things seemed to matter less now. Was it since he had learned about her sister?

'See up there?'

In the darkness she pointed up the estuary. The tide was full. In the far distance, miles down towards the sea, lights reflected off the water.

'The Beatles stayed there last year. In a hotel. When they were filming *Magical Mystery Tour*. Imagine that. The Beatles coming to this godforsaken backwater. Alexandra would have been in heaven.'

'Did you see them?'

He had an impulse to take her hand, but she had already started walking again, squelching through the mud. He was glad he hadn't done it. It was the drink, like last time.

'Me? I was in London, worse luck. Always in the wrong place at the wrong time, me.'

The lights of the farmhouse were ahead of them now, a single bulb lighting the farmyard.

Mr and Mrs Tozer were in bed by the time they got in, the house dark and silent. The kitchen was still warm, though. Tozer started opening cupboards. 'I know they got some bottles stashed away somewhere,' she said. 'Here. I found some Martini. Do you like that?'

'Not for me.'

'There's a drop of whisky. Want that?'

'A little, then.'

Breen sat at the kitchen table and pulled out the three photos of the dead girl again: the morgue photograph, and the two he had taken from the house.

She sat next to him, so close he could smell the alcohol and cigarettes on her breath. 'Promise me one thing. You won't let my mum and dad see those, will you?'

He took off his left shoe and removed his sock. It was sodden.

'Hang it on the range,' said Tozer.

He sipped the whisky and pulled out his packet of cigarettes. In the last couple of days, he had taken to writing marks on the packet to remember how many he had smoked. Today there were four downward strokes and a fifth, crossing them out. He had already smoked five. He went to put them back in his jacket, then thought better of it.

He smoked the sixth cigarette flicking through the pages of his notebook, glancing up occasionally to look at Tozer, sitting by the range, bare feet up on the surface warming her long legs. It tasted particularly good.

When he came to the address of the solicitor he had found, he asked, 'Do you have a phone book?'

TWENTY

Breen sat up slowly in bed and looked out of a small, square window onto the estuary below. He slept later here than he ever did at home. His head felt thick and slow.

A cold, bright day. Seagulls wheeling in a blue sky. A group of swans dawdling on the tide, a small red boat chugging against the current in the estuary below. The prettiness of the scene was unnerving. The domesticity reminded him of what he had never had. His good mood was gone. He wished he was back in London, amongst the grey of it. Sighing, he got up to dress. Mrs Tozer had washed a shirt, a pair of underpants and a pair of socks for him, leaving them neatly folded and piled on a chair.

He was shaving when he heard a car coming down the lane towards the house. He pulled the curtains to one side and saw it was a police car, slowly weaving through the puddles.

When he came down to the kitchen there was a man sitting at the table drinking a cup of tea. Mrs Tozer was cooking bacon.

'Sergeant Breen?' said the man. He wore a suit that looked too small for him, and had a thin moustache on his upper lip.

'Yes?'

'Sergeant Sharman,' he said. 'Plymouth CID.'

'Sharman?'

'A little birdie told me you were involved in a bit of drama. I thought I'd find out what was up.'

Mr Tozer was there too. His corduroy trousers were tucked into the thick woollen socks in which he stood. He must have just come in from the farm and left his boots outside.

'You spoke to Sergeant Block?' asked Breen.

Sharman shrugged. 'You're in the country now. Everybody knows everyone else's business round here.'

Mrs Tozer put the bacon into a sandwich and put it down before Sergeant Sharman. She looked pale. 'Fred says you're here to investigate a dead girl,' she said to Breen. 'Only, Helen had said you were down here looking into people who were making dirty films.'

Sharman laughed loudly, 'She said what?'

'She said you were looking into a pornography ring.'

'Round here?' said Sharman. 'Making smut films?'

'That's what Hel said.'

'First I heard of it, round here.'

'She told you that because she didn't want you to know about the case we were working on,' said Breen. 'In case it upset you. I'm sorry.'

'Only you're really down here about a girl that was killed?'

'Yes.'

'A young girl?'

'Seventeen.'

Mrs Tozer nodded. Her husband was sitting stonily, looking straight ahead, eyes focused on the kitchen wall.

'How was she killed?' There was a flicker in Mrs Tozer's eye.

'She was strangled.'

Mrs Tozer nodded.

'Naked too,' said Sharman. 'I looked it up. That's right, Breen? Nasty business. Got any ketchup?'

Helen's father stood, rangy and tall, tweed jacket fraying at the cuffs. 'I noticed one of the cows had pink-eye this morning. I better go and check,' he said.

He left the mug in the sink and opened the door. Leaning on the frame, he tugged on his wellington boots. Cold air filled the kitchen.

'Poor old bloke,' said Sharman when he had gone. 'He's not doing too well, all things considered. It's a bloody shame.' He scratched the back of his hand.

Mrs Tozer said, 'I expect you two need to talk.'

'Lovely grub, Mrs T. As always,' Sharman called after her. When she was out of earshot, Sharman said, 'You should have stayed in a hotel, instead of bothering them here. It's only going to upset them, bringing this kind of business into their house.'

'Is that why you came? To tell me that?'

Sharman took a gulp from his tea. 'I spoke to Block this morning. He's not had a sign of Mrs Sullivan yet. Nor has anyone else.'

'Did he call up Marylebone CID this morning?'

He nodded. 'She hasn't turned up there, either.'

Breen sat down at the old kitchen table opposite Sharman, watching him take another bite from his sandwich. Sharman chewed his mouthful, swallowed, then said, 'I expect she'll turn up, sooner or later. So. You and Helen, you going out?'

'Sorry?'

'Interested, that's all. I know she doesn't think that much of me these days.'

'No. I mean, we're not going out.'

'She's a great girl. My trouble was I was too keen, I suppose.' Sharman smiled. 'Frightened her off. I should have been more patient.' He wiped his mouth on the back of his hand and belched quietly. 'To business. Supposing it was Julia Sullivan that did it, what do you think it was you said to them that made her blow his head off?'

'I thought this was Block's case.'

'We're all in this together down here. It's not like the Met.'

'Block is sure it was Julia Sullivan?'

'It's a theory,' Sharman said. 'Apparently he was in London the day before their daughter was killed. So you think he was involved in the death of his daughter?'

'Somehow. But he was back in Devon by the day she was actually killed. So it doesn't make sense.'

'And why would he kill his own daughter?'

'I have no idea.'

Sharman nodded.

'I think the major was covering something up too,' said Breen. He told Sharman how the major had lied to his wife about reporting their daughter missing to the police.

'Probably thought you lot at the Met are useless anyway.'

Helen Tozer clattered into the room. She glared at Sharman. 'I thought I heard your voice. What are you doing here?' she said, looking at his empty plate in front of him. 'Isn't your wife feeding you enough?'

Sharman stood again. 'Nice to see you too, Hel. I was just saying to Sergeant Breen. I would have thought he would have stayed in a hotel rather than here.'

'What's wrong with the farm?' She cut herself a slice of bread and buttered it thickly.

'I heard you were down. Val called me up last night. Said she'd seen you in town. I came to talk about your case.'

'I knew she wouldn't keep her mouth shut.' She took a jar of honey from the shelf. 'Did you see Dad?'

'Yes.'

'I suppose you talked to him.'

'Of course. We're old friends, him and me.'

She stuck the knife deep into the honey. 'Tell him about our girl that was killed and everything?'

Sharman leaned back on his elbows. 'Your dad seemed to think you were investigating some nudie movie set-up.'

'Did you tell him?'

'Why not?'

'You're such a prannock, Fred. Where is he now?' She spread the bread thickly with honey.

'Just gone out. Something about a cow with pink-eye.'

She walked to the window and looked out into the yard.

'You heard I got a baby now?'

'Good for you.'

'A boy.'

'Naturally.'

She took a bite out of the slice of bread, laid it down on the counter, then picked up the kettle and filled it at the tap; it hissed when she placed it on the range. Then she picked up an apple from a bowl on the windowsill and set about cutting it into quarters with a small knife.

'Another thing,' Breen said quietly. 'Where did the major get his money from?'

'What money?'

'They were in debt. But he's got a brand-new Jag.'

Sharman nodded. 'Good point.' He picked up a silver salt pot from the table and turned it upside down so that salt poured out onto the wood. 'Very good point. So where do you think she's gone?'

'Assuming it was her who killed him . . .'

'Yes.'

'Maybe to London,' said Tozer. 'That's where her daughter's body is.'

'What you still doing down here if she's up in London, then?'

'Our car got wrecked. You remember?' The kettle started to whistle.

'Let's say, for a moment, that she killed him because something you said made her realise he'd killed their daughter.'

'Brilliant work, Sherlock,' said Tozer, lighting a cigarette.

'Only like I said, Major Sullivan wasn't in London the day she was killed,' said Breen.

'I got a feeling, though,' said Sharman.

Tozer said, 'That's what makes you so great at catching murderers, then.'

'Don't be hard on us poor country boys, Helen. You used to be part of the gang too.'

Breen had been enjoying witnessing Tozer's spikiness directed at someone else, but the longer it went on, the more he felt like an eavesdropper at a lovers' quarrel. He shut his eyes and rubbed his temple.

'Is he all right? He looks a bit peaky. Don't you think?'

'He's fine,' said Tozer. 'Are you done now?'

After his car had gone up the track to the main road, tyres crunching on gravel, Tozer said, 'I think he still fancies me, don't you, sir?'

Breen just said, 'He was right, wasn't he? I shouldn't have stayed here.'

Tozer pulled on a pair of boots and went to find her father.

The house was empty. Breen picked up the phone and called the station. The ordinary daily noise of the office in the background made him want to be there.

'Bailey's had Devon and Cornwall on the blower complaining about you for not letting them know what you were doing down there,' said Marilyn.

'Is he there now?'

'No.' Even the familiar sound of one-fingered typing in the background sounded sweet to Breen. He thought of the thick-smoked air of the office and the dark floorboards.

'What's going on, Paddy?'

'We'll be back Monday morning. Can you get us train tickets for the weekend?'

'Us?'

'Yes. Constable Tozer and me.'

'Thought you had a car?'

'It got smashed up.'

'Prosser said you've been letting her drive. Did she do it?'

'It was nothing to do with her. We were rammed.'

'You're getting a reputation as a man who breaks things, Paddy. Bailey is going to kick up a stink about paying for a hotel for those extra days.'

'He doesn't have to. We're not staying in a hotel.'

'Where are you staying then?'

'I'm staying at the Tozers' farm.'

'At Helen Tozer's house?'

'Yes.'

'Oh.' Pause.

'I'm just staying here. That's all. It's convenient.'

'What you do is your own business, Paddy. Why would I care?'

'What's the news?'

'Nothing much. Uniform are up in arms because leave is cancelled this weekend.'

'Why?'

'On account of the Vietnam demonstration at the American Embassy coming up next weekend. You getting anywhere with the dead girl?'

'I'm not sure.'

'So did Tozer invite you to stay at hers? I mean, there's got to be plenty of B and Bs. It's famous for them.'

'We're in separate rooms if that's what you're asking.'

'I didn't mean that,' she snapped.

He dialled again, this time the number of the solicitor whose name he'd found amongst the Sullivans' letters. Afterwards he searched in his pocket for a couple of shillings to put in the tin marked *Phone*.

At the top of the farm, he found a path that led up over the hill, away from the estuary. Helen hadn't returned from going to meet her father so he had gone for a walk alone.

The earth was red and wet. It clung to his boots and doubled their weight. There were still blackberries in the hedgerows but when he reached out, plucked a fat one and put it in his mouth, it was bitter so he spat it out.

It felt good to stretch his legs, though. The slope steepened and the path became slippery.

At the top of the next ridge he hoisted himself up to sit on a gate to get his breath back and looked down towards the farm. He could see the path they must have walked along last night, on their way back from dinner, and the flat dark water of the estuary. The cows were lined up across the green of the field. He could now see Helen behind them, shooing the last ones into the yard for milking, her father lagging behind them.

He looked back up the path, wondering if he should continue. That was when he noticed the rabbit, just a few yards away, squatting down in a clump of long grass at the side of the hedge.

He sat still, not wanting to disturb the animal, wondering how long it would be before it saw him, or smelt him. It didn't move. He remembered how his father talked of snaring rabbits as a child in Ireland. Breen could not remember the details, only that you had to set the trap exactly right. In the couple of years before he had stopped making much sense, he had talked a lot about his childhood in Ireland.

Breen realised his behind was aching from sitting so still, and stepped down. Undisturbed by the sudden noise, the rabbit still sat there motionless. Breen tiptoed closer until he was standing right next to it, close enough to see the thick discharge from its closed, reddened eyes and its slow, laboured breathing. The creature didn't seem to see or hear him; it just sat, ears pinned back against its body, waiting to die.

'You should have taken a rock and killed it,' said Helen, sitting in the kitchen, a cup of tea in her hand. 'It would have been a kindness.'

'Myxomatosis,' growled her father. 'Keeps them down. Best thing that happened round here.'

'Dad,' chided Helen.

When he'd gone back out to the yard, she said, 'When we were little girls the fields around here used to be full of rabbits like that . . . dying. It was horrible. Hundreds of them, there were. Alex sneaked one up to her bedroom once and tried to care for it under her bed, but it died, of course. Dad said she could have caught something from it.'

The solicitor turned out to be an old friend of Julia Sullivan's. His office was in Exeter in a Georgian house on the edge of a small green, with a brass plate on the door worn from polishing, and a dark entrance hall lined with oil paintings.

They had borrowed the Tozers' rusting Morris Oxford to drive up there. The leather seats were dry and cracked. It smelt of sheepdogs and there were stacks of yellow receipts stuffed into the glovebox. Smoke poured from its exhaust.

'I won't shed a tear,' said the solicitor. 'I always thought he was a blackguard.'

His name was Percy Manville and he must have been at least sixty years old. He sounded out every consonant. 'The Metropolitan Police? How very grand,' he said.

He was a neat, thin man with a trimmed moustache who wore a grey suit and waistcoat with a gold watch chain. 'Mallory Sullivan was a spendthrift who squandered all of Julia's inheritance on cars, gambling and idiotic investments.'

An elderly woman in pearls and twinset had placed a teapot with three china cups and saucers on Manville's desk. 'Will you pour, or shall I?' he asked Tozer.

'Oh no. You go ahead,' said Tozer.

'Julia Sullivan, on the other hand, is the love of my life. Always was. Me and half of the county. I was her father's solicitor. Lovely man. Very good bridge player. Dead now, of course. Aneurism on the golf course. Lucky fellow. Best way to go. Sugar?'

'Loads, please,' said Tozer.

'Good girl. I can't play golf any more, unfortunately. Buggered up my back. Agony.'

He poured the tea into the delicate china cups and handed them around.

'Spendthrift, you say?' said Breen. 'They were heavily overdrawn at the bank.'

Manville sat back down in a leather-studded chair and rocked it back and forwards.

'Let me tell you something in absolute confidence,' he said, like a man who enjoyed sharing others' secrets. 'In the summer he marched in and asked me for the deeds for Fonthill. "What for?" says I. Of course, I knew. He was planning to mortgage the place to raise some money. So I told him the deeds were in both of their names and I couldn't just hand them over without Julia's permission. I'd made sure of that when they bought that stupid house. With her money, I might add. Should have seen the look on his fat face. A delight.'

'Did she give permission?'

'I doubt he even told her, frankly. He always did things behind her back. He was terrified that he'd disappoint her.' He picked up the small teacup and lifted it, little finger crooked.

'What did he want the money for?'

'Oh, it's been a long, steady slide. He owes money left, right and centre. I saw him in town the other day. Brand-new car. Some idiot had lent him some more, I expect. Well, they won't be getting it back now, will they? I shouldn't laugh. Poor Julia. It makes me sad to think of it. So is it true she shot him, then?'

'We don't know.'

'Awful, really. Can't say I blame her. Still, it'll be hard on her, I suppose.'

'Why have you got all those handcuffs?' said Tozer, pointing to the wall.

There was a mahogany wall cabinet mounted on the wall. In it were about a dozen pairs of handcuffs, mounted in four rows of three, some brass, some iron, some chrome, all different shapes and sizes, each with a delicate label beneath them.

'I'm a collector, my dear,' said Manville.

'Of handcuffs?'

'He told us he was in London on business a few days before his daughter was killed,' said Breen. 'Do you have any idea what that would have been about?'

'No, no idea at all, I'm afraid. Are you interested in handcuffs, my dear?'

'Only professionally.'

'I have several from the 1800s. All in working order. You can try them out if you like.'

'No thank you, sir,' said Tozer.

Manville smiled, 'They're wasted up there in the cabinet. They'd look lovely on you, I'm sure.'

'No, really, I'm fine, thank you.'

While they were talking, Breen had taken out the photographs of Morwenna standing in her tree house. He pushed them across the table towards Manville.

'Yes. There she is. Poor Morwenna too. An unfortunate girl. Her father's looks instead of her mother's. And his temper too. And dead now.'

'Do you recognise where that photo was taken?'

'That would be The Last Resort.'

'What?'

'That's what Julia called it,' said the solicitor. 'The Last Resort. It was just a glorified summerhouse, really. Beautiful spot up on Dartmoor. It was a kind of artistic commune. Wild parties. Orgies, I expect. She holed up in there with all these bohemians and beat poets. I visited her there sometimes. She was very refreshing, a very poetic person, if you understand me. And then that bore Sullivan came along and elbowed in and the moment they were married he insisted they move into somewhere grander off in Cornwall. He was an arse. He never understood her.'

'She sold it?'

'No, no. She refused. Good for her. But she had to rent it out because they needed the money.'

Afterwards in the car, Tozer said, 'What a sicko. All those handcuffs. What do you think he does with them?'

'He just collects them, I suppose.'

'He's kinky, if you ask me,' she said.

Compared to Cornwall, Devon seemed almost comically green. The lumpy hills and neatly trimmed hedgerows. The prettiness left him ill at ease.

'Was your dad OK after this morning?' asked Breen.

Tozer nodded. 'He said he was checking some cows for mastitis, but I think he was finding some reason that he didn't have to talk to me. I swear he used to talk all the time when we were kids.' She chewed on her sandwich some more. 'Sometimes I find myself wondering if he'd be hurt as bad if it was me that was dead. I'm not sure he would. Alex was his favourite, see?'

'You don't know that.'

'I do,' she said. 'It's always like that, really, isn't it? There are always favourites.'

'I don't know. I was an only child.'

'This the right one?' said Tozer.

Breen looked at the yellow notepaper in front of him that the lawyer had given them. 'According to the map.'

'Funny-looking place.' Tozer peered at it through the trees.

The Last Resort turned out to be tucked away from the road. A chocolate-box wooden house, green and white paint peeling. It sat on the bank above the lane, hidden by trees. They had parked the Morris on the edge of the narrow lane, close enough to the hedge to let other vehicles pass, but only just.

'We should have told Sergeant Block we were coming out here,' said Breen.

'Why?'

'That's what you're supposed to do.'

'This is 1968, sir. There aren't any "supposed to's" left.'

'That's not true.'

'What's the chances we find anything up there, anyway?'

The gate to the footpath that led up to it was not locked; the path was choked with fallen leaves.

'Do you think there's anybody in?'

'Doesn't really look like it.'

The chalet's faded curtains were closed. Breen went to the front door and knocked, then called, 'Hello?'

Nobody answered. He walked round the wooden building. There was a fresh log pile stacked against the back wall in readiness for winter. Lying on an unruly lawn, a fallen tree trunk had been carved into the shape of a Picasso-ish reclining nude, arms stretched above her head.

'No sign of anyone,' said Tozer, face pressed up against a windowpane.

At the rear of the house, a series of water butts gathered rain from the roof, green mould streaking down their sides.

'Well, it was worth a try, I suppose,' said Tozer. 'What now?'

'I don't know.'

'We could go for a drive on the moors. See if we can find somewhere to have a bit of lunch.'

A jar full of paintbrushes stood on a bench, filled with more rainwater.

'Well? What else is there to do? It's not like the Constabulary want us poking our nose into any of this anyway.'

From the back of the house, a pathway led into the woods. Breen was in his brogues. He wished he'd brought a pair of wellingtons from Tozer's collection.

'Where are you going?'

'Just looking around.'

The path was narrow and led to a small stream that cascaded down the hillside. It was dammed. Someone had built a small pool into the surface of the hill, collecting the brown water off the moor. Dark leaves rotted below the surface.

'I expect she used to swim naked here. What do you think?'

She had followed him down the path.

'I imagine her as being the kind of woman who swims naked,' said Tozer.

The path continued up the hill.

'Nobody would see you here,' she continued. 'You could pretty much do as you please. All them orgies that solicitor was talking about, probably.'

Breen followed the path up past the stream, skidding on the rocks and mud in his leather soles. The place was dank and rotten underfoot.

'Oh, wow. There are little sculptures here,' said Tozer. 'Did you see them? They're a bit overgrown.'

Breen was walking up the pathway, about twenty yards away now, in the thick woods. The light filtered down through autumn trees. Something caught his eye among the bracken and bramble that lined the narrow path. Leaning down, he picked up a piece of rubbish that someone seemed to have dropped by the pathway. He unfolded it carefully and held it up to the light.

'Tozer?' he whispered.

She was too far away. 'Oh, Lord. Naked people. Little statues of nudie people dancing.'

'Shh.'

'Nobody's got bosoms that big. Not even Jayne Mansfield.'

'Tozer. Quiet,' he hissed.

'What?'

He held up the piece of rubbish and waved it at her.

Through the branches, she looked at him, puzzled. 'Wait there,' she said, starting to crash through the undergrowth towards him.

He held his finger up to his mouth but it didn't lessen the noise she made tramping through the undergrowth.

'What is it?' she asked when she was next to him.

He held up the wrapper.

'So?'

He pulled out his notebook awkwardly and thumbed through it, then opened the page. 'See?' he said. He held the page book towards her.

'I can't really read that.'

'Rich Tea biscuits,' he said.

Abruptly, she burst out laughing, loudly enough to startle a magpie that flapped up into the tree canopy. 'I'm sorry,' she said.

The shot was not loud, but it felt like it was close. A muffled pop that could have come from yards away.

Tozer's laughter stopped dead. She dropped down onto her hands and knees and crawled to the tree behind which Breen was sheltering.

'It might just have been someone hunting pigeons,' she whispered. 'It might.'

They were pressed against each other. Breen was conscious of the bony warmth of her, her short breaths. After a minute, she said, 'How long are we going to stay here?'

Breen said nothing.

'What if we go back to the car and find a phone? Then call up the Devon and Cornwalls?'

'Like you said, it might just have been someone hunting pigeons.'

'Or rabbits.'

'Right.'

'Want me to go?'

He shook his head, then peered out from the tree. 'You reckon it came from over there?'

She nodded. He stood up. 'Hello?'

No answer.

'Hello?' he called again.

The usual sound of the woodland had reasserted itself. A two-note birdsong. They had heard nobody moving, nobody running away.

He moved forward; the crack of a stick underneath his foot almost made him throw himself to the ground. 'Is there someone there?'

Nobody answered; nobody moved.

'What was that, then?' Tozer finally said. 'I could have sworn that gun was close.'

Gaining confidence, they spread out, peering behind the larger trees, into thickets of bramble. The woods were a long strip of land, maybe thirty yards wide, that stretched around the contour of the hillside. Breen saw small, strange, brightly coloured fungi, orange tentacles forcing their way through the leaves, big blobby pale lumps, small bright red upturned cups. There were small piles of droppings, and the half-eaten carcass of a wood pigeon. The rich smell of rot. But no sign of another person; not even a sign of footprints or broken branches. The biscuit wrapper must have just been a coincidence.

'That was weird,' said Tozer.

Breen wondered if they had imagined it. Or maybe it was some strange trick of the local air currents that had made a distant hunter's shot seem closer than it was; maybe the air really was thicker in Devon.

'I'm hungry,' said Tozer. 'Can we get some lunch?'

They started to retrace theirs steps back towards the pool and the small chalet.

'I thought she'd be here,' said Breen.

'The locals are probably right. She's long gone. We should go. It's starting to rain, I think. I just felt a raindrop.'

They walked back, past the chalet to the car. The key was stiff in the lock, and Tozer spent some time struggling with the door. When she opened it and leaned across the seats to open Breen's door, he noticed some colour in her hair.

'You're bleeding,' he said.

'Where?'

'On your head,' he said, getting in beside her.

She touched the top of her head and brought her fingers down; there was a small smear of redness.

'Here,' he said, pulling her head towards him. There was a little spot of blood in her hair, but no sign of any wound.

'What the . . . ?'

Breen was out of the door, running back up the narrow path past the pond. By the time she caught up with him, back in the woods, he was staring upwards. Twenty feet above their heads was a small tree house, built around the trunk of a tall beech tree.

'My God.'

There were planks across the bottom of the structure. Something dark had made an oval stain on the wood. Slowly, drop by drop, it fell to the ground.

TWENTY-ONE

Breen stamped his feet in the cold to try and get his muscles back under his control.

'They'll be here soon,' said Tozer, looking up at the tree.

'They'll be here soon,' Breen shouted, hoping whoever was in the tree house could still hear.

Walking towards the edge of the woods to try and get a better view of the tree house, they found the Jaguar covered in a green tarpaulin. She had driven it up a muddy track and left it at the side of the field. Breen lifted the tarpaulin; the front driver side light was smashed.

'You think she shot herself when she heard us?'

He nodded. 'I think so. She pulled the ladder up after herself so no one could see she was up there.'

'She's almost certainly dead, sir.'

Breen had nothing to say.

Tozer stamped her feet to keep warm. 'So, what do you reckon? Major Sullivan goes up to London, has some sort of argument with his daughter. Ends up killing her. When we come down here and tell Julia Sullivan her daughter's dead, she figures out he's killed her, takes a shotgun and shoots him and runs away here, because it's a place she used to live with her daughter. Then she shoots herself?'

Breen's neck was aching from looking up at the tree house. 'It's possible.'

'You think it was hearing me, seeing us, that made her do it?'

'I don't know.'

'God. Everything we do is wrong, isn't it?'

Breen didn't answer. The view from here was no better. He walked back into the woods. The blood at the base of the tree house looked black in the dimming light.

Sergeant Block stood below, collar turned up. 'Unbe-fucking-lievable.'

It was almost dark by the time a fire engine had arrived with ladders. The blood had stopped falling a long time ago. On the uneven ground the firemen were trying to wedge chocks under the base of a long ladder to make it steady enough to reach the tree house.

Tozer had fetched a tartan rug from the boot of the Morris Oxford. It was covered in dog hair, but she'd placed it round Breen's shoulders to try and stop him shivering.

'Why didn't you tell me you thought she was here?' said Block.

Breen pulled the blanket tighter round him. 'You know, I wish I had. Then it would have been you here, instead of us.'

'You didn't tell us you were coming down to interview the Sullivans. You turn up there and one of them ends up dead. You didn't tell us you knew where Julia Sullivan was hiding and now she's probably dead as well.'

'I didn't know for sure she was here.'

'You obviously had an idea.'

'She'd still have shot herself the moment she saw you coming.'

Block spat onto the leaves on the ground. 'Maybe I wouldn't have just blundered in without knowing if she was here or not in the first place. If it is her.'

'Move please, gents,' said a fireman, carrying a long coil of rope to the ladder.

They stood back a little way. The fireman slung the rope over his shoulder and began to climb the ladder. It was dark now and another fireman trained a strong torch up to help him see. In the beam of light, the blood on the timbers shone red. At the top of the ladder, the fireman spent what seemed like minutes tying the top rungs to the tree. Breen trod impatiently below. Eventually the man switched on his own torch and put his head up into the trapdoor.

He shone the torch down, dazzling them. 'It's a woman,' he called. 'I should take a look,' said Breen.

'You can read my report. I'll send you a copy. Now get out of here.' Breen shook his head. 'I should see the scene.'

'Don't be ridiculous,' said Block. 'Get out of here, the pair of you.'

They stood a while longer, while the firemen tied pulleys to the tree so they could begin to lower the body down, before Breen turned his back and walked to the car, Tozer following behind.

'Tosspot,' said Tozer, turning on the engine. 'Block.'

She switched on the interior light and leaned across to Breen's seat, her body across his, and pulled down the sun visor. She tried to peer at the top of her head in the vanity mirror. 'Is there blood there? I can't see.'

She flattened her dark hair down onto her head and stretched her eyes upwards, but could see nothing.

'I want a bath.' She released the clutch and the car lurched forward. 'I feel like Lady Macbeth.'

The car shot down the small lanes.

Breen sat, hand gripping the side of the seat. 'He was right, though. We made a mess of it and because of that she's dead.'

TWENTY-TWO

Three in the morning, Tuesday night, the only customer in Joe's All Night Bagel Shop was listening to the music Joe was playing on his gramophone. Tonight he was playing jazz.

'You should find another job,' said Joe. 'Something with a night shift.'

'You're just trying to get someone to replace your daughter now she's had a baby.' Breen read a copy of yesterday's *Times* that someone had left on the counter. It was full of the American election.

Joe took a pull from his tiny rolled-up cigarette and coughed. 'You couldn't even wash up. I wouldn't let you in a million miles of my kitchen anyway. You'd turn the milk sour.'

'My dad was always telling me to get another job.'

'It's best left to the stupid ones. The ones who have no imagination.'

'Is that a compliment?'

Joe snarled. 'Go home to bed. You've got to be up in four hours to go to work.'

The bell over the door rang and a policeman came in. Breen recognised him from several nights before, and he said exactly the same thing: 'Turn that racket down.'

'Talk of the devil,' said Joe, taking the needle off the record.

He took an aluminium teapot off the shelf and spooned tea leaves into it.

'Can I have the key to your bathroom, mate?' asked the constable. Joe took it off a nail by the till and handed it to the policeman.

Breen turned over a page with the headline 'Vietnam may lose Hubert Humphrey the Presidency'; the next announced, 'Nigeria's

General Gowon says "Final Offensive" Will Be Decisive'. He read the article; it was about the Biafran war. It said the general had been trained at Sandhurst. His Federal troops had encircled Biafra, cutting the secessionist state off from the sea. The Biafran advance on the Nigerian capital had been turned back. Instead, the rebel troops had been pushed back inside their own borders. The journalist seemed to think it would all be over in a matter of weeks. 'You know anything about this Biafran war, Joe?' he said.

'Since when have you been interested in foreign affairs?'

'I met a Biafran man. A doctor.'

'Very educated, the Biafrans. They call themselves the Jews of Africa. Though I'm not sure having a persecution complex is enough to make you the Chosen People.'

'The man I met thinks they will win the war. This article here says they don't have a chance and that it will all be over in weeks.'

'Which do you believe?'

'The newspaper, I suppose.'

'There will always be people who say a war will be over by Christmas. We could have stopped it all if we'd wanted to. What happened to your sidekick?' Joe asked Breen.

'Sidekick?'

'That girl.'

'Helen? She's been assigned to another murder squad.'

Breen had not seen her since they had come back to London. All the previous week she had been at Harrow Road Station, working with Sergeant Prosser; an incident room had been set up there to deal with a domestic murder in Kensal Town. She had not called him.

The copper came out of the bathroom and sat at the far end of the counter. 'Got any biscuits to go with that?'

'What happened to that case you were on with her?'

'You're very conversational tonight, Joe.' Breen closed the paper and folded it.

'My daughter said I should try and be more friendly to our customers.'

'Ha.'

'I can be friendly, you know.'

'It's possible that the murderer is already dead.'

'You should be happy then instead of sitting there with a face ache.'

'Should I?'

'You liked her, didn't you?'

'Who?'

'The copper girl.'

Breen shrugged.

Joe looked at him. 'She seemed nice to me.'

'You have her, then. You could do with a woman in here.'

Breen put on his coat.

Joe tutted. 'Expect she'd had enough of you, anyway.'

'Is all this part of your charm offensive?'

'Bugger off home to bed, Paddy. You're like a stone in a shoe.'

The night was cold, the pavement slippery from dead leaves. He walked back slowly, let himself in and switched on the light. His two-bedroom flat seemed unlived in, despite the mess. The living-room floor was particularly bad now, the floor covered with pieces of paper. He missed the cosy domestic muddle of the Tozers' house. The women's things he had never lived with. Lace doilies on shelves. Pictures chosen simply because they were nice. Dried flowers.

He looked at all the mess of paper. The single sheets had turned into piles around the room. Laid out. Organised. Arranged. Rearranged. Some words underlined. Others crossed out. Maps. Lists. Questions. Photographs of Morwenna Sullivan, alive and dead. A drawing he'd made of Alexandra Tozer in her John Lennon hat. Sometimes he moved them deliberately, like a chess player moving his pieces. Other times he shifted a pile randomly to see if it would make any sense in a different place in the room.

Breen tiptoed carefully through the paper and took his place in the chair, surveying his work. He wondered if he should call Constable Tozer tomorrow. A couple of times in the last week he had put his hand on the receiver to call Harrow Road and ask to speak to her, but he hadn't dialled the number. He wasn't sure what he'd say.

From where he sat now, the sheets of paper radiated outwards in circles. On the pile straight in front of the chair was one titled 'Major Sullivan'. There was an empty space between that and another single sheet that said: 'Morwenna Sullivan. Killed 13 October'. He stared at the empty floor space as if waiting for it to speak to him.

'Major Sullivan comes to London, kills his daughter. You have evidence to prove he was here around the time she died.'

'Before.'

'Around. His wife killed him because he killed her daughter. She killed herself because she killed her husband. Three cases solved. You just won the treble.'

They were sitting around Carmichael's desk. Marilyn had said she was on strike, so Jones had lost the toss and had to go out to buy the digestives.

'But what's his motive?'

Carmichael went on, 'Like I said, you don't need one. He's dead. We only need to prove motive if we're prosecuting them for murder. Which we're not on account of you can't prosecute a dead murderer. *Finito. Va bene.*'

'Aren't you even slightly curious about why he killed her? I mean, what had she done that was so bad that it made him want to strangle her?'

'I'm curious about things that matter.'

'Who's stolen my stapler?' said Prosser.

'You should be glad. A man who almost certainly killed his daughter is dead.'

'So what did I say that made her turn round and kill him?'

'Who gives a stick? She's dead too. Listen. Of course I'm curious. I'm also curious about what Marilyn looks like without her jumper on, but it doesn't keep me awake at night. Some things don't bear thinking about.'

'It keeps Jones awake at night,' said Prosser.

Marilyn pretended not to hear.

'You're not going to get on if you get bogged down in cases like that. We've got work to get on with and it doesn't get done by thinking about stuff that doesn't matter.'

'You? Work?' said Prosser. 'Pull the other one.'

Prosser whistled the first four notes to *The Good, the Bad and the Ugly*.

Jones, arriving with the digestives, chimed in with an imitation guitar. 'Wah wah wah.' Prosser pointed a finger at Jones and pretended to shoot him, then replaced his finger in the imaginary holster.

'I've promised myself I'll just have one,' said Marilyn. 'I'm on a diet.'

'You're not having none,' said Carmichael. 'You didn't go and get them.'

'You never go and get them and that don't stop you scoffing half the packet.'

'I never.'

'You do.'

'I do not.'

'Shut up,' said Breen. 'Please.'

Everybody looked at him. He looked around, all of them staring at him. As calmly as he could, Breen stood up and took his coat off the hook.

'Where are you going?'

'Out,' he said.

'Paddy? You OK?'

'Where is he going?' said Bailey, emerging from his office.

Nobody answered him.

'Biscuit, sir?' said Marilyn, holding out the packet.

There was a newspaper shop on the corner of Portman Square. Breen went in to buy a new notebook. He had never gone through so many. His office drawers were stuffed full of them.

A Number 13 bus to Golders Green rounded the corner just as he was coming out, so he ran after it and caught it at the Great Portland Street stop, flashing his warrant card to the conductor as he boarded. Struggling to get it back into his pocket as he lowered himself onto his seat, he almost lost his balance and ended up in the lap of a plump woman with a feather hat.

He rode the bus up until St John's Wood station and then got out and walked west to Abbey Road and then down to Cora Mansions.

He had been away a week, but the flats looked much the same. Miss Shankley was pegging out her washing on her rear balcony. She looked down at him.

'You got him then? And he's dead now, isn't he? So what are you still doing around here, then?'

He looked around him at the London skyline of chimney tops and cranes. 'Just tying up a few loose ends.'

'Loose ends?'

'Yes.' He pulled out the photograph of the major, standing next to his wife. 'Did you ever see him around here?'

'He the man who did it? Quite a handsome man, wasn't he, really?'

'Would you recognise him if you'd seen him?'

'I don't think I've seen him before. What sort of man kills his own child? You can't rely on anything any more. The world is full of all sorts.' She nodded her head towards a figure on the stairs.

At the end of the walkway he turned and saw Mr Rider approaching, a small briefcase in hand. Seeing Miss Shankley and Breen talking about him, he hurried on away.

'Mr Rider?' called Breen after him.

He caught up with him on the fourth-floor walkway.

'What do you want now?' he said.

'I just want to see if you recognise this man.'

'They all talk about me, you know.'

Breen took out the photograph of the major.

'He's dead, isn't he?' said Mr Rider. 'I read it in the papers.'

'Yes.'

'Lucky bugger.'

'But you don't recognise him?'

'People are laughing at me. Sniggering like schoolchildren behind their backs.'

'Do you recognise him?'

'No. Now please leave me alone.'

The rest of the afternoon Breen spent buttonholing anyone on the streets. People shook heads. Tutted. Nobody recognised the major.

The next day at University College Hospital, Prosser and Breen watched as Wellington prodded charred flesh.

'Any other clues?' asked Breen.

'He's still dead, I can tell you that.'

Skin on the torso had been roasted till it was black, tightening around his body to become almost shiny. Extremities had been burned clean away. Lipless, his teeth seemed unnaturally white. His left arm and other bones sat in a pile at the other end of the slab. The dead girl, Morwenna Sullivan, would be taken away to be cremated soon, thought Breen. No friends or relatives had come forward to reclaim her body. The man in the fire was the same; nobody had noticed he was missing either.

'I'm not sure what else you want me to find, Paddy.'

'I was just thinking maybe he was worth a second look.'

'This is pointless, Paddy,' said Prosser. 'Wellington's got better things to do.'

'Not much else to go on. The fire must have been hot. These bones –'Wellington pointed to his exposed upper arm – 'where they were exposed by burning, have fractured in the heat. Are you sure you don't need a bowl, Paddy?'

'No. I'm OK.'

'Apparently you had a little vacation with a lady officer.'

Prosser snorted.

'I wouldn't call it a vacation, exactly.'

'Quite the talk of the station. Have you seen much of her since you've been back?'

'Can we just hurry it up?'

'Whatever you say.' The pathologist picked up a fragment of bone. 'I can't find any evidence of trauma that would indicate that he was killed first and put in the fire second. Not that he's exactly a perfect specimen.'

'Too damaged by the fire to be sure?'

'Yes. But then we found this melted into the skin of his lower abdomen.' He held up a twisted bottle, melted in the heat; a swirl of opaque glass, shattered at the neck, fused with pieces of ash and stone.

'He's a no-fixter, right, most like?' said Prosser.

'My guess is he was probably roaring. Covered himself in newspaper in there to keep warm. And it did keep him warm, after a fashion. There was a can of lighter fuel on the floor too. He'd probably squirted it at the fire to get it going.'

'What about the clothes?'

'Ah yes. Oxides of calcium and silicon. Lots below the knee.'

'What's that?'

'Concrete dust to you. His trousers were thick with it.'

'Builder maybe?'

'I'd say so.'

'Height?'

'Hard to be exact. Five foot six to five foot eight, I'd say,' said Wellington. 'He's in bits. It'll take a while.'

'Age?'

'Thirties. Maybe twenties. What are you going to ask next? Eye colour?'

The man had no eyes left.

'Not much to go on, Dr Wellington?' said Prosser.

'No.'

'Breen's probably wasting his time on this one. What you reckon?'

'That's your call, Sergeant.'

'Poor bastard,' said Prosser. 'It shouldn't happen to anyone, should it?'

'Amen,' said Wellington.

They left Wellington putting the pieces of the man back into plastic bags. As they walked along the dark corridor to the stairs, Prosser said, 'Don't get me wrong, I respect you not giving up on this one.'

'And?' said Breen.

Prosser put his hands in his pockets. 'Don't be like that, Paddy. I'm just offering a word of advice. I've been around. You know. I've been on D longer than you. I'm a survivor. I know the way things work. Don't waste your effort on jobs that nobody's going to thank you for.'

Breen nodded. These were the silent rules Prosser understood. Not the regulations that Bailey always tried to enforce, but the rules by which things really worked. A nod and a wink. The regular you-scratch-my-back-and-I'll-scratch-yours that Breen never felt part of. It was why he never trusted Prosser, and why Prosser didn't like him. But there was no point in rubbing Prosser up the wrong way. 'How's that murder in Kensal Town?' he asked.

'Open and shut. We got the husband. You OK to walk back to the station? Only, I have something I have to do.'

'Constable Tozer OK?'

'She's keen, I'll say that. Bit mouthy. She'll be one of the boys in no time at all.'

Breen doubted it. He still hadn't called her. He hesitated, then said, 'I was thinking maybe of going up to St John's Wood High Street one day, to have a look around at Martin and Dawes. Where you were stabbed. You want to come some time? I could do with a lift.'

Prosser shook his head angrily, looked away. 'There you go again,' he muttered.

'What?'

'You're wasting your effort. It's my case. I'm looking after it.'

'I thought if I was there I might notice something I hadn't on the night. I was tired. Or I might remember something.'

'I remember you legging it clear enough.'

'I want to have a word with the shopkeeper too. He might have heard something.'

'What are you trying to do, Paddy? Piss me off? I thought we were just starting to get along again.'

'I just thought I might—'

Prosser stopped suddenly in the corridor. 'Look. You made a cock of it that night and I almost got killed. You made a cock of it arresting the wrong bloke in the murder of that girl by Abbey Road. You made a cock of it down in Cornwall by all accounts. Don't you start making a cock of my cases too, OK?'

And he poked Breen hard in the chest.

'OK?'

Breen stood in the lobby looking out through the swing doors. Rain was falling hard outside. Prosser had driven off with his rain-coat. As he waited for the rain to ease off, he noticed a man he recognised standing in a corridor to his left.

'Mr Ezeoke,' he called.

Ezeoke's head turned. He frowned, as if at first the surgeon did not recognise him. He was in conversation with a dark-haired woman of about thirty who wore a lime-green minidress and a gold necklace. Ezeoke towered over her.

'Detective Sergeant Breen,' Breen said, holding out his good hand to Ezeoke in case Ezeoke did not remember him.

'You look pale, Mr Breen. Is there anything the matter with you?'

The woman smiled. 'A detective, Sam? You've not been doing anything you shouldn't?'

'Always,' said Ezeoke.

Breen turned to the woman. 'Mr Ezeoke was helping me with an investigation.'

Ezeoke smiled. 'Where is your eager young assistant today? Have you had any luck tracking down the killer of that poor girl?'

The woman said, 'A killer? Sam, what are you involved in now?'

'We think her father may have killed her,' said Breen. 'Mr and Mrs Ezeoke's house is close to where the body was found,' he said to the woman.

'My God. Why didn't you tell me about this, Sam?'

The surgeon looked down at his feet and nodded his head. 'Her father? How terrible.'

'Yes.'

'Have you arrested him?'

An orderly walked past, pushing an empty trolley. 'Unfortunately he is dead too. He was killed by his wife.'

'How terribly Shakespearean,' murmured the woman.

Ezeoke looked past Breen. 'I am glad of that. All the same, you must be pleased to have solved the crime.'

'I'm not sure I have.'

Ezeoke smiled. 'Does that bother you, that you are not sure?'

'Of course.'

'Really? Perhaps it should not. There are many crimes that go unpunished. Why should another one make a difference? You can only do what you can do. I am a doctor. I cannot save everyone.'

'Of course it makes a difference,' said Breen.

'Behave, Samuel,' said the woman.

'Forgive me if I seem hardened. Or cynical even. I am an African. There are many, many crimes against Africans that have gone unpunished. Crimes that are happening right now. Do you care about those too? Or just the ones that happen in your own jurisdiction?'

'The officer is just trying to do his job. Samuel is a revolutionary.' She smiled. 'He loves to get on his high horse about African politics – don't you?'

'I am sorry,' said Ezeoke. 'It was not a fair question. You must forgive me.'

'And how is your war?' asked Breen. 'I read an article saying that the government troops were making advances.'

'The Federal army have been conducting a major offensive, but their gains are only temporary. Their lines of supply are very vulnerable to attack. We will see them beaten back soon.'

'The Federal troops are committing atrocities, Mr Breen,' said the woman. 'Children are being starved to death. Tens and tens of thousands. It is mass murder. If you're interested, you should come to our fund-raiser. We should invite him, Sam.' She reached into her shoulder bag.

'My good friend Mrs Briggs helps me fund-raise,' said Ezeoke.

She handed Breen a gilt-edged card. In copperplate script, it read: *The Pan-African Committee for a Free Biafra invite you to a Dinner Dance. Donations will be accepted*. There was an address of a club in Soho.

'Mrs Briggs. You were dining with Mr Ezeoke on the Sunday night?'

'How did you know that?'

'Because I told him,' said Ezeoke. 'In case he suspected me of the crime. After all, I am a black man. Who knows what atrocities I am capable of? Mr Breen is a policeman, Frances. Which means he couldn't possibly make a donation.'

'Well, he should come anyway,' said the woman. 'Support the cause. We'll make a revolutionary out of him yet.'

Ezeoke smiled. 'Mrs Briggs is an enthusiastic supporter of Biafra. She wants to convert you too.'

'Are you married, Mr Breen?' asked the woman. 'Do please bring your wife. Or a girl. We have an awful lot of men but not enough women. There will be dancing. Not just boring British dancing. African dancing. It's very exciting.'

'Come, Mr Breen. You would be welcome,' said Ezeoke.

'By the way, have you had any more problems with your neighbours?' Breen asked.

'I have not invited them, if that's what you mean, though I'm sure Mrs Briggs would like to. She would invite the whole world.'

Breen returned from work one evening to find that the drain outside his front door had blocked, filling the space at the bottom of the stairs down to his flat with rainwater. It had seeped in through the door, ruining the brown carpet in his hallway.

He spent the evening moving furniture and pulling the sodden carpet up off its tacks and stacking it outside. A box of his father's books had been sitting in the hallway since he had moved in. Those at the bottom were sodden. A copy of Keats's *Complete Poems* with his mother's name written on the front page in a fine cursive. A thick-looking James Joyce. He put them in the dustbin outside. It felt good to be doing something physical.

He looked around the flat and realised that he had done nothing to the place for years. Perhaps it was time to redecorate, anyway. He should rip out the old brown carpet and maybe paint the floorboards. Bring a bit of colour into the place. Some modern furniture. Start over again.

Later that evening he watched television, eating tinned spaghetti and sardines from a tray on his lap.

He slept well too, dreamlessly, and woke so late he had to run for the bus.

Bailey was standing there in the middle of the office, looking at his watch as he walked in. 'Glad you could join us, Breen. Anyone seen Prosser? This isn't a holiday camp.'

'Package for you, Paddy,' interrupted Marilyn.

The package was covered in eight 4d stamps and done up so well with Sellotape that he had to go and find a pair of scissors to open it. It was from Detective Sergeant Block of the Devon and Cornwall Constabulary: a report of their findings into the murder of Major Sullivan and the suicide of his wife. There was a thick bundle of roneoed documents, photographs, carbon copies and transcriptions. As far as Breen could see it was thorough and efficient.

Breen read the covering letter. The shotgun Julia Sullivan had killed herself with was the same one that had killed the major. There was no doubt at all that she had been the killer. 'Given the fact of her husband's presence in London close to where Morwenna Sullivan's body was discovered, confirmed by the Road Traffic Violation Notice issued on 13/10/68 at 4.30 p.m. [8849/88/1168], we believe it highly likely, without wishing to prejudice the investigation by the Metropolitan Police, that Major Mallory Sullivan was responsible for the death of his own daughter.'

A photograph of the traffic notice was there in the bundle of papers. Breen leafed through them. There were copies of the major's bank statements, which showed considerable sums of money entering and leaving his account, but no explanation of what it was the major had done for a living.

He pulled out the photograph of Julia Sullivan's body, lying on the floor of the tree house. Labelled '886M/88/1168', it was overexposed, the flash too bright for the small cabin. The white of her skin was snow-like, the blood merely a thin grey. Her head, or what was left of it, was propped against the wooden wall. Her legs lay awkwardly, one tucked under the other. A half-eaten loaf of bread and two bottles of vodka lay on the floor beside her, alongside a pile of unopened packets of Rich Tea biscuits.

And all around the walls of the tree house were photographs. Breen opened his drawer and pulled out a large, old-fashioned magnifying glass. They appeared to be photographs of children, dozens of them, held up by drawing pins. A boy and a girl. Almost certainly her son and daughter, both dead under awful circumstances, both of whom she had outlived, but not by very much.

Tommy Nutter Suits from £12 19s. 6d. Drip-dry shirts in stock. Lurex – The Latest Top Gear 59 shillings. The shop window was crowded with signs, handwritten on white card.

Breen stood outside, looking in. There was a plain blue shirt with a button-down collar. It was not his usual style, but maybe he should start to move a little more with the times. He went inside to see if they had it in his size.

'Got it in a fifteen-and-a-half. That do?' said the man in the shop. He was smartly dressed in a pinstripe suit with wide lapels and flares, and a pink shirt with a high collar.

'Are you Martin or Dawes?' asked Breen.

'Both,' said the man. Parted neatly on the side, his hair was slicked down with Brylcreem.

'What?'

'Martin Dawes. I just thought it sounded better if I was two people. Martin and Dawes. That's me.'

Breen pulled out his wallet and pulled out two pound notes and his warrant card.

The shopkeeper took a look at it and said, 'What? You expecting a discount?'

'You were broken into on a Monday night a while back?'

'"Broken into" makes it sound like they had to try.'

'What do you mean?'

'Like I said to the other coppers. They didn't break in. Someone opened the doors.'

Breen remembered wondering why the shop's back door was open, yet apparently undamaged. *Ask about the doors.*

'Have you got the buggers, then?'

'Not yet.'

The man nodded. 'Well, there's a surprise. I stopped by Hoxton Street market on Saturday. There was a guy selling my suits there. Cocky bastards, they hadn't even bothered to take my labels out. Why should they? None of your lot are going to do nothing about it. You want a tie with that?'

'Did you call us to let us know? We would have pulled him in.'

The man laughed and set to wrapping the shirt. 'Course you would. Tell you what, though. One of your lot did OK. He stood up to them. Got himself stabbed, I heard. Hold on. That wasn't you, was it?'

'No. It wasn't me,' said Breen.

'At least he put up a fight. Other guy ran off. Typical. I don't know why we bother paying our taxes.'

Breen took his change and picked up his shirt. 'So you've not met him at all then, the copper who was stabbed? He hasn't been in here since?'

He shook his head. 'I'd shake his hand and tell him thanks for trying, at least. Unlike the rest of you. Couple of uniform blokes came in the day afterwards. That's the last I've heard of until you turned up.'

'No phone calls or anything?'

'Not a dickie.'

Breen wrote down his name and a phone number. 'Let us know if you see any more of your suits going on sale, will you?'

The man ignored the card, leaving it on the counter.

'Got a nice V-neck jumper that will go a treat with that shirt if you like,' he said.

He took stairs two at a time now. Panting, hand on the brass railing, he met Constable Tozer on the way down. She was carrying a mug full of tea in one hand and a rock cake in the other.

'Hello,' they both said.

'How've you been?' he asked, getting his breath.

'OK. Busy. You know.'

'You've cut your hair.' It was shorter than before. The sides now barely covered her ears, giving her an even more tomboyish look than usual.

She moved her head to the left, then the right to give him a proper view. 'The girls say I look like a feller.'

'I like it,' he said.

'Thanks.'

'You still at Harrow Road?'

'All done there now. How's the shoulder? Getting better?'

'Pretty much.' Stilted conversation. The familiarity they had had when they were away together had gone.

'You going to court tomorrow to watch Pilcher?'

'What's that?'

'The John Lennon thing. He's up for sentencing for that drug raid.'

'Are you going?'

'Might do. Bunk off. Never know, might get an autograph.'

'Mind you don't get into trouble.'

'I don't care.' She grinned. 'All the hippies are saying Pilcher probably planted the drugs anyway, and it's not too unlikely, let's face it. It's sick.'

A throng of uniformed men came barging down the stairs. 'Oi, oi, Helen,' one of them said. 'Coming round my place later?'

'Bugger off.'

'Mind you don't spill your tea, love.'

When they'd gone, she said, 'Any luck with your man in the fire?'

'He was a dosser, Wellington reckons. So does Prosser.'

'What's Prosser got to do with it?'

'Bailey put us both on to it. Trying to knock our heads together, I think.'

'Prosser's still mad at you, you know. He came into the section house last week calling you a . . . name.'

'What name?'

'A prick, if you want to know.'

Breen smiled. 'I hardly see him. He's never around. Always off on some business. I don't ask.'

'He's been visiting his son, I expect. He's not been well.'

'His son? I didn't know . . .'

'A spastic. He don't talk about it, but everyone knows. He pays for him and everything. His wife looks after him. His ex, I mean. He's still got the police flat, though. I don't think he's told them. That way he keeps it to himself.'

'I never knew.'

She nodded. He put his foot on the next step up.

'What about the girl?' she asked.

'Nothing new. Sometimes these things just grind to a halt.'

'I know.' The hardness in her face again.

'Of course.'

They both stood there, waiting for the other to move on. Police men and women came and went up the stairs. 'It's an awful shame. Do you think her father did it?'

'I don't know. I don't suppose we ever will.'

'That's the way it goes, isn't it? Well,' she said. 'My tea will be getting cold, sir.'

'Yes,' he said, and went on his way, up the stairs. When he got to the office he kicked himself for not having the balls to invite her to come to Ezeoke's party. In case she said no.

Not knowing where to go next with Morwenna Sullivan, he concentrated on the unidentified man, walking around the building sites in the neighbourhood where the body was found. 'You want to come?' he asked Prosser.

'No. You're OK.'

'Everything OK with you?'

'Why shouldn't it be?'

'I heard your son was ill.'

'Mind your own fucking business,' said Prosser.

Not for the first time, London was being built by the Irish. The men Breen met on building sites were young and muscular, still brown from a summer under the English sun.

'No. No one gone missing from here,' they'd say automatically, not meeting his eye.

They were nervous of the police, unwilling to talk. Only when he told them he was trying to find the identity of a dead man did they start to open up.

'Anyone gone missing?' said a young man from County Offaly. 'Sure. We've all gone missing – haven't we, boys?'

As a teenager he'd asked his dad for summer jobs working on the building sites. His father had always refused. He hadn't wanted him mixing with these men.

He was standing at the bottom of a block they were creating as part of the new Abbey Estate. A tower of concrete rose upwards; a spine onto which the flats were being attached, like ribs to a backbone.

'Is there anyone from this site who's been missing since October the second?' he repeated, above the churn of a cement mixer.

Heads were scratched. The workforce was often a fluid one. Men would leave if they received a better offer from another foreman. Or they would simply disappear.

'Joey, maybe.'

'No, Joey was in yesterday. He had busted his toe,' said a man with a voice that sounded much like Breen's father's. 'That's why he'd gone a bit quiet.'

'Are you a Kerry man?'

'God sakes no. I'm from Cork.'

'Close.'

'That's libellous talk.' The man's smile showed broken teeth. High above them a crane dangled a great wing of precast concrete.

'Detective Sergeant Breen. Is that an Irish name?'

'My father was from Tralee.'

'And you're a policeman now? Oh God. There's hope for us all.'

He wanted to say his father had been a builder too. Instead he asked, 'How big is this one going to be?'

'Eighteen floors,' said the man. 'Four flats on each floor. Seventy-two homes on as much land as it takes to keep a horse.'

'If it was you, Spanky, you'd take one of those flats and keep a horse in it too, I expect.'

'Now how would I get it in the lift?'

'What about Paudie?' said another voice.

'You could lure it in with a lump of sugar.'

'Paudie? No. He's working over Hammersmith this week, I believe.'

239

'Working? When did they start to call what Paudie did work?'

'It would have to be a fuckin' big lump of sugar to get a horse into that tiny lift.'

'Is it a missing man you're after looking for?'

'We have found some remains of a man. We can't identify him.'

'God there. That's no good.'

'Poor bastard.'

Breen nodded.

'And you think it may be an Irishman?'

'Maybe.'

'Why not? The odds are great, I would say.'

The Cork man took off his red woollen hat and rubbed his thinning hair. 'The unfortunate truth of it is, nobody would really mind a fuck if any of us went missing, 'cept for the publicans,' and he spoke with such a sudden sadness in his voice that all the big men around him were quiet for a second.

Until one of them said, 'Speak for yourself, you cunt.' And they all started laughing again, louder than before, as if they were all really having a great time.

For a while he stayed there and watched the crane swing the huge hunks of concrete skywards. He wished he had asked his father which buildings he had made. It would have been good, seeing them still standing and knowing that his father had built them.

That night he pulled out his father's address book. It had lain untouched for the last couple of years in the drawer beside his bed. It was a small one, the black leather worn and cracked, bought from Boots years ago. His father had been a quiet man; he had not had many friends. Though he had worked with them on the building sites, he had not liked the younger Irishmen who had arrived in waves in the '50s. He had thought them too loud and wild.

The entries were made in his neat, elaborate handwriting, learned in some small schoolhouse in Kerry. Some names, those with whom

he'd lost touch or who had died, had been crossed out. A couple
of those Breen recognised he copied into his address book; his
handwriting was so different from his father's.

TWENTY-THREE

There was a crowd pulsing around a light grey Bentley. A surge of people trying to get close to the man at the centre of the crowd. A burst of flashbulbs going off as a young man with long hair lifted his head a fraction. A babble of voices.

He spotted Tozer on the stairs leading up to the front entrance and pushed his way through the crowd towards her.

'This is horrible,' she shouted above the racket.

A ring of police helmets showed above the rest of the crowd. Somewhere in the middle was the pop star, making his way slowly to the waiting vehicle, a tiny dark-haired woman in a fur coat that made her look even smaller clinging to him.

'Do you feel you've let your fans down, John?'

'Were you set up?'

'John?'

'Down with the pigs!'

It was a short walk from the steps down to the waiting vehicle, but the police could not get through.

'Over here, John.'

'Since leaving your wife, have things fallen apart for you?'

Men in macs with notebooks pressed forward against the flow. Others holding Leicas and Hanimexes above head height were hoping to snatch a photo.

'Come on now, give us some room.'

Cars slowed to watch the goings-on. Others, behind them, honked, trying to get past. Idle passers-by craned necks.

'John! We love you!'

'What a farce,' said Tozer.

They stood on the steps of Marylebone Magistrates' Court, looking down on the crowd. Breen hadn't been able to squeeze into the courtroom it was so full. Tozer had been there early and seen it all.

'What did he get?' Breen shouted in Tozer's ear.

'Magistrate fined him one hundred and fifty, plus twenty guineas costs.'

'Not much, then. Carmichael must be hopping mad. And Pilcher too.'

'They were. Should have seen their faces. Here he is now.'

Carmichael came out of the courtroom looking sullen. 'All right, Paddy?' A group of fans stood on the steps near them, teary-eyed.

'His girlfriend had a miscarriage on account of all this,' said Tozer.

'What's that?' said Breen.

'They said it in court. That Japanese girl Lennon is going out with. She had a miscarriage because she was so upset by it all.'

'Her fault for hanging around with a druggie, then,' said Carmichael.

'He looks smaller in real life, doesn't he?' someone said.

'He looks scared silly.'

'Pilcher just wanted to nail him, that's all.'

Carmichael looked at Tozer. 'He broke the law, darling.'

'She lost her bloody baby, they said.'

'He's a pop star. He's got millions of pounds. He drives a bloody Rolls-Royce for God's sake. People like him would say anything to get off. People like him . . . It's one law for him, another for the rest of us.' Breen had never seen Carmichael so angry.

There was a bunch of fans still trying to get close to Lennon. Breen pointed at them. 'Who are they?'

'That lot? They're the scruffs,' said Tozer, craning her neck.

'Scruffs? Who are the scruffs?'

'They go round everywhere. Camp out on their doors. Rich daddies, mostly.'

'You couldn't tell by looking at them, though.'

Breen looked back towards them. They were the ones wearing sheepskin coats and screaming, 'John!'

The pop star had made it to the car now. They were struggling to close the door behind him. The car started moving through the crowd even before the door was properly closed.

A girl in a Doctor Zhivago coat leaned forward and kissed the glass of the window.

'He's spoken for, love.'

'Stupid cow.'

The Bentley moved slowly through the crowd until it was free of them, and as soon as it was gone, merging with the traffic on Marylebone Road, people started to move on.

'There,' said Tozer. She dug into her handbag and pulled out a photo. It was the photo of the three prizewinners that Tozer had brought from the Beatles Fan Club.

'It's Penny Lane. Look.'

Breen took the photo out of her hands. He looked at the photo of the three girls. 'This why you came?' he shouted over the noise.

'Partly.'

He could feel his face break out into a grin. She had not given up on the girl either. By the time he looked back at the girls who had been pressed against the car, the one from the photo was now walking past with two friends. Tozer was right; it was the girl in Miss Pattison's photograph.

'Excuse me,' Breen called out to them.

'What?' The girl must have been about seventeen. She was long-haired and wore a lot of eye make-up.

'I just want to ask you something. I'm a policeman.'

'Go away,' she said and walked on, her two friends beside her. They all dressed the same. All three wore sheepskin coats; each carried a large, bulging, cloth shoulder bag. One had a camera around her neck.

'No. Wait.'

He walked after them, but they walked faster.

'Please. I just want to ask you some questions.'

The three girls broke into a run, shoes clattering on the Marylebone paving. Breen sped up too, almost enjoying loosening the muscles for the first time in months. The girls barged their way out of the crowd, down the pavement.

'Penny Lane!' called Tozer.

Breen soon lost sight of them, but he could tell from the startled expressions on pedestrians' faces that they weren't far ahead. The girls all wore sandals with big heels. He would catch them easily as they wove their way through the crowd.

He caught them up faster than he thought he would. The one who'd called herself Penny Lane stood with her friend at the corner of Balcombe Street next to the fallen body of a third girl. She was lying on her back, eyes wide, panting and whimpering.

Breen pushed past the other two and knelt down. A crowd of shocked pedestrians stood on the pavement watching, doing nothing. The driver of a Peugeot 204 pulled up in the middle of the traffic said in a loud voice, 'It wasn't my fault.'

'Where did the car hit you?'

'Leg.'

He took her hand. 'Can you squeeze my hand?'

'Get off her,' screamed Penny Lane, kneeling down beside him, trying to push him away.

'It's all right,' said a woman's voice. 'He knows what he's doing. She needs looking after.' Breen looked up. Constable Tozer had followed and was leaning down beside them.

'Can you wiggle your toes?' Breen asked.

The girl did, but burst out crying from the pain. She clenched Breen's hand hard. Mascara dribbled down the side of her face.

Tozer always seemed to have a handkerchief on her. She handed it to the girl, who took it with her free hand and scrunched it into her eyes.

'Get an ambulance,' said Breen to the man in the Peugeot. 'I think she's broken her leg.'

The man, who wore a sports coat and a tweed cap, hesitated a second, about to object, then walked off. Traffic was backing up on the main road now, horns starting to sound. Someone offered a coat. They laid it over the girl.

'Don't worry,' said Tozer, kneeling down beside her. 'It'll be all right.'

'Don't worry, Carol,' repeated the other girl. Short curly hair, face rounder than Penny's.

'Why did you run?' Breen asked the girl who'd just spoken. 'I only wanted a chat.'

'My bloody leg,' whispered the injured girl, through pale lips. ''Cause you're police. Obviously.'

Breen nodded.

'Hospital's only just over the road,' said Tozer. 'Ambulance will be here any sec. Detective Sergeant Breen here knows the place well. He's in there so often they give him Green Shield Stamps. Swears by it.'

'Back again? You're a liability, you are.'

Breen recognised the nurse who had been there when they had set his shoulder.

'Not me this time.' He thumbed backwards towards the side room where the injured girl was being treated.

'What's she mean?' asked the girl with the short curly hair.

'Detective Sergeant Breen was recently injured in the line of duty,' said Tozer.

'Serves him bloody right.'

'You didn't have to run. He only wanted to ask you a question.'

'He didn't have to chase us. Are we in trouble?' The girls huddled together, leaning against each other.

'No.'

'Don't say anything, Fi.'

The injured girl was being examined by a doctor while they waited outside, sitting on hard plastic seats.

'What was the question?'

'Shut up,' said the other girl.

'Who's your favourite Beatle?' said Tozer. She took out a packet of Polos.

'You chased us to ask us that?'

'Go on. Who's your favourite?' She unwrapped the mints and offered them to the girls. They both shook their heads.

'I wouldn't tell her. She's a copper.'

Tozer laughed. 'Don't tell me then.'

'George,' said Penny Lane.

'Mine too,' said Tozer.

'Really?'

'You like George?'

'Yes. Detective Sergeant Breen here is a Paul McCartney man. Mint, sir?'

'Never,' said the curly-haired one, who seemed to be called Fi.

'No. I really do like George.'

'Fibber.'

'Test me.'

The girl bit her nails for a second, then asked, 'What was the first song George ever wrote for The Beatles?'

'"Don't Bother Me". It was on *With The Beatles*.'

A pause, then the girl with short hair whispered something in the other's ear.

'Come on. I'm waiting.'

More whispering, until: 'Who played banjo on the soundtrack disc he's just released?'

'Peter Tork from The Monkees. Rubbish, in't it?'

'Yeah.' The girls both laughed.

The short-haired one said, 'I been to George Harrison's place.'

'You never. Inside?'

'Have so. He invited us in one time when we were outside and it was weeing down. He's nice. He made us tea.'

'What's it like?'

'Fabulous. He had a chair that hung from the ceiling.'

'You lucky cow.'

The girl smiled. She nodded at Breen. 'He really a Paul McCartney fan?' she asked.

Breen shrugged. Tozer wrinkled her nose. 'Not really, no.'

'Thought not. He's a square.'

'Hear that, sir? You're a square.'

Breen said, 'You quite done now?' But he was smiling at her when he said it.

'You won that "Hey Jude" competition that the Beatles Fan Club ran,' Tozer said to the girl with the long hair. 'Penny Lane.'

The girl's mouth dropped open. 'How did you know that?'

Tozer pulled out the photograph of the three winners again. 'Miss Pattison gave me this. I tried to find you at the address you gave. That squat. But the people there said you don't live there any more.'

The girl wrinkled her nose. 'That dump was horrible. The toilets don't work.' Then, 'Oh my Christ. This is about Morwenna, isn't it?'

Breen reached inside his jacket pocket and pulled out the photo of Morwenna Sullivan. 'You recognised this picture when you visited the Beatles Fan Club, didn't you?'

The girl took the picture and stared at it, then looked at him suspiciously. 'Why do you want to know?'

Breen turned to the other short-cropped girl, Fi.

'What about you? Did you know her?'

'I'm not saying anything.'

They were suddenly quiet again. Nurses walked briskly past in sensible shoes on the work-grey lino.

'You see,' said Breen, 'Morwenna was murdered last month. Possibly by her own father. We don't know why. We're trying to find out. If you can tell us anything at all, it would be really helpful.'

'God.'

'God.'

And they held each other's hands, squeezing them tight.

Eventually the one who'd called herself Penny Lane said, 'Well, we knew her, yes. But not that well.'

'She was just around a couple of times.'

'Quite a few times.'

'When you said she was around,' said Breen, 'around where?'

'The Apple shop mostly. And EMI sometimes.'

'The Apple shop?'

'The boutique. In Baker Street,' said Tozer. 'You know. That shop with the big wizardy mural thing on the corner of Paddington Street. Went bust after six months.'

'We all got some clothes when it went bust. Did you?'

'No,' said Tozer. 'I was on bloody duty that day.'

'It was a bit of a riot, wasn't it?'

'What did you get?' Tozer asked.

'I got a shirt. It was a men's shirt. Don't really fit me. I give it me brother but he says it's too like what a wog would wear for him.'

Breen said, 'What about the girl?'

'She was just around. That's all.'

One girl said, 'She was a George girl, wasn't she? I saw her outside George's a couple of times, I think. You should ask Carol. She's the number one George girl. She knows all the George fans.'

'Isn't the girl who was knocked over just now Carol?'

'That's Carol-John. She means Carol-George.'

'Everyone's got their own Beatle.'

'What do you mean?'

'There's Sue-Paul and Sue-John, for instance. She's Sue-John –' the short-haired one pointed to her friend – 'because she's a John girl.'

The girl nodded solemnly.

'Carol-George. Haven't seen her for a bit.'

'Where's the best place to find her?'

'Where do you think?' she asked.

'Kinfauns?' said Tozer.

The girls nodded.

'She's always there. A bit weird if you ask me. She never goes anywhere else,' said Sue-John.

'*She's* a bit weird? What about you? You sleep outside John and Yoko's flat.'

'Not every night, though.' She pulled out a packet of Juicy Fruit and offered one to Tozer. She took one. 'You want one?'

'Who's Kinfaun?' asked Breen.

The girls burst out laughing.

'Kinfauns. It's the name of a house.'

'George and Pattie's house.'

'Pattie?'

'George's girlfriend.'

Breen shook his head. 'So, what? You just wait outside their houses?'

The girl nodded. 'Or the recording studio, yes.'

'Why?'

The girls looked at him like he was from Mars.

'Because they're the Beatles.'

A nurse emerged from the room where they were putting a plaster cast on the broken leg of the injured girl. 'You lot still here?' she said.

'How is she?'

'She's not going anywhere today. Do you have her parents' telephone number?'

Breen asked, 'How do I find out where George's house is?'

'I thought you were a policeman. You knew everything. Bet she knows where George's house is.' She nodded at Tozer.

Tozer looked at the ground like a bad schoolgirl. 'I might do.'

The other girls laughed. 'See?'

Tozer took out a packet of Bensons.

'Can I have one?' said the short-haired girl.

'Me too,' said the other, taking her chewing gum out of her mouth and attaching it to the underside of her chair.

'Do you want to go in now?' the nurse asked the two girls.

They left the girls with their injured friend. The lift was at the end of the corridor.

Breen and Tozer stood by it, waiting for the doors to open. Once the lift came close, only to disappear down to the basement.

'Let's take the stairs.'

'I'm in no hurry to get back to the nick,' said Tozer.

When the lift finally arrived and the doors opened, Frances Briggs was standing there, clutching an expensive-looking handbag in one hand and examining her face in a make-up mirror that she held in the other. 'Well, if it's not the detective. Going down?'

They stepped into the lift. 'Back with us so soon?'

'Just delivering a patient.'

'Nothing serious, I hope?'

'Nothing serious.'

'And will you be coming to our shindig on Saturday, darling?'

'Well . . .'

'Oh, don't be shy.'

'I'm not sure if you really need any more single men, by the sound of it.'

'Well then, bring a friend.' She looked from Tozer back to Breen.

It was only when they got out onto the Marylebone Road, where a horse-drawn dray was patiently trotting slowly along, forcing the traffic to crawl slowly behind it, that Tozer asked, 'What was that lah-di-dah in the lift saying?' They walked across the road, making their way between the honking cars.

'Would you like to come with me?' Breen asked.

'Is there a party? How super. I'm game for any shindig, darling.'

'Shut up.'

'Don't be shy, darling.'

He stopped, mid-traffic. 'Do you want to go?'

'Are you asking?' she said.

'It would be useful,' he said, thinking that might be an encouragement.

'Useful?' She frowned. 'You want me to go to a party? To be useful?'

'It's Ezeoke's party. I'm only going because of the case.'

'Useful?'

Why did he find it so difficult to come out with it and ask her to the party? 'I haven't been to a lot of parties in the last few years.'

'You surprise me,' she said, walking on ahead.

Had he always been so bad at this? he wondered as he walked back across the road to the police station.

TWENTY-FOUR

In Hammersmith, Breen tiptoed through the mud to the wooden
shed at the back of a building site. He wished he had worn different shoes.

'Come in,' said a voice when he knocked on the door.

The foreman sat behind a desk in a wooden hut crammed with
filing cabinets and map chests. The makeshift room was heated to a
fug by a pale green paraffin stove.

'God there,' said the man. 'You look the very spit of him.'

Breen wiped his shoes on a newspaper on the floor. His father
had always insisted he had his mother's looks.

John Nolan wore a brown jacket over blue overalls; he stood and
came towards Breen to take his hand and shake it. 'I'm very pleased
to meet the son of Tomas Breen.' A rough hand, like his father's
used to be before the old skin softened. 'Take a seat. Just move them
papers.'

Breen sat on the wooden chair opposite the desk.

'It is terrible news. I would have liked to come to the funeral if
you'd have told me.'

'I'm sorry. I should have called you before.'

'I understand, of course. You had things you had to do.'

That felt like a reproach.

'But he was a great man. Very, very respected.' John Nolan opened
the drawer of a filing cabinet and pulled out a bottle of Bell's and
two glasses.

'Was he?'

'Naturally. Doing what he did for us, you understand.'

'What do you mean?'

Nolan offered a cigarette. 'Your father was the man who gave me my first job in the building trade here in England. He gave a great many of us our first job. I hadn't seen him for years. I wish I had kept in touch with him, but when he retired it was as if he disappeared.'

The man was awkward now; he fiddled with a yellow pencil, flicking it from hand to hand. 'And educated, so. He could quote from every one of the works of Shakespeare, you know.'

'Yes, I know.'

He poured two glasses and gave one to Breen, then raised it solemnly. 'Tomas Breen. A great man,' he said, chinking his glass against Breen's, then downing it in one.

Breen did the same; the alcohol scalded his throat.

'I am a Kerry man myself. To men like me who came over here, it was a pleasure to find an Irishman who knew the way things worked. He took us under his wing. He knew how to look after us. We all knew Tomas Breen. There's not a ganger in London who wouldn't have spoken respectfully of him.'

At home, Breen's father had been quietly dismissive of the Irishmen he worked with. They arrived by the boatload, desperate and uneducated, carrying dreams of sending fortunes home. Many of the gangers treated them badly, keeping them in beer but paying them a pittance. The English hated them and put up cards in their windows: *No Blacks, No Irish*. 'Ignorant bogtrotters' his father called them, but Breen never knew whether this was part of wanting to put his son off a manual trade. His father had imagined Cathal as a doctor, a scientist or an academic of some sort.

'You must be feeling the loss still.'

'I am,' said Breen.

'He would have been proud of you,' said the foreman. 'You being a policeman.'

'You would think so,' said Breen.

Nolan looked around fifty, his skin darkened from the work

outdoors. 'He was, I am sure of it. He raised you on his own, did he not? A remarkable thing.'

'He did. My mother died when I was young.'

'Of course. We knew that, but he didn't talk about it a great deal. That was a terrible loss to him. And he too proud to accept help from the Church.'

Somewhere outside a piledriver started its regular thumping.

'My father didn't think much of the Church.'

'No, he did not,' the foreman said. 'But I'm sure St Peter will forgive him that on account of his goodness. He had reason, naturally.'

'What do you mean?'

Nolan looked wary. 'On account of what happened to him and your mother.'

Breen frowned. 'What was that?'

The foreman paused. He picked up the glasses and put them back in the cabinet, unwashed. 'It's of no importance. You said on the phone you were trying to find the identity of a missing man.'

Breen took out a notebook. Nolan crossed to a grey filing cabinet, pulled out a sheet of paper and handed it to Breen.

'It's a worksheet. If you're a foreman you fill one in for each week. Payday on Friday.'

Breen looked at the name on the top of the sheet. Patrick Donahoe. The worksheet consisted of seven boxes, one for each day of the week. The sheet was headed, 'Week commencing September 30 1968'. The boxes marked Monday and Tuesday were ticked but all the rest were blank.

'I asked around like I said I would. It's a small world. You only have to be in London a couple of years and you know everyone on the building sites. That's the name I came up with.'

'Where was he working?'

'Paddington. Not so far from where your man was found.' He pointed to the worksheet. 'As you can see, he didn't come in on the Wednesday. They thought it must be because he had a sore head. It was his birthday, you see, on the Tuesday.'

There was a calendar on the wall advertising a plant-hire company. A topless girl sat uncomfortably astride a blue moped in November's picture. Somebody had circled her nipples with a biro.

'But he didn't come in on the Thursday either and they haven't seen him since?'

'That's right. And he's never been in to collect his wages.'

'Do you have any record of an address for him?'

'I do. He was a first cousin of the foreman there from back home. They had took him on here as a favour to his father.'

'Have they contacted his father to ask if he's been in touch?'

'Naturally. And no. I'm afraid he has not.'

'How old was he?'

'It was his twentieth birthday. And they bought him a bottle of whisky to celebrate it.'

'A bottle?'

'Yes.'

Breen said nothing, but took down the man's father's address.

'They said he was a nice fellow too.'

'And was he in the habit of going missing?'

'They are all missing men, after a fashion. They should be at home looking after the farms and chasing girls, but instead they're here building flats and getting drunk.'

Halfway back across the building site he stopped. The mud was almost up to his socks.

'You should have worn boots,' said a man in a flat cap.

'Bugger off.'

The slow regular thud of the piledriver seemed to shake the ground he stood on. But instead of heading forward towards drier ground, he turned back through the ooze, towards the foreman's hut again. Mud sucked at his feet. He could feel the moisture seeping into his socks through the gap around the tongues of his shoes.

A second time he opened the door to the shed. Nolan looked up. 'Did you forget something?' he said.

'You were going to say something about what happened to my mother and father.'

The man's face stayed blank. 'I said it wasn't important.'

Breen picked up the newspaper and wiped the mud off his leather shoes. 'If it's not important, what is it then?'

The man changed tack. 'If he hadn't told you, he didn't want you to know.'

Breen balled the dirty newspaper up and threw it into a bin, then started on his other foot with a fresh sheet. The man took a cigarette from his shirt pocket, offered one to Breen, who refused it. 'I'm not sure it's my place to say, if he did not tell you.'

'My father is dead.'

'Yes. But I would like to respect his wishes.'

Breen sat in the chair in front of Nolan's desk. 'Respect my wishes. I have no relations. My parents are both dead. No one to tell me if you don't.'

'True enough,' said the foreman. He sucked on his cigarette a minute, blew smoke out through his nose, then said, 'So you don't know why your father and mother left Ireland?'

'Because he hated it. He thought it was a backward place.'

'Maybe so. But there was more to it than that. Your mother was a schoolteacher in the local village. She was ten years older than him, a married woman herself. She fell pregnant by him. Did you not know any of this?'

'No.'

'Can you imagine the ruckus?'

'I didn't know any of it. Only that they were in love.'

'When you were born, it would have been a terrible scandal, of course. The Church wanted to take you into an orphanage and raise you so they could brush the whole episode under the carpet. The stink it would have caused in a little place like he came from.'

'I never knew.'

Nolan stubbed the cigarette out and immediately lit another. 'Your mother's husband was a dry old stick. He worked on the railway, I believe. There was no such thing as divorce, of course. And so they eloped with you to England.'

Breen tried to imagine his quiet father leading such a daring, romantic life, but could not.

'She died not long after they were here. You wouldn't remember her, I don't suppose?'

'Sometimes I think I remember her. I'm not sure though.'

'You would have been only one or two, I think. Maybe three. I'm sure she's been there, looking after you. Of course the Church offered to take you in again. But your father would have none of it. He thought them a bunch of lousy hypocrites for the stink they caused in the first place. So he raised you on his own. And looking at you, he did a very fine job of it, I would say.'

'He never told me any of this.'

'I don't think he was proud of taking another man's wife. I don't think he was proud of having a son out of wedlock. He was a very proud man, Tomas Breen. He was very proud of yourself too. He talked about you all the time at work, you know. "Cathal has done this", "Cathal has done that".'

'He did?'

'Of course he did. A fine boy like you.'

Breen looked into the older man's eyes. There were little pale crescents below each pupil, veins in the yellowed whites. Breen would have liked to believe the foreman was not just saying this out of kindness.

A workman in a donkey jacket knocked on the door and threw it open. 'Someone's only gone and put diesel in the big cement mixer. The engine's jiggered.'

'Jesus. I'll be along in a minute,' Nolan called. 'Leave us alone a second.'

Breen stood up to go. The old foreman shook his hand warmly. 'And now somebody else's son is dead. I hope you find the truth of it. You'll excuse me for saying that most of the police in England could not give a one-legged fuck for another dead Irishman.'

★

'No,' said Bailey.

'This lot, they're girls, sir. Sixteen, seventeen years old. They're not going to want to talk to me. If I had Constable Tozer with me . . .'

'Firstly, there is no need,' said Bailey. 'We know who killed Morwenna Sullivan.'

'I've turned it over and over, sir,' said Breen. 'I can't see how Major Sullivan could have done it.'

'Secondly, there are plenty of other lady police constables. CID is not a matchmaking agency, Sergeant.'

Breen stood in front of Bailey's desk, blinking. 'What, sir?'

'You heard what I said. Any woman constable will do perfectly well.'

'Tozer really understands this world, sir.'

Bailey quivered as he spoke. An old branch about to fall from an older tree. 'It is not our job to understand their world. This is precisely why . . .'The older man looked him in the eye. Breen stared into the pale flecks around his iris. 'Precisely why I've been opposed to women officers doing men's work all along. Any more questions?'

'Bugger that for a game of soldiers,' said Tozer, when Breen told her what had happened. 'Miss the chance to be outside George Harrison's house on official business?'

'Why don't we go at the weekend? You wouldn't be on duty then.'

'You really don't like breaking the rules, do you?'

'Saturday?'

'I can't do tomorrow. One of the women in A4 is getting married. A bunch of us promised to go shopping with her. I can't imagine anything worse.'

'Sunday then?'

'Sunday and Monday I'm on shift. How about Tuesday?'

'OK. See you then.'

'What about the shindig?' she said.

Breen looked at her. 'Are you coming? I thought . . .'

'After you said I could be useful, how could I refuse?'

Breen wondered if he had time to go to the barber's before the party on Saturday. On second thoughts, maybe he should let his hair grow a bit.

He was looking around for a constable to drive him to the building site in Paddington when a car drove into the car park at the back of the station, high speed, siren blaring, breaking to a halt behind the back door. Carmichael leaned out of the window of the Escort. 'There you bloody are. Jump in.'

'What's going on?'

'You seen Prosser anywhere?'

Breen stood on the stone stairs that led up to the main police building. 'He's gone out somewhere. He didn't say where.'

'Never mind. Get in.' Carmichael reached back and opened the car door.

'Why?'

'Just get bloody in.'

Breen got in the back. Jones was behind the wheel.

'Go, Batman,' Carmichael ordered Jones. Jones floored the accelerator and the car roared onto the road, siren wailing, cars scattering to left and right. On Seymour Street, Jones braked to let a schoolteacher anxiously herd a crocodile of schoolchildren off a zebra crossing, then accelerated past.

'What's happening?'

'Surprise,' said Carmichael, leaning backwards from the front seat.

The car zigzagged between a lorry and a motorbike. 'Out of the way,' shouted Jones.

'Tell me.'

'Like I said, surprise.'

Breen pressed himself into the back seat, feet wedged against the base of the seat in front. 'Slow down. What's the hurry?'

'Don't be a girl,' said Jones.

'You've got blood on your collar,' Breen said to Carmichael.

'Where?' Carmichael turned and pulled down the sunshade on the passenger side and examined his pink-striped shirt. There was a splodge of blood on the right point. 'Shit. So I have. I'll never get that out.'

'Soak it in vinegar when you get home. That's what my wife does,' said Jones, sawing in and out of the parting cars, heading south down Great Portland Street and across Oxford Street.

'Relax,' said Carmichael. 'It's a bit of fun, that's all.'

Jones switched off the siren. 'That's better.'

They swung right into Wardour Street and then cut back to the bottom of Berwick Street where the market was just packing up. Jones pulled up behind another police car.

'Come on,' said Carmichael.

Breen got out, clammy from the speed. The air was heavy with the scent of discarded meat and vegetables from the market. A man was hoicking unsold sacks of potatoes back into a Morris van. Another was stacking up cages full of budgerigars. A radio playing pop music full blast was blaring from another stall.

It was a narrow shop, unoccupied, windows blacked out what had once been a cobbler's. Some street trader used it now for storing his groceries. Cardboard boxes of tinned tomatoes were piled against the wall. There were stairs at the back. A uniformed policeman was sitting on the bare stairs, smoking a cigarette. 'Is this one of the fellers?' he asked.

'This is him.'

'Enjoy yourself,' said the copper, shifting to one side to let the others pass him on the stairs. 'Give the bugger what he asked for.'

Breen pushed open the door at the top of the stairs. 'Ta-da!' said Jones, like he was presenting an act on a stage.

A small room, probably a bedroom once. The pink-rose wallpaper was old and stained. Pinned to the wall was a picture of Jayne Mansfield sitting on a bed in a white fur bikini.

Tied to a chair was a Chinese man. Breen recognised him straight away. He was the man who had threatened Prosser and him with a knife at the clothes shop; the man who Breen had run from. The Chinaman was bleeding from his lip and there was an ugly cut under his right eye. Snot and blood bubbled from his nose and had stained his light blue shirt and brown nylon trousers.

'We saved his legs for you,' said Carmichael, holding up a cricket bat. 'On account of you won't have to run so fast next time if you break his.'

Breen looked back at Carmichael, and Jones, hopping up and down behind him like a child.

'Joke. Seriously, though. Don't hit him too hard. Just a bit of fun.'

'How did you find him?'

'Fridays this Chink runs a clothes stall in Berwick Street outside. You know that shopkeeper from St John's Wood High Street? He was down here this morning and spotted this bloke selling Italian suits of his. They've still got the bloody labels in and all. Martin and Dawes. He called you up this morning, only you weren't in. Don't know where he got your number from. Anyway, Marilyn took the call and passed it on to Jonesy here. Bingo. Picked him up a couple of hours ago. What's up between you and Marilyn, by the way? She called you a miserable piece of shit. I thought she always had a thing for you. This is the fellow, isn't it?'

'Yes, that's him,' said Breen.

'Go on then, give him one,' Carmichael said, pushing the end of the bat into his belly. 'They should learn you can't go round threatening coppers with knives.'

Breen kept his hands by his side. 'Where's Prosser?'

'Tried to reach him but I think he's off with his son somewhere. He takes time off on the sly. Everybody knows, but it's OK. Don't you worry, he'll have his turn.'

Carmichael prodded him again with the cricket bat. 'Go on. Take it.'

Breen grasped the bat, but didn't move. 'Give me ten minutes alone with him.'

'What's wrong with you?' said Jones. 'You windy?'

The Chinese man didn't even look scared, he just looked tired. Above his temple, there was blood caked in his black hair. His brown nylon trousers were torn at one knee, and there was something unpleasant about the way the little finger on his left hand was twisted. He looked Breen in the eye sadly.

Breen tried to remember him with the knife in his hand, threatening Prosser. He tried to replay the scene in his head. Him bursting into the back of the shop; Prosser standing there with the Chinese man; the Chinese man wielding the knife. 'Give me ten minutes,' he said again, weighing the bat in his hand.

'Can't we watch?' said Jones, disappointed. 'I found him, after all.'

'Come on.' Carmichael tugged his arm. 'Leave Paddy alone.'

They left the room and closed the door behind him. Breen stood there holding the bat, looking at the Chinaman. The man looked at him resignedly, knowing what to expect.

'Let's talk,' said Breen, putting down the bat against the wall.

The man looked warily at Breen for a second, then shook his head. 'No talk.'

'Yes talk,' said Breen.

'Go hit me. I don't mind. You can hit me. I am not afraid.'

'No,' said Breen. 'I don't want to hit you.'

Breen sat down on the floor, his back against the floral wallpaper. The Chinaman looked puzzled.

'I want you to start telling me what really happened the night I found you filching coats in St John's Wood High Street.'

'You were afraid.' The man giggled. 'You very afraid. You run away.'

'That's true. What else?'

'I don't understand.'

'I want to know what was going on.'

The man shook his head, becoming agitated now. 'Hit me. It's OK.'

Breen shook his head. 'I'm not going to hit you.'

'I was stealing clothes. I'm a bad man.' The man smiled. 'You and Sergeant Prosser caught me.'

There was a singing in Breen's ears. 'So you know Detective Sergeant Prosser, then?'

'I don't know anything. I was just a stupid Chinaman. I got out my knife. "Come near and I kill you." You run away like a little rabbit.' He giggled again. 'That's all. Cross my heart.'

'You're not a very good liar,' said Breen. 'Why was the back door open? The door to the shop. There was no sign of a break-in. Who opened it for you?'

'You must hit me, please.' The man was starting to sound increasingly desperate.

Breen stood and walked over to him. He laid the cricket bat on the floor and started to untie the sash cord that bound the man's wrists.

Breen stepped out into the busy street still holding the cricket bat. A pair of kids were sitting on an old armchair that someone had chucked out, listening to a transistor radio. Louis Armstrong sang 'What a Wonderful World'. The copper put out his cigarette on the pavement and smiled. 'All done in there?'

Leaning against the police car, Carmichael said, 'Shall we fetch him and take him down the station, or are we going to wait for Prosser to have his turn?'

'What's left of him,' smirked Jones.

A white-haired man dressed in black, with a sandwich board that read *Repent ye evil doers for the Kingdom of the Lord is at hand*, joined the crowd that stood watching the policemen.

'I let him go,' said Breen.

'You let him go?'

'Out the back. He's long gone now.'

Carmichael opened his mouth wide. Neither of them seemed to know what to say. A blast of music came from an open window from one of the flats above them.

Jones said, 'You absolute blinking tosser.'

'Can you drop me back at the station now, or shall I make my own way?'

'I got him in for you and Prosser. I got him in.'

'Paddy. That man, he's the worst sort,' said Carmichael woundedly. 'He stabbed a copper. And you let him go.'

'Prosser'll be bloody mad with you. He stabbed Prosser in the arm and you let him bloody go.'

'I expect he will be mad with me, yes.'

'I can't believe you did that,' said Jones. 'You're ridiculous, you fucking Irish arse.'

Carmichael looked puzzled and said, 'What's going on, Paddy? What are you doing?'

The small crowd pressed round the group of policemen, curious to know what so many of them were doing here in their street. Carmichael stood, frowning.

Jones said, 'You've really lost it,' and pushed angrily through the crowd, back to the police car.

TWENTY-FIVE

Tozer had suggested they have a drink before the party. 'Dutch courage. Where shall we meet?'

Breen had opted for the York Minster in Dean Street, a known hang-out for writers, artists and painters. It was a smug little bar that celebrated its own eccentricity; there were cartoons of French politicians on the wall, and the barmen refused to serve beer in anything other than half-pint glasses, all of which made it the sort of pub where the police would never drink. Which was why Breen chose it. He didn't want to be in a police pub this weekend, around policemen talking police gossip.

Tozer was not there when he arrived, so he took a stool by the bar, within earshot of a fat man who was talking to half a dozen listeners who laughed at all his jokes. A couple of elderly queens played chess in the corner, ignoring the noise, each with their elbows on the table in front of them.

It was a Saturday night. The pub was full, the air so rich already you could hardly see from one side of the small room to the other. He caught snatches of conversation. A man in a tweed jacket with arm patches telling another man, 'In the next ten years we're going to see worldwide mass starvation. Believe you me.' 'Judy Garland,' said a short fellow with a quiff. 'So drunk she couldn't get her coat on.' A man holding hands with a young woman who wore a blue felt hat said, 'What about Kettner's?' She pulled her hand away and said, 'You know I hate Kettner's.'

Tozer arrived at 8.30 and said, 'Double brandy. Sorry I'm late. Why are you only drinking a half?'

Breen had never noticed her wearing full make-up before. Blue eyeshadow and pinkish lipstick. She had dressed for the occasion, wearing a knee-length green frock and heels that Breen thought looked too feminine on her, though he said, 'You look nice.'

'Do I? I feel ridiculous. I never wear dresses. I didn't know what the code was for a shindig. The girls made me buy it today. You look nice yourself. That shirt suits you. It makes you look younger.'

The blue shirt he'd bought from Martin & Dawes. He should buy more new clothes, he thought.

The pub was crowded, so Breen offered her his stool to sit on. She shook her head and stood. She leaned over towards him so he could hear above the noise and said, 'There was talk this morning at the section house. About you.'

'My ears were burning,' he said.

'They were saying you'd gone mental again yesterday.'

Breen nodded.

'Why are you smiling? It's serious.'

'I'm not smiling. I know it's serious. I can't help it.'

'What's going on?' she asked.

'Jones had arrested this guy for a robbery, but he hadn't charged him yet. I let him go.'

'So he was innocent?'

'Not exactly.'

'What then?'

'I was doing Prosser a favour.'

'By letting the guy who stabbed him go?'

Breen paused. 'Sort of.'

'I don't get it.'

'Can we leave it just for now? I don't want to say. Not yet.'

'You still don't trust me, do you?'

She was wearing earrings too. Small silver birds that hung from each ear.

'I do.'

'No you don't.'

267

'You think everything is about you just being a policewoman, don't you?'

'You're not going to tell me why you let that guy who stabbed Prosser go, are you?'

'No.' He paid for her drink and another half-pint.

'Well, you keep it all to yourself, then,' she said. 'Keep it all bottled up in there.'

'I will.'

'One day you'll go really mental. Really, really mental. You'll explode.'

'Are you Sigmund Freud now?'

'It's no wonder you don't have any mates.'

'I do have mates.'

She laughed. 'Who exactly?'

'Carmichael for one.'

'I see more of him than you do.'

'What do you mean?'

'None of your beeswax. So when did you last meet up with your great friend outside of work?'

He tried to remember. 'The last few months have been different.' She made a face.

He said, 'And I'm out with you, aren't I?'

'Aren't I the lucky one?' She took too big a gulp of brandy and then burst out coughing until Breen slapped her on the back. 'Went down the wrong way,' she said when she'd got her breath back.

'Maybe this party isn't such a good idea.'

'Sorry, Paddy. I'm in a bad mood. All day shopping for clothes in Oxford Street. Give us another brandy and I'll be nicer. What's that white stuff they're drinking? Maybe I'll try that.'

He turned back to the bar, trying to attract the attention of the barman who was filling a tray with glasses of Pernod.

She made a face after the first sip, but after the second she decided she liked it.

★

The basement of the St Moritz was already full by the time they arrived. The crowd was mostly black, but there were a few white people there. There was loud African music, full of drums and spiky guitar lines. A long table down one side of the room was piled high with food that included a big bowl of rice with unfamiliar looking meat in it and a large pot of dark brown stew. Breen peered in. 'Groundnut stew,' said a voice next to him. 'It's very spicy. Very delicious.'

Breen recognised Mrs Ezeoke; she held out her hand to him.

'I didn't know Sam had invited you,' she said. She was wearing a loud pink-and-gold floor-length African dress with a matching cloth headwrap.

'He didn't. Mrs Briggs invited us.'

Breen noticed how Mrs Ezeoke's smile disappeared at the mention of her name. 'Are you a friend of hers?'

'No. We just met her at the hospital . . . She gave us tickets.'

At the end of the table was a large silver bowl, full of coins and notes. A sign read: *Donations*.

'And you have brought your policewoman friend. How nice.' Mrs Ezeoke held out her hand to Tozer. The African woman wore a thick bangle on her wrist. It looked huge next to her small hand. 'You look very pretty, my dear,' she said to Tozer.

'I love your bracelet,' Tozer said, fingering the metal. It was a heavy piece of patterned bronze. Breen wondered how drunk she was already.

'Thank you.'

'And your dress is fabulous,' Tozer went on. 'A British woman would never dare wear anything so gorgeous. Where did you get it?'

Mrs Ezeoke's smile remained fixed. 'I think you have met Mr Okonkwo?' she said.

Breen recognised him as the man they'd met at the Ezeokes' house; older than the Ezeokes, a short, wiry man holding a plate of food.

'Ah, the detective. We meet again. Did you find your murderer?' He laughed.

Mrs Ezeoke was not the only woman there in traditional dress. Every black woman in the small club was wearing voluminous bright clothes and elaborately folded headdresses. A few were dancing together, holding one hand up in the air, shuffling their feet around in circles.

A young black man in a suit approached. 'You are much too thin. Eat, eat. We have plenty of food. You need African food,' he said to Tozer. 'Have you ever eaten jollof?'

Tozer laughed. 'I need a drink first.'

Okonkwo said to Breen, 'Do you think it strange to see us dancing while our brothers are fighting a war?'

'What are you raising money for?'

'We must convince the politicians and the journalists of our cause. We must let them know about the crimes being committed by the Federals and by the British. Money helps change minds.'

'British crimes?'

Okonkwo smiled. 'Don't look so shocked. Even the British are capable of crimes. Our Biafran people are being systematically starved to death by an army that your government is supporting. Even in the Second World War the women and the children were spared. Not in our war. You are supplying an army that is creating a total blockade. It is indiscriminate warfare. Their original intention was to kill us all. Now they have found a way to do it with the world's approval.'

There were banners on the wall: *God bless Biafra – Free Biafra – Biafra ga adi ndu!! – Biafra win de war!!* Balloons hung from the ceiling.

'But I am sure you are a good man,' grinned Okonkwo. 'You would not support this. Your government keeps you ignorant. Nobody in Britain has heard about how tens of thousands of our Igbo people have been slaughtered in the north by the Moslems, urged on by the Federals. And when people are ignorant, a word is worth a thousand guns.' He paused and looked at the dancers. 'Although not everyone agrees. They would rather just have the guns.'

Breen spotted Ezeoke on the dance floor, in the middle of a circle of women, dancing with one hand on his belly and the other in the air.

'I am sorry. You are a policeman. You are not interested in politics. Come and sit with me while I eat,' said Okonkwo. He took a chair against the side of the room. Breen looked around for Tozer, but she was still talking to the young African man, so he found a seat beside Okonkwo under a large handmade red, black and green flag, fixed to the wall with drawing pins.

'I do not enjoy parties any more,' said Okonkwo. 'I am too old. The music is too loud and you can never hear people speak properly.'

It was hot. Condensation ran down the walls. Behind the bar a middle-aged woman hoicked the tops off bottles of beer and laid them out on the counter.

'And tonight is to raise money for the Pan-African Committee for a Free Biafra?'

'It was Mrs Briggs's idea. She believes that all causes must throw parties.'

'She is on the committee?'

'She is a friend of Ezeoke's. Her husband is the Senior Registrar at the hospital. She is the Secretary, of course. I am the Chair and Sam is the Treasurer. It helps to have someone respectable on board.' He smiled. 'And she is in love with Sam, of course.'

Breen looked around for Frances Briggs. She had been standing by the entrance, welcoming guests, but now she was on the dance floor with the others.

'You are an art dealer, I seem to remember,' said Breen.

'Art, artefacts, antiques. I sell the culture of Africans to Europeans. It is very fashionable. And to men like Sam Ezeoke, who want to become more African.' He laughed.

'How could Ezeoke be more African?'

'You see? It works.'

'What do you mean?'

'I am sorry. I am teasing you. You did not know that Ezeoke was raised in Britain? That is why he is my best customer. I sell him African paintings and African masks so he can become more African.' Okonkwo was picking at his plate of food, taking delicate mouthfuls.

Tozer came by with two bottles of beer and handed one to Breen. 'Don't thank me,' she said. 'My admirer over there bought it.' She turned and waved to the young man in the suit. Breen raised a hand in thanks.

'How come Ezeoke was raised in England?'

'He was adopted. His father was a chief, a friend of the British Colonial Governor. He died before Ezeoke was born, and his mother, thinking she was doing her child a service, asked the Governor to adopt him. So he did. They took him to England to civilise him. He went to Rugby and Cambridge. We grew up hunting snakes and birds,' Okonkwo said. 'He hunted foxes. Why do you think he is the most successful man amongst us? You English adore a black man who talks the Queen's English. They wouldn't let an ordinary African man become a consultant in your hospitals.'

'He doesn't talk about it.'

'He does not advertise it. He did not have a happy childhood. He once told me he did not even know he was black until his parents sent him to an English boarding school. Can you imagine not knowing what you are? That is why he is desperate to be African. Can you blame him?'

'How terrible.'

Okonkwo looked at Breen. 'You have sympathy for a man who feels out of place?'

'I suppose I do,' said Breen. He watched Ezeoke, bending at the knees, descending lower and lower as the others danced around him.

'He is a great man. This committee would be nowhere without him. He has given more to the cause than any of us. Of course, he was much richer than any of us to start with.' He laughed again. 'But perhaps he won't be soon. He sold his house for the cause, you know. I don't think his wife has quite recovered from it.'

'I wondered. When we visited them they had far more packing cases than seemed to fit into the house.'

'I shall have to be careful of you. You are a very observant young man.'

Breen looked across the room. Mrs Ezeoke was standing by the food table still, watching her husband buying drinks for a large crowd, passing the bottles around to eager young men. Her arms were folded, a look of intense disapproval on her face. 'Mrs Ezeoke. She was born in Biafra?'

Okonkwo smiled. 'Oh yes. She is African. One hundred per cent. Sam wanted to be African, so he went and got an African wife. My niece, you know.'

'She is very beautiful.'

'Isn't she? The most beautiful girl in the world,' said Okonkwo.

Now Tozer was on the dance floor, led there by the young man she had been speaking to earlier. The young man's face remained serious as he danced, his motions much less effusive than Ezeoke's; Tozer danced around him like a teenager on *Ready Steady Go*. Ezeoke was wiping the sweat from his forehead, grinning, as five women danced around him. One of them was Frances Briggs, who danced closer than the others, pushing her body against his.

'See. Now he is a very modern African,' Okonkwo said drily.

Breen looked around to find Mrs Ezeoke. She was leaning against the wall, glowering at her husband as he danced with Mrs Briggs and the other women. Breen looked from one to the other: Frances Briggs flirting with Sam Ezeoke while his wife watched. Ezeoke saw them looking at him and broke away from the dance floor, pushing through the tightly packed crowd. He leaned down towards Breen. 'Your girlfriend is a good dancer,' he shouted.

Breen said, 'She's not my girlfriend.'

Ezeoke reached down and took Breen's arm. 'Why are you talking to this old man? You don't come to parties to talk. Come and dance with her.' He took Breen's left arm and yanked him up, away from Okonkwo.

Tozer was grinning broadly, sweating on the dance floor. 'I didn't think you could dance,' she said. The brass and drums were deafening. Compared to this, Irish dancing at the Garryowen looked like croquet.

'What was Eddie Okonkwo talking to you about?' Ezeoke leaned in towards him.

'You,' said Breen.

'His favourite topic of conversation.'

'He admires you.'

Ezeoke began to dance as Breen stood woodenly on the dance floor. 'He was telling you that I was not a true Biafran, I expect.'

'He said you were raised in England.'

'The mother country,' he said, unsmiling.

A cheer went up from the Africans as a new record started. 'Do you like high-life music?' shouted the dapper young man dancing with Tozer. Above the polyrhythmic tumble of guitars and drums Breen could hear a chorus singing in a language he did not understand.

'Be careful of Okonkwo. He is a wily old devil,' said Ezeoke. 'Come on. Dance. I will teach you.' He took Breen's hands and started to pull him one way and then the other.

'You don't like him?'

Ezeoke was shouting so Breen could hear, but the words were indistinct. 'Of course I like him . . .' Ezeoke talked on, but his words disappeared into the roar of voices and the pulse of the music around him. The dance floor was full now with people jostling for space, bumping into each other, not seeming to care. If it had been sweaty before, the air was now thick. Breen's shirt stuck to him.

Breen had hardly ever danced. He tried to follow the movements of the Africans, making small, quick movements with his feet, but despite their encouraging shouts he was conscious of looking absurd. He tried copying Tozer's wild gyrations, but that was worse. He caught sight of Okonkwo grinning from his seat at the side of the small room. Was that an encouraging smile, or was he laughing at him?

Frances Briggs was leaving the dance floor. Breen followed her.

'Are you enjoying yourself, Mister Policeman?'

'This is not like any other fund-raiser I've been to,' he shouted above the music.

'It's not exactly a village fete, is it?' She laughed. 'The Biafrans are marvellous people. Africans still have the connection. It's like being set free. You should do it more often.'

'Do I look like I need to be set free?'

'Oh yes. I suspect you're terribly like my husband. Very English and correct. And dull. He just sits in the corner looking awfully uncomfortable. And he doesn't approve of politics. I don't invite him to our parties any more.'

'I'm not English,' he said. 'I'm Irish.'

'You've no excuse at all, then.' She picked up a gin and took a gulp. 'Come on and dance.' She took his arm.

'I don't think so.'

'Don't be boring.' She was dragging him into the dance floor again now.

He was saved when, with a loud bang, the amplifier blew a fuse. The music stopped abruptly, the lights snapped off, and the room was filled with a giant groan of disappointment. The dancing wound to a halt.

'There will be a short interval,' somebody quipped in the darkness.

'Someone go fix the gen.' A laugh.

A girl's abrupt scream was followed quickly by a slap and a shout: 'E netulum aka! Keep your filthy hands to yourself, old man.'

'Give me a kiss!'

'Go away. The darkness does not stop you being ugly.' An even bigger laugh.

A couple of people found their lighters and dark faces shone in the blackness.

'Blackout. Now I am homesick.' More hilarity. More matches lit.

They stood there in the thick, sweaty darkness, waiting for the lights to come back on, jostling for space, until someone started to sing a slow, solemn song.

'All hail Biafra, land of the rising sun,' came a rich baritone. Voices joined in. 'We love and cherish.'

Soon the whole room was filled with singing. In the dim light Breen could make out a young man with diagonal scars cut into his forehead raising his arm in a stiff military salute. Breen watched eyes stream with tears, damp cheeks that shone in matchlight. 'We have vanquished our enemies, all hail Biafra.' Voices quavered. Harmonies thickened the song. Men reached out and held hands with other men. Breen looked over towards Okonkwo. In the darkness he could just make him out too, standing, almost shouting the song. 'We have emerged triumphant from all our foes.' And Ezeoke, holding Frances Briggs's hand, chin jutting out, chest full, crying like a child as he sang.

Afterwards, the party moved outside onto Wardour Street, where Ezeoke handed Breen an opened bottle of beer. Still hot from the nightclub, women fanned themselves with leaflets about the war, men leaned against the shop windows and smoked cigarettes. The amplifier had blown. The music was over. After the singing, the atmosphere was subdued.

Breen found Tozer talking to Mrs Briggs.

'Of course it's a real photo,' she was saying, 'The boy is starving.'

Tozer was holding a bottle of beer in one hand and a leaflet with a photo of an African child on it in the other. She had kicked off her heels and was standing on the pavement in her bare feet. 'If he's starving, how come his belly is so big?'

'Have you heard of kwashiorkor? It is one of the few West African words to have entered the medical dictionary,' Mrs Briggs said. 'It says something that while we make Africans learn Shakespeare, all we take from them is a word like this. It's from Ghana. It's a type of starvation. You should get Sam to explain why it leads to the distended belly. It's something to do with the failing of the liver function, I believe.'

'That's terrible. Is that taken in Biafra?'

'In one of the relief camps. Yes. There are hundreds of thousands of young children there. That boy died two days after the photograph was taken. Hundreds are dying every day. It's inhuman.'

'That's awful.'

'It is a monstrosity,' said Okonkwo, joining them. 'Let me ask you. What does it make you feel?'

'I don't know. It makes me angry, I suppose.'

'Does it make you angry that your government is helping this to happen?'

'I suppose it does,' Breen said.

'Yes. You should be angry. I can give you copies of the leaflet if you like. We are printing them. We want everyone to see the truth about what is happening in Biafra. You see? He did not die in vain.'

'That's an awful thing to say,' said Tozer. 'It's like you're almost glad he died.'

Ezeoke came and snatched the leaflet out of Tozer's hand.

'I was looking at that,' she protested.

'Have you progressed any further with your investigation?' In the orange street light Ezeoke looked tired and drawn.

'Not since I saw you last.'

A boy on a scooter rode past, pausing to look at the unusual sight of a group of black people in the middle of Soho, then revving on down Broadwick Street.

Ezeoke said, 'You don't strike me as the kind of man who goes to parties. Perhaps you're investigating now?'

'He's not the kind of man who goes to parties,' said Tozer. 'I brought him.'

'That explains why you are a much better dancer than him.'

Tozer laughed. The young man was next to her still. He attempted to put his arm around her waist and she pushed it back, wriggling away from him. 'Get off.'

'Why?' he said. 'I'm just being friendly.'

'I know your type of friendly,' she said, still laughing, but she didn't move away from him.

'Are you OK?' Breen asked her.

'Of course I'm OK.'

'You are neglecting your beautiful Biafran wife, Samuel,' said Okonkwo.

'Yes, mazi-Okonkwo. You are right. You are always right. Let me tell you a little about Mr Okonkwo,' said Ezeoke. 'He is our minister of propaganda. He sees every starving Biafran baby as a present from God. He believes he can shame the British into changing sides. He does not understand the British have no shame. But with him the objective is everything. He cares nothing for whether people live or die.'

'Are you drunk, Sam? Go home before you say something you regret,' said Okonkwo.

'I'm not drunk.'

'Didn't your wife tell me you had a plane to catch tomorrow morning? Ezinwa? Shouldn't you take your husband home?'

His wife was talking to another woman, ignoring Okonkwo.

'I am fine.'

'Where are you flying to, Mr Ezeoke?' asked Breen.

'Belgium. I am attending a conference on causal links between heart disease and cigarette smoking.'

'Which means you should go to bed.'

A light blue police car turned into the top of Wardour Street and drove slowly towards them. The men moved off the street onto the pavement to let it past. As it drove by, the policeman behind the wheel wound down his window and looked sideways at them. The Africans shuffled their bottles of beer into their coats and behind their backs.

The car passed on and turned round to Broadwick Street.

'Smoking does not give you heart disease. It makes you strong,' said Tozer's young man.

'You got a cigarette I can smoke?' said Tozer. 'I'm feeling weak.' The man laughed and pulled a crumpled packet from his trousers. Breen was surprised at how jealous he felt.

A minute later the police car was back, returning from the north and crawling past them again. This time when it reached Broadwick Street it stopped. 'Go back into the club,' said Okonkwo. The younger Africans hesitated. 'Go back downstairs. Now.'

A few of them had begun to move just as the car started to reverse back towards them, rapidly. It braked right outside the nightclub and both doors flew open.

The copper who had been driving was a lanky fellow. He unfolded himself from the car, saying, 'Right. What's going on here?'

Okonkwo stepped forward. 'We were having a party, sir. We are going home now.'

The other policeman eyed them across the roof of the car. 'Is that beer you're drinking?' he called.

'Sorry, sir. We were having a party in the nightclub, but the electricity broke.'

One of the partygoers giggled.

The first officer shouted, 'I'm going to give you one minute to get out of here.' Breen could see Ezeoke's jaw clenching. 'Move. Now,' said the copper.

Breen was about to intervene, to tell the officer that he could vouch for these men, when Tozer gave a small high-pitched yelp. 'Get off!' She slapped the young man's hand away for the tenth time.

'Stand back!' the policeman shouted, pulling his truncheon out. 'Get your hands off the woman.' The other policeman was back inside the car now, on the radio, calling for support.

'For God's sake,' said Tozer. 'It's OK. I can handle him myself. He's just a kid.'

But the policeman's face was already reddening as he held up his truncheon. 'Get away from her.'

The young black man's face hardened; he cocked his head back, eyes narrowing.

Breen saw Ezeoke step between them, fired up with patriotism, beer and song. 'Leave him alone,' he blurted, feet planted firmly apart.

'Don't, Sam,' shouted Ezinwa.

'Don't be stupid, Sam,' said Okonkwo.

The policeman put his face right up to Ezeoke's. 'Get out of my way, nigger.'

'Leave us alone, white man.' Ezeoke shouted back, raising a fist and shaking it in his face.

'Just try it,' taunted the policeman.

Ezeoke was quivering with rage, eyes wide. For the first time the young policeman suddenly looked uncertain of himself, scared even. Before he could land a first blow, Breen pushed between Ezeoke and the copper, sending Ezeoke staggering backwards towards his wife. He held up his warrant card a foot in front of the policeman's face.

'It's OK,' he said. 'Calm down. Everything's OK. He's just a bit drunk, that's all.'

Okonkwo was ushering the young men off the street back into the nightclub as the sound of a police siren approached from the south.

'Do as the man says,' said Breen. 'Go home, everyone.'

Some descended back into the club to collect their coats and bags. Others drifted away into the night. The policeman stood by his car, glaring at them as they dispersed.

The other police car pulled up behind, light flashing, policemen piling out of it.

'I was fine,' said Tozer. 'Honestly. Big bunch of boys, you are. Do we have to go home now?'

'We could get a taxi. I'll drop you off,' said Breen.

'I don't want to go home yet,' said Tozer.

'Come on,' said Breen. 'Everything's closed now.'

'I can give her a lift,' said the young man. 'On my motorbike.'

'Get lost,' said Tozer. 'I'm walking. On my own.'

'In your bare feet?' said Breen.

As his wife pulled him away up the street Ezeoke turned and said: 'I did not ask for your help, Mr Breen. I can fight my own fight.'

Mrs Ezeoke tugged at his arm. 'Shut up,' she said. 'Just shut up, you stupid man.'

TWENTY-SIX

It was a bad-tempered week. On Monday, Prosser called in sick. Breen wrote up a report about the fire investigation suggesting that the dead man was probably a labourer called Patrick Donahoe and handed it in to Bailey. On Tuesday morning, Bailey stuck his head round the office door.

'Where's Prosser?' he asked.

'Sick still,' said Marilyn, giving him a glare.

'What's wrong with him?'

'Cold.'

'I'm disappointed rather than surprised,' said Bailey, retreating behind his door.

At lunchtime Breen went down to Woolworths and bought the new double disc *The Beatles* and an LP by the Modern Jazz Quartet that the man behind the counter said he should try.

'Who are they for?' said Marilyn when he was looking at the covers on his desk.

'Me,' said Breen. He put the discs down on the floor by the side of his desk.

'I just didn't think you were into that stuff.'

Carmichael was in court, but he came in just after lunch and said, 'Where's Prosser?'

'Off sick still,' said Marilyn.

'You seen him, Jonesy?'

'No. He hasn't been outside his front door since the weekend.'

Breen spent the early afternoon going through the report from the Devon and Cornwall police. Jones said, 'What's this I hear about you and Tozer going to a darkie club at the weekend?'

Almost immediately, Marilyn dropped a pile of suspension files on the floor, sending papers everywhere. When Breen went over and knelt down beside her, picking up pieces of paper, Marilyn snapped. 'I can manage on my own.'

He went back to his desk and studied the photograph of Julia Sullivan's body, trying to see clues in it about what it was that made her kill her husband. When he looked up, Marilyn was holding a piece of paper out in front of him to be signed.

'What's this?'

'Form you got to fill in about the car. The one you and laughing girl wrote off in Cornwall.'

'Do I have to do it now?'

'You should have done it last week.' She dropped it on his desk. 'What's that about you and Tozer being at a nightclub together?'

He picked up the sheet of paper. 'You couldn't do it, could you, Marilyn?'

'You bloody do it yourself for a change.' And she turned round, shoes clattering on the bare floorboards, stamping off through the doors out to the ladies' toilet.

Breen looked up, puzzled. 'What's got into her?'

Jones put his hand over the mouthpiece of the phone he was talking into and said, 'Probably, like the rest of us, she's finally figured out that you're a cunt.'

Around two, Breen caught the Circle Line down to Notting Hill Gate and walked back to the police flats.

He searched the doorbells. He found, written on a green label, *Mr & Mrs Prosser*. He hadn't changed the names since his wife moved out.

He pressed the button but no one answered. Stepping back, he looked at the windows, trying to work out which flat was Prosser's.

He went back and rang Prosser's bell again. This time he held his finger on the buzzer until it started to ache. It must have been a minute before he spotted a face peeking from behind a net curtain on the second floor. It was there just for a second and then it was gone.

Police flats, two to a floor. He rang all the doorbells until someone buzzed him in, then he walked up the stairs and banged on the second-floor door. There was no answer. 'Michael. I know you're in there,' he called.

He knocked again.

'Michael Prosser, it's Paddy Breen. Open the door.'

He banged louder.

'I haven't told anybody about what you did,' Breen said. 'But I will if you don't talk to me.'

He sat down in the hallway, back to the door.

'I'm not going until you let me in. Anyone who sees me is going to ask me what I'm doing here. They're already wondering why you haven't made it in to work this week.'

A couple of seconds later he heard the bolt on the door being drawn. Prosser hadn't shaved and he was wearing a cardigan over a string vest that hung down over his narrow shoulders. 'You better come in then,' he said.

The flat was a mess. There were dirty plates and mugs on the living-room floor and piles of clothes pushed into the corners of the room. The ashtray hadn't been emptied in a while and grey ash and stubs were overflowing onto a small glass coffee table. Empty bottles of Pale Ale were lined up on the windowsill.

Breen stood by the front door.

'Everything OK, Paddy?' Prosser looked at him curiously, rubbing his unshaven chin with his fingertips.

'Jones caught the guy you were in the shop with that night you were stabbed.'

Prosser nodded. 'I heard,' he said. 'I heard you let him go too.'

'I did.'

'I suppose I should be grateful for that.'

'You should,' said Breen. The walls of the room were bare except for a painting-by-numbers picture of a galleon and a photo of a boy, about four years old, on the mantelpiece.

'They thought I was a bastard for letting you get cut up and now they think I'm worse for letting the Chinese guy go.'

Prosser nodded. 'And you haven't grassed?'

'No.'

'Not to no one?'

Breen shook his head.

Prosser said, 'Thanks. I appreciate that. We coppers should stick together.'

'Yes. You said that.'

'I owe you an apology then. I'm sorry, OK? Things just got out of hand.'

Breen's arm started to ache. He rubbed his collarbone and said, 'I spent weeks thinking it was my fault you got stabbed. Do you have any idea how that made me feel?'

Prosser said nothing.

'The door was open. But there was no sign of a forced entry. I didn't even think of that until a few weeks ago. I thought it was all my fault.'

Prosser smiled. 'He was supposed to make it look like a break-in. What a tosser.'

The sort of smile a man makes to another man when he knows he has ballsed something up. Almost like he was saying, 'You really can't get the staff these days, can you?'

'Did you get him to stab you or did you do it to yourself?'

Prosser sat down on his sofa, put his head in his hands and said, 'I did it. I thought it would make the whole thing look proper. And suddenly I was a bloody hero. Even Bailey called me a hero. I'm up for a medal. Funny, isn't it?' Breen followed him into the room. Prosser picked up a cigarette packet and shook it. It was empty. 'Got a cigarette?'

'No,' Breen said, though he knew there were still four left in his packet.

Prosser sighed.

'It was a coathanger job, wasn't it? You sold the keys to the Chinese guy. He went in to take the clothes and you took the money.'

Prosser nodded. 'I'd caught him stealing cars last Easter. A car, leastways. He offered me money to let him off. I never done it with anyone else, promise. I'm not one of those coppers. I know it looks that way, but I'm not. And then I met these CID guys from Peckham who were running a coathanger team, selling the keys to gangs and taking their bit and they were making a fair whack of money. And the shopkeepers were all insured, so where's the harm? Because we were the ones who had to tell the insurance whether it was a crime or not anyway. And they showed me how easy it was. I mean, we've got the keys to half the shops in Marylebone back at the station. I only did it the once, promise. Once or twice, leastways. And never places that couldn't afford it. That guy Martin Dawes, he's loaded. You know how much those insurance companies rake in. I really needed the money. Only the Chink turned out to be so stupid he was spotted. Just my luck.' He smiled. 'What are you going to do, Paddy? It's your call.'

All the time he'd been in CID Prosser had never treated him as one of them. He was the Paddy. Now he had one on him, they could be pals.

'Depends. How much would you pay me to keep quiet?'

Prosser's face fell. 'I can't give you money, mate. I owe a bit here and there. That's why I was doing all this in the first place. I've got this kid—'

'Put a figure on it. What if I said a hundred?'

'I never thought you were like that, Paddy, to be honest,' he said. 'I'm disappointed.'

'Two hundred.'

'Christ, Paddy. I haven't got that much. Hundred maybe. Possibly. I could do favours for you. Take bits of work if you like.'

Breen rubbed the back of his neck. 'Do you have any idea what it's been like for me? I ran away from a copper who was about to be killed. I don't want money. I need to know what happened.'

Prosser looked relieved. 'I knew you weren't like that, Paddy. Look. I know we haven't been particularly friendly, up till now . . .' He stood up and went to the window and peered through the nets. 'You want some tea? It would have to be powdered milk. I haven't been out of the flat since I got back on Friday. No? I'll have to go out now, I suppose. I'm out of fags. Would you go for me?'

'Bugger off. Go yourself.'

Prosser winced, then went back and sat on the sofa again. 'Fair enough.'

Breen said, 'You got any aspirin?'

'In the cupboard in the bathroom.' Breen picked past the damp towels on the floor and found a small bottle on a shelf.

'I knew he was doing the job on Sunday night,' called Prosser. 'I made sure I was on shift in case anything went wrong.'

There was a filthy-looking tooth mug on the sink. Breen took the pills and swigged water from the tap in his hand instead.

'I was in the car parked up on Old Portland Street eating a bag of chips when it came on the radio that somebody had seen somebody in Martin and Dawes.' He tugged at stuffing that was already coming out of the arm of the sofa. 'Stupid Chink switched a light on. And I thought I better get there first. And I wasn't far away so I thought I could do that. Which I did. Only you arrived about a minute later. And I thought, what happens now?' A large piece of stuffing came away. Prosser dropped it onto the floor. 'But I knew this Chink always carried a knife so I told him to get it out and wave it at me. Which he did. And you came in. And then you scarpered. Luckily. That's all. And so I just gave myself a couple of cuts with the knife for good effect. Didn't even hurt that much. Not then. Let the guy out of the front door. It wasn't your fault.'

Breen nodded.

Prosser picked up the empty cigarette packet and shook it again. 'What's Bailey been saying? About me not being in?'

'Not that much.'

'And what about the others? Have they been wondering why I'm not in?'

'You're ill, that's what they're saying.'

'I really appreciate this, Paddy. I don't deserve it. You're a good mate. I behaved really badly. A disgrace. Know what I mean? But I can make it right. What if I told people that Jones had got the wrong guy? That's why you let him go? What if I told them you fought the Chink too, as well as me, only it was just me that got injured? You could be a hero.'

Breen looked at him and said, 'We don't have to tell them anything. You just have to go into the office tomorrow and tell Bailey you're throwing in the towel.'

Prosser frowned. 'Sorry?'

'You tell him you're leaving.'

'Me? Resigning?'

Breen nodded.

'Me?'

'Yes.'

'Quitting the job?'

'That's what I said.'

'Why?'

'Because otherwise I'll ring the bell.'

Sitting on the sofa looking up at Breen, Prosser, the big hard London lad, seemed like he was about to cry. 'Paddy. I've been almost twenty years on the force. What else am I going to do? I'd lose my flat and everything. And my kid. His mum relies on me. I got obligations. I really need the money.'

'You'll lose your pension too if I tell them what really happened. And they'll put you away. That would be worse.'

He crunched the cigarette packet in one hand. 'It's my life, Paddy. It's my fucking life.'

288

'I won't tell anyone. Think what would happen if the press found out. They're just waiting for something like this. Corrupt coppers. They'd have a field day. It's best if you go quietly.'

Breen stood up. He wanted to get back to the station.

'Paddy. We can talk. I'm really sorry for what I did to you.'

Breen didn't look back at Prosser, just headed for the front door.

'You're a bastard, Paddy Breen.'

'By tomorrow. Or I'll go to Bailey.'

Prosser lurched up off the sofa and grabbed Breen's arm, bunching his other fingers.

'Just try it,' said Breen.

'I might,' said Prosser. He stood there for a second with his fist held in the air. 'All this doesn't change the fact that you were windy, Paddy. You should have seen the look on your face. When he pulled the knife on you you were dirtying your ruddy pants. You're a fucking coward, Paddy Breen. A lousy Mick coward.'

Breen let himself out and walked away, relieved to be out of the place, keen to put some distance between himself and Prosser. After the hum of dirty laundry and stale cigarette smoke, it was good to get some fresh air in his lungs.

It was a short walk to Pembridge House. Three Victorian houses had been joined together to create the women's section house. Behind the big front door there was a row of pegs and underneath each one hung a wooden tag with the resident's name on both sides, green on one, yellow on the other. He tried the door at the bottom of the stairs but it was locked.

'Can I help you?' called a middle-aged woman from the living room. 'Men aren't allowed upstairs.'

'I'm looking for Helen Tozer.'

The woman came to the door and scanned the tags. Tozer was in. 'And who are you?'

Ten minutes later Tozer emerged down the stairs.

'You took your time,' said Breen.

'What's got into you? I had to choose the right clothes. I mean, for God's sake. What if George is actually there? The girls made me buy this on Saturday. What do you think?'

A striped frock with two pockets at the front.

'You look nice,' he said.

She wrinkled her nose. 'I feel a bit daft in it, to be honest,' she said.

TWENTY-SEVEN

Tentatively, they walked past rhododendrons, up Claremont Drive, past the gates with the painted notice: *Private*. 'You sure?' said Breen.

'Positive.'

An elderly-looking man in a tweed jacket was piling leaves onto a smoking fire in one of the gardens. He looked at them suspiciously.

'It doesn't look like where a pop star would live.'

'And how would you know?'

The driveway curved round past small recently built bungalows until it reached a last one.

'There,' she said. 'I told you so.'

But for the swimming pool and the hippie paintings on the wall, it would have been like any other new suburban bungalow. It was an ugly building, plain and oddly proportioned; it looked as if it had perhaps borrowed its window frames from another house, or maybe the pitched roof was just too big. It seemed an unlikely home for a member of the world's most famous pop group.

The murals were florid and ugly. Bulbous swirls of pink and orange covered the bland walls, wiggles morphed into flames or faces, flowers and zigzags crawled over the plaster. In a few afternoons of stoned brushwork, people had attempted to prove that the person who lived here was not a stockbroker or a retired dentist like the neighbours.

'This is really George's house?'

'Yes.'

'Where are all the fans, then?'

'I don't know.'

There were no girls outside; it looked like the bungalow was empty inside too. Breen and Tozer sat on a low wall that had the words 'MICK AND MARIANNE WERE HERE' written on it in bright yellow paint.

'I've never been around that many coloured people in my life,' said Tozer. 'You danced. I never thought I'd see that, either.'

'If you can call it dancing.'

'It was fun. I enjoyed myself.'

A petrol engine spluttered into life in a nearby garden.

'That man you danced with . . .' said Breen.

'He said he wanted to marry me and take me back to Biafra when they'd won the war.'

'You liked him,' said Breen.

'You jealous?' Tozer grinned.

'No.'

'He was a bit fast, you know what I mean?' she said. 'Only I never been to an African party before. It's an experience, isn't it? Where I grew up there ain't nobody dark. So I thought . . .'

'When in Rome?'

'I suppose.'

A hedge trimmer started gnawing the branches of a cypress hedge that bordered Harrison's garden.

'Did you mind?'

'Why should I?'

'He said Ezeoke is having an affair with a white woman.'

'Mrs Briggs?'

She nodded. 'All that Africa stuff he goes on about all the time. Apparently everybody knows.'

'Yes,' said Breen.

'My guy at the party said he wanted to try an affair with a white woman too. I told him he'd have to find another bloody one, then. I'm hungry,' said Tozer. 'I didn't have any lunch.'

'You reckon anyone's going to turn up?' asked Breen.

'I don't know.' Tozer lit a cigarette and said, 'My mum asked after you. She always does, regular as clockwork. "How's that nice policeman?" she says. I told her you were improving.'

'What do you mean by that?'

'I don't know. You're loosening up. Letting your hair down. You danced on Saturday.'

'You call that dancing?'

'Not really.'

'What about your dad?'

'Not so good,' she said.

'Why?'

She didn't answer. Instead she said, 'How is your other investigation going? The guy in the fire.'

He told her about the meeting with the foreman; about how it was probably the body of a young Irishman who had got drunk on his birthday.

'That's so sad,' she said.

'The foreman used to work with my dad,' said Breen. 'I found his name from one of his address books.'

'Your dad was a builder?'

'Yes. And he knew my dad well, it turns out.' Breen told Tozer the story the man had told him, about his father and mother leaving Ireland.

Tozer sat on the wall, swinging her legs, smoking a cigarette. 'And you never knew that. About your mum and dad eloping?'

'No. I suppose he must have been ashamed.'

'He shouldn't have been.'

'It was different then, though.'

'That's amazing. You only just found that out.'

'Yes.'

'How do you feel about it?'

'I suppose . . . I resent the fact that he never told me about it.' He looked around at the bungalows with their neat lawns and hedges, wondering what the neighbours thought of having a Beatle living here.

'You should feel good. You came from love. That's important,' she said.

A man in blue overalls appeared around the edge of the cypress hedge, holding the trimmer. He looked at the pair of them for a minute then bent down and tugged on the starting cord. It burst into life straight away and he started cutting back the branches on George Harrison's side.

'My family have been on the same farm for generations,' said Tozer. 'At least he got away. He gave that to you. I think it's why you're quite good.'

'What?' The sound of the trimmer was deafening.

'You don't fit in anywhere, do you? That's why you're good at what you do. You don't carry any weight with you. 'Scuse me,' she shouted at the gardener, but the man didn't hear.

Tozer stood and waved at him. This time he stopped and switched off the engine.

'That's better,' said Tozer.

'You're a bit old, aren't you?' said the man.

'What do you mean, old?' Tozer said.

'It's teenagers usually, hanging out around here.'

'Thank you very much,' said Tozer.

'We're police,' said Breen.

The man looked her up and down. 'You don't look like police.'

'We were looking for a girl called Carol,' said Breen.

The man pulled a tin from his overalls and dug inside for a packet of tobacco. 'Carol-George?'

'That's the one.'

He looked at his watch. 'She comes after school. She should be here any minute.' And he started up the trimmer again.

He was right. Not long after, she came walking down the driveway, dressed in a sheepskin coat and a pink crocheted hat. She was tall, almost scarily thin, with a long pale face framed by dark hair.

She frowned when she saw them there. 'Who are you? Are you reporters? He doesn't like reporters.'

'You waiting for George?'

'Free world.' The girl took off her hat. Her hair fell in front of her eyes; she took a strand, put it in her mouth and started sucking on it.

Tozer said, 'Pattie and George not in?'

'No.'

'They away?'

She shook her head. 'Not sure when they're back.'

'So you just stay here?'

'Why shouldn't I? I like it here.'

'What do you do?'

'Nothing much. What's it to you?'

'Nothing,' said Tozer.

'Don't your parents worry?' said Breen.

The girl snorted. 'What's it to do with them?'

'You're Carol, aren't you?' he said.

She frowned. 'Are you the policeman who was asking about Wenna?'

'Morwenna?'

'You showed some girls a photograph of Wenna and said she was dead.' Her expression didn't change. 'Is she dead?'

Tozer dug out the photograph of the young girl standing in the doorway of the tree house; the place where her mother had killed herself.

The girl nodded 'Wenna, we called her. She really is dead then?'

'Yes. She is.'

The girl nodded. 'I heard that.'

'I'm sorry,' said Breen.

The girl said, 'I feel I ought to cry, but nothing's coming out.'

'That's fine,' said Breen. 'I know that feeling. It'll come out when it needs to.'

'Don't think it will,' said Carol.

Breen sat on the wall. 'What was she like?'

'Why?'

'I want to know.'

The girl nodded again, sombrely. 'She was all right,' she said. 'She hated her dad. She was like the girl in "She's Leaving Home".'

'What?' said Breen.

'The song on *Sergeant Pepper's*,' said Tozer.

'I was thinking of buying that,' said Breen.

'Really?' said Tozer.

'Maybe. What about the girl?'

'Her mum was OK, she said. But her dad was really strict. She hated him. He hated her too, she said.'

'She told you this?'

She nodded again. 'Yes. A lot of us scruffs have had trouble with our parents. She went the whole way, though. She ran off.'

Tozer sat down on the wall and patted it. 'To meet a man from the motor trade?'

The girl sat down beside them. 'I don't think so, no. I never saw her go out with any blokes.'

Breen must have looked puzzled because Tozer said, 'It's in the song. She runs off to have it off with a man from the motor trade. Detective Sergeant Breen here's mother did much the same.'

'Did you like her?' asked Breen. 'Morwenna?'

'Course. She was one of us. We're all friends. OK, sometimes we get a little bitchy amongst ourselves, but we're all the same really. We're a gang.'

'Did she spend a lot of time here?'

'What do you mean by a lot? As much as me? No one spends as much time here as me.' She laughed, brushing hair away from her eyes. 'But at the beginning she was down here loads.'

'When was that?'

'It was just when "Hello, Goodbye" came out.'

'What?' said Breen.

'That would be November,' said Tozer. 'A year ago.'

'She was here almost every day around then. Haven't seen her for weeks. Months, really. Not since around the time Paul called it off with Jane Asher.'

'That was June,' said Tozer.

'Did you used to go to EMI Studios when they were recording the last disc?'

'Sometimes.'

'You never saw her there then?'

'That's where I must have seen her last, I think. Outside of there. But then she drifted off.'

Tozer said, 'You were there in October when they were finishing the record?'

'A few times, yes.'

'But you never saw her then?'

The girl shook her head. A flock of starlings swooped overhead. Simultaneously, the three looked up at the chattering bubble of birds. When they had gone, Breen asked, 'How would you describe her?'

'What do you mean?'

'I mean, to someone who'd never met her before?'

'Don't know.'

'Think of one word,' asked Breen. 'One word that says who she was.'

'Fierce.'

'Fierce?'

'She was fierce, you know? She didn't let anybody treat her like a child. She even had a go at George once.'

'What did he do wrong?' asked Tozer.

'See them roses?'

A line of rose bushes, neatly pruned after flowering.

'One of the girls picked one of them. You wouldn't have thought there was much harm in it, only he saw her. Grabbed her arm and gave her a mouthful. He's really proud of his roses, you know.'

'George Harrison?' said Tozer.

'Yes. He is. You'd be surprised.'

'I am.'

'Wenna went right up to him. She was quite tall, really. Put her face right up to his. She told him that men should never hurt women. You should have seen him apologising. He was totally remorseful. It was amazing. We're all in awe of them, you know. They're our idols. But she wouldn't have it, him being so angry with her. He told Wenna she was totally right. Know what he did? He cut a rose and gave it to the girl and then gave another one to Wenna.'

They heard a car coming down the driveway.

'That him?' A Mercedes drove past slowly, the driver eyeing them.

The girl shook her head. 'No. He's driving a mini right now. You'd know it if you saw it. It's all painted up.'

'Like his house?' asked Breen.

'Kind of. I don't think he's coming today, though.'

'Why are you still waiting, then?'

'Just in case, I suppose. I like it here. I spend a lot of time here. It's like home to me. Better than, as a matter of fact. She didn't come back so much after that. After that row with George. I think it upset her.'

'For having a go at George?'

'No. Not that. We said she shouldn't cry because he probably respected her even more now. But later, when she and her mate were staying over on my floor, they talked about how she always used to row with her dad. That's why she left home. I just don't think she liked it here so much after that.'

'Did she ever talk about her father using violence against her?'

'Maybe. I don't remember. She said he had a right temper. I remember that. You think it was him that did it?'

Tozer looked like a teenager herself, in her plain sleeveless dress. 'I do. He can't make up his mind.'

Breen said, 'We don't think anything, right now.'

'We've got him in London the day before she dies,' said Tozer.

The girl put her arms round herself to keep warm.

'Know any good cafes around here? I'm starving,' said Tozer.

They walked silently back along the lane, through the low white gate to where the car was parked.

'I never been in a police car.'

'I should hope not,' said Tozer.

'Can you put on the siren?'

'No.'

'Go on, sir. Just for a second,' said Tozer.

'No.'

'Spoilsport,' said Tozer.

They found a tea room open in Esher. Inside, Breen felt suddenly ravenous. Confronting Prosser had felt like a weight lifting from his shoulders.

He sat and looked at the menu and ordered chips, beans, double egg and toast. A budgie sulked in a golden cage. A trembling vicar slurped soup alone at a nearby table.

Breen said, 'Who was the other girl?'

Carol-George said, 'Who?'

'You said she and another girl came to stay on your floor. Her mate.'

'Oh, Izzie?'

'Was that her?'

'Izzie was her best mate. The darkie.'

'Darkie?'

'She and Izzie were a team. They'd share sleeping bags outside EMI. They'd turn up at George's together, most days.'

'Izzie was a black girl?' Breen and Tozer glanced at each other.

'Yes.' In his mind's eye, Breen was rapidly rearranging the piles of paper on his front-room floor.

'Where's Izzie?'

'I don't know. Haven't seen her for weeks neither.' She looked up from her sandwich suddenly. 'Oh God. You think she's OK?'

Breen looked up at Tozer. She was leaning across the table now, brow furrowed.

'Have you got a photo of her?'

The girl shook her head. 'Someone's bound to. Not me, though. I'm no good with cameras.'

'What's her last name?'

The girl shook her head. 'She never had one. We just called her Izzie.'

'Think hard. Who might know where she lives?'

The girl chewed her lip. 'I'm sorry.'

'Think. Please.'

'We spend a lot of time together, us fans. Girls mostly. Just a few boys. We're waiting for stuff to happen.' She looked away, then back at the detectives. 'We're the sort of people who never fitted in. And then along came these pop stars and we realised we never wanted to belong anyway. So we don't always tell people about where we're from.' The girl had left her bacon sandwich on the plate. 'Do you think she's dead too?'

Breen looked at Tozer; she looked back at him. 'How can you find out if anyone's seen her?' he asked.

She pulled out a small Letts diary and turned to a page full of phone numbers.

'I could try calling. Only, I've not got no change.'

This time, on the way to the police station, Breen put the siren on as Tozer weaved through the traffic, cars pulling to one side.

'She's a good driver, isn't she? Look at them cars bloody move,' said Carol from the back of the car. She wound down the window and stuck her head out, feeling the wind in her hair.

The station was quiet. Carol sat at Breen's desk calling her friends. 'Three guesses where I am.'

Most of them were in at this time of day but not one of them had seen Izzie for the last month.

A boy who lived in Palmers Green had a photo taken in a photobooth, but he said they couldn't really make out Izzie clearly as there were six of them all trying to squeeze into the shot. The only girl who might have had a proper photo was away in America, visiting her parents.

The girl sat at Breen's desk, doodling.

'Were they girlfriends? You know?'

The girl nodded. 'Didn't bother me,' she said. Breen watched Carol write her name in big rounded letters and put a heart in place of the 'o'. Tozer said, 'You want a lift home, then?'

'Can you put the siren on again?'

'I want you to drive me to the Ezeokes' house after,' said Breen.

'Oh. Right. God.'

'Just a minute.'

He opened his desk drawer, pulled out the envelope Devon and Cornwall police had sent him, took out the photograph of Mrs Sullivan's body and examined it again.

'What's that?' said Carol.

'Nothing,' he said.

Carol-George lived with her uncle in a terraced house in Belsize Park.

'I'm home,' she shouted loudly. 'I've got two friends with me.'

He was in the kitchen at the table with the wireless on, a thin, silver-haired man in a grey sleeveless jumper. There were Beatles pictures stuck all around the walls.

'I'm hungry,' he said, not looking at them. 'You're late.' The whites of his eyes showed as he talked; Breen saw he was blind.

'I'll make tea in a minute,' she said, kissing him on the forehead. 'Toad in the hole and gravy.'

'Delicious,' the blind man said, smacking his lips. 'Introduce me to your friends, then.'

'This is Helen. I don't know his name.'

'Cathal,' said Breen.

'They're not any of the ones I've met before, are they?'

'No, Uncle.'

301

She put the electric kettle on. 'Come here,' she said to Tozer. 'I want to show you something. Back in a minute, Uncle.'

There were bits of newspapers and magazines cut out everywhere around the house, pasted to the walls. The four Beatles getting into an aeroplane. A headline saying 'George Says I Love You Yeah Yeah Yeah'. A picture of John next to a bulldog. An old picture of the group playing in the Cavern. 'The house is like a big scrapbook,' said Tozer.

'It's OK. He doesn't mind,' said Carol. 'I think it brightens up the place a bit. Come on. I want to show you this.'

'You look after him?'

'My auntie died a couple of years ago. I moved in then. It's better than home. Home is rubbish. Here I get to do what I want.'

She led them up to a back room on the first floor. 'This is where I bring all the fans I like,' she said shyly to Tozer.

She switched the light on.

'Oh my God,' said Tozer. 'It's incredible.'

The wall was plastered, floor to ceiling, in photographs, each overlapping the other, pasted there with glue. Thousands of faces looked out at them. It must have taken her weeks. Breen realised that each Beatle had one wall. Ringo's wall had a small sash window in it. Paul's wall had the door they walked in through. John's was the wall to their left.

'Wow,' said Tozer.

'My pride and joy,' said Carol.

'It's super,' said Tozer.

'Thanks.'

'You did all this yourself?'

Carol nodded, smiling.

There was a pile of cushions in the middle of the room, from which you could look at the walls. And there were candles stuck to the floorboards with wax around the edge. Tozer walked in and stood in the middle, looking slowly round. Breen stayed by the door with Carol.

George had the wall opposite. In the middle, a large picture of George, surrounded by flowers. Breen watched her revolving slowly in the centre of the room. By the time she came round to face them, her eyes looked red.

'Are you OK?' he said.

'I'm fine,' she said.

TWENTY-EIGHT

Breen rang Mr Ezeoke's doorbell. After a minute or so, Mrs Ezeoke opened the door.

'Can we come in?'

She shook her head. 'My husband is away. He is at a conference.'

'When is he back?'

'Tomorrow morning.'

Breen nodded. It was late; they had stayed too long at Carol's.

'Are you sure you are well? You don't look well to me. Have you come to ask my husband a medical question?'

'No. It's just something to do with the case.'

'Can I offer you a Coca-Cola?'

'If it's no trouble.'

She opened the door and led them through into the living room. 'I am bored when he is not here. I do not have many friends in London. I miss my country.'

'Will you go back there after the war?'

'My husband tells everyone that we will.' She smiled. 'But he has never lived there. I have. Your hospitals are full of Nigerian doctors. They all talk about how they will go back to make the country great, but they all prefer to work here.'

The living room was the same as it had been last time, boxes still unpacked, record sleeves scattered around the floor. She returned from the kitchen carrying three glasses of Coke on a tray. 'I must apologise for the mess. I had meant to tidy up, but I have not got around to it yet. Sit, please.'

She sat on the sofa; he perched on a chair; Tozer sat in a modern-looking chair that looked like it came from Habitat.

'How is your husband's war?'

She laughed. 'My husband's war. I think that is a good name for it. He believes he alone can win it from the distance of so many thousand miles.'

'He's a very passionate man.'

'Yes. A very passionate man. We have given all we have to the war. If it was me, I would not have given so much.'

'What do you mean?'

She smiled. 'I do not like this house. I do not like our new neighbours. They are not educated people. We used to have a good house. We have sold it to raise money for the committee. He says we will get our money back when Biafra wins the war. As you say, he is a passionate man.' She was silent for a while, then said, 'What did you want to ask my husband?'

'It's an odd question.'

'I expect it is odd. You are looking for a murderer. There is nothing normal about your job.'

Breen hesitated. 'I have a photograph of a woman wearing a bracelet. I think it may be African. It's like the bracelet you're wearing now.' He had remembered her wearing it at the party. 'I was just wondering if he could tell me anything about it.'

'Why can I not help? I am more African than he is. Show it to me.'

'It isn't that simple. The bracelet is being worn by a dead woman. She committed suicide with a shotgun.'

'So?'

'So it's a very disturbing photograph.'

'This photograph. Is it something to do with the dead girl? The one you found by our house?'

'It's the girl's mother.'

'She has killed herself? My God. The girl and now the mother?'

'Yes.'

'So you found out who the poor girl was?'

'Yes.'

She held out her hand. 'Show me the photograph.'

'Your husband is a doctor. He would be more used to seeing things like this.'

Mrs Ezeoke smiled. 'You underestimate African women. We are much stronger than English ladies.'

'It's gruesome.'

'The girl is dead. Have you found the killer?'

'I'm not sure.'

'If I can help I should help. You should let me help. Show me the photograph.'

Breen lifted his bag onto the wooden coffee table and opened it. The photograph was still in the brown envelope that Block had sent it to him in. He pulled it out and handed it across to her.

At first her face didn't register shock; it was calm. But that composure only lasted a second or two. Her eyes widened and the hand that wasn't holding the picture went up to cover her open mouth.

'I warned you it was bad,' he said.

'It is the bracelet.'

'I had been wondering if you or Mr Ezeoke could suggest where it might have come from.'

The woman eyed him suspiciously. 'When was this photograph taken?'

'Several weeks ago.'

'This is my daughter's bracelet. My mother bought it for her from a Hausa trader, before the war, when she was just a little girl.'

'Your daughter?'

'My daughter Ijeoma.'

'Izzy,' said Breen.

'What?' said Mrs Ezeoke.

'You never told us you had a daughter,' said Breen.

'She does not live with us any more.'

'You're sure it's her bracelet?'

'One hundred per cent. It is a very unusual bracelet. My mother bought it for her. In our country, the Hausa traders come from the north. They are Moslems. They buy goods and travel south with them to sell to us. Since the war, the Moslems and the Igbos hate each other. But when I was pregnant with my Ijeoma, things were friendlier.'

She reached up and touched her earring. 'An old Hausa man came every year and he set up a stall outside our house, out on the street. Every year, soon after the rainy season, he would appear and lay out his goods. He knew if he needed water to drink he could come to our house. Every year he would bring us a little present. As a girl I always used to like his jewellery. When Ijeoma was christened, my mother bought a bracelet from him as a christening present. It was too big for the baby Ije to wear, but I wore it for years. When she was big enough I gave it to her, and bought another for myself. See?' She showed the photograph of the thick bronze bracelet. 'Why does this dead woman have my daughter's bracelet?'

'Her daughter gave it to her before she died.'

The woman nodded sombrely.

'When did you last see your daughter, Mrs Ezeoke?'

'Three months ago.'

He rubbed his forehead hard, then cleared his throat. 'Mrs Ezeoke. It seems she was friends with Morwenna Sullivan, the murdered girl. I'm afraid that means there is a chance she might be dead as well.'

'Nonsense,' Mrs Ezeoke said abruptly. 'She is in Ivory Coast.'

'Ivory Coast?'

She frowned. 'It is a country in West Africa. Many Biafran refugees are there. She has gone to look after them.'

'When did she leave?'

'In the summer. In August.'

'And you know she's there?'

'Of course.'

'Can we contact her?'

Mrs Ezeoke laughed. 'You can send a telegram. Or write a letter. She writes to us sometimes, but not often. She is angry with us. She will not forgive her father for sending her there.'

'Mr Ezeoke sent her there?' asked Tozer, looking at Breen.

'Yes.'

'Why?'

'To save her.'

'I don't understand,' said Breen.

Mrs Ezeoke said, 'My husband is a very complicated man. He grew up in this country. But he is black.'

'We know.'

'He did not have a happy childhood here.'

'I can imagine.'

'I don't think you can begin to imagine it. He told me that until he was thirteen he never met any other black people. Can you imagine that? Can you imagine? It would be like being a ghost in a land of the living,' she said.

There was a hardness in her voice now. 'He never knew what it meant to be an African. You English grew up with an Empire. You believe black people are like children. It is why he worked so hard all his life. He didn't want to be like one of those lazy, childish black people. When he told his foster parents he wanted to come back to Africa to find his true family, you know what they told him? "It would be better if he didn't."' She laughed. 'But he came anyway. It is when I met him. He was full of excitement at being home in the country of his ancestors for the first time. Our town threw a big party for him when he returned. Dancing, beer. He drank palm wine for the first time and it made him sick as a dog.' She giggled. 'Poor Sam looked so happy, and so confused and lost at the same time. Even the water we drank made him sick. He wants so much to be African, but he can never be properly African. Because of that he will always be angry with you. Everything is the fault of the English. It is the English's fault he was taken away from Africa. It is England's fault Biafra are not winning the war. They support the Federals who are killing us.'

308

'And your daughter?'

'My daughter was born in England. She grew up in England. She has never lived in Africa until now. She does not share her father's obsessions.'

'And she liked pop music.'

Mrs Ezeoke laughed. 'It would make my husband angry that she would not listen to African music.'

Tozer said, 'He sent her back to Africa because she liked The Beatles?'

'Our people need help. We have many refugees in Ivory Coast. He wanted her to help.'

Tozer said it again. 'He sent her away because she liked The Beatles?'

She looked at the carpet sorrowfully. 'No no. It was not just The Beatles.'

'What?'

'This has nothing to do with the murder of your poor girl,' said Mrs Ezeoke. 'I have nothing more I can say.'

'She was friends with the murdered girl. She gave her your bracelet. That must mean she was close to her.'

'Yes,' said Mrs Ezeoke, still looking at the carpet. 'I am a mother too. I wore that bracelet myself.'

'Why did he send your daughter away?'

'He wants her to find a husband. An African man.'

'She and Morwenna were lovers,' said Tozer.

The woman stood and turned away, started pulling books out of one of the boxes and arranging them in piles. After a minute she spoke again. 'She never brought her friends to us. It is wrong for a man to lie down with a man or a girl to lie down with a girl. My husband says that only white people are like that. He believed it was just a teenage infatuation. An illness, you could say. She had to be cured of it. He is a very proud man, you understand. Everything can be cured. I would have forgiven her. It is more important to be happy. He wanted it fixed.'

Breen nodded.

She abandoned the books and sat down again. 'She is gone. I am not sure she will ever come back to us. I think we have lost her for ever,' she said, sitting straight-backed.

'And so your husband has sent her away from temptation?'

'He believes girls like that do not exist in Africa. Africa is a perfect place for him. It is Eden. He thinks for a girl to love a girl is just a Western corruption. In some ways he is a very innocent man.' She closed her eyes and breathed deeply.

'You never mentioned you had a daughter the same age as the dead girl.'

'I do not speak about her much now. It makes me too sad. It makes him too angry.'

'Did your husband ever meet your daughter's lover?'

'My daughter was careful to keep her away from us. She knew her father would not forgive her. I know he met the girl's father once.'

'When?'

'After he sent Ijeoma to Africa. He went to clear her belongings out of her flat and the other girl's father was there too, doing the same. Moving his girl's things.'

'Did he talk about him?'

'Why do you need to know this?'

'Please.'

'Yes. They had a lot in common. They both wanted to save their daughters. This other man, he was a military man. Sam liked him. Said he was on our side. He supported Biafra. He wanted to help. They were both men.'

Breen and Tozer looked at each other.

'When will your husband come home?'

'Tomorrow.' She looked around the room. 'Could I get you some more Coca-Cola? Or perhaps some cake?'

Breen shook his head.

Mrs Ezeoke stood suddenly. 'Excuse me,' she said, leaving the room. They heard her bustling in the hallway outside. She returned with a pale blue envelope.

She handed it to Breen. It was an airmail letter addressed to Ijeoma Ezeoke. There was a stamp on it, but the address was not filled in. On the back was the sender's return address: *Morwenna Sullivan, 118c Edgware Road, London.* On big letters on the front, underlined, *Strictly Private!!!!*

'She came here?' said Breen.

'I did not see her,' said Mrs Ezeoke. 'She left the letter in our letter box to post to my daughter with a note asking us to post it to her. I did not post it. I thought it was best if Ijeoma forgot about her.'

They sat in silence for a minute while the darkness outside pressed in at the room.

In the car: 'Ivory Coast. That sounds beautiful, doesn't it?'

Breen said, 'It does.'

Breen opened the letter. It was dated 17 August 1968.

Darling, darling Izzie,

I miss you so much. I cry every night and every day. I hate your father for what he has done. Both our dads are EVIL. I hate everybody. I love only you.

Please don't worry. I know what you are like. Everything is going to be FAB. I'm moving out of the flat to a squat to save £££, and I'm going to get a job as a shop girl or a secretary or even a DANCER so I can earn even more £££. (I told you my mummy was a MODEL – if she can do it so can I!!!!)

I asked my dad for money but of course he's useless LIKE ALL DADS. (If you've opened this Mr Samuel Ezeoke then know that I HATE YOU (sorry Izzie darling but it's true)).

Don't worry. I am going to come and save you. I promise We can live in a mud hut together. I have worked it out. There are cargo ships from Liverpool that take passengers to Aberjan (sp???) for only £45 (I called up the Embassy and a Nice Girl told me).

My love for you is bigger than the planet. I promise. All we need is ❤! You are always my SUPER FAB GIRL 4 ever.

There were hundreds of little 'x's covering the entire bottom of the thin blue airmail paper.

'You think it was him, then? I do.'

'I don't know if he killed the girl. But the murder victim was found right next to his house. And he knew the major.'

'And now we know that Morwenna knew where the Ezeokes lived.'

'And he's been keeping it from us. He has to be able to tell us something.'

'I think it was him.'

'Don't jump to conclusions, Helen.'

'Yeah, but I still think it was him.'

TWENTY-NINE

He went to bed exhausted and slept dreamlessly. A thick, honeyed sleep that was hard to emerge from when the time came.

Tozer's knocking woke him eventually. He fumbled in the dark for the flex to his bedside light. The brightness of the light stung his eyes.

'You said you'd be ready,' she shouted through the letter box.

Half asleep, he struggled to remember why Tozer was there. He had overslept. The travel clock by his bed said it was already past seven in the morning. He remembered how, last night, he had phoned Bailey at home to tell him about Ezeoke; that he intended to bring him in for questioning. With Bailey's blessing, he had called the police at London Airport to request their assistance.

He shaved while Tozer put toast under the grill, then struggled into his clothes, Tozer helping him yank a shirt past his shoulder. 'Is that all the butter you got?' she complained.

At 8.20 the winter sun was starting to light up the buildings around them.

'I'll drive,' he said.

'You sure?'

The roads were surprisingly empty but for bread wagons, newspaper lorries and the occasional red GPO van. Breen felt nervous but he no longer had Tozer's driving to blame for it. He would have felt happier if he could have called up control to ask them to check that the London Airport police had received their instructions from last night's shift, but it was not a radio car, so he could only hope.

'You OK, Paddy?'

'I think it's him,' he said as they sped up the Great West Road, past dark rows of offices and factories.

'And I thought you weren't one to jump to conclusions.'

There were roadworks on the A40 and the traffic moved slowly, single file, behind a bus that stopped every couple of hundred yards to pick up people who were on the early shift.

Once they were past Gillette Corner the traffic moved more quickly. They parked outside Terminal 1. The policeman on duty there, a sergeant, strode over straight away. 'You going to be long?'

'We called up last night. We're picking up someone for questioning from the ten-forty flight from Brussels.'

'That space is for emergencies only.'

'Where can we stop, then?'

'Car park.' He pointed towards a concrete building.

The car park faced the main terminal building. The attendant came out of his hut wearing mittens, and took an age to issue a ticket. 'Don't matter if you're police or not. You got to have a ticket.'

When they returned to the terminal on foot the same policeman was still there. He looked at his watch. 'Ten forty? Cut that a bit fine, didn't you?'

'So we should hurry.'

The sergeant spoke into his walkie-talkie and then said, 'Come with me then. Gate Number Seven. Don't worry. They're expecting you. We do this all the time.'

The policeman led them into the terminal and through a small anonymous door to the left hand of the check-in desks, where weary businessmen queued with briefcases and children clambered over mountains of luggage. They passed down a narrow corridor, past a row of interview rooms and through a locked door into the back of a duty-free shop, squeezing between a queue of passengers clutching large packs of Peter Stuyvesant cigarettes and bottles of Johnnie Walker.

'Can we hurry?' said Breen.

'Not supposed to run,' said the policeman. 'This way.'

They were in a public corridor now, passengers coming the other way, lugging carrier bags, holdalls and kids.

Tozer broke into a trot.

'You're not supposed to run,' said the policeman again, panting, but Tozer was too far ahead, flat shoes clacking on the lino.

Ahead was Gate No. 7. A man stood there in a blue BOAC uniform; he waved Breen and Tozer on, down the concrete staircase, to the door that opened out onto the runways.

After the brightness of the inside of the terminal, the world outside was abruptly cold and dark. A couple of lights shone onto the gangway. The passengers were already pouring out of the Britannia and up into the main building.

'Where are the other police?'

'They're on their way,' said the sergeant, gasping for air.

'But they're already getting off the plane,' said Breen.

'Any sign of him?' Policemen started to arrive. 'Who are we looking for?'

'The plane got in early. They didn't let us know,' complained the sergeant. 'Don't worry. Chances are, he's still on board. Is he important?'

Businessmen clutching leather briefcases, yawning, families tugging fractious children, an elderly lady carrying a cat in a basket, all moved slowly down the staircase, single file.

A jet roared into the black sky.

The stream of passengers soon slowed to a trickle. The cabin crew started to emerge.

'You sure he's on this plane?' the sergeant asked.

Breen grabbed a startled air stewardess. 'Was there a black man on this plane? A large man, about forty years old?'

She said, 'In First. We let First Class off before the rest. He's already gone, I think. – Hey? Did that big black man get off already?' she asked a colleague.

'He'll be heading for immigration,' said Tozer.

As Breen started to run back towards the main building he heard the seargeant saying, 'E–Z–E – oh, bugger it. Black bloke,' into his walkie-talkie. He looked over his shoulder and saw Tozer running behind him.

They ran back up the stairs they'd descended only a few minutes earlier and were suddenly in amongst the throng of passengers arriving at the airport from around the world. Tozer barged ahead. 'This way,' she shouted. 'Passports.'

They ran fast now, following the line of passengers. 'Police!' shouted Tozer. 'Make way.'

Breen dashed after Tozer, who seemed to know her way around airports, following the signs for *Passports*. Ahead, a long queue of people craned their necks towards a row of desks. Breen pulled out his warrant card, ready to flash it.

'Excuse me,' he said, moving through the crowd.

A large woman in a white hat said, 'Wait your turn like anyone else.'

'Sorry, ma'am. Police.'

'That doesn't mean you shouldn't wait your turn.'

Breen apologised again and firmly pushed past her.

'Absolute cheek.'

Breen spotted him. Dressed in a grey business suit, Ezeoke stood in front of one of the desks, holding out his passport, smiling to the young man sitting behind it.

Breen pushed on through the crowd of waiting people.

'Oi, who you shoving?' someone shouted.

In that moment Ezeoke looked up to see what the fuss was about and spotted Breen. The big man's first expression was puzzlement, as if he was trying to remember where he knew him from. His second was a frown, as if he were processing the new information. He turned back to the young man at the desk who was holding out his passport, smiled back at him, took the passport and set off briskly.

'Police,' called Breen loudly, holding up his warrant card.

People looked round.

'Let us through.'

Reluctantly people pushed their bags aside as Breen and Tozer barged through.

The man on the immigration desk looked startled as they held up their cards. 'Can you get them to close the customs doors?' Tozer shouted.

Breen didn't understand airports. He wasn't sure what she was asking. The young man on the immigration desk looked equally confused. 'I could ask.'

She pushed past an Indian man and his family and ran into the clear space behind, Breen following.

Looking down the corridor lined with gaudy photographs of Buckingham Palace and the Changing of the Guard, Breen could see no sign of Ezeoke. They both started to run again in the direction they had seen him disappear into – following signs that read *Baggage Reclaim*.

They were in a corridor that somehow seemed to be suspended above the tarmac. Windows to the left-hand side looked out over runways and planes, where passengers streamed downstairs into waiting buses.

They rounded a corner and before he knew what was happening, Breen went flying into a mop bucket that a cleaner had left by the side of the wall, falling awkwardly. He came down on his bad side. Pain exploded through his shoulder.

He looked up. The cleaner was standing there, mop in hand, an angry look on his face.

Tozer had stopped, looking back at him, then down the corridor where they had been heading before he fell. 'Go on,' Breen shouted. 'Catch him.'

Tozer hesitated, then something caught her eye out of the window. 'Bloody hell. How did he get there?'

Breen struggled to his feet, shoulder throbbing.

She was gazing out of the window at the airport outside. He looked too. There, running steadily across the tarmac between the planes, Samuel Ezeoke, briefcase still in hand, weaving his dogged way between the queues of waiting passengers. They watched him pass a Lockheed Constellation that was taxiing slowly onto the runway. For a while he disappeared behind a BP petrol tanker, then appeared again, still running into the far distance.

They sat in the small office that served as the police's Airport HQ while the inspector talked on the phone.

'If they'd been here on time, as agreed, we would have been at the gate to apprehend the gentleman,' he was saying.

'You had his name and the flight he was on,' snapped Tozer.

The inspector looked at the woman police constable disapprovingly.

On the wall above a set of filing cabinets was a framed picture of the Leeds United squad from last year's season. It was signed by a few of them. Breen recognised Norman Hunter, Jack Charlton and Don Revie's signatures; he couldn't make out the rest.

'You don't get many coons running around London Airport runways,' the inspector was saying. 'Even you should spot him easy.'

He put the phone down, shook his head. 'We have work enough to do without having to run around looking for someone you chased out onto the runway. For God's sake.'

'If they'd been there on time we wouldn't have been chasing him,' muttered Tozer. 'It was him. It proves it. He ran. And we lost him.'

The inspector caught Breen looking at the poster. 'You a United fan?'

Breen shook his head. His father had always been Manchester United. He rubbed his shoulder. It ached.

'Nor me, really. I'm Crystal Palace, but I got them when they came through from an away match in Amsterdam. Not bad, eh? I got Sonny and Cher the other day. Lovely couple.'

'He could be dangerous. It's possible he's killed a woman.'

'We're professionals here.'

'Right,' said Tozer.

'Can we help look for him?' said Breen.

'You two stay put. We had to stop all flights from Terminal 1 because he got away. Do you have any idea how much money that costs? We're here to ensure the smooth running of the airport, not to turn it into a circus. You two stay right here. We'll get him. You'll see.'

He pointed to a map of the three terminals. 'This is the future of transport, right here. And it's just beginning. Air travel is within the reach of ordinary men and women. Spain. Greece. Soon they'll have passenger planes that can travel faster than the speed of sound. Getting to New York will be like getting on a bus to Reading.'

The phone rang. 'That'll probably be him caught now, you'll see.' The inspector picked up the phone and said, 'Yes?'

Tozer said to Breen as the inspector answered the phone, 'I hate Leeds United. What's your team?'

'I don't really have a team.'

'I can't say I'm surprised.'

'Thanks.'

'Christ almighty,' said the inspector. 'Oh, good God. Christ al-bloody-mighty.' Tozer and Breen stopped their conversation. 'What with? Oh God. Did you get an ambulance? I see. I'll be right there.'

THIRTY

The policeman lay in a wide culvert by the side of the road, legs sprawled upwards, head down in the ditch. A swallow tattoo showed on the exposed flesh of his arm. Drizzle covered the serge of his uniform in a light sheen. It looked like there had been a struggle, but not a very long one. There was a large dark stain on his tunic where the knife had punctured his heart.

A couple of other officers stood in the misty light, looking down at their fallen colleague. One eye gazed skywards, the other was covered by his helmet, knocked askew.

Nearby a blackbird flew down into the culvert and pecked among the weeds.

'It was his birthday yesterday,' said one of the coppers.

'That's right.'

The inspector looked furiously at Breen. 'He was a good man.'

His voice was drowned by the roar of an airliner passing what felt like only a few feet above their heads. Breen turned in time to see the wheels bouncing down onto the tarmac beyond them, sending up a blurt of black smoke. The runway shimmered with the heat haze of the plane's jet engines' deafening reverse thrust. He watched the plane sway and shudder as it slowed.

Low-ranking policemen wandered around the scene, uncertain of procedure. An ambulance arrived, but the body had not yet been photographed, so the crew waited inside the vehicle looking bored.

Unperturbed, the blackbird continued foraging at the weeds close to the dead man.

★

They crossed London, siren nee-nawing. Breen marvelled at his own calm as he weaved through the traffic.

By the time they arrived at the Ezeokes' house there were two police cars already outside. Breen got out and tapped at the window of one of them. 'Anyone been in?'

'There's a copper in there now with her. Our orders was just to wait here and keep an eye out for a big black bloke. There's a couple of officers around the back and all.'

Breen left them and walked up the steps and rang the bell. He heard it echo through the house.

He banged on the door. It was opened by a policeman. Mrs Ezeoke was there by his side, trembling slightly, but straight-backed. 'My husband told me you would come back,' she said.

'He's here?'

'He telephoned. Half an hour ago. Before your colleagues arrived.'

'Where from?'

She stiffened. 'I do not know. He would not tell me.'

'Was he in a call box?'

She frowned. 'Yes.'

Breen nodded. 'What did he say?'

'He said you would come here and tell me he had done a terrible thing. That I was to stand by him. Of course I will stand by him. He is my husband.'

Breen nodded. A young boy stopped outside on a bicycle, peering at them, wanting to know what was going on.

She said, 'You don't have to tell me. I know it. You believe he killed the girl.'

'Well, it's a mite more serious than that now, missus,' said the uniformed copper standing next to her.

'So it wasn't serious before?' Tozer asked him.

A woman with a wicker shopping trolley stopped by the boy on the bicycle. It wouldn't be long before a crowd formed. 'May we come in?' asked Breen.

Mrs Ezeoke hesitated, then held the door open for them.

'Can I get you a Coca-Cola?' Always polite. Always dignified.

'No, thank you.'

She led them back into the Ezeokes' living room.

'Can I offer you a cigarette?'

There was a copy of a magazine called *Ebony* lying on the coffee table. 'On the phone just now, did he tell you he had killed a policeman?'

'Why would he do such a thing?'

'You tell us,' said the copper.

'Please,' said Breen. 'Do you mind keeping out of this?'

'Don't mind me, I'm sure.'

There was a pinging noise. Then again. Wondering vaguely what it was, Breen asked, 'Why did you move into this house?'

She sat down on the sofa, straight-backed. 'We used to have a very fine house, you know.'

'I know.'

'So why did you move here?'

'Because we could no longer afford our old house.'

Breen sat on a chair opposite her. 'Your husband must make a great deal of money as a senior consultant.'

'Yes.'

'So why do you live here?'

That ping again. Breen realised it was the sound of a stone, half-heartedly thrown against the glass window.

She put her hands face up in her lap and said, 'We have given everything we have to the cause.'

'The cause?'

'The motherland. Biafra.' He stood up and went to the window. There were about ten people outside now, staring in. He wondered which one of them had thrown the stone. Seeing a face at the window, a man started jeering, waving his fist at him.

'You don't sound as enthusiastic about the cause as your husband, Mrs Ezeoke.'

'When men fight, women suffer.' She looked down at the floor.

'What exactly happened to your money, Mrs Ezeoke?'

She glared at Breen. 'Please. Do not expect me to know the details. This was my husband's business.'

'Who was he giving the money to?'

'I do not know.'

The news would be on the radio now, and in the latest editions of the *Evening News* and the *Evening Standard* there would be reports of a murdered policeman.

'You must have some idea, Mrs Ezeoke.'

'Why are you asking me this?' she said.

'Mrs Ezeoke. A girl is dead. A policeman is dead.'

'I do not think this has anything to do with our donations.'

'So who did he give your money to?'

'My husband is a good man.'

'And your own daughter has been sent away from you, which means that we can't interview her.'

She put her hands over her ears. 'I do not want to listen to any more of this.'

'Did he tell you where he was going, Mrs Ezeoke?'

'Even if I did know, I would not tell you.' Her chin rose.

Tozer said, 'We can arrest you for obstructing our enquiries.'

'I do not care. Whatever he has done, he is my husband.'

'I think he killed your daughter's lover,' said Breen.

A tear rolled down her cheek. 'I would not tell you, even if I did know. And I do not.'

Breen stood up again and walked to the window. A woman with a pram had joined the small crowd. 'Armed police will now be searching for him, you realise that? They are the sort of people who shoot first and ask questions later. They really don't like people who kill their colleagues. If we can get to him first and persuade him to give himself up, he'll be OK. It's his best chance. Where will he have gone?'

Breen looked at the poster: *Biafra victorious*.

'I am not going to talk to you any more,' she said. 'He is my husband.'

'There are men stationed outside the house at the front and back. If he comes anywhere near here he will be arrested.'

She turned her head aside, pretending to look out of the window.

'If he tries to get in touch with you, we will expect you to ask him to give himself up. I'm sure you don't want anyone else hurt, Mrs Ezeoke.'

'I never wanted anyone to get hurt,' she said.

In the distance, police sirens, gradually getting closer and louder. The cars arrived in the road outside. When they were switched off, the world seemed suddenly silent.

Bailey was out in front of the house, sitting in his Rover, talking to other officers. He was wearing his old grey mac with a cloth cap and had a pipe in his hand. A man out of time. 'London Airport cocked it up, then?'

'Yes, sir.'

'They're a new force, I believe.' This seemed explanation enough for Bailey.

Policemen were streaming into the Ezeokes' house to begin searching the place. From the front door, Mrs Ezeoke glared at them, arms folded, muttering.

Sitting in the back seat, Breen told him everything that had happened since he had come to this house yesterday afternoon. Bailey pulled out the cigarette lighter and held it above his pipe, sucking at it from the side of his mouth.

'Scotland Yard are taking the whole thing over.'

'I'm still investigating the death of Morwenna Sullivan, sir. That's a different murder.'

Bailey frowned. 'You met this man. What did you make of him?'

'He was one of those men who fill the room, if you know what I mean.'

'And you're sure?'

'I wasn't this morning when we went to pick him up, but I was when he made a run for it. Now I'm sure.'

'Why? Why did he kill the girl?'

Breen hesitated. 'Ezeoke blamed Morwenna for . . . corrupting his daughter,' he said. 'Though I'm not sure if that's all there was to it.'

'Corrupting?'

'The girls were lovers, sir.'

'Ah,' said Bailey stiffly. 'Right.' He looked away, then said, 'Don't go round thinking said, 'Don't go round thinking it's your fault, you know. It was good work. You did the right thing.'

'Thank you, sir.'

'After what happened to Prosser, they'll think you are responsible for that policeman's death. It'll be the talk of the canteen.'

'Yes, sir,' said Breen.

'They're an unruly bunch. I don't feel I have control of them any more.'

Breen didn't answer.

'There's a different way of looking at things, I suppose. I'm probably too old for it all now. But I don't think much of it. They're like a bunch of football hooligans. Not like members of a police force at all. Talking of Prosser, I expect you heard he resigned?'

'Yes, sir.'

'Good riddance to bad rubbish. Do you know why? He wouldn't say.'

'No idea, sir.'

'Right.'

On the doorstep, a constable was shouting at Mrs Ezeoke to get out of the way. He swore at her as she chewed the inside of her cheek, looking past him.

Inspector Bailey sighed, 'Better get on with it then.'

More policemen kept arriving, cars blocking the street.

When he got out, Miss Shankley was standing in the growing crowd, as always in her housecoat and slippers. 'See. I told you it was the darkies. You wouldn't have it, though, would you?' she shouted loud enough for everyone to hear. 'I told them what I thought weeks ago. And what did they do?'

Someone shouted, 'Spazzers.'

He looked at Miss Shankley, arms crossed in front of her. Her smile was bitter and triumphant. 'What you got to say to that, Sergeant Breen?'

It was true. She had been right all along in her single-minded bigotry. He, on the other hand, with his fascination for the anomalous, his feeling of kinship for the immigrant, had failed to see Ezeoke for what he was: a murderer; a madman? Breen looked away, saying nothing, and walked back into the house. A policeman was yanking paper out of Mr Ezeoke's desk in the living room. 'Be tidy, please,' said Mrs Ezeoke. 'There is no need to make a mess.'

'Shut your mouth,' snapped the policeman.

'You don't talk to me like that,' shouted Mrs Ezeoke.

'I'll talk to you like I bloody well like.'

Bailey stuck his head round the door. 'There's no need to act like that, Constable.'

Mrs Ezeoke looked down her nose at him and said, 'Grow up and act like a man.'

The other policemen in the room sniggered. 'Yeah, Smithy. Grow up and act like a man.'

Bailey retreated again.

'There's no need to act like that, Smithy,' mocked the other policemen.

Tozer appeared, eating a cheese sandwich. 'Lunch,' she said. 'You want some?'

Breen shook his head.

'How was Bailey?'

'Could have been worse.'

'Look at all these coppers. Sad, isn't it?'

'What?'

'It takes a copper to get killed to get all this attention. When it was just our girl, nobody cared. Now it's going to be all over the evening papers.'

From the far side of the room, Mrs Ezeoke tightened her lips. She seemed to grow larger and more immovable the angrier she became.

Breen crossed the room towards her. 'I'm sorry,' he said. 'For all this.'

'You're sorry,' she said. There was almost a laugh in her voice.

'But we have to look for anything that might let us know where he has gone.'

'Oi,' said one of the coppers going through Ezeoke's belongings. 'Look at this. He's only got a medal from the Queen.'

'That'll make a great headline, that will.'

Mrs Ezeoke closed her eyes and sighed.

'Your husband has killed at least one person. Probably two. A girl the same age as your daughter. Why?'

'I have nothing to tell you. Your people have no respect at all.'

Breen looked behind her at the *Free Biafra* poster.

'I think he killed the girl in your own house,' said Breen. 'That's why her body was left by the sheds next to it. You were cooking dinner for your uncle. He was trying to find somewhere to hide her so you wouldn't find out what he'd done when you came home. He knew the sheds were unlocked because he had complained about the doors banging. Or he thought he knew.'

Her faced turned grey, but her expression didn't change beyond a tightening of the lips. 'Why would he kill anyone?'

'I don't know,' said Breen.

'He is my husband.'

'What will you do?' he asked her.

'What do you mean?'

'Your husband is a fugitive. Your daughter is a long way away in Africa. Do you have anyone who can look after you? Your uncle?'

'I do not need anybody,' she said. 'I am perfectly fine.'

Breen nodded. 'If he does get in touch again, will you tell him that the best thing he could do is just to give himself up?'

'My husband does not like to be told what is the best thing for him.'

There was a loud smashing of glass. A constable, leafing through the papers on Ezeoke's desk, had nudged a crystal brandy decanter, sending it crashing to the floor, pieces spinning across the polished floorboards.

'Sorry,' he said.

'Get out of my house,' screamed Mrs Ezeoke. 'You are all animals. Get out of my house.'

Everybody ignored her, returning to their tasks, leaving the shattered decanter on the floor. A thick, rich smell of brandy filled the room as Mrs Ezeoke sat down on her sofa and began to cry.

The Afro Art Boutique was a small shop on the Portobello Road between a dry cleaner's and a newsagent's. The windows were full of strange trinkets and carvings. A cardboard box piled with small metal sculptures, each different; some were tiny men holding sticks or spears, others were shaped like chairs or cars. The box was labelled *Ashanti gold weights 3 Guineas*. A huge, black mask with massive cowries for eyes hung from two pieces of string, raffia streaming from the edges of its face. Old black stools of odd shapes and sizes, ancient and worn, were piled haphazardly everywhere. A rusting model of a cruise liner made from tin cans lay at a perilous angle, perched on top of a box carved with intricate zigzag patterns.

Okonkwo's unshaven beard was greying and his eyes were red and tired. He sat at a desk with a tin of Brasso and a dark rag, buffing a ceremonial bronze spoon. Somewhere, a record player was playing Bach's suites for cello.

'Good afternoon. I was expecting you,' said Mr Okonkwo, putting down the rag.

Like the window, the shop itself was piled full of African carvings, boxes, stools and totems. There were masks everywhere, some hung on the walls, others piled untidily on the floor. A heavy looking

328

black stool, seat curved in a gentle 'U' shape, sat on a table. On top of it, a clay statue of a small boy, squatting.

'We've come about Ezeoke.'

'Yes. Of course you have.'

On the wall behind Okonkwo, Breen recognised the same poster as he had seen in Ezeoke's house. There was another too: *Save Biafra*. A picture of a young boy looking up at the camera with dead eyes, stick-thin hands folded around his massively distended belly.

He picked up his rag again and started polishing. 'Ezeoke told me the police were looking for him.'

'You've seen him?'

'He telephoned me. About an hour ago.'

'Where did he call from?'

'I asked. He would not say.'

'You should have called us right away,' said Tozer. 'He's a fugitive.'

The man shrugged. 'I knew you would be here.'

'We could arrest you for withholding information,' Tozer continued. 'You know he's killed two people?'

'Two?' Okonkwo frowned. 'I only heard he killed a policeman.'

'Why did he call you?' asked Breen.

'He called to confess. Oh, and to beg for money and for me to hide him.'

'And?'

'And what?'

'Did you offer to help him?'

'I told him to go fuck himself.'

Okonkwo spat onto the spoon, then continued buffing it.

'Why?'

'You have to understand. I loved Ezeoke like a brother. He was the most successful among us. But now I learn that he has lied to us and cheated us. I told him to go fuck himself.'

'What do you mean?'

'What I understand now is he never was one of us. He is just playing at being one of us. He never listened to us.' Okonkwo seemed to be staring at a single spot on the spoon. 'He always thought he was better than the rest of us because he was raised in England.'

Breen looked around. The bookshelves were full of thick books with weighty titles: *Shakespeare Criticism 1919–1935*, *Hamlet and Oedipus*, *Ashanti and The Gold Coast*, *Tristes Tropiques*.

'Cheated?' said Tozer.

'He has taken our money.'

'I don't understand.'

'He called to say sorry. "I have lost sixty-two thousand pounds of your money. Please, Eddie. Save me. The police are after me." Go fuck yourself, Samuel Ezeoke.' He peered at the spoon and then put it down on the table.

'God,' said Tozer. 'Sixty-two thousand pounds? Your money?'

'Not just my money. The committee's money. All of us contributed. Expatriates over the world. Sam Ezeoke is our treasurer.'

'That's a great deal of money for propaganda,' said Breen.

Okonkwo smiled.

'You gave him the money for Biafra and he embezzled it?' said Tozer.

'Oh, no, no, no. It is far worse than that. Embezzling it would at least have been an African thing to do. No. He lost it.'

'He was conned out of it,' said Breen.

Okonkwo banged the table loudly with the spoon. 'Exactly.'

He stood, went to the front door and locked it, turning the sign that said 'OPEN' round, so it faced the inside of the shop.

'There is nothing as dangerous as a man who imagines himself superior to the rest of us.'

'What is the money for?' asked Breen.

'What we were doing is not illegal.'

'What *were* you doing?'

'It is completely legal.'

'What is?'

Okonkwo spat into a dustbin. 'How much do you know about Africa?'

'Very little.'

'You ruled us until eight years ago but you know nothing about us.' He smiled. 'Our history and our culture mean nothing to you. You have heard of Rhodesia, I suppose?'

'Of course.'

'As a continent, we rarely agree with each other. However, one thing all black Africa agrees on is we hate Rhodesia. It is ruled by a white man. Ian Smith. And you have heard of him too?'

'Is he being lippy?' Tozer asked.

'Rhodesia supports Biafra. South Africa too. Ironic, don't you think? White men in Africa suddenly find it convenient to support the cause of ethnic self-determination.'

'We're in a hurry, Mr Okonkwo,' said Tozer.

'Publicly we are raising money for propaganda. But we are also raising money to pay for mercenaries. Rhodesia supports us. Rhodesia supplies mercenaries.'

'So that party we went to. That was really raising money for mercenaries?' Tozer said.

'Yes.'

'Bloody hell.'

'Ezeoke is an idealist,' said Okonkwo. 'From the start he has never liked the idea of us paying white men to fight our war.'

'You're *not* an idealist, I take it?' said Breen.

Okonkwo opened a drawer and pulled out a small white stick, opened his mouth and dug it into a crevice between his teeth several times. 'Of course I am. But the Rhodesians are the best mercenaries in Africa.'

The phone rang. Okonkwo ignored it. 'We already have some Rhodesians in Biafra. The Federals are scared of them. We Africans have not had proper training. You English made sure of that. A few dozen properly trained men can run rings around a hundred Africans. And, with good reason, given what you have done to us, we Africans still fear white men more than our fellow black men.'

331

'You should answer the phone,' said Breen.

'It's probably no one.'

'Pick it up.'

Okonkwo picked up the ringing phone. 'Hello?'

He listened, then said, 'I am closed, I am afraid. It will not be convenient. Try again in an hour.' He put the phone back down abruptly.

'Who was it?'

'Just a customer.'

Breen wondered if he was lying, but he could see nothing in his expression. 'You were saying. Ezeoke doesn't like the idea of giving money to Rhodesians.'

'Sam Ezeoke is a very passionate man. He wants Africans to show other Africans how we can create a noble post-imperial era. We can control our own destiny. All we need is some guns. He does not understand the first thing about modern warfare.' He dug the stick between his teeth again. 'The Rhodesian mercenaries are racist devils. But they are greedy racist devils. They are our racist devils. Sam has always argued against the rest of the committee. He believes in African solutions for an African continent.' Okonkwo sighed. 'It turns out he had a better plan. One he didn't want to tell us about because he thought we were not true Africanists. We had become corrupted. So he decided to use all our money to buy the arms himself. He met with an arms dealer. A supposed arms dealer.'

'Major Sullivan,' said Breen.

'Is that his name? I did not know this. You can always find a corrupt Englishman somewhere.'

'Major Sullivan?' said Tozer. 'Oh God.'

'It's my guess,' said Breen.

Okonkwo spat a wad of chewed stick into a dustbin at his feet. 'You might expect me to hate this man for stealing our money,' he said. 'I do not. The English are always the English. It is Ezeoke who I hate. I hate him for being stupid and not trusting his fellow Africans. It is the same with all these people, all these Pan-Africanists.

Nkrumah. Nyerere. We Africans are all in this together. At least, we Africans are all in this together as long as you do it my way. And now look what happened.'

'Sullivan probably met Ezeoke through his daughter,' said Breen. 'He was up to his eyeballs in debt. He may have strung Ezeoke a story about being able to get him guns.'

'I don't know who he gave our money to. I don't care. All I know is that he had our money. And all of it is gone. All of it.'

'Did you lose much?'

'Me. I did not have much. Two thousand pounds. I don't care for myself. We all gave it freely. It was like a fever. "Take our money. Take all of it." Ezeoke gave the most, of course.'

'How many of you?'

'There are fifty-six of us. Some are rich. Others, like myself, are not. But we all gave what we could to the cause. And it's all gone. Dogs eat shit, but it's the goat that gets rotten teeth.'

'What?'

'An Igbo saying. It suffers a little in translation.'

'So what's the connection with the girl?' Tozer asked Breen.

'What girl?' said Okonkwo.

'You said he wanted you to hide him?' asked Breen, ignoring his question.

'Yes.'

'And . . . ?'

'Of course I refused. I am not a lawbreaker, Mr Breen.'

Breen walked slowly around the shop. On one shelf, to the right of Okonkwo's desk, there was a worn wooden board with two rows of little cups. There were beans in some of the cups and none in the others. Breen reached in and scooped up the beans and dropped them back into the cups, one by one. 'If you were Ezeoke, where would you go now?'

'I am not Ezeoke.'

'If you were.'

'If I was Ezeoke I would go back to Biafra.'

'How?'

333

'I would go back to Biafra and let a Federal soldier put a bullet into my brain.'

A woman, head covered in a scarf against the cold, tried the door, rattling the handle.

'Go away,' said Okonkwo, waving his hand angrily. 'I am closed. Can't you see the sign?'

The woman disappeared down the street.

'Ezeoke told me it was only a matter of time before the Federal troops collapsed.'

Okonkwo laughed out loud. 'We have lost Port Harcourt. We have lost Nsukka and Enugu, our capital. We are fighting from the bush. What does he think? This is some strategic retreat to weaken the enemy? Our only strategy is to prolong the war until the tide of opinion turns to our side.'

'But all those children are going to die,' said Tozer.

'It's not us killing them. It is the Federals,' said Okonkwo.

'If you were Ezeoke, how would you go back?'

Okonkwo picked up his polish rag, poured some Brasso onto it and started polishing the metal spoon again. 'The country is surrounded. The coast is cut off. There is only one way left to get there now.'

'By air?'

'Yes.'

'Who flies there?'

'Which airlines, do you mean?' Okonkwo laughed. 'No airlines fly to Biafra. Only aid. And only from Portugal now. He would take a plane to Bissau. And from there to the island of São Tomé. That is where the French are flying their aid planes from.'

'So he's probably trying to head to Portugal?'

'How could he get there? You are watching out for his house?'

'He wouldn't dare go near there. There must be half the Met there,' said Tozer.

'What about the committee?' said Breen. 'He must have some friends on the committee.'

'He has no friends on the committee,' said Okonkwo angrily. 'Even before he stole our money, we had argued. He did not approve of our tactics. He is a traitor.' He put down the spoon, pulled another cloth from a drawer and dusted down his desk. 'You should try the hospital. He could borrow money from a colleague.'

'Do you have any idea where he was when he phoned?'

'It was a phone box. He reversed the charges. He could have been anywhere.'

'Did you hear anything in the background that might have given you a clue?'

'It was in a street. There were cars. That is all.'

Breen stood silently in the shop for a minute, looking at the clutter around him. A white-faced wooden figure, standing like a toy soldier on a shelf. A chess set made of tiny wooden carvings of Africans.

'Maybe we should go to the hospital,' said Breen. 'Take a look there.'

'You seriously think he'll have gone back there, sir? It'll be crawling with our lot.'

Breen looked at the poster that said *Save Biafra*. The same picture of a young boy who had starved to death for the cause.

It was dark when they left the shop and walked to the car.

'So. We going to the hospital now? I don't think he'll be there, sir, honest.'

Breen said, 'Just get in the car.'

'What?'

'Drive up a little way and park somewhere out of sight.'

Avoiding a man walking past on the pavement, struggling with an enormous brass candelabra, they got in.

'Why, sir?'

'Act normally and just drive away a little bit.'

'Is he still watching us?'

'Probably. Don't look. Just drive.'

335

Tozer did as he'd said, pulling up down an alleyway next to a launderette.

'What are we doing?' Ishe asked, switching off the engine.

'Did you recognise the woman who knocked at the door of the shop?'

'No.'

'I think it may have been Mrs Briggs. Her face was covered up with a scarf but she ran off the minute she saw us in there.'

'You think Ezeoke is in the shop? Hiding?' Tozer asked.

'I don't know. Something's going on.' It was a small road. People around eyed the police car, wondering what they were doing parked up in their street.

'But he said he hated Ezeoke.'

'Well he would, wouldn't he?'

'Oh. I see what you mean. God.' She looked at Breen. 'So what are we going to do?'

'The shop has a front and a back entrance. Did you see the corridor at the back? We'll split up. You take the back. There's a pub opposite Okonkwo's shop. It should be open. I'll call up the station from there. That way I can keep an eye on the front of the shop.'

'Great. You get to sit in the pub and I get to stand on the street.'

'You're in uniform. You'll be more conspicuous out front.'

'I suppose.' They walked back down the street towards Okonkwo's store. Ten yards before the shop was Blenheim Crescent, which led down into an alleyway.

'That's the back door to the shop there, isn't it? I'll be OK here.'

Breen said, 'Don't worry. The station will send people soon. If anyone moves, don't follow. Just tell us who it is and which way they're headed.'

'I've always wanted to do surveillance,' she said. 'Like in the films.'

Waiting until he could conceal himself among a crowd of people moving up the street, Breen walked up as far as The Prince of Wales. It was a big square Victorian building on the corner, with large windows from which Breen could get a good enough view of Okonkwo's front door, a little to the right and across the road.

336

He went into the pub and ordered a half-pint of best, keeping one eye on the street outside. He sat with his back to the bar. 'You got a phone?' he asked the barman.

The barman nodded towards the toilets. The payphone was in a corridor. He wouldn't be able to see Okonkwo's shop from there. Breen split a ten-bob note for change. 'Five bob if you keep an eye on that door. If anyone goes in or out give me a wave, OK?'

He took a last look. The sign on the front door still read 'CLOSED'. Dimly through the glass, he thought he could make out the dark silhouette of Okonkwo moving behind the muddle of bric-a-brac in his window.

Leaving his position at the bar, Breen got through to Marilyn. 'How are things?'

'Prosser just came in and resigned.'

'So I heard,' said Breen.

'No reason. Just jacked it in. Weird, hey?' He looked over to the barman. He was polishing glasses, but his eyes were fixed on the street like they were supposed to be.

'Weird.'

Breen told her about Okonkwo. 'Tell Bailey. Tell him we need some officers here. Discreetly. And as soon as they can. I think they might lead us to Ezeoke, wherever he is.'

'Is that Constable Tozer woman with you?'

'Just give him the address. I've got to go.'

He made it back to the bar; the shop looked the same, still closed. 'All OK?' he asked the barman.

Breen must have been away from the window a couple of minutes. He peered into the dark behind the junk in the window and tried to make out if there was any movement, but couldn't make out anything. He wondered if Tozer had found a safe place from which she could keep an eye on the back of the shop. A light drizzle had started to fall. If she hadn't found a shelter she would be getting wet.

The barman took the ashtray off the bar in front of Breen and emptied it, then wiped it with a beer towel. The pavements were filling again. He looked at his watch; it was just past five o'clock. They had been watching the shop for just ten minutes. Shopkeepers were switching off lights. Men were returning from work clutching evening newspapers and umbrellas.

'Like another?' said the barman.

'No. I'm OK.'

Another voice said, 'It's Breen, isn't it?'

He was conscious of someone taking the bar stool next to his. Breen tore his eyes away from the window for a second. He recognised the big Irish man at the bar; it was John Nolan. He was holding his hand out towards Breen and it looked like he had been drinking all afternoon.

'Give this man a whisky on me.'

'No, I'm fine.'

'Great news, isn't it?'

Breen looked away from the shop again. 'What?'

'You've not heard?'

'Which news?'

'The best news. I left you a message. Did you not get it?'

'I'm sorry. I don't know what you're talking about.'

'About Patrick Donahoe. The fellow who I thought must have fried in that fire. Do you remember? I'd been trying to contact his relations in Mayo.'

'I remember.'

'You haven't heard then?'

'No.'

'Patrick Donahoe. He worked for me on the building site. He'd gone missing. You were afraid—'

'I was.' Breen looked back at the doorway of the shop. A large blue Pickfords lorry obscured his view, crawling so slowly through the early evening traffic that it seemed like an age for it to move. 'You said it was good news.'

'I got a letter back from his mother this Friday. The stupid bastard was in prison the whole time, thanks be to God.'

'In prison?'

'Pentonville. He'd only got arrested for trying to hold up a petrol station, stupid bollocks that he is.'

'Really.'

The lorry had passed the shop, finally.

'You'll like this. He attempted to rob a petrol station with a fork.'

Breen couldn't help but look at the Irishman again. 'A garden fork?'

'No. Just a table fork. Honest to God. A garden fork would have been better, I should say. He was drunk, I believe. And all he wanted was some cigarettes. So he threatened the guy on the petrol pumps with a fork. Like an ordinary table fork that you'd eat your dinner with. True story. And now he's inside for armed robbery. All for a packet of ten Bensons. Can you imagine?'

'With a fork?' He turned his head. Still no one across the way.

'That's right. And of course he was so ashamed he didn't want to call nobody. So that's why we never heard a whisper. You *would* be ashamed, really, I'd imagine, under the circumstances.'

'Yes.'

'It would be hard enough in prison. "You're in for armed robbery. You must be a tough nut. Was that a double-barrelled shotgun you used?" "No, it was a fork."' The man burst out laughing. He signalled to the barman for another drink.

Breen had seen nothing moving behind the glass since he'd returned from the phone call. Maybe Okonkwo was still at his desk at the back of the shop.

'I can't say I wasn't relieved to hear he was alive, at least,' said Nolan. 'I'd have felt terrible if it was him. Did you find out who the poor bugger under the bonfire was?'

Breen shook his head. 'I thought I had.'

'Well, I'm awful sorry to spoil that for you.'

Breen shook his head. 'Sometimes you don't find out.'

'That's a terrible thing. A poor man dying and nobody caring enough for him to notice he's gone.'

339

'Isn't it?'

'Let me buy you a drink, Sergeant. It would be an honour to buy a drink for the son of Tomas Breen.'

Breen didn't want a drink, but he asked for a pint of Heineken just the same so as not to offend the man and then, to be polite, took a sip from the top of it.

He had drunk almost a half by the time Carmichael arrived, with Jones in tow.

'I have to go,' he told the older man.

'Good luck, Mr Breen,' he replied, swaying gently on his stool.

When they reached the shop, Breen couldn't see anyone inside. Cautiously he tried the door. It was locked.

The hairs on his neck were prickling now. He started walking up Portobello Road, then broke into a run as he rounded the corner into Blenheim Crescent.

When he reached the corner where he'd left Tozer to stand, she was not there. He turned on his heels and started sprinting back up to where they'd left the police car.

'Paddy?' said Carmichael. 'Where are you going?'

Running up the pavement, Breen careened into a woman pulling a shopping basket across the pavement. The basket tipped on its wheels. A cabbage rolled out onto the pavement.

'Oi!'

He didn't stop. But when he reached the small side street the police car was gone.

THIRTY-ONE

'And she hasn't called in?'

'Don't think so,' said Jones.

'The radio wasn't working,' said Breen.

'Typical.'

'She'll phone in,' someone said.

'Oh, Christ.'

The CID room was full of noise. Everybody in the station seemed to be crowding in there. 'It's been the best part of an hour already. You'd have thought she would have had time to call in by now.'

'She's just gone off somewhere, I expect,' said Marilyn. 'You know what she's like. She's done it before anyway. I'm sure she'll be fine.'

Breen glared at her.

The rush-hour traffic had been torture. Even with the sirens blaring it had taken them over half an hour to crawl back to the station.

'Jesus. You think she's OK?'

Bailey said, 'What in heaven's name was she doing on surveillance anyway? She's a woman.' He looked pale.

'She wasn't on surveillance. It was just till back-up arrived.'

'A plonk on a stake-out?' said Jones. 'For God's sake.'

'It wasn't a stake-out,' said Breen.

Carmichael turned to him and said, 'She was doing a sight more than you ever do, Jonesy.'

Breen was surprised by Carmichael coming so strongly to Tozer's defence. Breaking the brief silence that followed, Carmichael said, 'What are we going to do, then?'

'Can I remind you that the murder at London Airport and the subsequent disappearance of Officer Tozer are a Scotland Yard operation now?' said Bailey. 'They are coordinating this.'

A groan went round the room.

'I'm sorry, but that's procedure.'

Carmichael ignored him. 'We can assume he ran because he was guilty, yes? Of killing Morwenna Sullivan. Right, Paddy?'

'In his own house, I'm pretty sure.'

Okonkwo had said Ezeoke would try and make it to Portugal, but then Okonkwo had almost certainly been lying all along. Where could Ezeoke be now?

'He's already killed one woman we know of,' said Carmichael.

'You can't just lose a bloody police car,' someone said.

Breen cornered Marilyn in the kitchen. 'Are you quite sure she didn't phone in?' he said.

'You mean, you think I wouldn't tell you?' she said, turning her back to him as she spooned coffee into a cup.

'You've made it pretty clear you hate her.'

She spun round so fast he had no time to raise his hand to protect his face before she slapped him.

'For fuck's sake, Paddy. I think she's an arrogant bitch, but you think I wouldn't tell you?'

He stood there blinking at her.

'You're such a moron sometimes, Paddy bloody Breen. You don't have the foggiest, do you? You're the most heartless man I ever met.'

She was still shaking with anger when he left her, standing in the kitchen, spilling the sugar she was trying to spoon into a cup.

'She ever come back to your place?'

Carmichael and Breen were standing on a traffic island, marooned by speeding cars. Carmichael picked his moments to talk about this stuff.

'Yes.' Breen was looking at the westbound traffic, waiting for a

342

gap. The skin stung on his face from where Marilyn had slapped him.

'Bit weird, isn't she, Tozer? Did you an' her ever . . . ?'

Breen shook his head. He would have asked Carmichael the same question but he wasn't confident he'd get the answer he wanted to hear.

'I always thought you had,' said Carmichael. A motorbike roared past, just a foot away from them. 'Thing is. She's a pain in the arse. But . . .' Carmichael changed the subject. 'This traffic is ridiculous. In ten years London will have ground to a halt. They're thinking about building monorails above all the streets.'

When they made it across the road there was a uniformed copper in front of the steps outside the hospital. Scotland Yard would have stationed him there to keep a lookout for Ezeoke. 'You been here all day?'

The copper nodded. 'It's not like the man's going to try and walk in the front door. Not after what he's done.'

Carmichael grunted again and they strode on. 'Prosser came in this morning.'

'Marilyn said.'

'What's that all about?'

Breen shrugged.

'Don't do that, Paddy. There's been something going on between you and Prosser. He's jacking it in.'

'So I heard.'

'And?'

Breen shrugged.

'I'm supposed to be your mate, Paddy.'

'I can't say.'

'Did Prosser tell you why he was going?'

'Sort of. I can't say, though. I promised.'

'Don't get me wrong. I'm glad to see the back of him. Just tell me.'

Breen didn't answer. However much he loathed Prosser, he'd made a deal with the man.

'Fine,' Carmichael said. 'Suit yourself.'

The lobby was busy. A patient on crutches leaning against a wall in his striped pyjamas. A white-coated doctor talking to a young woman. Staff trotting past with determined steps. Breen turned to the woman on reception. 'Where's the Senior Registrar's office?'

'Third floor,' she said, cigarette dangling from her lip. 'It's thick with all your mates up there.'

Carmichael took the stairs two at a time. When they reached the front door, a nurse pointed the way down the corridor to a door on which was a polished brass plate: *Professor Christopher Briggs. Senior Registrar.*

A middle-aged secretary in cat's eye glasses looked up from her electric typewriter. 'Yes?'

'Is Professor Briggs in?' Breen held out his wallet.

'He's busy. He will be free in half an hour.'

'It's important.'

She called through to him on the intercom. 'Two more policemen to see you, sir. They say it's important.'

They had to wait five minutes before they were buzzed into a large office. An Afghan rug covered a polished wood floor. A portrait of the Queen hung from the wall behind his desk.

The professor's hair was thick and grey; it flowed dramatically back from his forehead. He wore a pink shirt and a grey woollen suit and sat at a large oak desk, opposite another man who was taking notes on a clipboard.

He nodded at Breen, checked the time of his watch. 'Yes?'

'I'm sorry, sir. But do you know where your wife is?' asked Breen before he'd even sat down.

The professor frowned. 'Could you leave us for a minute?' he told the other man, who got up hastily, dropping the clipboard and then scrabbling for it on the floor.

'I beg your pardon?' continued Briggs. 'Is this concerning the investigation into Mr Ezeoke?'

'Yes, sir. It's possible she knows the whereabouts of Samuel Ezeoke.'

Professor Briggs picked up a fountain pen from his desk and screwed the lid on slowly. 'Why would she?'

'She is Secretary for the Committee for a Free Biafra.' Breen sat in the empty chair; Carmichael stood behind him.

Briggs fiddled with his pen. 'She is very keen on politics,' he said carefully. 'Enthusiastic, the word would be.'

There was a photograph on the registrar's desk, turned halfway so that anyone coming into the room could see what a beautiful wife he had. A black-and-white portrait of a young, confident woman with a look of Audrey Hepburn about her: Mrs Briggs.

'And she was close to Mr Ezeoke.'

'I wouldn't say close.'

'Really, sir? They seemed quite friendly last time I saw them.'

'Are you trying to insinuate something, officer?'

'Do you know where she is?'

'At home, I expect, cooking our dinner.'

Breen leaned across the desk, picked up the telephone and held the receiver out across the desk. 'Can you call her for us?'

Briggs frowned. 'Why?'

'Call her, if you don't mind, sir,' said Carmichael.

'I do mind. I'm not particularly happy about policemen coming into my office giving me orders.'

Breen said, 'We are looking for a senior consultant from your hospital in connection with two murders, one of a policeman, another of a young woman. She knows him well, I believe.'

Briggs coloured. 'As you said, she is on a committee with him,' he said.

'And are you involved in the committee?'

'Of course I'm not. She has her own business, I have mine.'

'Call her, please.'

'Are you seriously suggesting my wife might be harbouring a criminal? I should warn you that I know the Commissioner of the Metropolitan Police well.'

'Of course not, sir. We just want to know where she is,' said Breen.

'At this point,' added Carmichael.

'Please, sir,' said Breen.

Briggs eyed them both for a second, then took the receiver from Breen and dialled a number. Breen watched his face as the call connected. His eyes betrayed nervousness, flickering from the phone to the two policemen, and back again.

'Well?' said Breen.

'It's ringing.' He held the receiver to his ear a while longer. They could hear the regular burr of the tone. On the other end nobody picked up the receiver. 'She could be out,' he said, still holding the telephone.

'Out where?'

'The shops perhaps?'

'Which shops?'

'How would I know? She is an independent woman.'

'How independent?' said Breen. Briggs put down the phone. Breen noticed that his hands were shaking slightly. Seeing Breen looking at them, Briggs placed them on his lap out of sight.

'What my colleague means,' said Carmichael, 'is do you know if she is having an affair with Samuel Ezeoke?'

The man pursed his lips. He picked up the glass jug and poured himself a glass of water. A little water spilled onto the oak desk; he swiped it off the surface with his hand. 'Don't be ridiculous,' he said.

The registrar opened a drawer and pulled out a jar of large white pills. He dropped two into the glass where they fizzed, loud as a dentist's drill, rising and falling in the clouding water.

Frances Briggs was not at home. The house in Russell Square was a large Georgian building, four storeys tall, and she wasn't in any of the rooms. Her Hillman was not outside either. They sat with Professor Briggs in his living room while he slowly worked his way through his address book, calling friends, dialling the numbers, a glass of Glenfiddich by his side.

'Just wondering if you'd seen Frankie . . . No?'

They had no children; it was just the pair of them to fill this massive house. The place was very modern, very up to the minute. There was a huge abstract painting above the chimney, and next to it a screenprint of a girl in a white bikini under which were the words 'BABE RAINBOW'. A pair of modern chairs in front of a white television. The walls were white. A huge domed orange lampshade hung from the ceiling. A couple of African carvings that had probably come from Okonkwo's shop. She did the decorating, Breen guessed. This was not the professor's taste.

'No? Nothing important. Yes. A dreadful business. Listen. Must go. Lunch? Of course. Next week maybe. Goodbye.' A man keeping up appearances.

Another number. 'Teddy? It's me. Ah. You've heard? Yes. Awful for the hospital. No, he'd always seemed so in control. It's been a shock for all of us. Quick question . . .'

Every now and again, the professor poured a little more whisky, turned another page and dialled again.

'What now, Paddy?' said Carmichael.

The professor was talking into the phone: 'No. I've tried her sister. Not a peep. Yes, of course I'm sure she'll turn up any second. Of course I'm not worried.'

Breen looked at Carmichael. 'I don't know.'

'No one has seen her,' said Professor Briggs, replacing the receiver. 'I don't understand it. You don't think she's in any danger, do you?'

'How much time did she spend with Ezeoke?' asked Breen.

'I'm tired of these innuendoes, Detective Sergeant. She was very committed to the cause. Of course she spent time with him.'

'Where would she have gone?'

'I don't know,' Briggs said. 'I don't understand.'

Breen and Carmichael sat side by side on a chesterfield; Briggs had not offered them a drink. 'Have you checked her clothes?' asked Breen.

'Why would I do that?'

'You'd better go upstairs and see if she's packed a bag.'

347

Briggs's face twitched. He upended the glass into his mouth and stood.

'Do you think she's OK?' said Carmichael. They sat outside in the car.

'Briggs or Tozer?'

'Either. Both.'

Breen picked up the radio. 'Delta Mike Five,' he said. 'Requesting a radio car to keep an eye on 19 Russell Square. One, nine, Russell Square. Over.'

It was past eight o'clock. Breen had been up since seven in the morning, but he was wide awake. Today had been relentless, from chasing Ezeoke at the airport, to the discovery of the murdered policeman, to the disappearance of Helen Tozer. After the slow days since returning from Devon, events had cascaded around him, but if anything, his senses were clearer, his shoulders lighter. Tozer might be dead. The thought made him feel physically ill. Yet he felt more alive than he had done in months.

'So maybe this darkie from the shop would have come out and met Mrs Briggs. Or maybe he had Ezeoke with him in the shop. And they came out. And Tozer didn't have time to call you.'

'Something like that,' said Breen.

'Delta Mike Five,' said the woman's voice. 'Delta Mike Three on the way. With you in ten to fifteen minutes. Over.'

'So she just went to the car and followed. Because if she'd have gone to get you, she'd have lost him,' said Carmichael.

'Probably. Possibly.'

'This is a mess, isn't it?' Carmichael lit another Benson & Hedges, though one was still smoking in the full ashtray. 'I'm not blaming you, but you've got to admit. It is, isn't it?'

Breen said nothing. He looked at the Briggses' house.

'So. Like I said, what now?'

'It should be here in a minute.'

'Delta Mike Five,' barked the radio.

'That's us,' said Carmichael.

Breen picked up the handset.

'Thought you'd want to know. They've found Constable Tozer's car, sir. Over.'

'Where?'

'Walthamstow. Over.'

'Walthamstow?'

'Right.'

'And what about Tozer?'

Crackle and fizz. 'Hold on.'

Carmichael said, 'Oh God.'

The radio went quiet for a while. Carmichael leaned forward and banged his head twice on the steering wheel.

It seemed like an age before the woman came back on the air.

'No sign. Over.'

'Bollocks,' said Carmichael.

Walthamstow was way to the east, miles from where Breen had last seen Tozer.

Carmichael already had the blue light flashing.

'Repeat that address,' Breen said, trying to write the street name down as Carmichael tore away.

The car was parked in a cul-de-sac a little way up Chingford Road from the greyhound track. It was nothing more than a short, rubbish-strewn path leading to allotments. The doors had all been locked and the police had had to smash a quarter-light to get into it. Apart from a lipstick on the dashboard and the wrapper from a packet of Polos, there was nothing of Tozer's in the car.

'No sign of blood or anything,' said a copper, standing by the car. 'No sign of a struggle.'

'That's good, right?' said Carmichael. Local police had spent the last half-hour knocking on doors in the area, talking to people on the allotments, but no one remembered seeing the police car arrive.

'Did she drive it here, or someone else?' said Carmichael. 'Why here? Where were they going?'

Breen and Carmichael drove around the streets themselves, peering at endless post-war terraces and semis, looking over cypress hedges and larch lap fences, hoping to spot something. The streets were empty now. People were at home watching the news on television, or on their way to bed.

'I don't mind saying, I'm quite worried now,' said Carmichael.

Breen was too; he just wasn't inclined to say it out loud.

At one point they found a couple of black teenagers riding around on a bike, one sitting on the handlebars. When they asked them if they'd seen a couple of black men with two white women the boys said, 'We haven't seen nothing.'

At around ten they passed another police car coming the other way. Carmichael wound down his window. 'Anything?'

'Not a sniff,' said the other cop.

It was pointless just driving around, but the alternative was to go home, which felt like giving up.

At ten-thirty Carmichael parked outside a corner pub and returned with three packets of Bensons and a box of matches. Around eleven, he said, 'You hungry?'

Breen had eaten nothing since Tozer had made him toast that morning but he didn't feel hungry in the slightest.

'I could eat a donkey and still have room for a doughnut,' said Carmichael. 'Shall we take a break?'

'I know a place. It's not far.'

'This better be good,' Carmichael said, parking outside. 'It looks like a dive.'

'It's good,' said Breen.

Aside from a fading Rembrandt print on the yellowing walls, the cafe was normally a plain place. Tonight, though, there were flowers. Some flowers were in jugs, others in old coffee tins, or oil cans. There were red roses and yellow lilies. One bunch of orange delphiniums was propped in a glass measuring jar.

He couldn't see Joe anywhere. His daughter was behind the counter working with an elderly man Breen didn't recognise.

'What's with the flower shop?' Breen asked.

'Joe's in the Homerton. He had a stroke.'

'Joe? A stroke?'

He noticed now her eyes were red-rimmed and raw. She spooned Nescafé into a couple of cups and held them under an urn. 'Night before last. I got a call around three in the morning. One of his regulars came in and he was sitting on the floor down there.' She pointed behind the counter. 'He couldn't speak or move.'

'I'm so sorry.'

She nodded.

'How long had he been like that?'

'Nobody knows.'

'I'm so sorry,' he said again.

'I shut the shop. I had to.'

'Of course.'

'Joe wouldn't have liked it, but there was only me.'

She opened the counter and walked out to put the coffees on a table in the far corner.

'How is he?' asked Breen when she came back.

She busied herself deliberately wiping the counter. 'He's going to need a bit of looking after.'

'Are we getting some food?' called Carmichael. 'Or what?'

'How are you going to cope?'

'I don't know. A couple of old friends of Joe's have offered to help.' She wiped her eyes.

The cook yelped as he burned himself, trying to pick up a sausage from a pan with his bare hands.

'When are you going to see him next?'

'They don't let us in till after eleven in the morning. I'll go down then.'

Breen looked around. Half the late-night regulars were in. The biker couple whom he'd seen here a few weeks ago were sitting in a corner talking to one of the Pakistanis. When the man caught Breen's eyes he nudged his pretty girlfriend and they waved hello.

'Who's looking after the baby?'

'She's with friends. Everybody's being so kind,' she said, crying again. Breen put his arm around her, but it only made her cry more.

Carmichael ordered double eggs, sausages, chips, beans, tomatoes, mushrooms and fried bread. Breen ordered a smoked-salmon bagel.

There was a gust of smoke from the kitchen.

'It's something, though, isn't it?' she said. 'People coming to help.' She returned to the kitchen to help the temporary chef, who was struggling. He had a bandage on his finger when he brought the plates over, from when he had tried to slice tomatoes. Carmichael's sausages were barely cooked; his egg was black around the edge; there was a dark greasy thumbprint on one side of the plate.

'Bloody hell. I'm sending this back,' Carmichael said, staring at it.

'Over my dead body,' said Breen. He picked up his bagel and took a bite from it.

Carmichael set about cutting the burned part of the egg away. 'Oh God. Did you see the state of his hands? By the way, I handed in my request for a transfer,' he muttered.

'Scotland Yard?'

Carmichael stuck his fork into the firm yolk of the egg. 'Yes.'

'Drug Squad?'

'Yes,' he said again. 'You're not coming, are you?'

Breen took a sip from his coffee. It was watery and unpleasant, but hot at least. 'No. I'm staying put.'

'You'll be stuck in a dead-end force with Bailey.'

'I'm OK there.'

'Pilcher says I can make another six hundred quid in a year.'

'Best of luck.'

The bagel was too dry. Breen picked off the salmon and ate that on its own.

They ate quickly. Breen left a big tip. 'Give Joe my best,' he said.

Carmichael got on the radio as soon as they were back in the car.

'Any news on Constable Tozer?'

'Any news on who?' the woman on the other end of the radio said. 'Over.'

'Fuck sake,' said Carmichael, then to Breen, 'What if she's dead?'

'Shut up, John, for Christ's sake.'

'OK. I was just saying, that's all.'

They went back to Walthamstow and drove round aimlessly for a while longer. 'I could drop you home,' said Carmichael. 'It's not far from here.'

'What about you? Are you turning in?'

'I don't know.'

'I'm OK. I don't feel like sleeping.'

'Me neither. I wish we could bloody do something. This is driving me nuts.'

'If I hadn't told her to keep an eye on the back of the shop, this would never have happened.'

'You can't say that, Paddy.'

On Billet Road they were flagged down by a middle-aged woman in a fur coat. When they pulled over she asked, 'Have you seen my husband?'

They both got out. Her breath reeked of brandy. She was tottering on patent leather heels. 'Where do you live, love?' said Carmichael.

'London,' she said.

'Can you be a bit more precise?'

The radio crackled. 'Delta Mike Five?'

Breen ducked back into the car.

A brief crackle, then: 'Delta Mike Three just called in. Have a message. Over.'

Breen checked his watch in the green glow cast by the radio's light. It was half past midnight.

'Is Mrs Briggs back at the house? Over.'

'Negative. Delta Mike Three says her husband has just got into his car. Requests urgent instructions. Over.'

'Follow him.'

'Say again.'

'Follow him,' shouted Breen. 'Tell him not to let him out of their sight.'

The operator went silent while she relayed the message. When she came back on the air, Breen said, 'Tell them to let us know where they're heading.'

'Will do. Out . . .'

'Wait. What about Constable Tozer?'

'Nothing so far. Out.'

He called through the window. 'Get in.'

Carmichael returned to the car. 'What?'

'Briggs is on the move,' he said, replacing the handset in its holder.

Carmichael got in and started the engine. 'That toff in the pink shirt? Bloody hell. He's gone looking for her?'

'It looks like it.'

'Where?'

'They're following. They're going to let us know.'

'Hey,' said the woman in the coat. 'What about my husband?'

'Go home, love,' shouted Carmichael.

'I'll report you,' called the woman. 'I'll bloody report you buggers.'

Everything else she said was lost to the roar of the engine.

THIRTY-TWO

The next call they received told them that the professor was driving a blue Daimler Sovereign heading out on Whitechapel Road. 'Registration Golf Romeo Tango One Nine One Foxtrot.' Breen scribbled it down as they roared off down the Chingford Road.

'Bloody hell. He's coming our way,' said Carmichael.

'That's something,' said Breen. 'It means he's heading in the same direction as whoever got Tozer.' He could lead them to her still. Breen was flicking through a road map and traced the A11 towards where they were headed. 'Can we make it to Leyton High Road in five minutes?'

'You bet.' Carmichael gunned the car southwards, slowing only for red lights, but not stopping.

They were there in good time; Carmichael swung a U-turn, reversed the car into a side street and turned off the headlights.

'If it's coming our way.'

'Delta Mike Five. Quarry stopped for petrol on Bow Road. Over.'

'Reckon he's going far, then?' said Carmichael. 'If he needs a full tank?'

'If he's heading out of London it's going to be harder once we have to relay the radio with Essex.'

A moment of stillness as they waited in the car, watching the traffic pass. Carmichael lit another cigarette and belched. 'My guts are killing me. Bet it was those bloody sausages. If he's heading out of London we might lose him. We should pull him up.'

'Could do,' said Breen. But if they stopped him they might lose the chance of finding out where he was heading.

'I mean, odds on, if it's out of London he'll spot he's being followed.'

It was true, thought Breen. In the dark, on country roads, you noticed if you were being followed.

'So should we pull him?'

'Let's wait and see what he does.'

He switched on his torch and shone it on the road atlas. If Briggs wasn't heading for East London itself, he could be heading anywhere further north or east.

'Delta Mike Three now heading up . . .'

The radio faded away to nothingness.

'Say again. Over,' said Breen.

Nothing. Breen and Carmichael looked at each other. 'Bloody hell,' said Carmichael.

'Say again. Over,' said Breen. 'We're losing you.'

'I don't feel that well, to be honest,' said Carmichael.

'Say again.'

Nothing.

'Bloody mess.'

The receiver fizzed and buzzed; ghost voices from some ham-radio conversation drifted into the police frequency.

'Get off the airwaves,' Carmichael thumped the radio in frustration.

'Quiet,' said Breen.

The operator's voice faded back in. 'Rom . . . Road. Over.'

'Say again.'

Again the interference obliterated the reply.

'Jesus.'

'Say again,' Breen repeated.

And then the voice cut through: 'Romford Road.'

Breen studied the map. 'There.' He pointed. The car had turned east.

'Shit,' said Carmichael, switching on the headlights and putting the car into gear.

He turned on the blue light and roared out of the side road, right in front of a milk float, which had to swing out of the way, a milk crate toppling off onto the tarmac. Carmichael blared his horn and spun away on down the road.

Water Lane was thankfully deserted. Carmichael turned off the police lights as they approached Romford Road. 'Right,' shouted Breen.

Carmichael swung the car round a red traffic light and slowed down to a less conspicuous speed. 'We've got to be behind them both now,' he said.

'What's the latest from Delta Mike Three? Over.'

No answer; just the crackling of static.

'Bollocks,' said Carmichael. They tore through junctions and zebra crossings and past closed shops and pubs.

In the centre of Ilford he stopped in the middle of a junction. 'Where now?' The road divided. 'Quick, Paddy.'

'Hold on.'

Breen peered at the map, his finger tracing the yellow lines. Where? He had to make a guess which route they would have taken. North or east?

'Right, then first left.'

'Got you.'

If they had come this far they would still be heading east, Breen was hoping. The A12 was beyond them, stretching out towards Essex and beyond. Post-war semis lined either side of the road ahead, each house like the last. London edging ever outwards.

'Bingo,' cried Carmichael, braking suddenly.

Ahead of them, stopped at a red light, was a police car. And about 150 yards beyond that a Daimler, moving away on the far side of the lights. They were following at a distance, letting it stay well ahead of them.

Carmichael pulled up alongside the police car, and Breen wound down his window. A pair of young uniformed men sat in the car, grinning broadly, thrilled by the chase. 'Hey-ya,' the driver said, and waved.

'We're pulling him over,' shouted Breen from the passenger seat.

'Now?

'Yes.'

'Do we have to?' said the constable. 'We're having fun.'

'We'll get in front.'

The moment the lights changed Carmichael shot up the road. They caught up with the Daimler easily; Briggs had had no idea he was being followed. Breen caught a quick glimpse of Briggs's face as they passed, hands clutching the wheel, and then Carmichael had the siren on and the lights blazing, brakes on, forcing the car to a stop as the other policemen's Austin boxed it in from behind.

Breen was out of the car, torch in hand. He shone the torch in Briggs's eyes.

'Morning.'

Professor Briggs blinked into the light. 'Oh,' he said. 'It's you.'

'You know where she is, don't you? Your wife?'

They were stopped by a big roadside pub whose sign creaked in the wind. Briggs looked back at the steering wheel. 'Sort of. I think.'

Carmichael called over from the driving seat of the police car, 'Get in the back. We'll take you there.'

Sitting in his Daimler, gloved hands on the wheel ahead of him, Briggs hesitated. 'All this mess,' he said. 'You don't have to make it public, do you?'

Breen said, 'Out of the car, please.'

'I don't really care for myself,' said Briggs. 'It's just it would embarrass Mrs Briggs if this got out. I'll put in a word with your boss. I do have some influence, you know. I know the Commissioner very well.'

'Out,' shouted Breen.

It was a house by the sea in Suffolk. Their getaway place; the couple spent weekends there in the summer.

'Did she take Sam Ezeoke there?'

Briggs didn't answer.

Later, in the dark of the A12, Carmichael driving down the empty road, headlights on full beam, he said, 'We have a caretaker. I called her up after you'd left my house and asked her to look in on the place. She said, "Oh. I thought you were there. The light was on."'

They travelled east into the darkness.

'Why here?' asked Breen.

'I don't know. We have a boat. A twenty-six-foot Seamaster. Perhaps she wants to get him away in that.'

As they got closer to the coast, the mist hung in patches. Carmichael looked pale. He said little beyond swearing at a cattle truck that was blocking the road and asking Breen to light his cigarettes.

'What if they've taken the boat already?' said Breen.

'They haven't. I asked the caretaker to check for me.'

'Can she handle the boat on her own?'

The professor laughed drily. 'I'm the landlubber. The boat is her toy.'

They were doing around forty down a narrow, straight black road, short hedges on either side, when Carmichael braked suddenly, sending the professor hurtling off the back seat and into the space between the two front seats. 'For God's sake,' he shouted. 'Be careful.'

Muddy water splashed up as Carmichael pulled the car into a lay-by.

'What's wrong?' said Breen

Without answering, Carmichael kicked open the door and dashed out into the blackness.

'What the devil has got into him?' said Professor Briggs.

'I don't know,' answered Breen, getting out to follow Carmichael. It was a dark, starless night and it took Breen a minute for his eyes to adjust. He leaned back inside the car and pulled the torch from the glove compartment.

Carmichael had clambered over a fence and disappeared into a newly planted field.

'John?' called Breen.

A faint groan returned from the black field.

'Are you all right?' asked Breen.

Another groan. Breen switched on his torch; dazzled by the light, John Carmichael was squatting on the brown earth, trousers about his ankles, the pale skin of his legs luminous in the bright beam.

'Switch it off!'

'What's wrong?'

'Don't laugh. I just shat my trousers,' said Carmichael.

'I'm not laughing, I promise.'

Carmichael groaned. 'Go away,' he said.

The night was cold; wind came unhindered over the flat land. An owl screeched somewhere. Breen returned to the car.

'What's wrong?' asked Professor Briggs.

'Detective Sergeant Carmichael is ill,' Breen said, rummaging again in the glove compartment. There was a pad of licence-producer forms but the paper looked flimsy.

'What's wrong with him?'

'Food poisoning, I think.'

'Oh for pity's sake.'

Breen went round to the boot, opened it and shone the torch inside. A set of spanners lay wrapped in a copy of the *Mirror*. He took the newspaper and clambered over the fence with it. 'Best I could find,' he said, offering it to Carmichael.

'Thanks.'

Breen and Professor Briggs waited in the car, heater on. The land around them was flat and empty. There were no lights on the horizon. No cars came past.

'I suppose I should call someone at the hospital and let them know I'm going to be late,' said Professor Briggs, pushing his hair back from his eyes. 'What time should I tell them I'll be in?'

'I haven't the slightest idea.'

'That is not particularly helpful.'

Breen turned round and glared at the man in the back seat. 'There would have been no need for any of this if you had told us where you thought your wife was in the first place.'

The professor turned his head away, as if looking at something of great interest beyond the blackness outside the car.

Breen got out of the car. 'How are you doing?' he called.

'I feel like shit,' said Carmichael.

Breen looked at his watch. It was almost three in the morning. They still had at least three hours to drive.

'Are you going to be long?'

'I keep thinking I've finished and then I start again.'

Breen peered into the blackness around them and wished they had contacted the Suffolk police before they'd left civilisation.

Eventually Carmichael rejoined them; his eyes looked sunken, his hair was matted against his forehead. He slumped into the driver's seat, put the car in gear, then took it back into neutral again. 'Not sure I can drive,' he said.

'Good grief, man. Is that you? You smell to heaven,' said the professor. 'What did you do to yourself?'

Breen turned to the professor: 'Right. You drive,' he said. After the fall that morning, he wasn't up to a long session behind the wheel.

'You must be ruddy joking,' said Briggs.

'I wish I ruddy was,' replied Breen.

In the darkness, the professor was a nervous driver. He paused at every corner or junction; if any vehicles approached from the opposite direction, headlights shining into his eyes, he slowed to a virtual standstill. As dawn approached, the roads became fuller; huge lorries packed with beets loomed within feet of the rear bumper. Their presence slowed Briggs down even more, sending the truck drivers into a rage of impatience. One blared his horn until Briggs found a lane he could pull over into.

Carmichael lay on the back seat, groaning occasionally. By the time they stopped at a small all-night petrol station somewhere in Suffolk, a thin line of deep blue light was starting to form to the east.

The attendant was asleep in a chair inside. Breen banged on the window to wake him. He emerged, rubbing his eyes, dressed in a long brown cotton coat with *Esso* written on the chest pocket. 'Fill it up,' said Breen. 'Oh. And you got a key for the toilets?'

Breen passed the key to Carmichael, who tottered out to the back of the station clutching it.

'Is he going to be all right?' asked Breen, as the attendant put the nozzle into the tank.

'How would I know?' answered Briggs.

'Well, you're a doctor, aren't you?'

The professor didn't answer.

When Carmichael returned he was looking a little less white, though he still got into the back seat. He sat up straight this time in the corner and lit a cigarette. 'Drive,' he said.

'I'd rather you didn't smoke,' said the professor.

'I'd rather you just shut up,' said Carmichael.

THIRTY-THREE

The greying light revealed flat, dull land. The roads were straight and the hedges were even. Small pockets of fog loomed in fields filled with flocks of lapwings and geese.

And then the sea was ahead of them: a grey line beyond the dark fields. They pulled up a hundred yards away from the house, a small white two-storey cottage at the end of a thin strip of village lying along the coast. The road lay between the houses and a shingle beach; a few black-hulled fishing boats were pulled up on the stones alongside tar-painted sheds.

'That's her car,' said Briggs. A new Hillman Minx, parked a few yards away from the house.

He opened the driver's door and got out.

'Are they still there?'

'I'm not sure.' He walked hesitantly towards the house. The air blowing off the North Sea was bitterly cold. His long grey hair flew about his face.

'Shut the door. It's freezing,' complained Carmichael.

Breen leaned over the driver seat and pulled the door to.

Briggs returned to the car, opened it again and leaned in, brushing his hair back. 'I think they're in there. The curtains are drawn but there's a light on. Shall I knock?'

'No,' said Breen.

'Why not?'

'Get in and shut the fucking door,' said Carmichael.

Briggs sat back in the driver's seat. 'There's no need for language like that.'

'Sit down,' said Breen, 'and don't do anything.'

'I need to know if she's OK.'

Breen picked up the radio and searched the frequencies but he could hear nothing. There was a red phone booth about fifty yards past the house. 'Stay here.'

'I want to die,' said Carmichael.

After he'd phoned the local police, he returned to the car and waited. Wind hummed in the telephone wires. Clouds scudded low across the sky.

They sat and waited. 'My God, you stink,' said Briggs, winding down the window.

'I can't help it.'

'That's enough,' Breen hissed at Briggs. 'Keep your voice down.'

After around twenty minutes, a police car approached quietly from behind them, lights off.

'You the ones from London?' whispered the senior officer, a thin-faced sergeant with pointed sideburns. He leaned down into the open window of the car. A couple of gangly constables got out and stood behind him.

'Yes.'

'You've got a warrant?'

'No time,' said Breen.

The sun was peering over the horizon, turning the white cottages along the seafront a rich red. Seagulls whirled in the greying sky above; more sat on the beach, pointing beak-first into the sharp wind.

'How many in there?' asked the policeman.

'Possibly two men and two women. One is a police officer who may be being held against her will.'

The sergeant nodded thoughtfully. 'I got two men,' he said. 'We could send for more, only there aren't too many of us on duty in these parts this time of day.'

Breen considered for a second. 'Two should be OK,' he said.

Carmichael leaned forward. 'Is there a toilet round here?' he called through the open window.

'Public toilet down there,' said the sergeant.

Carmichael opened the door and stood, bent from the waist, holding his stomach.

'It'll be closed now, course,' the sergeant said.

'Of course,' said Carmichael. He got back into the back seat and lay down again.

'He OK?' said the policeman.

'He's sick.'

The officer nodded again. 'So just two of you then?'

'One,' said Breen. 'He's a civilian.' He nodded towards Briggs, who scowled back. 'Shall we go then?'

Breen got out of the car and walked towards the house, aware of the sound of each footfall. There were two sash windows on the ground floor, one on either side of a front door over which straggled a weedy, blackspot-covered rose. The garden had a large abstract granite sculpture in it that looked a little like a Henry Moore; old pieces of driftwood were strewn around the gravel that surrounded it.

Between the Briggses' cottage and its neighbour was a small, thin alleyway. The mast of a sailing boat lay down the length of it, varnish peeling. Breen walked as silently as he could along it; behind the house he found a small concrete yard, full of old paint cans, a rusting bicycle and a pile of firewood. A low flint wall separated the yard from the pathway. Behind, another line of houses backed on to them.

Breen tiptoed back round to where the sergeant was standing.

'Two men at the back?' the sergeant whispered. Breen nodded.

A brown-feathered gull sat on the chimney above them, eyeing the two policemen as they moved down the alleyway to cover the rear of the house.

Breen went up to the door, looked over to the sergeant, who nodded; then he knocked loudly on the door with his fist. 'Open up,' he shouted. 'Police.'

Nothing.

'Sam? I know you're in there. Open up.'

There was a clattering sound; someone moving behind the door. 'Who is this?'

'It's me, Sam. Cathal Breen. Open up.'

'Mr Breen?'

'Yes.'

'I am glad it is you, at least.' It was Mr Ezeoke's voice. He sounded tired.

'We've got you surrounded, Sam. There's no way out. Where is Constable Tozer?'

There was a long pause.

'Don't be stupid, Sam.'

There was a weariness to his voice when he said, 'It is too late to tell me not to be stupid.'

'Where is Constable Tozer?'

'She is here. She is safe.'

Breen was filled by a sudden sense of lightness. Everything could be OK. Until he heard Ezeoke say that, he had not been aware of how tense he had been for the last fourteen hours.

'Let her out, Sam.'

'She is asleep now.'

'Wake her up, then.'

'I can't. I've given her a pill, Mr Breen. If I give her back to you, will you let me go?' Breen's heart started thumping again. His respite had been short-lived.

'You killed two people. You need to come out.'

No answer.

'What did you give her?'

'I will kill myself first.'

'What drugs did you give her?'

'Nitrazepam.'

'What's that?'

'A sedative to make her sleep. She will not be harmed by it.'

'Is that how you got her here?'

366

Ezeoke sighed. 'She was following us.'

'You forced her?'

'There was a small struggle, but she was not hurt.'

'Is that what you did to Morwenna Sullivan?'

A pause. 'I did not mean to kill the girl. It was a mistake. She made too much noise. People would have heard.'

'You strangled her.'

'I did not mean to kill her. All I wanted to do was to keep her until her father gave me the money that he stole off me. But she shouted. She screamed and shouted.'

Fierce, her friend had called her.

'What money, Sam?'

'The money he stole from me. Money to buy guns.'

'So he knew you had his daughter. She was a hostage.'

'I lost my daughter because his daughter perverted her.'

'But he didn't go to the police because . . .'

'Because he'd stolen our money.'

There was a longer pause. There was a rattling and two barrels of a shotgun pointed out from the letter box. Breen stepped quickly aside, and moved behind the granite sculpture. The sergeant scrabbled his way back down the short path to the road, shouting, 'Jesus! He's got a bloody gun.' He started gabbling into his lapel radio.

'Let the girl go, Sam,' said Breen from behind the cold grey stone.

'Go away.'

'We can't go away, Sam.'

One barrel of the gun exploded into the air, sending the gulls on the beach squawking suddenly into the air.

'Fucking hell,' said the sergeant, bent over double, scuttling down the street away to the police car. The barrel moved sideways along the small slot of the letter box towards Breen. He closed his eyes, then heard the sound of the barrels withdrawing from the letter box, followed by the sound of the shotgun being reloaded. He took his chance and ran.

★

One of the policemen from behind the house came hurtling down the alleyway.

'He's a nigger. He's got a gun. Nobody said,' he complained.

'Did you see him?' asked Breen.

'I poked my head up and he was there in the kitchen. He pointed the fucker right at me. Nobody bloody said.'

'Why didn't you say he had a gun?' hissed the sergeant, still crouched below the low wall.

'I didn't know he had,' said Breen.

He walked back to the police car where Briggs was still sitting, and yanked open the door.

'Do you keep guns in the house?' he demanded.

Briggs said, 'Is she OK?'

'Tell me about the guns. How many?'

'Three. Duck guns,' he said. 'My wife. Is she OK?'

'Christ,' said Breen. He put his head in his hands.

Five minutes passed. 'How long before any more police get here?' said Breen.

'Twenty minutes,' said the sergeant.

'The longer he's in there, the harder it will be to get him out.'

'Not exactly simple right now,' said the sergeant.

On the far side of the Briggses' house, an elderly man appeared in a red woollen dressing gown. A woman peered out from behind him with a small Yorkshire terrier in her arms. She wore large wellingtons under her pink dressing gown. 'Get back inside,' Breen shouted.

'Can someone please tell me what the hell is going on?' called the old man, wandering towards them.

'Go back,' shouted the sergeant.

The man paused. 'Good grief. Is that Chris Briggs in the police car?' the man said. 'What's going on, Christopher?'

Bending low, Breen ran towards them. Putting his arms around the old man, he pulled him back, away from the house.

'What's going on?' he demanded.

'There's a man with a gun. Go back inside and shut your doors,' Breen said.

The man seemed to take orders well. He turned and walked back, taking his wife and their dog with him. Their house was two doors along from the Briggses', a bigger cottage, but with paint peeling from the woodwork.

The sergeant came up. 'Colonel? Do you have a gun?' The man hesitated.

'Of course he has,' said his wife. 'Haven't you, dear?'

It turned out the colonel was a retired military man who kept a revolver in a cigar box. He returned with the box and opened it; the gun was covered by a handkerchief. 'You won't tell anyone, will you? About the gun. Only I never bothered getting a licence,' he said, unwrapping it.

'Course not, sir,' said the sergeant.

It was an elderly Webley service revolver. There were a few rounds lying in the box around it. The sergeant released the cylinder latch and pushed four bullets into the chambers.

'It's been a little while since I used it,' said the old man.

Breen returned to the far side of the house. The barrels of the shotgun had been withdrawn from the door. There was no sign of any movement.

A moth flew into Breen's face, startling him. He brushed it away. Briggs got out of the car. 'What's going on?'

'Get back in the car.'

'What about my wife? Is she OK? Maybe if I spoke to her?'

'Get back in the car.'

'Frances?' shouted the man. 'Are you in there?'

The shotgun emerged from the letter box a second time. 'Jesus Christ,' said Briggs. Revolver in hand, the sergeant pulled the professor back towards the police car.

'Sam?'

'Go away, Mr Breen.'

'Do you have Mrs Briggs in there?'

The barrels poked out of the door again. 'Yes.'

'Have you drugged her too?'

'No. Mrs Briggs came willingly.'

'That's a lie,' shouted Professor Briggs.

At that moment there was a sudden commotion behind the house. A man's scream, followed by a crashing noise. 'Help me!'

In that moment the sergeant turned. The revolver's quick pop was remarkably quiet compared to the shotgun.

'Got the bugger,' the sergeant shouted, still pointing the gun down the alleyway.

Breen ran towards the alley; a man was sprawled on the bare earth, face down. Breen could see from the grey hairs on his head that it was not Ezeoke. The constable emerged from behind the house, white-faced.

'He came right at me, Sarge. I couldn't stop him,' he said. 'Is he dead?'

They had dragged Okonkwo into the street, away from the side of the house where he had been shot.

He was wearing the same clothes as the day before and was bleeding thickly through them from a wound in the stomach.

'How was I to know there was two of them in there?' protested the sergeant.

'Sorry,' whispered Okonkwo to Breen. His head was propped against a wheel of the police car. Breen took off his jacket and put it over the man. 'He is mad. I had not thought he was so mad.'

'He was coming right at me. I thought it was the other one. It's not my fault.'

Okonkwo's face looked the colour of stone. 'I am so sorry.'

'What about Constable Tozer?' Breen asked.

'What about my wife?' demanded Professor Briggs.

'Ezeoke is mad,' said Okonkwo. 'Your wife is an idiot, Mr Briggs.' His breath was shallow. 'She thinks Ezeoke is a god. A revolutionary god. He can do no wrong.'

'Shut up,' said Professor Briggs.

'You should have told me where he was yesterday,' said Breen.

'I'm sorry. I thought I should help him.'

Blood was bubbling from his mouth now. Okonkwo did not seem to notice. 'I think we will lose the war. What do you think, Mr Breen?'

Okonkwo's skin had turned grey.

'What war? What's he on about?'

Okonkwo closed his eyes. Breen leaned closer.

'What is the layout of the house?' he asked. 'Where is Tozer?'

Okonkwo didn't answer. His breathing slowed. His hand was opening and closing slowly.

'We have to know. Where are they?'

The sound of sirens came from across the marshland, louder and louder, until their wailing filled the air around them.

By the time they had arrived, Okonkwo had stopped breathing altogether.

The policemen complained of the cold. They stamped their feet. 'We could take him.'

'What's going on?'

'Nothing, I don't think.'

'You're the copper from London. What's up with your mate?'

'He's got food poisoning.'

From inside the house, Ezeoke shouted, 'What is happening?'

'Eddie Okonkwo is dead,' said Breen.

Ezeoke didn't answer.

'What's he going to do?' The local inspector had brought guns. Police crowded round the house with .303s. They were excited. Things like this happened once in a local policeman's life.

'Shoot the cunt, I say,' said one lanky policeman.

Some police were pushing inquisitive locals down the street. There was an inevitability to what was about to happen now.

He thought of Okonkwo and Ezeoke, men filled with a fervour

371

for politics. The world was suddenly full of people like them, shouting for change, willing to see blood spilled. The kind of men who didn't run from knives but towards them; who were sure about what the world was and what it should be. Breen could never be like that. For him, the world was a place seen from a distance, a curious puzzle. He thought of Tozer, comatose in the room just a few yards away. He could fight for her, he knew, but never for a country or an idea. Maybe it was just a lack of passion; a lack of imagination. But he only wanted to save one person.

He thought of his dead father and the woman his father had lost. He felt he had never known him as well as he did now. They were not so different.

'Sergeant?'

Breen walked over to the local inspector. He was a round man with a moustache and a mournful expression on his face. He shook hands with Breen. 'Nasty old day,' he said.

'Yes, sir.'

'Professor Briggs says you know the man with the gun.'

'That's right, sir.'

He nodded. 'Go and talk to him.'

'Why, sir?'

The inspector looked at him. 'Just go and talk. You'll know the kind of thing to say.'

'Yes, sir.' He knew what would happen now. Darkness filled his chest.

It had started to drizzle. The ambulance man had tried to give him his jacket back but he hadn't wanted to wear it; it had Okonkwo's blood congealed on the cloth by the vents.

He looked out towards the grey light on the eastern horizon. A pair of fishing trawlers was setting out from some nearby port. They looked small against the big sea. Waves slapped onto the shingle, out of sight, below the cottage.

'Go careful. Keep him talking as long as you can.'

'Yes, sir.

'Good luck.'

Constables with rifles were surrounding the house.

He walked slowly down the short path towards the shotgun. As soon as he could, he tucked himself back behind the sculpture.

'Sam,' he called. 'You there?'

No answer.

'Did you hear? Eddie is dead. He was shot. They thought he was you.'

'You killed him. You English people.'

'You'll die too.'

'Why should I care?'

'It's pointless, Sam. There's nothing to be gained. Please.'

No answer. Breen heard a noise behind him and turned. A policeman with a gun was crouching just behind the wall, pointing his rifle past Breen. Breen shivered. There was no shelter. His white shirt stuck to his skin.

'Please, Sam. Send out the women at least.'

'If they are harmed, it will be your fault. You killed Eddie Okonkwo. You shot him like a dog.'

'You killed Morwenna Sullivan. That was your fault.'

'It was her father's fault. He stole our money. He promised me guns. He was a liar and a thief. It was him I wanted to hurt.'

The police had stopped moving now. They were all in position, he assumed.

'So you kidnapped Morwenna?'

'Our entire country is being held as a hostage. Hundreds are dying every day.' Breen was shivering uncontrollably now, his jaw juddering with the cold. 'He took our money. I am tired of talking, Mr Breen. All I want is to go home to Africa. All I want is to go home.'

'You can't go home, Sam. You don't have a home any more.'

'I have to.'

Breen thought he could bear it no longer. Rain trickled from his hair into his eyes. This was taking too long.

'Your daughter loved her,' said Breen.

'That is not love,' shouted Ezeoke.

A gust of wind rattled the windows of the house, sending raindrops flying down the collar of Breen's shirt.

And then the shooting started, and the screaming. Wild, lurid, loud, pained screaming. Seabirds flew up from the shoreline. Breen crouched down below as the bullets flew, shattering wood and glass, smacking into brickwork. Dust sprayed all over him, sticking to his dampened shirt. His eyes stung. Glass sprayed out onto the gravel behind him. The smell of cordite stained the air.

All that was left was the sound of a woman still screaming, pausing briefly for breath, and then screaming again.

THIRTY-FOUR

The terrible screaming gradually faded in volume and then stopped. As he crouched by the sculpture, he heard wood splintering; the sound of men breaking down the front door.

Breen could not see. Only by keeping his eyes closed could he stop the excruciating pain of the brick dust in his eyes. He took in the world in brief blinks, each one feeling like sandpaper was passing across his corneas. His ears still rang from the gunshots, but he heard well enough to make out the sound of policemen breaking down the front door, tramping inside and shouting. 'Keep Briggs out of here. His wife is dead.'

A hand touched him. 'You all right, chum?'

Painfully he looked. A young police constable was standing over him. 'Who was screaming?' Breen asked.

'Don't know. It's a bloody mess in there.'

Breen stood and looked around. He stumbled through the broken door of the cottage. In a series of blinks he viewed the living room. The walls were cratered by gunshots, and glass and splintered wood from the window lay across the floor. He noticed Ezeoke first. The man was slumped against an ottoman, blood soaking through his trousers from a wound somewhere in his leg. His hands had been cuffed. He had a dazed look on his face, as if he was just waking from a sleep.

Mrs Briggs was just behind him, sprawled across the small living-room floor. She was dressed in a black polo neck and a mini skirt and, yes, she was dead. A bullet had smashed part of her jaw away. White teeth protruded through a bloody mess. Her top was spattered with blood.

'Where's Constable Tozer?' he croaked.

No one answered.

Louder. 'Where's Constable Tozer?'

He pushed through them into a dining room at the back of the little house. Unlike the front room, this was completely untouched, six chairs tucked neatly in around a dark mahogany table, dried flowers in a vase on the sideboard. A painting of a man on a horse. The room looked bizarrely normal, unaffected by the catastrophe that had just taken place.

The sergeant was in the kitchen at the back of the house talking on his radio. 'Leg wound. He'll live.'

It was as wrecked as the living room. He looked at Breen and said, 'Nothing like this has ever happened round here,' making it sound like an accusation.

Police had smashed down a stable door at the back to break in; windows had been shattered by the gunfire. The remains of a hasty breakfast of cornflakes and toast lay on a pine table.

'Where's Constable Tozer?'

The sergeant didn't seem to hear him; he was talking to his lapel radio again.

Breen returned to the living room. Two ambulance men were crouching over Ezeoke, who lay, eyes shut, on the floor now. They had torn away his trousers and were pressing gauze onto a wound just below his blood-soaked underpants. His skin looked grey.

'Fuck you,' he said to no one in particular.

Breen noticed a small, narrow staircase at the back of the room. To reach it he had to pick past Mrs Briggs's body, eyes wide, looking up at him as he stepped over her.

He found Tozer upstairs in the back bedroom, fully dressed in her uniform, lying on top of the covers of a single bed, a tartan blanket over her. Her hands and ankles were tied with cord to the side of the metal bed, her eyes shut, her mouth slightly open. He leaned over her and put his face next to hers.

She was warm. He felt her soft breath on his unshaven face. He stood there leaning over her for some time, feeling her breathe in and out, grateful, occasionally running the sleeve of his shirt across his eyes. Groans and complaints rose from below as they lifted Ezeoke onto a stretcher. He stayed with her, his face against the warmth of her skin, until the inspector appeared at the door.

'She alive?' he said.

Breen jumped back, as if he had been caught doing something he shouldn't have.

'She's OK, I think,' he said.

As two coppers lifted her awkwardly down the stairs, still unconscious, Breen found the bathroom and started to rinse his eyes, splashing ice-cold water up onto his face from the basin.

They had given Ezeoke a painkiller and handcuffed him to the small bed in the ambulance.

'Shame they stopped hanging people, in my opinion,' said the ambulance man.

Breen and a constable sat opposite, jerking from side to side as the ambulance navigated the narrow Suffolk lanes. Ezeoke's rage at the world seemed to shine from him, even in semi-consciousness. Breen's failure had been not to recognise that anger. Ezeoke had kept it half-hidden inside him. Perhaps it was the immigrant's trick. The ability to exist in two places at once. Two halves of a mind, each not recognising the state of the other. His father had learned to hide so much of himself. Breen was only now learning how much he had kept secret.

Ezeoke opened his eyes. 'You,' he said.

'Mrs Briggs is dead,' said Breen.

Ezeoke nodded. 'She wanted to go to Africa with me. To fight.'

There was a notice that said *No Smoking*, but the young constable ignored it.

'Jesus,' said the copper. 'It shakes you up a bit, doesn't it? Did you see her?'

Ezeoke's right hand was handcuffed to the side of the bed he lay on. They had dressed the wound on his leg.

'Did you really ever intend to make it back to Africa?' said Breen.

'Of course,' said Ezeoke, though his eyes flickered with what looked to Breen like doubt and he turned his head away from them.

'I don't think you'd have lasted five minutes,' said Breen.

'You're a liar.'

The ambulance's bell rang briefly, clearing cars away ahead.

'Did I kill any of your police?' Ezeoke said, when the noise stopped.

'No.'

'A pity,' said Ezeoke. 'I should have killed you all. You English.'

'Fuck's he on about?' said the young policeman sitting next to Breen, blowing out cigarette smoke. Breen noticed the young man's hand was shaking.

When Tozer returned to Marylebone Police Station, two days later, the coppers lined the corridors and clapped her.

'Oi, oi. Sleeping Beauty's back.'

'Well done, love,' said Carmichael.

'I heard you had a spot of bother too,' she said, kissing the big man on the cheek. 'They said you were on the bog the entire time.'

'Shut up.' Carmichael grinned like an idiot.

'Aye, aye.'

'Think he fancies you, darling.'

'Who said that?'

Somebody started singing, 'For she's a jolly good fellow.'

'Save it for the pub,' said Tozer.

'I don't know why you're making all this fuss for someone who got themselves caught,' said Marilyn. The song petered out.

The office quickly returned to normal. Marilyn made tea. Breen went back to his desk to do paperwork.

Tozer followed him to his desk. 'I called you yesterday,' she said.

'I was out,' said Breen, 'helping out at Joe's over the weekend. He's had a stroke. A bunch of us are keeping the place open.' He had visited Joe in hospital; he had spent an hour listening to the slurred words before Joe had fallen asleep, exhausted from the effort of trying to make sense of the strange words and growls that tumbled from his lopsided mouth. He'd looked frightened and thin.

'That's sad. Is he OK?'

'Not too good.' It was too early to tell whether he would get better, the doctors said. 'What about you?'

'I'm OK.'

She pulled out a cigarette and lit it. Bailey came out of his office and opened his mouth to say something, but thought better of it, and walked on. When he was out of earshot, Tozer said, 'On the news they said it was a gunfight. They said Ezeoke killed Mrs Briggs.'

'I know. It wasn't really like that.'

'Nobody will tell me what really happened.'

Breen stood and walked round to her side of the desk.

'They said Ezeoke was shooting at you.'

'Yes,' he said. 'That's true.'

'Why?'

'I think he felt he had nowhere left to go.'

'Tell me, then. I need to know what happened. It's like being in a dream, still. Only the opposite. I'm asleep and all this stuff that makes no sense going on around me.'

He sighed. 'To be honest, I don't know where to start.'

'I need to know. It's driving me bloody nuts.'

Tozer stole an ashtray from Prosser's empty desk and came back, holding it in her left hand.

'I went to find you,' he said. 'But you were gone.'

'I was outside Okonkwo's for about five minutes and she turned up. I didn't know whether to run and find you or what. Only, right away, Okonkwo came out and Ezeoke was with him.'

'He was in the shop when we were there.'

'I suppose. The moment they were gone I went up and got the car and followed. I couldn't stop to phone.' She talked quietly so her voice could not be heard by the others in the office. 'He pulled into a breaker's yard near Walthamstow. I waited a while, then followed him in. Bloody stupid. I'll never make a copper. Not that it matters any more. He was waiting for me inside the gates.'

'What do you mean, you'll never make a copper? You did great.'

'He stabbed me with a needle full of something. When I woke up we were in that car I'd been following. That Mrs Briggs was driving. What did happen to her?'

'A police bullet. Got her in the face. Carotid artery. They said Ezeoke shot her but they're just covering their backs. It was never a shotgun. I saw it. It was a bullet wound.'

'It's so strange to have slept while all that was going on around you.'

'I was scared for you,' he said. 'I didn't know if you were dead or alive.'

She looked away. 'I can't say I'm sorry, whoever did it,' Tozer said. 'She was a cow.'

In the house, she said, Frances Briggs had held Tozer's mouth wide while Ezeoke had forced the tranquillisers down her throat. 'It was horrible. I was kicking and struggling. Look.' She pulled up the sleeve of her tunic. 'I kept thinking about my sister. What it must have been like for her.'

Breen nodded. There were still marks on her wrist from where the ropes had cut her. 'Frances Briggs enjoyed it,' Tozer said. 'I swear.'

'What was it like?'

'It was like being in this nightmare.' Every few hours she had woken and tried for as long as she could to pretend to be asleep, hoping that they would not drug her again. 'They were rowing. Shouting at each other. Okonkwo wanted them to give themselves up. He's dead, isn't he?'

'The police shot him. As he was trying to escape.'

She nodded. 'One time he untied me. I'm not sure when this was. He told me to get away, but I was too tired. I couldn't move. I kept falling asleep. And then Mrs Briggs kept saying she had this boat and they could get away to France on it. It was crazy.'

'Why didn't they go? They had plenty of time. They were a day ahead of us.'

'I don't know. It was weird. Ezeoke kept delaying. Said he wanted to get some money. Said they could take their time. You know what I think?'

'What?'

'He was afraid. You know, big African man. But he'd never actually lived there or anything. He'd only been there once to bring back his African wife, you know?'

'Maybe. I think you're right. I think he had built up this big thing about Africa in his head.' He thought of his father: a man who had never gone home.

'I think he was nuts all along, you know. Right from the start. Right from that first time we met him.'

They sat at his desk and Breen told her how he had found her missing from Portobello Road, and how it had taken so long to find her car.

'It was horrible,' he said.

'Really?' she smiled. 'You and Carmichael?'

'Yes.'

'I was wrong about him,' she said.

'Yes.'

And how they had searched the neighbourhood until they heard that Professor Briggs was on the move.

'Lucky,' she said.

'Lucky. We were very lucky.'

That night after the pub and the drinks and the retelling of stories and rowdy cheers, they caught a taxi to his flat and had sex in his single bed, Tozer clinging to him fiercely.

Afterwards, as she lay there, he took a towel and wrapped it around his waist, then went to the living room and put on one of the new records he'd bought, and turned the record player up, full volume, so they could hear it from the bedroom.

The record started with a roaring noise that dissolved into a thumping song with pianos and guitars stomping out a rhythm, almost childishly. They lay on the bed together, listening. It felt good to move on. A new him. Everything beginning.

'This is the one,' she said, as another track started, a single note ringing out on a piano, overlaid by a wailing guitar. 'I'm not sure if that's George or Eric,' she said, as if they were both personal friends.

'Eric?'

She stood and started to dance, naked, leaping from foot to foot. 'Eric Clapton,' she shouted. 'It's incredible, great, isn't it? So fab.'

Laughing, he watched her dancing shamelessly above him. Her skinny body jumping around the small bed next to him so the springs creaked. He hoped the neighbours could hear. Sex had never been like this before. It had always been wordless and in darkened rooms.

She dropped down onto the bed, laughing too, and pulled the sheet over her. 'How long is it, since you ... did it?' She laughed.

'Three years,' he said. 'You?'

'Three years? That's ridiculous.'

'And?'

'I'm not telling. Not three years, that's for certain.'

He picked up the album's sleeve. It was a plain white square, inscrutable and blank. It seemed to say, 'Think nothing.' He was envious of Tozer's ecstatic reaction, her thoughtless lust for the music. The distance between them remained.

'I like it,' he said. 'It's good. Even the eight minutes of noise.'

She leaned down and kissed him on the forehead. 'To be honest,' said Tozer, 'I think that one is total rubbish.'

'Really? I thought it was, you know, good.'

'I'm a bit disappointed, really,' said Tozer. 'I mean, there's good stuff on it, but it doesn't really sound like The Beatles. Most of the time it sounds like four blokes doing weird stuff. It's not really The Beatles any more, know what I mean?'

'I liked it.'

'It makes me feel sad. It sounds like they're falling apart. Shall I turn it over?'

When she was back, he said, 'What did you mean when you said you'd never make a copper?'

She leaned over and felt for her packet of cigarettes. He looked at the long line of vertebrae twisting down to her buttocks as she padded her palm around the floor under the bed looking for the matches. The beauty of her bone beneath the skin.

'Want one?'

He shook his head. He had smoked his five cigarettes for the day.

'I've decided I'm leaving the police,' she said. 'I don't fit in.'

'Of course you do,' he said, though he didn't really believe it. She didn't fit in. That was what he loved about her. It was what she stood for: the importance of not having to fit in.

'You look shocked,' she said.

'I am.'

'I'm sorry about that time at Paddington in the rain. I felt really bad, leaving you there. I was acting like a big kid.'

'Yes,' he said. 'You were.' She hit him on the arm.

'I'm going back to the farm,' she said. 'I'm going to look after it for my dad. Mum says he's getting worse. He can't cope any more.'

He sat up and looked at her. He had only just slept with her for the first time and now she was going away. 'I thought you didn't want to live there any more. I thought you couldn't stand living there.'

'I didn't. I don't. But I'm allowed to change my mind, aren't I?'

Breen was silent. The music next door seemed too loud now.

'It's what I know. I can make a go of it, I think. Do things differently.'

He wondered at her ability to be one thing one minute, another the next. 'Why?'

'I used to think I had to save the world to make up for what happened to my sister. I don't really think that any more. The world carries on without me. And people get killed all the time, don't they? Besides. I don't think my mum can cope any more with Dad.'

She got up, naked, and said, 'I'm just going to the toilet.'

He lay in bed, breathing in the scent she left behind. She came back a few minutes later with a bottle of Scotch she had found in his kitchen and poured two small glasses. He brushed his hand over her face, past the plaster on her forehead.

'I don't have to save anyone any more. Just myself. I'll leave saving people to you,' she said.

His clothes were folded neatly by the bed. Hers were scattered across the floor.

'Don't you want to find her killer any more?'

'Course I do. But I realised that we may never find out who he is. That's the reality, isn't it? It's too long now. And it's so horrible it makes me cry, but I've got to live with that. We don't always know, do we? Even when we do. Even when we arrest people. Or shoot them. It's a lot messier than we like to say.'

He couldn't bring himself to say, 'But what about me?' Instead he said, 'I was thinking I was going to take a holiday. A long one. I've got leave owing.'

'You?'

'What do you mean?'

'I didn't think you knew how.'

She was teasing him, but it was probably what she thought as well, he realised. 'I'm going to go to Ireland,' he announced. 'I've got some money in the bank from my father. I thought I could go and find out where he was from.'

She nodded. 'That's good,' she said. 'You should do that.'

'I was thinking, you could come too,' he said.

She licked the rim of her whisky glass. 'I've heard it's like Devon only wetter.'

'Probably.'

'I don't think I'd like it then. I don't think so, Cathal. You go.'

He tried not to show his disappointment. She was young. Uncommitted. Maybe this was the way it was now with girls.

'When are you going back home?' he asked.

'Gave in my notice today. Four weeks,' she said.

He tried to imagine her bringing in the cows day after day, but couldn't see her in that role. He tried to imagine himself down there with her, but that was no better.

'If you don't fit in, what makes you think I do?' he asked.

'You? You fit in fine,' she said.

It was just a careless comment, but he was stung by it. He chewed it over for a while. It was fine for her to change her mind from one day to the next, but he was set in stone. He was about to ask what she had meant by it, and perhaps start some childish argument of the kind that lovers might have, but they were not lovers, they had just had sex because they were two people who had gone through something terrifying together. He had wanted more, but he realised this was all there was. And when he turned to her, she was asleep, mouth open, eyes closed.

He lay there a while, watching her naked chest rise and fall, feeling a weight pressing down on him. The bed was too small for the both of them. He tried to sleep, but he couldn't.

From 1966–7, tens of thousands of Igbos died in pogroms in the Muslim north of Nigeria.

Britain had ruled the vast ethnically diverse country, with its arbitrarily drawn borders, using the age-old principle of divide and rule. The hasty exit of the British in 1960 left a country primed for civil war. Six years later, with an inexperienced government descending into increasingly fractious regional disputes, a group of bright-eyed young army officers stepped in with a cack-handed, stupid military coup. The fact that most of them were Igbo triggered long-held resentments and the blood-letting began.

Responding with equal parts hubris and genuine fear of obliteration, Igbo leaders founded Biafra in May 1967. Civil war was now inevitable. Britain followed the oil, as it always does, backing Federal Nigeria in the hope of securing access to the riches in the Niger delta. Cabinet papers of the time reveal the stark cynicism of British policy. Commonwealth Minister George Thomas wrote in August: 'The sole immediate British interest is to bring the economy back to a condition in which our substantial trade and investment can be further developed.' Officially, Britain turned a blind eye to the Federal state's blockade of Biafra, fumbling the opportunity to broker peace talks. By the time the war ended in 1970, as many as three million had died, mostly of disease and starvation. Up to a million were children.

The year 1968 saw another post-Imperial car crash: the arrival in Britain of tens of thousands of Kenyan Asians, disenfranchised by the government of Jomo Kenyatta. With racist sentiment being stoked by the press, the British government hastily cobbled together the Commonwealth Immigration Act, withdrawing the right of entry of Commonwealth passport holders without British ancestry – a coy way of restricting non-white immigrants. Two months later, in April, Enoch Powell exploited the growing racism with his poisonous 'Rivers of Blood' speech, giving voice to fears that 'within ten to fifteen years the black man will have the whip hand over the white man'.

In September 1973, Detective Sergeant Norman Clement 'Nobby' Pilcher was convicted on a charge of conspiracy to pervert the course of justice after it became clear that he was extorting money from victims he had framed for drug offences. In a five-year career on the Drug Squad, Pilcher was responsible for arresting Donovan, Mick Jagger, Brian Jones, Keith Richards, George Harrison and John Lennon. His appetite for busting rock stars led to *Oz* magazine calling him 'Groupie Pilcher'. Pilcher was given four years by Justice Melford Stevenson who told him, 'You poisoned the wells of criminal justice and you set about it deliberately.'

Twelve years of heartfelt thank-yous must go to Roz Brody, Mike Holmes, Janet King and Chris Sansom for their enduring support, encouragement, insight and wisdom. Several police officers were generous with advice: Jancis and David Robinson, Tanya Murray, as well as Sioban Clarke of the Metropolitan Women Police Association. My fellow members of All Saints School Enugu Alumni 1966 remain an inspiration. Finally, thanks to those who commented so perceptively on the manuscript. They include Joshua Kendall, Jane McMorrow, Jeff Noon, Hellie Ogden, Paul Quinn, Rose Tomaszewska, Nick de Somogyi, my editor at Quercus Jon Riley and my agent Karolina Sutton.